Sue Sully grew up in Yorkshire and now lives in Somerset. Her previous novels are *The Barleyfield* ('an adroitly orchestrated symphony' *The Sunday Times*), *The Shingle Beach* ('both an enjoyable story and, in the universality of its themes, a thought-provoking one' *Wiltshire and Wessex Life* magazine) and she has published short stories in magazines such as *Me* and *New Woman*.

The Scent of May

Sue Sully

KNIGHT

Copyright © 1992 Sue Sully

The right of Sue Sully to be identified as the Author of the
Work has been asserted by her in accordance with the Copyright,
Designs and Patents Act 1988.

The rights to the Knight chess piece reproduced on this book
are the property of Hodder and Stoughton Limited
and it is reproduced with their permission

First published in 1992
by William Heinemann Ltd

First published in paperback in 1994
by HEADLINE BOOK PUBLISHING PLC

This edition published 1999 by
Knight an imprint of Brockhampton Press

10 9 8 7 6 5 4 3 2 1

All characters in this publication are fictitious
and any resemblance to real persons, living or dead,
is purely coincidental.

ISBN 1 86019 6969

Typeset by CBS, Felixstowe, Suffolk

Printed and bound in Great Britain by
Mackays of Chatham PLC, Chatham, Kent

Brockhampton Press
20 Bloomsbury Street
London
WC1B 3QA

Rise like lions after slumber
In unvanquishable number –
Shake your chains to earth like dew
Which in sleep had fallen on you –
Ye are many – they are few.

Percy Bysshe Shelley,
from *The Mask of Anarchy*

One

There's nothing happier than the days
In which young Love makes every thought
Pure as a bride's blush, when she says
'I will' unto she knows not what . . .

Coventry Patmore,
The Angel in the House

Bertrand woke on his wedding day to the sound of the rooks cawing in the elms. Too late that the world was full of adventuring and beautiful women, tomorrow he would open his eyes in a hotel bedroom and see his wife by his side. He groaned into the carpet and remembered the still, warm nights under the gas-lit greenery of the Paris boulevards, the laughter and wine and the boulevard women who offered their bodies with such ease. How did he woo the chilly piece of porcelain soon to be his bride? He sat on the floor holding his head, wishing he had drunk less port the evening before. He cursed his best man and hoped he felt ill this morning and that he would muff his part in church on account of it. Serve him right for being such a clown and plying him with drink all night.

The housemaid brought hot water and drew the curtains, letting the sun stream on to the carpet and making him wince. She expressed no surprise to see him on the floor. 'It's a grand day for a wedding, sir.'

'It's a terrible day. Won't you run away with me, lovely Ellen, and rescue me from a fate worse than death?'

The girl blushed at the look of exaggerated anguish on Bertrand's youthful face. It was an open face, thin, with a delicately shaped jaw, a straight nose and the eyes dark-fringed and appealing. She bobbed a curtsey and backed from the room. He was a terror for flirting was Mister Bertrand, even worse since he had come back from France.

Bertrand clambered to his feet when she had gone and washed and dressed slowly, shivering though the air was not cold. He pulled on the light grey wedding trousers and tucked in his wedding shirt, fastened it and the buttons of the white silk waistcoat and attempted to knot the blue necktie. He abandoned the tie and sat on the bed, trying to resign himself to the notion that he wanted nothing more from life than a sensible and virtuous wife. He thought of Paris with a sweeping nostalgia for the sparsely furnished studio on the fourth floor of a dilapidated, yellow-washed house, too close to the Gare du Nord to be respectable or even fashionably squalid, where for a year his father had allowed him to pursue the activities of a sculptor. From there he had attended a public studio each morning, where young men and women gathered together and drew from a life model. At lunch-times a few of the students had mixed with radical workers in the cafés, listening to the opinions of those opposed to the régime of Napoleon III. And in the evenings . . .

Bertrand remembered the cafés and establishments of Montmartre, where '20 sous' women flirted and smoked cigarettes and a man with a pointed moustache and shining accordion sang filthy songs. He thought of the tiny rooms upstairs with their iron bedsteads, cracked mirrors and

2

broken window blinds. On rare occasions, if Antoine, a fellow student of more indulgent family means, was paying, or – even more rarely – if he had sold a piece of work, they had visited the gilded and red-plush cafés of the *grands boulevards*, mingled with Society and lusted after the high-class courtesans.

'A man needs a woman at regular intervals,' Antoine had said. 'She does not have to be beautiful, beauty is for sculpting and painting, but she must excite the senses.'

If his friend could see him now. He took the short blue coat from its hanger and laid it on the bed, then laid his new lilac gloves on top of it. Other memories rose one upon the other: the lunch-time discussions in the crowded café with its red checked table cloths, where the trains on the railway line shook the plaster from the walls and the air was dense with radical talk and tobacco smoke. What would Maurice, fanatical defender of the proletariat, ranter against all that smacked of middle-class extravagance, have made of all this? The worker's image was strong: the squared and scarred fingers, the downward droop and sensual sneer of his mouth with the deep line from left eye to top lip – the result of an accident at his workplace, though some had hinted that it was a wound from a sabre or a knife, won during a skirmish between workers and militia or more sordidly in a lovers' brawl. Maurice – with his consistent two-day growth of black stubble, who always looked and smelled none too clean and wore a filthy red scarf knotted round his neck. Bertrand had been conscious of his own superiority as an Englishman and the son of a prosperous Yorkshire industrialist, yet he had been more than a little in awe of the Frenchman. Maurice was dangerous. No doubt of that. He was a true Parisian.

'The instinct for rebellion is inscribed on the heart of every Frenchman,' one of the students had ventured as an opinion one day, a typical Bohemian with paint-spattered clothes and long hair which hung over his face.

Maurice had lowered his gaze wearily and drawn with a blackened and calloused forefinger in the beer spilled on the café table. 'Are you a Parisian, my friend?'

The student shook his head.

'Then may I suggest you are talking through your arse. Without *Paris* there would have been no revolutions in France.'

The other occupants of the café, who knew Maurice Chaudet and his mocking tongue, laughed and banged their glasses on the tables. Antoine said, 'Well spoken, Maurice. Long live Paris.' Maurice did not respond and drank his beer slowly to the bottom of the glass, then stood. Obeying his signal the other workers stood too, their blue smocks setting them apart from the students and artists.

'Why the hurry?' The student with the Bohemian air had attempted to restore his damaged ego with a cynical laugh.

'They have an emperor to assassinate,' someone joked when they had gone, but Bertrand had not laughed with the others.

He stared at the lilac gloves on the bed. They looked incongruous, as did the velvet coat collar and edging of lilac silk cord – hardly the garb of a man who felt he was on his way to the guillotine. He smiled at the irony of it: Antoine had written that Maurice was raging at fate from behind his prison bars. Maurice was in Paris, caged like a lion for offences against the Empire, and here was he, voluntarily submitting himself to a matrimonial life sentence.

He went on to the landing to look for Phoebe to ask her to arrange his tie for him. His sister was filling a bowl with sweet peas on the hall stand downstairs. She did not look up and did not hear him as he leaned on the metal balustrade to watch her. The smell of the flowers was very sweet. The

4

stand, a massive piece of furniture made from cast bronze with a marble top and a mirror above, dominated the dark hallway. Curlicues of serpents provided ingenious pegs and enclosures for coats and umbrellas. It was linked in his memory with the foundry and his father and Bertrand recalled his childhood fear of its looming presence.

Phoebe's hair was tied back neatly in a knot. She wore a plain dark dress and apron, not the outfit she would wear as chief bridesmaid. The sight of his sister's silent preoccupation with the flowers was reassuring. Phoebe and flowers: the two images were utterly compatible.

He thought of his fiancée's decorous and undemanding letters, sent with weekly devotion, filled with news of Griseley and the occasional optimistic reference to their wedding at some unspecified date in the future. He was not ready for marriage, he protested silently. And yet he supposed that it had been inevitable. Phoebe and Christina had been close, he had gone to school with Christina's brother. They had all four been friends since childhood. Everyone had expected it. And, he reminded himself, Christina possessed a handsome income. She was – despite an unfortunate resemblance to one of her father's hunters – also refined in manner and not flighty. A steady, wealthy wife would be an advantage to a man determined on a career as an artist. 'You tend naturally to the bourgeois life, Bertrand,' Antoine had told him, 'a sentimental pastel-coloured little wife would suit you. You try to be a Parisian but you do not have the Latin temperament.' Christina would be a pastel-coloured wife – water-coloured even: she would arrange his household prettily and sympathetically and stay in the background so that he could devote himself to his work. He remembered, a little shamefaced now, the desperation with which he had written to Phoebe, to ask her to plead with their father against his return.

Why had he come home? Why had he succumbed once more to the tyranny of this household? 'What choice is there?' he had appealed to Antoine, who had shrugged and agreed there was none. 'I shall come back to Paris,' he promised, but he did not think Antoine had believed him, and he had not really believed it himself.

The return of the prodigal. They had all come from chapel to the station to meet him. One moment there was the remembered view of sooty houses, mill chimneys and the clock tower of Griseley's town hall and the next he was stepping on to the platform, nervousness squeezing his stomach as he saw the figure of his father beside his brothers.

His father had aged visibly, the mass of hair a little whiter, but his figure still strong and muscular and his authority familiarly daunting as he called to a porter to remove the luggage from the roof of the train. Only when this was done did he turn to face him: his eyes, a faded blue, were sharp and somewhat cold. He had crushed him against his huge chest as if very moved by the occasion and unwanted tears had started to Bertrand's eyes.

Gerald, heavily built, beginning to look like Father, stood beside his carriage with his wife. There was the familiar broad smile on his solid face and his blue eyes were softened by genial amusement as he spread his arms. 'Brother – wander no more. The bosom of your family awaits.' Olive had kissed him gravely, a flicker of a smile on her beautiful lips, her cheek cool to the touch.

Charles shook his hand with a rigid formality and Bertrand had searched his brother's face for evidence of a change in him, for Charles had caused a scandal in his absence by putting some girl in the family way and then marrying her. There was no sign of his wife. *The circumstances of the marriage are, to say the least, unfortunate*, Phoebe had written. A *harlot*, his father had recorded with less charity.

6

The boy is even more of a profligate than yourself. Charles, an unlikely subject for profligacy, handsome and bland, had averted his eyes as he stepped aside.

Bertrand had looked anxiously for Phoebe. Was she angry with him and so had refused to come? She had sounded angry in her letters. *How dare you ask me to speak for you after you have treated Christina so high-handedly! It would be more than you deserve if the Underwoods were to call off the marriage.* But in a subsequent letter she had written, *How can I plead for you to stay in France when my heart and soul know that it is right for my brother to come home?*

He had seen her at last, hurrying along the platform in her dark blue chapel-going frock, a mass of foamy white may blossom clutched to her breast. Her strong expressive face was flushed with excitement under her black bonnet. She flung the bunches of may into the family carriage then stood before him, smoothing her gloved hands in characteristic fashion against her skirts. 'Eh, Bertie!' She stood very stiff and straight, lifting her face for his kiss, and the happiness in her eyes made him swing her round with exuberant relief. 'What a bad lad you are. You don't deserve such a home-coming, you know. I expect Christina will spoil you as well. I hope you realise how lucky you are.'

'An extremely lucky fellow,' he had replied when the luggage was packed on board and the family had climbed into the pair of waiting carriages. The scent of may blossom filled the air and at that moment he had believed in his heart that it was so and that there were no two finer girls in the whole of the West Riding than his sister and his fiancée Christina, though he was not worthy of either. 'I shall be the exemplary bridegroom, a reformed character.'

Phoebe glanced up as he came down the stairs in his wedding

7

clothes and stepped back to appraise him. He saw now that she had changed in the year he had been away: there was more of a hint of chapel austerity in her these days, yet her features were edged with tenderness, as he remembered, and beautiful, as women's faces should be.

'Not so bad, for someone who didn't come home before morning. Thank goodness Father knew nothing about it.'

'I feel terrible.' He held out the necktie.

'Isn't that how the bridegroom is supposed to feel?' She knotted the tie deftly for him.

'What am I going to do, Phoebe?'

'It'll be right enough.' She flecked an imaginary speck of dirt from his coat sleeve and gave him a little push. 'It will all be over in a few hours.'

She did not understand. Even Phoebe, who understood everything, could not see that he was in deadly earnest and that what she thought would 'soon be over' would have only just begun.

'Have some breakfast,' she said with what Bertrand considered a distinct lack of compassion. 'Philip has promised to see you to the church. I must get over to Chillingdale. I'll guarantee Christina is in a far worse state than you are.'

Phoebe's heart went out to her brother as she watched him cross the hall to the dining room. Though she had sided with her father about his return from France, she felt a perverse sense of disappointment in him because he had succumbed once more to the oppression of Griseley. Bertrand was twenty-one, Phoebe was twenty. Closest to her in years, he had always been her favourite brother. But they were all of them in their father's thrall, she thought as she finished arranging the flowers: Gerald, feeding an imagined notion of escape by pretending to be a theatre impresario in his spare time, but in reality trapped by his managership of the foundry; Charles, working for his father by day, banished for the rest of the time to a little house on Griseley Bank where he could keep his pregnant wife conveniently out of sight; and herself, attending chapel dutifully and ostensibly obeying Father in everything, though she might be biting her tongue for the things she wanted to say.

Phoebe had developed a self-sufficiency at an early age, for their mother had died when she was a child of ten. She had quickly learned that her brothers would look to her to take their mother's place. They always considered that they had indulged her, of course. She was their pet, their darling younger sister, somewhat limited in their eyes – for, though she played the harmonium with an acknowledged proficiency, she did not paint or sculpt or write poetry or plays and, since she was a female, their father could not make use of her at the foundry; but she was decorative and useful at arranging the house for Father and how could they in all honesty have managed their own more complicated lives without her? How indeed? Who, after their mother had died, would have tempered their father's criticism of Charles's and Bertrand's artistic efforts, or concealed Gerald's play-scripts?

Phoebe knew that certain occupations, such as Gerald's amateur theatricals, hovered on the edges of immorality for, though their mother had encouraged artistic pursuits and their father had indulged his wife's wishes when they were children, these days he made his disapproval of Gerald's plays increasingly plain. Charles's seduction of Tessa, one of Gerald's players, was undeniably sinful – though Phoebe wondered sometimes just who had seduced whom – yet she could see that Charles had made amends by marrying her. Other pursuits were less explicitly immoral: Bertrand's desire to be a sculptor, Charles's passion for drawing, her own

9

absorption with things non-spiritual like science and astronomy and reading about travel to far-flung parts of the world. They were not so much wicked – their mother would not have encouraged out-and-out wickedness – but they were frivolous. Did it follow that their mother too had been frivolous? Her father spoke bitterly against his dead wife these days, as if he blamed all that had gone wrong in the family on her early influence. And yet Phoebe sometimes wondered what was wanted of women. Was it not a mother's role to nurture the gentler, more creative aspects in her sons?

A mood of resentment entered her thoughts as she climbed the stairs, her back straight, her hands pressed firmly against her skirts. She did her best to please her father. She attended chapel and prayed regularly and earnestly for guidance, taught in Sunday school and played the harmonium on Sundays in the Ebenezer chapel. She visited the houses of people on the chapel sick-list and other unfortunates, towards whom the chapel elders and her father showed less charity. She acted as mistress of Belle Vue, directed the efforts of the small staff of servants, looked after her personal affairs without extravagance, dressed soberly and tended the garden. Who else would have taken on the unlovely task of running this cold ugly house and its servants so that her father and brothers need not trouble themselves about such things?

She knocked with an uncharacteristically irritable rap of her knuckles against the panelled door on entering her father's room. He sat in his dressing gown reading by the antiquated four-poster bed, just as if nothing more unusual was happening today than the fact that he had taken a whole Saturday off from the works.

For an instant Phoebe felt her irritation swell to a rebellious anger against him. He had pressed so hard for the marriage and persuaded her to urge Bertrand's return, the least he could do was acknowledge the importance of the wedding day now it was upon them.

'I'm off to Chillingdale now, Father.' Phoebe paused in the doorway, unsure of his mood. 'I'm afraid Bertie is in a bit of a state.'

Edwin looked up. 'We shall meet in *church* then.' He pronounced the word with a slightly derogatory note, as if church, unlike chapel, were some foreign, perhaps even heathenish place.

A nerve in his cheek twitched, as it did when he was agitated about something, drawing his mouth into a swift unconscious smile. Was he pleased because he had brought an erring son to heel? Or did the nervous tic betray a turmoil of emotion? She could not tell. For an instant Phoebe saw her mother sitting at the dressing table, her beautiful dark chestnut hair flowing down her back. How she would have loved the romance and sentimentality of a wedding. She would have allowed Phoebe to brush her hair for her as she used to do when she was small. 'A woman's hair is her crowning glory, my darling,' she had said with her curious rolling accent, which, Phoebe realised now, had been foreign to Griseley and Griseley people.

She regarded her father in his night-cap and dressing gown. What a strange couple they must have been. What had drawn them to one another? The one so steeped in respectability and hard work, the other colourful, exotic, like a tropical flower flourishing briefly among the gritstone hills. And the flowering must have been brief, for their mother's southern French constitution had weakened with each successive winter before she finally succumbed to the typhus epidemic which had taken her from them.

'Make sure Bertrand is all right, won't you,' Phoebe persisted. 'It's all a bit of an ordeal.'

'Christina will make a man of him.' Her father looked at

her for a moment as she waited. 'Phoebe – I shall be a very happy man the day it is your own wedding morning. Underwood would be a sound husband – and Chillingdale not far from home.'

'Stop matchmaking,' Phoebe said lightly.

'Think on it.' He gave her a straight look. 'You would have your father's blessing more than any of the rest.'

'A fine day for a wedding, Miss Phoebe,' called Henstridge over his shoulder. He had tied white ribbons to the sides of the pony carriage and the other servants had trimmed the horse's harness with flowers. They were dressed in their Sunday best this morning and looking forward to the spread which the Underwoods would put on later for the combined family and company employees. There were almost as many from the lower orders as there were worthies invited to the wedding breakfast, thought Phoebe wryly as she climbed into the carriage, and at what expense! Bertrand really should feel more appreciative. She glanced up at the austere sooty house with its narrow twin gables. Its claustrophobia was hard to define, but it was present in the very fabric of the gritstone building: in the impression of solid permanence, the plain sash windows, four above, four below, the staircase window of coloured panes of glass and the heavily studded front door. It was there too in the stillness of the garden, shielded from the road by rhododendron bushes, and in the lonely calling of rooks in the elms behind the house. Henstridge clicked to the horse and the carriage moved off, but Phoebe's sense of oppression did not fade until she had passed the stone gateposts and the crunch of wheels on gravel had changed to a more subdued rumble on the asphalted slope of Griseley Bank.

Belle Vue was at the very top of the hill, heading a series of similar detached houses with gardens set back from the road behind laurels and rhododendrons. The top of Griseley Bank overlooked open moorland; only by squinting from their first-floor windows might the well-to-do be reminded of the smoke-belching chimneys of the factories and woollen mills which filled the valley bottom. The carriage bowled down the hill past stone villas with gables and porticoed fronts and here and there a castellated turret. Half-way down the Bank the character of the houses altered and the smooth rumble of wheels on asphalt changed to a racket on cobbles; on the left-hand side a low wall separated the road from rhubarb fields; on the right a terrace of mean dwellings bordered the road.

Phoebe glanced swiftly at the little house of smoke-blackened stone, where her brother Charles now lived with his wife Tessa. There was no sign of life from behind the lace curtains; she hoped Tessa would not be difficult for Charlie today. But this was no time to consider her brother's troubles as the carriage drove on towards the foot of the Bank. Phoebe's attention sharpened as they passed the distinctive red-brick façades of the Nag's Head public house and, beyond it on the opposite side of the street, the Ebenezer. Phoebe did not even give a cursory attention to the chapel, where she played the harmonium each Sunday and where, if her father had his way, she would attend her own wedding. But, in the lingering glance with which she scanned the Nag's Head, a keenly thoughtful air occupied Phoebe's expression, as if she were looking for someone. Then a clatter of activity and voices from the inn yard made her check herself and she stared very intently at the back of Henstridge's broad neck. She smoothed her gloved hands on her skirt and the slightest hint of a blush graced her cheeks.

Phoebe reflected with a clear head on the institution of

marriage as Henstridge drove through the town and along the river valley to Chillingdale. She saw that Christina was more deserving of pity than Bertrand, for everything she had and was would now pass into the hands of her husband – her clothes, her person, even her children would belong to him. And all for love? Phoebe did not quite believe it, for she did not think that Christina had the look of a woman in love, and she sensed that though they had once been considered childhood sweethearts Bertrand did not really love Christina.

A group of servants was erecting a triumphal arch of greenery and garlands of flowers over the gates of Chillingdale. The carriage bowled past them, past the lodge which was to be the wedded couple's new home and up the long drive to the house.

Chillingdale, situated well to the west of the town, its gardens overlooking the river, always instilled a vague sense of inferiority in Phoebe and she sensed that her brothers, perhaps even her father too felt the same. The house stood in isolated splendour amidst parkland, like some ancient country seat which might have dated back to the estates and hunting forests of kings, though in fact it had been established little more than twenty years, built at a time when Gothic taste was at its peak. The house rambled with exuberant opulence but little sense of symmetry, throwing up turrets and towers at unexpected corners, with a frontage of mock castle walls and a glut of stone pediments and carvings. The interior was even more intimidating: it gleamed with polished oak floors, oak panelling and broad oak staircases. The entrance hall displayed a baronial-style fireplace with the Underwoods' family crest at its centre. All this 'ancient' dignity was overlaid, indeed almost swamped by a rash of interior decoration. Every item of soft furniture in the various rooms was over-stuffed and covered with antimacassars, every solid surface was carved, inlaid or otherwise elaborated upon. Mantelpieces were surmounted by huge gilded mirrors which reflected the backs of gilt clocks and photograph frames. There were cabinets enclosing photographs, whatnots displaying fine china, and tables at strategic intervals, as if placed there to trip the unwary visitor, and putting one in fear of destroying forever some precious work of art.

Feet echoed in the hall as Phoebe gave her box, containing her bridesmaid's frock, to the butler who handed it to a maidservant who carried it upstairs.

Bertrand did not know how he had got into this predicament or why. For Christina's three hundred a year and a house thrown in, a salary from his father and the prospect of working forever at the foundry? Or for old times' and old friendships' sake? How could he have let it go so far?

He helped himself to scrambled eggs and kidneys from the sideboard in the dining room at Belle Vue and sat at the polished oak table, staring at the hardening yellow mass on his plate without appetite. He told himself he did not blame his wife-to-be, indeed he felt himself to be unworthy of her humility. But there was no mystery in Christina's pale eyes, no fascinating past or promise of hidden joys waiting to be discovered.

Madeleine's more robust image flooded his thoughts. He saw again the half-finished statue of her which had stood in the centre of his studio in Paris. He had been disappointed with it: the figure was out of proportion – which he blamed on the imperfections of his model – yet he had known in his heart that its failure was due to his own ineptitude.

'Nothing like her,' Antoine had said with a mocking superiority, or, when he was in a more kindly mood, 'Get yourself a decent model.'

It was all very well for Antoine, who could afford women

who possessed the required comeliness. Madeleine was large and vulgar, sweaty from her work in the local bakery, and with lustrous black hair and a plump backside, but she was no beauty. She offered her body for him to model or to take into his bed free of charge. Bertrand had accepted that she did so because she was in love with him. It was an arrangement which had enlivened dull afternoons and now provided him with fond memories, but which at the time had not troubled him unduly.

He thought of Maurice again and a frown crossed Bertrand's face as he remembered the studio that after-noon when he had come to him, seeking refuge from the police.

Bertrand had been at the table by the window with inkpot, pen and notepaper trying to compose a letter to Phoebe, asking her to persuade his father that he should stay a further six months in Paris, when Antoine had burst into the room. 'My good fellow!' He was out of breath and agitated and turned apologetically towards the door. 'An accident! There have been arrests! Will you assist?'

Maurice stood, framed in the doorway, pale in the shadowy light, supporting the weight of one arm with the other. His wrist was bound with his neckcloth, dark and sodden with blood.

'We had arranged a strike meeting,' Maurice explained. 'The police were waiting for us and there was a little skirmish.' He looked in a detached way at his arm. 'As you can see, it is a scratch. It is nothing.' His sleeve was saturated and the blood welled through the improvised bandage as if to assist this studied bravado. He had wiped it with his other hand, red and slippery, and a drip of blood splashed the wooden floor.

'Can you keep Maurice here for a day or two until the fuss dies down?' Antoine had said. 'Nobody would think to look for him with you. You're not under suspicion as I might be.'

Bertrand had nodded, unnerved. He had believed himself an admirer of radicals, at least of atheists and flouters of social convention; he believed he was accustomed to the unrealities of the life of the artist, yet he had not supposed that Antoine, who always seemed so light minded, could be involved in activity against the Empire, nor had he ever seen so much blood. He watched Antoine fetch a bowl of water, place it on the table by the window and unwind the neckcloth from Maurice's arm. The gash was deep. He had looked away as the edges of flesh pulled open.

'I apologise.'

Bertrand had followed Maurice's gaze to where blood from the wound had formed a pool on the table and the corners of the pages of his letter to Phoebe soaked up the crimson stain.

'It doesn't matter. I can write the letter again.'

'Your betrothed?' Maurice regarded the photograph perched at the rear corner of the table, placed there for inspiration. He grunted as Antoine tightened the bandage.

'My sister.'

Maurice picked up the portrait with his free hand and studied it intently for several seconds. Bertrand expected him to say something complimentary, that his sister was pretty or the photograph, taken in a studio in Leeds, was well executed. People said the photograph reminded them of his mother. Phoebe's large, heavy-lidded eyes, unintimidated by the attentions of the photographer, stared straight into those of the onlooker. Instead Maurice handed back the picture saying only, 'My apologies to your sister for spilling my blood on your letter to her in this uncivilised way.' Antoine had finished binding the wound and Maurice touched the bandage experimentally. 'And if I ever catch the pig who did this—' he glanced up and a rare smile brought his face to life, though it did not light his eyes.

Antoine had said that he must leave. He would bring them news as soon as he was able. Bertrand had watched Maurice pace the floor restlessly.

'I'm sorry for the inconvenience I've brought on you,' he said. 'We Parisians can't keep away from a fight. As children we learned at our father's knees about the glorious uprisings of the thirties and 1848. We hoped that we too would man the barricades one day.' He turned suddenly and Bertrand had been afraid of the blaze of anger in his eyes. 'Another revolution will come. If you stay in Paris long enough you may witness it. We will crush Louis-Napoleon and his Eugénie just as we destroyed Louis and Marie-Antoinette in the days of the guillotine.'

All talk and swagger of course, and Bertrand had quickly wearied of harbouring a fugitive. Maurice's talk was incessant, his obsession with the mythology of past revolutions, fascinating in the milieu of the cafés, had been claustrophobic in the apartment, where Bertrand was a captive audience and Maurice a reluctant guest.

Bertrand discarded the memories of France. Maurice was a fanatic. Down with the propertied classes! Down with the masters of industry! He began to eat the cold eggs and kidneys. None of Maurice's revolutionary bluster had any place here.

Two

> . . . I should say that the majority of women (happily
> for them) are not very much troubled with sexual
> feelings of any kind.
>
> Doctor William Acton,
> *The Functions and Disorders of the*
> *Reproductive Organs in Childhood, Youth,*
> *Adult Age and Advanced life Considered in their*
> *Physiological, Social and Moral Relations*

Christina twisted and turned in front of her mirror. She did
not consider herself beautiful and was sceptical of her
mother's repeated assertions that Bertrand Clough had won
himself a prize.

The wedding frock fitted badly; she was too tall for its
narrow bodice and voluminous skirts. She looked at the
reflection which stared back at her in despair from the
mirror. She was not a particularly clever girl, no lively
intelligence shone forth from her pale blue eyes, but she
was astute enough to know that this marriage was not going
to be easy. She wished the whole business could be got over
without so much fuss and without the influence of her
mother on everything.

Beatrice Underwood was not a woman to neglect bringing

influence to bear; she felt her position keenly as the wife of a railway company director, who was currently mayor of Griseley Town Council, chairman of the Parish Church Council and numerous social and charitable committees. As such, Beatrice had a great deal of leverage on affairs in the town, though she satisfied herself with confining her chief influence to the lives of her children – her dear boy Philip, and Christina, soon to wed into the second most significant family in Griseley.

Her daughter's wedding was going to be an *occasion*: not for nothing was Beatrice known as a superior hostess in the West Riding.

'You look very pretty. Your papa will be right proud of you.'

'It's still too long in the waist,' Christina complained.

'You'll have your veil and head-dress, that will break the line up a bit.' Beatrice fancied herself as something of an expert on fashion and had always dressed herself in the best of taste – although when it came to headwear she was generally reluctant to expose her firsthand knowledge and intimate association with millinery. She wore a crinoline, flat in front and trailing voluminously at the rear, yet modest compared with the finery she would wear later on in her role as mother of the bride. Her very black hair was contained in a vast chignon, netted to prevent its escape and tied up with yards of tartan ribbon in the style of a young girl. She was stout and tightly corseted, the type of woman who had been strikingly good-looking in her youth, but who in middle age was intimidating rather than appealing.

Christina consoled herself with the fact that the veil would at least hide her face and disguise the fact that she was half scared to death of marrying the man everyone had assumed she was destined to marry, who, after a separation of a year, had become a stranger.

Bertrand's letters had been restrained and littered with gaps over his activities. Christina did not suppose that he had been faithful to her; she knew how artists and foreigners lived – or supposed she knew, for she had read about them in novels. But she was not supposed to think about such things. Nor did she want to. That aspect of the marriage filled her with even greater terror. Oh, why did one have to get married at all? Her image in the mirror blurred as her eyes swam with tears.

She remembered the dreadful reunion after Bertrand had returned from France. She had been trying on the wedding frock and her mother had hurried to the window at the sound of a carriage on the drive. 'Now look. He's here already. What an eager beaver, and you in all your finery. Isn't that just like a man! No sense of what's proper.'

Christina had hidden against the curtain. 'He mustn't see me in my frock!' Her panic rose not so much from a fear of being observed in her wedding gown as being seen by her future husband at all.

'Of course he shan't see your frock,' her mother had soothed. 'The very idea! We'll make him wait a bit, shall we? That'll cool his ardour.' Her mother was confident of her strategy when it came to handling men. In the drawing room, she had swept Bertrand in her arms against her broad bosom as if he had been her own long lost son. 'Eh, lad! What a sentimental silly-boots you must think me,' blowing her nose on a delicate lace handkerchief. 'We've been trying out the frock. She's going to look a picture on the big day. Well, Bertrand – and how has France treated you?' She had not waited for him to reply. 'Eh – is it really a whole year! Let me look at you. They say the Continent puts a veneer on a young man.'

Clearly relieved at the interruption of his future mother-in-law's embrace, Bertrand had stepped back and looked at

Christina and she at him. If Christina had hoped for reassurance from his smile she saw instead the forced grin of a man who was clearly determined to make the best of a bad job. She had wanted to run away, but held her ground and kept her eyes resolutely fixed on her lover's face, trying to recall the pleasure which his slender, sharp-edged features had once instilled in her and how she had mooned over the thought of those heavily fringed blue eyes – so affecting, so *extremely devastating* she had confessed boldly to her diary. A revelation had occurred in that moment: Christina recognised that Bertrand did not love her, but more significantly she realised that neither did she love him.

She remembered the agony of showing him over every inch of the Gatehouse where they were to live: the dining room, where they would face each other evening upon evening from opposite ends of the long oak table with nothing at all to say to one another; the drawing room where they would sit in silence at either corner of the fire. The house smelled of new paint and fresh plaster, the hall was dark and panelled, paved with black and white tiles, a fireplace occupied one wall complete with oak mantelpiece, an ornate grate and firedogs, high-backed tapestried chairs standing on either side and a Gothic-style bench between two doors on the opposite wall. The red-carpeted oak staircase reached into further heavy gloom upstairs.

Christina's taste in interior decoration echoed that of her mother: the walls of the sitting room were lined with hand-painted pictures and embroidered texts and the room was filled with every conceivable hand-embellished ornament – firescreens, wool-embroidered cushions and, on the tables, domes of wax fruits, collections of shells, arrangements of dried flowers and collages of leaves, shells and feathers. The curtains were of a deep-pink silk damask and heavily fringed with gold; they were drawn back from the diamond-leaded windows through which the sun streamed on to the polished floor, offering a view of the splendid façade of Chillingdale House.

'You've done all these?' Bertrand had said with a forced admiration of the bric-à-brac.

'I had to have some occupation to while away the days.' Christina had not meant to sound bitter, yet all her unhappiness lay in the remark.

'I'm sorry. It must have been very dull for you.'

'Papa says you're going to work on some scheme at the foundry.' She had changed the subject, wanting to dispel the awkwardness between them. They sat on a buttoned sofa and talked about the foundry and at last she said, 'I *do* want to be a good wife, Bertrand.'

The arrangement of the sofa was designed for intimacy. Bertrand had rested his arm on its curving back and moved to kiss her and she had instinctively drawn away before submitting to his lips on hers. His eagerness had frightened her. She had struggled in his arms and he laughed and held her more firmly, as if it was a game – she remembered how, when they were children, he and Phoebe and Philip had always wanted to engage in games of chasing, fighting and wrestling and that even Phoebe had laughed at her when she said that physical games were not feminine. 'Of course they're not feminine,' Bertrand had said. 'Phil and I don't want to be feminine.' And Phoebe had shrugged her shoulders as if she could not care one way or another what was feminine and what was not.

'You must show me the bedroom.' Bertrand tucking a strand of hair behind her ear made her blush a fiery red. He had reached for her again and she wriggled from his grasp.

'No, it wouldn't be proper to show you alone.'

He had frowned. 'My love. We shall be sharing a bedroom *alone* before long.'

23

'No Bertrand, we're not to share a bedroom. We're to have our own rooms, just as Mama and Papa do at Chillingdale.' She had seen his look of dismay. 'It's how things are arranged in proper society.'

Christina, remembering the humiliation of his silent disbelief, felt the tears slip down her cheeks. She looked in the mirror, seeing her pale face, made paler by the white of the wedding frock.

Her mother was looking at her in horror. There was an edge of hysteria to her solicitous, 'Poppet. Tell Mama. Whatever's wrong?'

Christina began to unfasten her wedding dress. She tugged at the buttons. Her tears turned to frantic sobs.

'I can't. I can't. It's all too horrible. Tell Bertie. The wedding's off.'

Phoebe followed the servant along soft-carpeted corridors and was startled to see Beatrice Underwood emerge from Christina's bedroom and slam its door before hurrying along the corridor. A second door slammed and the way ahead was empty again. Unperturbed, the maid continued to lead the way to the room which her mistress had hastily vacated.

Phoebe was quick to take in the scene in the bedroom, where Christina sat in her chemise and corset, weeping silent tears while Ratcliffe, her maid, dressed her hair. Her heart beat quickly: clearly this was a crisis which needed careful handling. 'Well, this is a nice to-do,' she said cheerfully.

Christina turned a face streaked with misery towards her. She began to sob again. 'Oh, Phoebe – I wish I could die.'

Beatrice acknowledged that her daughter was suffering from a bad case of the jitters, but no one seemed to consider that her own nerves were stretched unbearably. She knew she had done the unforgivable: she had lost patience with Christina, had shouted at her, 'What's the matter with you, girl! This is the happiest day of your life!' and had slammed from the room like one of the common herd. She shuddered at her own behaviour. She would look in on the young bridesmaids; a pretty spectacle would steady her.

The scene was not reassuring: the five well-bred nieces bounced about the guest-room and evaded the ministering hands of the maids and governesses who strove to add the finishing touches of flowered bonnets, white cotton stockings and buckled shoes to their attire. Baskets of posies littered the beds, the air was filled with shrieks and giggles, the harassed helpers looked at Beatrice, embarrassed by their impotence. 'I'm sure all will be well for the ceremonials,' said one of the governesses with a confidence which belied the desperation on her face.

Beatrice could not trust herself to speak. Her silence quelled the children's high spirits momentarily. With a choking sound she closed the door and heard the din begin again as she hurried along the corridor. She told herself that the mother of the bride must be dignified; the scale of Chillingdale's hospitality demanded a certain regality. 'Oh, such anxieties,' she moaned. 'Did ever any woman have to suffer such anxieties?' The tension of hosting the wedding of one's only daughter was enough to prevent any mother from acting as a mother should, and Christina was so strange. How could her poor mama help but be afraid for her? But it was too late to think like that – much, much too late. What of the disgrace? Imagine the humiliation if anything were to prevent the wedding. Beatrice saw that her hands were trembling and she could feel her heart pounding erratically. She rang for Ratcliffe to help her into her frock and sat on the bed to calm herself. 'Lord, make Christina pull herself together,' she prayed more earnestly than she had ever prayed before and then with a twinge of conscience added a more tender prayer for her daughter: 'Dear Lord, make my poppet happy. Make Bertrand Clough a devoted and considerate husband.'

'Miss Clough has come, ma'am,' said Ratcliffe as she bustled with comforting unconcern into the room. 'Miss Clough says she will deal with Miss Christina.'

Beatrice felt an immediate sense of her prayers having been answered. Phoebe would know the right things to say. She stood while Ratcliffe fastened the strings of her half-crinoline petticoat and lifted the heavy royal blue frock over her head. 'We are very fortunate in Miss Clough, Ratcliffe,' said Beatrice. '*Very* fortunate indeed.'

'Yes, ma'am,' said Ratcliffe, understanding that with weddings on everyone's mind the remark had more than a passing significance.

Beatrice straightened her shoulders and expanded her bosom and studied her reflection in the cheval mirror, feeling a gradual revival of self-confidence. She had worn well for fifty-five – a good figure still, no question about that. She preened a little and smiled at herself in the glass, the smile of a woman sure of her attractions.

Ratcliffe fastened the final hook and eye of the bodice and fluffed out the frills and lace. She stepped back to admire her mistress. They stood side by side – the one resplendent in silk with trailing skirts and yards of lace, the maid's finery restricted to a dark serviceable taffeta supported by a modestly curving crinoline and a nosegay of flowers pinned to her breast.

'It's going to be a lovely day for it,' Ratcliffe volunteered.

Beatrice smiled at her, woman to woman. 'I really think you might be right.'

'It's going to be a lovely day,' Phoebe insisted. She smiled as if to say, I have done all I can, it's your turn now, as Ratcliffe and a second lady's maid entered with the wedding frock over their arms, freshly ironed, the buttons mended.

She watched the women deck the rigid Christina in white. She had done well and had talked until her own throat was dry: the bride's only outward show of distress was her blotched complexion and an occasional hiccup. The dress at least was beautiful, a creation of satin and lace over whalebone with a skirt which dragged its Valenciennes lace across the carpet just as if it were so much curtaining. Christina's fine golden hair, worthy of the expression 'crowning glory', was swept up into curls and ringlets in a style reminiscent of the ancient Greeks, topped with a chaplet of wax orange-blossom and with a long veil hanging to the floor.

'Eh, she looks a picture,' declared Ratcliffe loyally. Christina twisted her thin hands and gave the woman a watery smile.

Beatrice swept into the room. 'How is the bride?' she said, as if the bride had not been declaring only half an hour before that she would sooner fling herself out of the window than go to the altar. Beatrice halted and threw up her hands in a genuine gesture of incredulity at the transformation. 'My precious chick, words fail me.' And she was indeed moved by the vision of her child robed and veiled in sacrificial white. She turned to Phoebe, who sat on the bed, exhaustion creeping over her. 'Phoebe love, could you do something about the bridesmaids? The scallywags are leading their governesses a proper dance.' Gratified by Christina's wan smile, Phoebe set herself to the duties of senior bridesmaid.

The whole town was out and celebrating. The railway station and surrounding streets were hung with flags and a band

27

had begun to assemble in the town square near the church with much clashing of instruments and the sun sparkling off polished brass.

Edwin Clough roused himself from his observation of the town hall and remembered that his destination was the church and that it was his son's wedding day. He had been thinking about another day, a visit to London some months earlier and the majesty of the four great lions around Nelson's Column.

Edwin was a large figure, somewhat lionlike himself, with a broad forehead and a mane of grey hair and side-whiskers flowing from under his top hat. They had been grand statues. 'Very fine. Very affecting,' he murmured. Edwin knew that the painter and sculptor Landseer had been responsible for the lions; he had a copy of 'The Monarch of the Glen' over his own fireplace in the dining room at Belle Vue. He had been struck by the coincidence of sharing the same forename with the great man and the fact that he and the artist were of the same generation, a generation which knew the significance of Trafalgar and had seen England rise as an industrial nation.

It was in London that Edwin had come to the conclusion that Bertrand had wasted enough time and money in Paris and the seeds of his idea had taken root. Had Edwin known that the sculpting of the lions had all but defeated his namesake, that the enormity of the commission had overtaxed the artist and was soon to hasten his decline into insanity, had he been aware that well-respected art critics had declared the statues flaccid and uninspiring, or even that Landseer had once resorted to using for a model the decomposing cadaver of an elderly lion from Regent's Park Zoo, his enthusiasm for the statues might have weakened – but perhaps not, for Edwin was less impressed by their artistic merit than the fact that they were cast in bronze. Edwin knew about casting bronze. There was a beauty in the metal which overwhelmed him at times; the smell and finish on a new locomotive wheel-bearing was almost sensual – though Edwin would not have used such a word. The perfection of a good casting invited the hand and eye in a way which most people did not understand. Statues they understood. Lions in a public square they understood, but the magnificence of a railway wheel-bearing was lost on them.

At any rate it was lost on his sons, thought Edwin as he made his way past the town hall towards the church, the prospect of Bertrand's wedding depressing him a little. Weddings reminded him of Annette, of his own mortality and the disappointments he had fathered. Annette would have argued for Bertrand to stay in France, never mind the practicalities of the boy turning his energies to the foundry or the suitability of the Underwood match. She had never quite forgiven him for wanting to live down her French family and her French ways.

He halted by the church. Crowds thronged the road, attracted by the band, the bunting and the rows of carriages and horses spilling out their guests. The Union Jack flew from the church tower, the motto *Long Life and Happiness* framed in flowers formed an arch over the gateway, and inside, hidden from view, the bell-ringers sweated as they pulled on the bell-ropes. The din and the colour and confusion made Edwin catch his breath. How Annette would have revelled in it all. For a moment his wife's zest for living flooded his memory and he felt a sob rise to his throat.

He still missed her. After ten years the pain of her death was still strong. Why did she have to leave him so soon and with the legacy of her wayward ideas – insisting that Gerald be encouraged to set up a theatre on her money, appointing drawing tutors, French tutors, music and dancing masters and encouraging Bertie, even when he was a boy of eleven, to believe he could be another Michelangelo? She had been a foolish woman, he saw that now, but beautiful, and full of joy and totally, wonderfully devoted as a wife.

The guests milled about in the sunshine near the church door, determined to be seen in their finery until the last minute. Men of commerce paraded with their wives, farmers mixed with leaders in local government and industry. The numerous tradespeople who had cause to be grateful for Underwood's continuing prosperity stood about with an air of slight agitation, born of the knowledge that the whole affair was costing them a day's trading.

Shortly before eleven o'clock people began to cram into the church, as if only now did they remember the reason for all the fuss and were suddenly afraid of committing a social blunder and not being inside when the bride arrived. The interior of the building was cool. The strains of the organ mingled with the rising murmur of people trying to find a place in the crowded pews and within minutes the building was filled to its doors.

Charles and Tessa, arriving late at the church, eased their way through the crowd. They were escorted by the ushers to a seat with much pushing and shoving and solicitous commands of 'Make way, make way' on account of Tessa's 'condition', unmistakable under her red-and-black striped costume. They sat next to Gerald and Olive and behind Edwin in a pew reserved near the front for the family of the groom.

Charles stared at the back of Bertrand's head coldly. Older by five years, he had never quite thrown off his childhood resentment of the interloper who had stolen his mother's affections. His father's too, come to that. Charles had always known that Edwin liked him the least, and yet he had been the one to play the dutiful son with the greatest concentration, trying so hard to please him, learning chapters of the Bible until he was word perfect each Sunday and throwing off his ambition to be an artist in order to work in the pattern office designing components for the foundry to cast.

Drawing was the only occupation for which he had ever shown any real talent. He remembered his mother's praise, her attempts to coax praise too from his father, and grudgingly, chiefly to please her, his father had allowed a few 'art' castings to creep into the foundry's manufacturing. But that was in the past, and long before he met Tessa. Even Charles found it hard to believe that he had indulged himself in a dalliance with one of Gerald's theatricals, yet it was typical of him that he should marry her, he thought with a touch of self-mockery. His father ignored him for the most part these days. He remembered the rejoicings, the readings from the Scripture of the parable of the prodigal, in celebration of Bertrand's home-coming. His younger brother's fall from grace had been less severe than his own.

Bertrand had quizzed him about Tessa with his superior smile. 'It's not like you, Charlie, to let a woman get her hooks into you.' None of them understood. How could anyone understand the way Tessa could rule one so completely, filling one's mind and senses? The scent of her frock and hair drifted into his nostrils, overpowering the musty smell of the church. He turned to look at her and she flicked him a smile. He felt the condemnation of the women in the pews behind, imagining their murmured comments. He heard again Bertrand's, 'A bit of a bobtail is she?' and clenched his fists against his knees. He had been as near as he had ever come to striking his younger brother. Why couldn't Bertie have stayed in France? Nobody wanted him here.

'You'd think it was the Prince of Wales marrying over again,' hissed Tessa. She adjusted the small red-and-black hat perched high on her head with a little push of her gloved fingers and sat back to look about her, regarding the figures in the front pew with interest and the rest of the congregation with critical eyes. Her fair springing curls, cut short to her forehead and massed in a wiry frizz under the velvet hat, surrounded a vivacious face. She held herself confidently despite her advanced state of pregnancy and with the physical ease of one who knew her own body well.

Tessa's views on love might have been called free-thinking or advanced had she moved in different social circles, for she believed that her body was her own to give to whom she pleased. As it was, Griseley folk knew very well what they thought of her: she imagined the tongues wagging in the pews behind. Tessa regarded Edwin Clough's massive frame in the pew in front disparagingly, his head bared, looking like one of the Old Testament prophets. Charles had told her how in the past they all used to attend family prayers – daughter and sons, sitting po-faced round the table while their father read them some long-winded sermon. She would never have subjected herself to that particular family ritual, even supposing Edwin Clough had allowed her into his house. Now there would be just Edwin and Phoebe. The mental picture of the two of them caused a sneer to settle on Tessa's features. Phoebe the dutiful daughter, with her pious, holier-than-thou looks. Why did she put up with it? She set her mouth. Just let Charles try making family prayers an institution in *her* household.

Tessa had returned to Griseley from her mother's house in Leeds by the evening mail coach only a few days before the wedding. She had not told Charles when she expected to arrive, had not even been sure that she would come at all

32

after their quarrel, though she could not remember now what it had been about.

She craned her neck for a full view of Bertrand, the reluctant bridegroom, who had gone to Paris, apparently with his father's blessing, only to be dragged back with his tail between his legs to marry Underwood's daughter. Did none of them have any guts? The wedding, according to Charles, was going to be the best event in Griseley all year. *Do come home, Tessa*, he had written. *It will look bad if you're not there.* Better than brass bands and choral singing, she had told herself. Some event! Well, then, she had supposed she must attend.

She remembered the travesty of her own wedding day, a hasty affair in a Leeds registry office. She had worn a discreet lilac dress and bonnet and her mother had cried all the way through the ceremony.

She despised Charles for marrying her. She could not even recall the occasion when he had got her pregnant. He had been a silent but surprisingly satisfactory lover and they had done it a lot in the early weeks. She despised herself now for not resisting him, for hanging around in Gerald's makeshift theatre after everyone else had gone home. She was sure he had only courted her to prove something: that he was as good as his younger brother, who would have been having a good time chasing women in Paris, or that he could be a rebel like Gerald.

Had he done it to spite his father, she wondered. Or to impress him? He had done that right enough. Edwin had been so impressed he had thrown a purple fit. She sighed, for it had been warm and cosy among the piles of old curtains and costumes and she supposed she had loved Charles just a little – though no more than she had loved so many men. 'The trouble is, Tessa my girl,' she told herself severely, 'you never could resist a good-looking fella.'

She shifted a little in the pew and looked at the groom with curiosity. She supposed she had expected some kind of pallid replica of Charles. She felt a response of slow pleasurable surprise as she watched Bertrand turn to speak to his groomsman. The family resemblance was noticeable, yet, where Charles and Gerald's faces were fleshy their brother's features were lean to the bone, with a clean-shaven firm jaw-line and straight nose complimented by a sweep of dark almost feminine eyelashes.

'The groom is prettier than the bride,' she murmured, recalling Christina Underwood's angular face and figure. Charles nudged her nervously and she giggled and fell silent. She amused herself by concentrating her full attention on his brother.

Bertrand's mind was curiously numb; he heard but did not comprehend the comments of Philip, his best man, his one-time best friend, by his side, yet he knew that he had responded to them for he was aware of his own voice from time to time, hoarse with nerves and very loud in his head. He heard the organ play and it evoked an evening at Belle Vue soon after his home-coming: Phoebe at the harmonium with Gerald beside her turning the pages of music, a log fire crackling in the fireplace, for a fire was always necessary against the wind off the moor right through until the end of May. 'Charles has his nose pushed out of joint because I need you for my latest venture,' his father had said, as if needing to explain Charles's hostility. 'He should have thought of that when he took up with the harlot. Come. I want to talk to you. We'll go into the study.'

Bertrand had followed him across the hall, hearing Phoebe strike up the introit to *Elijah* in the drawing room and Gerald's deep rich voice begin to sing. The scent of may from a vase on the hall stand had been slightly sickly in the air. His father had grumbled about the flowers, complaining that the petals were dropping and that it was bad luck to bring may blossom indoors but Bertrand had recalled his joy at seeing Phoebe run towards him along the station platform with the flowers against her breast.

They went into the study and his father indicated a seat by the fire-grate and settled himself in the leather wing chair opposite. He had seemed pleased with himself. A nerve in his cheek twitched, drawing his mouth into a smile. 'I was in London on business some time back. I got to thinking how the foundry might one day be sold outside of the family with no one to carry it on. You were in France. Charles had proved himself unfitted. Gerald called himself works manager but spent all his time laiking about like a great kid writing plays.'

'His plays are popular in the town,' Bertrand had defended.

'Popular! What's that! Nothing but vanity – *vanity and vexation of the spirit.*'

'Ecclesiastes.' Bertrand smiled, remembering how the reference had escaped automatically before he could prevent himself.

'So you've not forgotten quite all your teaching among those profligates in France.' The nerve had twitched again. It had been quiet in the study, the sound of the harmonium and singing were muted and the clock on the mantelshelf ticked slowly. His father said suddenly, 'I saw the lions in Trafalgar Square in London. It was as if their heads were lifted high because they were right proud of England and were looking to her prosperous future. I got to thinking to myself, Bertrand fancies himself as a sculptor. His mother wanted him to get a living from it. Why don't I give him something worthwhile to do? It might well be the making of him.' He leaned back in his chair and threw out his chest.

'Lions, lad. That's what it's all about. You and me, we're going to make the town some lions.'

Bertrand had been tempted to laugh, but his father's earnest expression had suggested that this would be a mistake.

'Think what it would do for the firm. Think of the honour of Clough's Foundry casting four great beasts to sit outside the town hall.'

'The town hall?' Bertrand had repeated stupidly.

'Leeds has lions outside its town hall. Why not Griseley?'

Why not indeed? The whole idea was bizarre. The old man had gone soft in the head. But no, his father was smiling at him, waiting for his opinion. As Bertrand sought to frame an excuse that he knew nothing at all about the anatomy of a lion, something unexpected had happened. Some aspect of the challenge, its eccentricity, its sheer novelty had touched a response in him. He was a sculptor, wasn't he? He had done menagerie studies, had once modelled a cat for his father when the foundry had taken to producing 'art' castings, and a sight more successful it had been than his statue of Madeleine. A cat was not so very different from a lion, just smaller.

'It won't be easy. A lion. It's very ambitious.'

'Charles will help you. You can work together on the drawings.'

'The town council would have to agree.' Bertrand's blossoming enthusiasm had wavered at the enormity of the undertaking, the public interest involved and the risk to his reputation as an artist if he should fail.

'I put the idea at the last council meeting. They were very interested. They thought it would put Griseley on the map.'

'Clough's Foundry too.'

'Naturally.'

'What if I were to refuse to do it?'

'You won't refuse. Your bread and butter depends on it and I've already told Underwood you're going to do it. Why else do you think he's still keen for you to marry Christina? His daughter, wife of the sculptor of Griseley's lions! What better prestige could there be than that!'

Bertrand could not imagine as he sat in church waiting for the future wife of the sculptor of Griseley's lions to arrive. Was the old man going daft in the head? Was he daft too to even consider it? The lion project would require Charles's co-operation and in his present mood of resentfulness that would be difficult.

His thoughts kept returning to Maurice. Why could he not get the notion that they were fellow prisoners out of his mind? He wondered whether he had left France only because he was afraid of his father? Had he perhaps been afraid of staying, afraid of the growing mood of unrest in Paris and, in particular, afraid of Maurice?

The Frenchman had paced the floor of his studio constantly, plucking at the grubby bandage on his wrist as if it itched or strumming one-handed on Bertrand's guitar. He had criticised his sculpting, the food he brought him and his clothes – which were 'too bourgeois' – and railed against the police, the government and the imperial family. He was excitable, he was vain and he was violent, and sometimes Bertrand had wondered if he was not also a little insane.

'It's impossible for me to live like this!' he would say. 'I feel trapped! Am I an animal? A fucking monkey in a cage?' Or he would look at his bandaged arm with hatred. 'Fuck the police! Fuck the Empire! I'll fucking kill the next policeman I see when I get out of here! I'll castrate the man who did this to me!'

'I know men who have fought alongside Blanqui,' he said one day, 'and others who have met him in prison.

There is a man who is dedicated to the spirit of revolution.'

'Some might call it fanaticism,' Bertrand had responded. He knew of Auguste Blanqui mostly from legend, the conspirator and revolutionary hero who had been in prison for his political activities more years than anyone could count.

Maurice shrugged. 'If fanaticism is necessary—' he had halted his pacing by the window table and picked up the picture of Phoebe; the portrait had seemed to hold some charm for him for he returned to it frequently. He set it down on the table with a display of reverence. 'English women are so self-contained,' he said as if to explain the fascination of the picture. 'Only an English woman can look truly feminine. French women are harsh, they are not tender-hearted.'

It was an observation which was to come back to Bertrand with particular irony a few days later when he returned to the apartment after an evening's wine drinking. He heard Maurice and Madeleine before he discovered them and was puzzled momentarily by the rhythmic thumping of the iron bedstead against the wall. He sat in the studio with his back to the shuttered window, the ribs of the wooden chair against his spine, staring at the statue with the oddly shaped breasts and hearing the grunting copulation between his house guest and his mistress in the next room.

He supposed that Madeleine had come to the apartment to find him and, disappointed because he was out, had decided not to waste all that pent-up energy. After a while he grew irritated with the complaining creak and bump of the bedstead and walked to the bedroom, flinging open the communicating door. He saw the tumbled bedclothes, Maurice's unnaturally white buttocks half covered by the blue workman's smock and Madeleine's reddened, sweating face peering over his shoulder. Their glances met before

Bertrand looked away and he heard Madeleine's shriek as he closed the door again.

Maurice came out to the studio first. He had dressed untidily, the buttons of his trousers still undone. He had shrugged, judging accurately that Bertrand would do nothing, and lit himself a cigarette. Bertrand reflected that if he had been a Frenchman he might have killed him – Madeleine too. The least he should have done was to kick Maurice out of the apartment and knock Madeleine about a little to teach her a lesson. He saw her through the open doorway, kneeling on the bed, naked and with her arms thrown out imploringly to him like the subject of a tragic or sacred painting, her breasts and thighs still rosy with the heat of Maurice's ardour. Smudgy tears streamed down her plump cheeks. 'Bertrand! He forced me, I swear!' Then, when she detected the scepticism in his silence, 'You weren't here! I knew you were with a woman!'

It had all been too much trouble – easier to laugh it off, to accept her subsequent offer of penance and take her into his bed. Maurice apologised the next morning. 'But these things happen,' he said, 'you mustn't blame the girl. I take it all on myself.' He was arrested that same day while Bertrand was at his art class. Bored with being confined, he had slipped out along the boulevard to buy cigarettes and was picked up at one of the cafés. Antoine said later that Maurice had been convicted of inciting fellow workers to riot.

Bertrand heard someone say that the bride's mother had arrived and that it would not be long now. The murmur of voices behind him had reached a fresh pitch of excitement, but he did not turn round, for his neck felt stiff and solid and his legs did not belong to him. He looked at his knees. Was he really sitting there in church or was he mercifully still in his room and had yet to wake? Was there perhaps still a chance of escape?

A hush fell on the waiting crowd and then a tumultuous shuffling and scrabbling. The congregation rose to its feet as the organ music changed to that of Handel's 'Processional March'. Bertrand too was standing and he turned to see an ocean of faces and a path between them, like the parting of the Red Sea, along which came Christina – pure, faithful Christina, shrouded in a veil like some ghastly white apparition – and behind her, bobbing from side to side, the various bridesmaids shepherded by his sister Phoebe. In that moment Bertrand awoke. There was to be no deliverance. His life from now on would be for ever altered. His gaze fixed in his despair on a face in the congregation. Among that crowd of townspeople, strangers he had known since childhood, a fresh, animated face with a wide curving mouth and laughing eyes shone out. A beacon of robust, healthy radiance seemed to illuminate the girl standing next to his brother Charles. So that was Tessa. She held his gaze, absorbing and – could it be? – recognising his despair? The encounter lasted perhaps no more than a few seconds, yet it seemed to Bertrand that a wealth of communication passed between them in that glance.

The church bells rang frenziedly, proclaiming the marriage ceremony over. The schoolchildren outside the church chanted a prepared anthem and hastily strewed their posies in the path of the bride before scrambling for the coppers scattered for them by the groom. The band puffed and blew and added to the din and the Rifle Volunteer Corps, receiving their awaited signal, fired off a cannon high on Griseley Bank.

The guests mingled and chatted and made haste for their vehicles, anxious not to miss the wedding breakfast; and then the bride and groom were off at the head of the procession of carriages.

Christina clung to Bertrand's arm with a vicelike grip. He suspected that she was close to tears. Her veil still covered her face and she did not speak – neither bride nor groom uttered a word from leaving the church to halting on the gravelled drive outside the doors of Chillingdale. It did not occur to Bertrand that there was anything odd in this, for his mind was filled with the recent memory of his sister-in-law. That face, those bold, challenging eyes! How had Charles, dull, prosaic Charles, managed to hook such a beauty? He thought briefly of Madeleine and wondered if she had found herself another lover. He had given her the statue, which had been too heavy and too embarrassing to bring home. She had sworn to smash it into a thousand pieces as soon as he had gone. Typical. Madeleine was a savage; everything about her had exuded a cheap vulgarity, but at that moment he would have exchanged this vigourless, pathetic creature beside him for just a pinch of Madeleine's vitality.

They climbed from the coach and only now did Bertrand think it a little strange that his bride remained so stiff and silent and invisible.

Phoebe ran forward to arrange Christina's gown. 'Throw back your veil,' she whispered. Christina shook her head violently and Phoebe suspected that she had again been weeping. She turned to Bertrand in exasperation. 'Can't you do something?' She was rewarded with a look of bewilderment. Were all men insensitive idiots or only her brothers?

Philip Underwood hurried inside the house and presently appeared at one of the bedroom windows. He held a pink and white plate high in the air and called to everyone to 'look out and stand well clear' if they didn't want to get their heads knocked in. The crowd watched to see whether the plate would break, for if it smashed into a satisfactory number of pieces the couple's married life would be one of great happiness, but if it remained intact their life together would be one of unbroken misery. Phoebe frowned and felt a sense of foreboding, and a wag called out, 'I hope that's not best bone china,' as the plate flew from Philip's hand.

Phoebe supposed he had meant it to hit the terrace, but he threw too wide and it skimmed the gravel drive and, bouncing, landed gently on the lawn. There was a moment's silence, an ominous pause in which superstitious thoughts took root in the minds of the onlookers, and then someone scooped up the plate and dropped it with a crash against a stone urn. Everyone cheered and Phoebe sensed the relief in the sound as the guests surged across the lawn towards the marquee. She looked up at the window and the distress on Philip's face made her pity him a little. She turned away with the others to the marquee and saw Charles with his wife on his arm and a curiously sardonic look on Tessa's face.

Three

Oh! lift me as a wave, a leaf, a cloud!
I fall upon the thorns of life! I bleed!

Percy Bysshe Shelley,
Ode to the West Wind

Jack Bateman, dressed like the Chillingdale staff in drab
knee-breeches and a scarlet waistcoat, stood alongside the
tent with his father and brothers. His father was over six
feet tall, with a chest like an ale barrel and an almost totally
bald head, which gave him the look of a criminal; he had a
reputation for throwing as solid a punch as his sons, yet he
held a successful balance between running the Nag's Head
Inn on Griseley Bank and maintaining an air of respectability.

Jack, at just twenty, was the youngest of the three sons.
Broad and tall in the company of most men, his muscular
build seemed almost slender in comparison with his father
and brothers and he was easily the most arresting in looks,
with a straight nose, as yet unbroken by brawling, and a
strong mouth and jaw. His brown hair, neither dark nor fair,
fell softly across his brow and an expression of dreamy
intelligence hovered about his brown eyes.

Phoebe passed the line of servers without looking at
him. He did not expect her to acknowledge him. She looked

prettier than all the other women put together, prettier than he had ever seen her, in a half-crinoline blue frock trimmed with blackberry-coloured flounces and ribbons. Her rich brown hair was gathered under a little hat trimmed with rosebuds. He could just see the perfect curve of her cheek and the downward cast of her heavy dark eyelashes. The gentry passed between the garlanded poles of the marquee and Jack went with his brothers to shift beer kegs from the drays into the shade.

'How's this for a day off at the masters' expense, lads?' said Joseph to his sons.

'Better than a day at foundry, but I'd as soon be at home,' muttered Matt, recently married, fair and pleasant-faced and the eldest of the brothers.

Walter hoisted a keg on to his shoulder and said with more venom, 'Trust the gentry to turn hard slog into some sort of charity. Buggers reckon they're doing us a favour.' Walter was handsome, there was no disputing the broad brow, dark eyes and high, slightly oriental cheek bones, but there was a vanity in his expression and an aggressive swagger in his tall frame.

The Bateman sons worked at Clough's Foundry and it was to the foundry, not Phoebe, that Jack now turned his mind. For what could be gained by dwelling on Phoebe Clough's attractions, when he was enlisted to perform the temporary duties of a servant and Phoebe, as chief bridesmaid among the wedding party, was to partner Philip Underwood at the top table?

'We shall have us some fun later,' Matt said, thinking of the festivities that evening. 'When all the fetching and carrying's done.'

Walter paused as he set down the barrel. He leaned forward and clipped Jack across the cheek. 'We shall have us some fun one day, lad. Isn't that right?'

He was meaning Edwin Clough's new scheme at the foundry of course. The men were grumbling about it already and threatening that they would strike rather than do the extra work for nothing.

Jack flinched from Walter's hand, neatly avoiding a second cuff behind the ear. 'You – you're all talk.' Griseley's foundry had never known a strike in its life.

'Am I, lad? Am I? We'll see about that.'

The tent had been the largest available, but it barely accommodated the Underwoods' guests. Distant family cousins and townspeople squashed themselves together at the long tables. Beads of sweat stood out on notable foreheads, the wives of important businessmen fanned themselves with the menus and the vicar declared he could eat a horse, though he trusted Alfred would serve them better than that.

'Heard you're having a bit of bother with your workers, Edwin,' said Alfred Underwood as the two families made their way to the top table. 'A few hotheads stirring up trouble?'

'A storm in a teacup.' Edwin hoped that Alfred would keep his voice down.

'Glad to hear it. We don't want anything to spoil this happy day.' Alfred had intended only a little malice in the observation and was in fact feeling magnanimous. It was not often one had the opportunity to bestow such visible largesse on the whole of the town.

Alfred Underwood's fortunes had flourished at the same time as Edwin's and the two men had remained friends for more than twenty years. Edwin and Alfred served on the town council and other local committees together, each had subscribed to the founding of charitable bodies – Edwin for the building of a reformatory, Alfred the almshouses and an orphanage. They were members also of various societies and institutions whose general aim was the improvement of man's leisure hours – Edwin via the Temperance Society and the Working Men's Scientific and Educational Institute, Alfred the Choral Society and the local brass band. In their religious loyalties they agreed to differ – Edwin being an elder of the Ebenezer Methodist chapel, Alfred attending at the parish church. Their wives had been friends in the early years, commiserating with one another over the foibles of husbands, the trials of pregnancies and of rearing young children. So, it seemed, the perfect association had been established: each paterfamilias enjoying respect in the town, their children growing to maturity together and now, thanks to Christina and Bertrand, the two families uniting in marriage.

Alfred seized Bertrand's hand and pumped it energetically. His grey hair was cropped with military severity, but he was a mild-mannered man, given less to exercising an iron will than to showing an occasional deficiency of resolution. The fact that his son Philip was employed at Clough's Foundry on an unimpressive salary was no act of paternal tyranny; it stemmed from a hope that the broader experience would stand his son in good stead when he eventually joined the board of the railway company.

Philip beamed at Alfred's side, as if nothing could have delighted him more than to be in the company of his family and his old schoolfellow. He was taller than Bertrand by several inches, a candid unsophisticated young man with the same long lugubrious face as his father; he sported fastidiously trained side-whiskers and a wispy, almost invisible moustache; his hair, a fine silky blond like Christina's, reached his collar. 'No escape now, Bertie,' he said, his clumsiness with the plate forgotten.

'It's good to see you and Christina hitched at last, lad,'

Alfred said. 'None too soon.' His only reproaches over Bertrand's long absence had been for the sake of form rather than heartfelt, and in the next breath he murmured, 'I've sowed a few wild oats of my own in my day, but I reckon you've got both feet firmly on the ground again.'

'If he hasn't, Christina will soon keep them there.' His wife, overhearing, came forward and hugged her new son-in-law. Crushed against whalebone and with Beatrice's hairnet and ribbons in his mouth, it occurred to Bertrand that the Underwoods approved of him, that he perhaps owed his marriage to nothing less than this fact.

Philip thumped Bertrand on the shoulder genially. 'Christina will keep you in order, Bertie.'

Bertrand wondered vaguely whether Philip had always been a blockhead without his noticing it. He looked enquiringly at Christina who was still hidden behind her veil. She did not appear to be listening. He felt a sudden desire to escape from the marquee and thought of Maurice, like a caged animal, restlessly formulating plans and discarding them, unable to contain his nervous energy within four walls. How would he survive in a prison cell? Bertrand did not care to imagine what life must be like in a Paris gaol.

'It must be grand to be back in Griseley.' Alfred's statement presupposed a superiority about Griseley, an acceptance that it was the best place any man could hope to live, the centre of the nineteenth-century universe and God's heaven on earth.

His wife, seating herself at the table, smiled at Bertrand and glanced at Christina with the implication that his reply should include some compliment to his new wife if it was to gain the approval of his mother-in-law.

Bertrand's swiftly murmured, 'It's very good to be back with old friends, sir, and to be in Christina's company

47

again,' did nothing to alleviate his feeling of being trapped nor convince him that he would rather be in God's Yorkshire heaven than far away in Paris. He surveyed the tables filling with guests and the girl in the red-and-black dress caught his eye again. A flicker of amusement played on her lips as she held his glance with heart-stopping intensity. Bertrand felt his spirits lift.

'You are looking especially lovely today, Phoebe,' remarked Philip as he sat beside her. 'It's a pity we can only hazard a guess at my sister's loveliness. Is she supposed to cover up her face all day?'

'She's very nervous,' defended Phoebe. She had heard one or two of the guests speculate already on whether Christina would manage the *déjeuner* by passing food under her veil, or perhaps she would be content with sipping champagne from a straw pushed through a hole in the lace. One guest had suggested rather too loudly that Bertrand had sneaked a French mam'selle in place of the bride and that if the girl threw back her veil he would be undone.

Phoebe saw Beatrice Underwood lean across Bertrand to speak to her daughter in an agitated manner; clearly the subject of the veil had become a burning issue. After an urgently whispered conversation Christina raised her hands to her face and a murmur of approval ran round the tables, followed by an audible sigh as the veil was lifted and Christina in all her pale anguish was revealed. Bertrand leaned forward and dutifully kissed her cheek and Christina lowered her eyes and blushed as the gesture drew forth a cheer.

Phoebe regarded the smiling faces and wondered why they all supposed the scene a cause for celebration. If she had glanced at Charles's wife at that moment she would have seen again the smile which hovered from time to time on Tessa's lips. She might have been alerted to the danger

48

in Tessa's expression and perhaps have noticed more – the covert glances which passed between Tessa and Bertrand, the surreptitious questioning appraisal of one another and once, a shared look, an expression of mutual certainty. But Phoebe had other matters to contend with: Philip was embarking on the subject of marriage. He spoke of the excellent way in which Phoebe had always managed her father's household affairs and mentioned casually his own preference for a degree of organising excellence in a wife. Too late to avoid it, Phoebe saw the direction in which he was heading and, making an excuse, she turned rather rudely to speak to a guest across the table.

Philip, feeling Phoebe's rebuff, bore her no malice but gave his attention to her brother. 'Well – the wedding breakfast. You've done it now, Bertie. Lord though, I envy you a year in Paris. Christina missed you like fury.'

Christina blushed and said nothing.

'I feared it would rain on the big day,' said Beatrice. 'It can be so wet sometimes in July. But there, I'm such an old worry-boots.'

'You always were,' Edwin said, remembering when Beatrice Underwood and Annette had been friends. *How that woman worrits and frets. It will be a miracle if the children survive her ministrations.* He smiled, recalling Annette's insistence that their own children run barefoot in the garden in summer and be allowed the fresh air of the moors even on the coldest of days. His mood of nostalgia faltered as he remembered that it was the Yorkshire winters which had attacked Annette's own less than robust physique.

The theme of matrimony was continued with the onset of the wedding speeches. Alfred assured everyone that marriage added a solidity, an objective and vigour to two young people's lives. The role of the husband was that of provider, he asserted, adding that his son-in-law was to fulfil that role

49

by returning to work in his father's business. The role of the wife – Alfred turned fondly to his daughter – was to be an adored sweetheart; it was her duty and privilege to help Bertrand all she could with her tenderness and love.

A pretty speech, thought Phoebe, prettier than her brother's: Bertrand gave a mumbling performance, barely adequate to the occasion and distinctly lacking in enthusiasm so that Phoebe longed to give him a good shake. Could he not see what was needed? Philip's response to the toast to the bridesmaids was by contrast a stirring effort; she might even have admired it, had it not contained so many references to bridesmaids becoming blushing brides and if she had not been so aware that everyone's gaze had settled with cosy indulgence upon her.

'It looks as if we shall be seeing a lot of one another, with you all set on the scheme at the foundry,' remarked Philip to Bertrand when the speeches were over.

'I don't know about *all set*.' Bertrand glanced warily at his father.

'You'll have picked up plenty of use to you about sculpting in Paris I dare say.'

'Oh – fair to middling.' Bertrand gave them a vague and watered-down description of his art classes and visits to art galleries. He watched Edwin leave his place and walk to one of the further tables to engage in conversation with one of the guests.

'The men at the works haven't cottoned on to your papa's idea of the lions, you know.' Beatrice lowered her voice so that Edwin should not hear. 'Ask Philip.'

Philip confirmed the remark. 'There's a small element of troublemakers at the foundry – fellows getting above themselves, shouting about fair pay for a fair day's work. You know the sort of thing.'

Phoebe turned to him suddenly. 'Perhaps the workers

would like to have been consulted too. Do you know that they are not to receive a penny more for the extra work which Father's statues will involve? There'll be a revolution one of these days. Mark my words.'

Bertrand looked at her in surprise and Phoebe flushed scarlet for she had surprised herself by the force of her opinion; she could only suppose it had something to do with the champagne or the strange mood of discontent which had been creeping upon her all that day.

'Who have you been talking to?'

Phoebe felt that Bertrand's scrutiny was tinged with disapproval and knew that she could not tell him; Bertrand, like her father, would think it odd if he knew that she had listened to the sentiments of the foundry workers.

Bertrand thought again of Maurice: the connection between the Frenchman and his sister jarred his sensibilities and talk of revolution was not pretty from Phoebe's lips. 'I don't think you should listen to complaints from the foundry. Father might think it disloyal.'

Phoebe turned a deeper red. She smoothed her hands on her skirt. 'You're right.' She stood up abruptly and left the top table to talk to an old acquaintance.

Beatrice explained to Bertrand with a hint of disapproval: 'Phoebe will no doubt have been listening to those Bateman boys. She has lately struck up an association with Sarah Bateman. The girl's mother was ill and I believe she's visited the family a few times.'

'The Batemans?' Bertrand, watching Phoebe bend her slim figure to speak to one of the chapel elders near the doorway, remembered how, when they were children, the Batemans had regularly lain in ambush for them at the bottom of Griseley Bank and how Phoebe had on more than one occasion fiercely defended herself and her brothers with her fists.

'The father is a decent enough fellow for a publican.' Alfred cut himself a slice of Stilton. 'And the wife and daughter are decent and hard-working, but the sons are getting a name for their lawless ways.'

'It's the Bateman brothers who are at the core of this group of troublemakers at the works,' added Philip. 'And Phoebe – dear, sweet girl that she is – out of commiseration with their sister has formed a misguided kind of sympathy.'

'Of course, it's quite proper for Phoebe to visit the girl and her mother,' Beatrice said with an emphasis which suggested the opposite.

Philip was moved to a peculiar anger. 'I can't abide the thought of that dear girl being taken in by those loutish ruffians.'

Bertrand looked at his old schoolfellow, at the red face and the hand which trembled as he lifted his champagne glass to his lips, and felt pity – not for Philip but for Phoebe.

The guests began to wander from the marquee, to stroll in the grounds, to view the wedding gifts and the bridal cake on show in the library or to rest about the house until it was time for dinner.

Phoebe escorted the young bridesmaids upstairs and, with their governesses, settled them to sleep in a bedroom so that they should not be exhausted when it came to the evening's festivities. It was over half an hour before the job of removing frocks and shoes and stockings was done and the maid drew the heavy curtains across the windows. Phoebe felt a longing to follow the children's example and slip bare-legged under cool sheets, for the day was turning out to be a hot and sultry one.

She glanced through the window on the stairs and saw Philip making for the house. The impression he gave of concentrated purpose made her turn abruptly on her heel as she heard him come in at the front door and across the hall.

The room she entered was Christina's. She had supposed it would be empty but Christina sat at her dressing table staring into the mirror.

'Shouldn't you be in the library watching everyone admire the cake?'

Christina turned from the mirror with a hopeless look. 'Phoebe, I can't face them all.'

'Bertrand will help you. You must ask him to be more attentive.'

'He went off. He said he wanted to smoke a cigar.'

Phoebe clicked her teeth in exasperation and began tidying clothes which were strewn on the chairs. 'You're going to have to be firm with him, you know. He's been allowed far too much licence living in France.'

Christina's chin trembled. 'I'm so afraid of him.'

Phoebe smiled. 'Nobody could be afraid of my brother.' She sat on the bed and fingered the travelling frock laid out for Christina to wear later; it was a beautiful moire silk, powder blue, which would suit Christina's pale complexion. 'He's a baby. You could manage him quite easily if only you would put more faith in yourself.'

'I'm afraid he won't like me. Mama says I must make him adore me, that I'm to do it by being tender and devoting myself to his wishes. But how can I make him adore me if he doesn't even like me?'

Phoebe frowned. 'I think people talk too much about tenderness in a woman. I'm sure most men admire a bit of spirit.'

Christina looked away and fiddled with the brushes on the dressing table. 'I seem to have so little of that.'

Phoebe could not answer; it was so painfully true. Why ever had Bertrand gone through with it? she thought, forgetting how, while growing up, they had all assumed Christina and Bertrand would marry, how she had helped to encourage it and that her influence might even have been to blame.

Christina dried her eyes. She saw by Phoebe's silence that she had strained the limits of sympathy far enough, and she had made her head ache with crying. 'At least I have my settlement to bring to the marriage. That's something. Perhaps it's everything,' she added with an ironic twist of humour – which might yet prove her saving talent, thought Phoebe, as she assured her that Bertrand would have far more to admire in her than a marriage settlement.

Bertrand walked alone in the shrubbery and smoked a cigar. He felt that he could breathe freely for the first time that day. The gravelled paths wound among the trees, all very artificially 'natural', with a statue placed here and there and a few benches at intervals where one might pause and admire a particularly attractive planting of rhododendrons or azaleas. He acknowledged the nods and murmured congratulations of the guests he passed, who were bent on the same purpose of a stroll and a smoke to help fill the long gap between the wedding breakfast and dinner; but Bertrand walked quickly, as if to indicate he had no time to become ensnared in conversation.

'Where is Charles's strumpet-wife? Have they hidden her away somewhere?' He smiled, remembering that first evening of his return and Phoebe's pretence at being shocked by his question. She had pursed her lips, like she did when she wanted to make it plain she should not be talking about something but could not resist divulging a piece of gossip.

'I think they've quarrelled. But if you ask him about it Charles won't say a word against her.'

'What is she like?'

Phoebe had considered for a moment, then said bluntly, 'Well, in Father's parlance, Tessa is common, lad. Common as brass.'

Bertrand had seen at once that his brother, handsome boring Charles, was besotted. Charles had avoided him that first evening, jealous of the fuss over his return. 'Tessa is very beautiful,' he had said with a fervour in his grey eyes when questioned. His face twisted as if with pain. 'She's a rare spirit is Tessa, a rebel. No one else understands her, nor her advanced ways of thinking.'

Bertrand had lowered his voice: 'Remind me to tell you about Madeleine one day. If we're talking of free spirits you should go to Paris.'

'I never had my chance to go to Paris,' Charles had said with a look full of hatred. 'I was the one who wanted to draw, who has talent as an artist, but I stayed at home while you were allowed to fritter away a year in France. A whole year of freedom and you wasted it.'

Was it true? He scuffed his feet on the gravelled path. Had Paris been an aberration? He entered the deepest part of the shrubbery and came upon his brother's wife seated on a bench and intent on coaxing a squirrel from a tree.

'Oh, now look – you've frightened it off.' She turned and held out her hand. 'I'm your sister-in-law, Tessa.'

Bertrand took her hand. 'I'm pleased to meet you, Tessa. It seems nobody's thought fit to introduce us.'

'They'd probably rather pretend I don't really exist.'

Bertrand stood holding her hand lightly before their fingers parted. He had known he would find her there; he had watched her walk away from Charles when the guests made their way up to the house. She looked into his eyes with an attentive expression, as if seeking confirmation of their earlier understanding.

'You're not a bit in love with her, are you?'

He tried to deny it, to say that of course he loved his wife. It was his wedding day, wasn't it? He knew that only by obeying the laws of convention now could he hope to avert disaster. His throat felt choked and he shook his head and drew deeply on his cigar to restore his self-control.

'I don't love your brother either.' Tessa glanced down at the pregnant bulge of her striped gown and patted it ruefully. 'This was all a mistake.' Again she looked into his eyes with that intent expression. 'Perhaps that's why we recognised one another – two loveless souls looking for a way out.'

'What are you going to do about it?' he said.

'What are you?' she countered.

'I shall concentrate on my work.'

'Ah – the lions. Charlie is full of them. He's obsessed with them.'

'I wish I was.' Bertrand sat beside her and ground his cigar into the gravel path with his shoe heel. 'I know it could be the making of me, but the more I think on it the less I want anything to do with it all.'

'What *do* you want?'

He looked at her. 'To go back to France. I have friends in Paris.'

'A mistress?'

He thought of Madeleine. 'Not really. I mean – that isn't the reason.'

'If you went to France I shouldn't see you again and you never know, that might be a pity.'

He laughed. 'And we've only just met today. I think you'd forget me, Tessa. I'm off to Scotland this afternoon for weeks and weeks on honeymoon. I'll guarantee you'll have forgotten all about me by the time you eat your dinner this evening.'

'Oh no, I won't.' Her look was direct and full of meaning.

He tried to laugh. 'And what about Christina?'

They heard footsteps approach on the gravel and they moved swiftly apart as Philip came into view, striding out in a determined manner. He beamed, 'Have you seen Phoebe? I've looked everywhere.'

'It's not likely you'll find her here,' said Bertrand. 'Why don't you try the house?'

'I've done that but no one seems to know.'

Bertrand shook his head with a baffled but helpful air and Philip walked on, too preoccupied with his mission to consider anything uncommon in the sight of the bridegroom lurking in the shrubbery with his pregnant sister-in-law.

'I hope Phoebe escapes,' said Tessa when he had gone.

'Do you think he has *intentions*? I've suspected it since I came home.'

'He looks like a man with intentions on his mind.'

'Poor Phoebe.'

'She'll speak up for herself.' Tessa's expression held the slightest trace of a sneer. 'Your sister has a mind of her own.'

'This is hopeless you know,' Bertrand said suddenly. 'I'd better go back to the house.'

'I'll come with you.' She eased herself from the bench. 'Must gawp at the silver tea services and the grand piano. Did they really give you a grand piano? Everyone's been talking about it.'

He put his hand on her arm to help her steady herself and fingered the seductive red-and-black silk of her sleeve. Her costume reminded him of Paris; she had the same self-possessed allure as the girls on the *grands boulevards* with their easy intimate manner. He wanted to kiss her. They stood for a moment with his hand on her arm.

'It needn't be hopeless,' she said in a low voice. 'Lots of married men do it.'

'We'd be found out.'

'Not if we were careful.'

'You might feel differently when I get back.'

'So might you.'

'I want you,' he said. 'Right now. I want to have you.'

'You shall,' she said. 'I promise. It will be something for you to look forward to when you come back.' She glanced round suddenly, placed her arms round his neck and kissed him on the mouth. 'I've been wanting to do that since church this morning. I thought, poor lad, he just needs a bit of loving.'

'You're a stunner,' he whispered.

'I'm big as a house.'

'You're beautiful,' he insisted. 'I wish it wasn't Charles. I wish I'd met you first. I wish—' he pulled her to him hungrily, letting the violence of the kiss obliterate all sense of guilt.

'You'd better go on.' She eased herself away from him. 'I'll follow you in a bit.'

'I think I'll die. Two whole months in Scotland!'

'No you won't. Now hop it before someone sees.'

Tessa sat on the bench and adjusted her hat, watching him go. What had she done? Was it just a bit of mischief-making or did she mean to take up with him when he came back? He made her tremble and got the juices flowing but she didn't want him to go mushy on her, not like Charles. She saw him turn at the curve in the path and he tipped his hat with a saucy look. No, she thought. This one was different.

It was quiet in the drawing room. There was a murmur of voices from the library where people were exclaiming at the presents and fussing around Christina. Gerald and Olive and a clique of Underwood aunts, uncles and cousins gossiped on the settees; they hardly noticed Phoebe in the window alcove from where she could see the servants moving to and fro carrying away the plates and food from the marquee.

Phoebe listened to Olive and Gerald's conversation: 'Is Bertie going to work for your father again?' Olive said.

'I hope so. Apart from this business of the statues, it will ease some of the load on me and Charles.'

'Oh, that *is* good. You'll have more time for the plays.'

Gerald smiled and patted his wife's hand. 'I thought a comedy next, Mrs C. What do you say? Three acts about the return of an erring brother.'

Olive put a hand to her mouth to stifle a smile. Her eyes, lustrous and almost always serious, gazed at him as if he had uttered the most intelligent witticism.

Gerald frequently referred to his wife as Mrs C., or sometimes the joy of his life, or his better half. He adored Olive of course, thought Phoebe, and Olive adored him; the endearments were part of the pattern of their relationship, but she wondered whether Olive did not sometimes find Gerald's air of condescension irritating. Phoebe studied her sister-in-law. Did she perhaps have some private defence against it?

Phoebe was puzzled by most married women's instincts to derive their identity from their husbands. She was sure that Olive overvalued Gerald's excellence both as an actor-manager and as a husband. Phoebe disapproved in principle of Gerald's amateur theatre and the company of players who lived with him; she was a little ashamed to be connected with such a demonstration of loose living and wondered whether her mother had known what she was doing when she had left Gerald enough money to pursue his hobby. She felt a perverse admiration for Olive, however. Her sister-in-law, like Tessa, had been a theatre player even before she met Gerald and should perhaps have been ostracised by decent society because of it. Yet, though some at the Ebenezer chapel mentioned her in hushed voices, Olive was liked, even respected in the more progressive circles in town. The chairwoman of the Ladies' Guild had asked her to join their society after seeing her perform as Lady Macbeth and had in sycophantic tones declared herself *inconsolable* when Olive declined with her regretful, rather mysterious smile. Phoebe, watching her sister-in-law, suddenly envied her unconventional way of life and knew that her own was in some way deficient.

She turned to the leaded windows which looked out on to the broad terrace. From here the garden descended in a series of balustraded lawns to a vista of open meadow. She tried to distinguish Jack Bateman from the other waistcoated figures near the tent but was distracted by the sight of Bertrand coming across the lawn from the direction of the shrubbery. At last. She would intercept him and give him a piece of her mind. She rose from the window and as she did so saw Philip come in through the drawing-room door. Phoebe stood very still by the curtain, hoping he would not notice her.

'Ah – Phoebe! There you are!' There was a slight agitation in his manner, for Philip had grown quite anxious about his search and had begun to convince himself – since he could not imagine that Phoebe had been avoiding him – that some accident must have befallen her. 'Would you care to walk with me in the garden?' He offered her his arm and, unable to conjure up any pressing excuse, Phoebe was obliged to take it.

'I've looked for you absolutely everywhere,' he said when they were outside. 'You've no idea what an elusive girl you are.'

'I thought I'd have a rest.'

'Are you too tired to walk?' He halted, immediately solicitous, a frown creasing his long forehead.

'No. No, I'm much refreshed now, thank you.' She walked more quickly, irritated by his concern. 'If anyone's being elusive it's Bertie,' she said after a while. 'I feel I should take him to task for neglecting Christina.'

'Christina will do her own taking to task,' Philip said with a confidence which Phoebe could not share. 'You ladies love to scold.' They walked a little way. 'I saw him with Charles's wife a moment ago.'

'Bertrand – with Tessa?'

'In the shrubbery.'

'How very strange.'

'She's a peculiar girl.' The remark was followed by an uncomfortable silence, for 'peculiar' hardly seemed an adequate description when one considered Charles's marriage.

Phoebe tried unsuccessfully to change their direction as the bustle of activity by the marquee loomed nearer.

'The servants will be looking forward to the supper,' Philip remarked.

'Your father was generous to include the foundry employees as well as the railway workers.'

'Aye, it'll be a noisy do. They are high-spirited today with no work on.'

'They seem to have worked hard enough fetching and carrying,' Phoebe answered sharply. They were very close to the marquee now and she could see Jack Bateman with his brothers among a small gang of men leaning against the side of a brewer's dray. They were watching the servant girls go in and out of the tent with stacks of crockery. The girls chatted and giggled with one another, aware of the attention.

The men fell silent and doffed their caps as they saw

61

Phoebe and Philip approach. Phoebe nodded to them and wished she did not have her hand so firmly tucked through Philip's arm and that Philip did not call out in quite so officious a manner: 'Have you fellows nothing better to do than ogle the women?' The men eased themselves lazily away from the cart and began to disperse.

'Do you still maintain they're hard-working creatures?' Philip said as they reached the iron fence which separated Chillingdale from the water-meadows. He turned to face her with a pleasant but supercilious smile.

Phoebe released her hand from his arm and gripped the rail of the fence, wanting to wipe the smirk from his affable face with a cutting remark. She said nothing but stared across the meadow into the distance where sheep grazed under the trees, their shapes distorted by the shimmer of heat.

'Phoebe—?' Philip said. 'Don't be angry.'

'I'm not angry,' she said distantly. But disillusioned, she thought – disappointed all at once with the pantomime of the wedding.

'You look so serious.' Philip had been hoping to set the scene for a proposal of marriage, but he did not feel that Phoebe was being co-operative.

'Weddings tend to make me sad,' she admitted. 'How can we all be so foolish as to believe in the happy ever after? It's a fantasy which can last only for an hour or two. It's like one of Gerald's plays – very pretty and stirring but we must soon see the reality again.'

Philip felt discouraged by this further obstruction to his plan. 'I think you're being unnecessarily gloomy.'

'Perhaps I am.' She turned away from the fence. 'It's so hot, do you think we might go back to the house now?'

Philip felt the rebuff keenly but he was resilient, he would ask her later: she would be in a more light-hearted mood after dinner and the dancing, he decided.

'Reckon we'll be hearing of another engagement 'fore long,' Walter said from the dray. He stood at the rear of the cart, under the canopy, poised to roll a beer keg on to Jack's shoulders and was looking over his head towards the distant figures of Philip Underwood and Phoebe.

Jack said, 'Aye, I shouldn't be at all surprised,' wondering which of them he would like to murder first, his brother or Underwood. The sight of other casual strollers and the colourful pageant they presented reinforced his jealousy of Underwood's class, who were at leisure to walk, sit or admire the scenery, while he and his kind must have 'better things to do'.

The tent was being prepared for the workers' supper and the women were laying fresh cloths to replace the good table linen. Jack finished unloading the beer and wandered inside the marquee, where the light was luminous and shady, the air humid and the smell of the grass rich with sap drawn out by the heat of the day.

The talk from the women was shrill as the Chillingdale servants in dark frocks, crisp aprons and with lace caps in their hair carried stacks of clean plates which they set down on the ends of the tables. Jack's sister Sarah wore a sprigged cotton frock and a country bonnet of white muslin which framed her broad hot face.

'Who are you going to dance with tonight 'fore supper, Jack?' she asked, setting down a stack of plates on the table and wiping the sweat from her forehead with her apron.

'The prettiest girl in the tent. Who else but my own sister?'

'There's plenty other pretty girls wouldn't say no if asked,' called one of the maidservants. The women shrieked with laughter and Jack wished he had stayed outside.

'Guess which of the gentry said I looked pretty as a painting?' Sarah laughed, covering her mouth and uneven teeth with her hand.

'Mister Bertrand,' said one of the Chillingdale servants. 'He's the worst of them all with his French ways.'

'Mister Philip,' said Jack bitterly. 'He smooth talks all the lasses.'

'Not Mister Underwood,' said Sarah, her face alight with enjoyment of the game she had set. 'It were Mister Gerald. He said my bonnet 'minded him of haymaking.'

'Hoo-hoo,' howled the other girls. 'We all know what he meant to say by that. Give us a kiss and a fumble in the hay. They're devils that lot. You don't half have to watch them.'

Sarah blushed and covered her mouth again. 'Oh, Lord. I never thought of owt like that.'

Jack left them and went out into the sunshine. The air was very still. The Cloughs were a strange family, he reflected. The father shoving chapel preaching at his men, yet hardly able to keep his own house in order. Gerald Clough was nothing like his father, except in looks, nor like his brothers. He was more flashy, a bit dandified; he called everyone 'my hearty' in that booming voice which could carry a mile, even when he was talking to the foundrymen. They were all a bit queer in the family – even Phoebe, Jack had to admit, remembering how, when they were children, she would stick up for her brothers and fight like a she-cat for them. He had joined in the baiting and taunting of children who lived at the better end of the Bank. He had disliked her in those days – a prissy girl with ringlets and a nasty temper.

He tried to analyse how his feelings had changed but it was beyond him. People said Phoebe Clough took after her mother, but Jack hardly remembered Edwin Clough's wife and it was difficult to imagine Clough marrying a

Frenchwoman, who, according to his mother, had possessed the manners and grace of a 'real lady'. Everyone said Edwin Clough had changed when she died, growing more inward looking and giving himself to nothing but the foundry and chapel. People said he blamed his missus's French ways for his sons' failings, but according to Jack's own mother, it was the lack of a mother's influence, however foreign, that had been the cause of all that had gone wrong in that family. 'Miss Phoebe has done her best,' she said. 'She's a good girl and tried to be like a mother to them.' Then she had shaken her head. 'It's a hard thing for a lass, to be left alone in a family of men.' Jack's heart had filled with pity for the poor, motherless Phoebe. Suddenly she had become a marvellous creature in his eyes. He wriggled with guilt at the thought of the insults he had shouted after her when they were small and the times she had fought him off as he caught hold of her ringlets. He tried to imagine how his own sister would have fared, or how he and his father and brothers could have borne it if they had lost their mother after her recent illness.

Phoebe had become a favourite topic for discussion with Sarah and his mother. He remembered how she had marched into their back kitchen and sat herself down – 'like Lady Bountiful on a sick visit', Walter had muttered – yet, after only five minutes she had been helping his sister Sarah chop up the carrots and onions to make soup for the inn customers and nursing his mother with beef tea. Even now, though his mother was fit again and Phoebe no longer visited, the family talked about her, speculating on the possibility of a double romance – Bertrand Clough and Underwood's daughter, Phoebe and Underwood's son – and Jack's jealousy of Philip Underwood had deepened.

The guests and a few servants were walking towards the house in a steady stream and Jack heard someone say that the newly married pair were about to depart for their wedding tour. He walked slowly towards the house.

Sarah came running past him with the other girls. 'Look sharp, Jack. We've all to be there to give them a proper send-off.'

Drawn by the excitement of the swelling crowd of spectators on the terrace, Jack quickened his step and was caught up in the jostling throng of servants and guests. Everyone pressed forward to see more clearly, servants and gentry, sweating in shirt-sleeves and uniforms, dark suits and silk dresses. The smell of mothballs and perspiration was strong in the crush. Jack found himself pressed forward and in an instant was standing not more than inches from Phoebe. He was so close that her dress brushed his body: he could easily have touched the mass of brown curls which lay against her neck, let his breath fall on the curve of her cheek or put an arm about her waist. He closed his eyes, faint with her nearness, prevented by the jam of people from moving from where he stood. Phoebe held a battered pink satin shoe in one hand, raised in readiness to throw it into the carriage when it moved off. Her hands were small, the fingers tapered and delicate, the nails a pale blush pink like small rose petals. He caught the scent of the silk of her frock, a faint trace of sweet perspiration and the warm smell of her hair. Oh, to move just an inch or more nearer and press his face against those rich curls and place a hand on her firm slender waist and whisper, *Phoebe, Phoebe my love—*

Phoebe turned. Her eyes were violet blue, wide and startled as they gazed directly into his, yet her look did not falter or grow cold. 'Jack—' she spoke a little breathlessly, a sudden catch in her throat. 'Jack, would you throw the slipper for me? I'm sure I shall miss the carriage.'

'Right enough, Miss Phoebe,' he said, just as if they

were not standing within two inches of an embrace and his legs against the silk of her skirts. He took the battered shoe from her hand, feeling the soft worn leather, loath to release it, for her fingers had caressed it. He lifted his arm as a cheer rose from the guests and the carriage began to move. He threw the shoe above the heads of the crowd and watched it fly to land on top of one of the corded boxes on the back of the carriage of the bride and groom.

Phoebe turned to him with a look of triumph. 'Eh, well done!' The words were brief but the warmth in them and in her eyes and the blush on her cheek were to be treasured. And then Jack's euphoria vanished as the crowd moved after the departing carriage and Christina tossed out her bridal posy. He saw it spin high in the air and begin to descend towards them. He heard the shouts of those nearby to 'catch it!' and prayed for divine intervention – a sudden gust of wind – but none came as Phoebe's delicate hands caught the flowers.

The cry went up, 'Another wedding! Another wedding!' and only then did Jack notice Philip Underwood standing a few feet from Phoebe. He turned away, not wanting to see more.

Four

E stands for England, that place of great fame,
The workers make wealth for the masters to gain.

People's Alphabet, c. 1870

Edwin sat at the enormous table in the banquet room at
Chillingdale, hearing the buzz and clatter of the guests
grow louder as the evening wore on. A heavy, gilt-framed
oil painting of Almscliffe Crag reared behind his head
against a red flocked wallpaper, and other pictures of rugged
landscapes and badly painted granite-featured ancestors were
placed around the walls.

Edwin envied Underwood the sense of permanence of
Chillingdale. He was of a naturally morbid turn of mind and
since his wife's death the notion of his own demise was one
which troubled him more and more. There was the comforting
prospect of eternal life for one's immortal soul, a prospect
Edwin had no cause to doubt, yet it was his life in Griseley
which he most desired to see immortalised. At fourteen he
had been apprenticed to an ironworks in Leeds and at
twenty-three had started his own business as an engineer
and bronze founder in Griseley. Clough's Foundry had
prospered during the railway boom of the forties and was
now one of the foremost foundry works in the West Riding.

Edwin knew that he had done well for himself; his Maker knew it and would no doubt congratulate him about it on the final day of judgement, but Edwin wanted Griseley and Yorkshire to know it too.

Alfred Underwood had Edwin's lions on his mind over dinner. 'It won't be an easy undertaking,' he said with confident gloom. 'You're an ambitious fellow, Edwin. Always were.'

'It will cost a pretty penny,' Beatrice remarked with a downward turn of her mouth.

The truth was that Edwin's scheme had exposed a flaw in the seemingly perfect affiliation between the two families. Gerald's marriage to an actress and Charles's hasty wedding to Tessa had shaken the relationship, and when Bertrand stayed on in France, an apparently reluctant bridegroom, alarm bells had sounded in the Chillingdale household. Beatrice had hinted that it was no more than she would have expected, considering Annette's foreign blood. Not that Edwin was as free from blame in passing on a streak of wildness as he made out. Beatrice could remember him as a young man, when chapel and profits had not been all that had occupied his mind, and chapel least of all. But that was a long time ago. They had all changed with time. One grew older and wiser and prosperity and respectability demanded heavy responsibilities.

It had taken Edwin's scheme over the lions to reveal the true depth of the fracture between the families, for though it meant that Bertrand had come home to a steady job in his father's business, and though Alfred expressed approval of the plan in public and had encouraged the town council to approve it, he had fallen victim to envy. As Beatrice said loudly and often – if only Alfred had thought of something as grandiose first.

'Nothing amiss with it costing a bit,' said Edwin,

reflecting that the day's wedding celebrations would have cost Underwood a fair sum, aye, and impressed a few folk in Griseley. 'All in a good cause, to mark the prosperity and pride of the town.'

'And as a testimony to the foundry,' added Philip ingenuously.

There was a significant pause in which Beatrice and Alfred looked at one another, a knowing look on Beatrice's part as if to say, *What did I tell you?*

'Well – nothing can come of it for a while at least,' she said without disguising her satisfaction. 'Not with two months of honeymoon before your Bertrand can get on with things.'

Edwin was looking forward to embarking on the lions; yet he saw that all three of his sons, even Bertrand, had disappointed him. Perhaps the lions would be a sort of compensation – a way for Charles and Bertrand to make up for past omissions. He looked fondly at Phoebe who stared at her plate and picked at her dinner next to Philip. Not for the first time Edwin wished that his only daughter had been his only son. The white lace window drapes behind her and the maroon curtains drawn back with deep, fringed and tasselled ties on either side, formed a kind of three-dimensional picture frame in which she was contained. A chill touched Edwin's spine. The image was Annette. He saw it increasingly of late. But with a difference, he reminded himself: his Phoebe was serious and dutiful, she was Annette without her mother's imperfections. Phoebe had inherited Annette's beauty, her generosity, her loving spirit, but Phoebe was not wilful; she had none of those strange notions about 'developing the inner person', as Annette used to call it. He remembered with a sense of unease the way she had looked at him when she had talked like that, with an expression of sadness in her

71

deep-set eyes, almost as if she had pitied him.

Tessa was bored after the bridal couple had gone. She had heartburn and the prospect of sitting through a long and tedious dinner was not appealing. Besides, two months of honeymoon was a long time and the episode in the shrubbery now seemed shabby and rather silly.

She was relieved to be seated near Gerald and Olive at dinner. 'All we Thespians together,' Gerald said. Tessa saw Charles's tight smile across the table, disparaging, forgetting that it was the life and colour of the theatricals which had attracted him to her in the first place. She knew that people were gossiping about her; they looked at her with that faintly shocked raising of the eyebrows and then looked away as though saying, was it really necessary to display one's condition at a ball in such an advanced stage of pregnancy? Couldn't she have gone home early like well-bred women did? It was more than that, thought Tessa: they were shocked by her effrontery in showing herself anywhere. It was all very well to have dragged oneself up by one's boot-strings through thrift and graft and call oneself gentry, but to have wormed one's way into the better classes by seducing the son of Edwin Clough was not quite the thing. She fanned herself with her hand and looked round the vast dining room with doors leading out on to the long terrace and enough space for an army to eat its dinner. She saw Phoebe next to Philip Underwood at the top table – the next pair heading for matrimony. Phoebe was frosty-faced and did not look as if she was enjoying her supper and Edwin Clough too had a glassy-eyed look. Sanctimonious old devil. Her father-in-law had not deigned to speak to her all day. He was struggling to keep up with Beatrice Underwood's stream of chatter. How that woman could talk! How they all talked – about business and money and progress, all very worthy and all such a bore.

Sounds of revelry drifted faintly across the grounds through the open french doors. 'The lower orders seem to be having more fun,' said Tessa in an undertone.

'*Go, Philostrate, stir up the Athenian youth to merriments; awake the pert and nimble spirit of mirth,*' declaimed Gerald.

'It sounds as if the Griseley youth are already up-stirred,' said Charles.

Olive placed a hand on Gerald's arm and looked into his eyes. 'An idea for our next production.'

'A three-act comedy of my own invention?'

'No, my love – *A Midsummer Night's Dream*.'

'The *Dream*. My notion exactly.'

'Aren't there too many leading roles?' said Charles with unusual sarcasm. 'Oberon, the Duke *and* Bottom. You can't do them all, Gerald.'

'Our little troupe is very versatile,' said Gerald.

'Will there be a part for me?' asked Tessa.

'But you'll have the baby to occupy you,' protested Charles in a low voice.

Gerald scrutinised Tessa's figure and her flushed face. 'When's the happy event to be?'

'Three weeks – maybe two.'

'You'll soon be on your feet again.' He rubbed his hands together. 'I see you, Tess, as Titania – Queen of the Fairies.'

Olive's smile flickered for she would have liked to play Titania, it had indeed been the inspiration behind her suggesting the play and she knew she was more suitable for the part than the robust Tessa. She bowed her head and only the merest flush of colour on her calm cheek betrayed her displeasure.

The dinner continued until Alfred Underwood rose unsteadily to his feet and announced that the floor would be cleared for dancing. The company spilled out on to the terrace as the hired servants filed into the room and began to clear the tables with a great clatter.

Charles drew Tessa aside. 'We should be going home.'

Tessa knew that even she must draw the line at quadrilles and that if they stayed she must sit with the old women, her feet tapping with the rhythm of the fiddles, longing to leap up and be pulled into the dance. Yet it was cool and pleasant outside on the terrace and she did not want to go home. The lights from the marquee seemed magical in the growing darkness. Shouts of laughter and fragments of song carried clearly on the still air; she could hear the raucous strains of 'On Ilkley Moor'.

'They're enjoying themselves,' said Phoebe, coming to stand beside them. 'Don't you almost wish we could join in?'

Tessa looked at her in surprise, wondering if she had misjudged her sister-in-law.

'I have an idea,' said Gerald. 'This is obviously a dull old do compared with what's going on down there. Let's join them.'

'Oh, let's!' said Tessa, her eyes lighting. 'Nobody would miss us.' She turned to Phoebe. 'Oh come on. It would be such fun.'

Phoebe looked across the lawn. She tried to picture Jack Bateman with the other workers – singing, laughing, perhaps drunk. She could not imagine it and did not want to; nor could she see herself as a participant in that scene, even less a spectator. 'I have to look after the bridesmaids,' she said. 'They'll wonder why I'm not there.'

'Tessa – we should be off home,' repeated Charles more urgently.

She shrugged off his restraining hand. 'Oh Charlie, don't be such a bore.'

Gerald and Olive were already starting across the lawn. Tessa hurried after them and Charles followed miserably in their wake. Phoebe watched them, then turned to the house again, but seeing Philip near the windows she stepped instead into the shadows on the lawn.

Jack listened to Walter making a fool of himself singing the ballad of 'Mary-Ann and the Coconuts'. The lines were rough and bawdy and there was a chorus of 'Oh-oh the Coconuts' in which everyone joined. Men sat on the tables and benches but many of the women had already been called back to help at the house. The smell of cheap tobacco and beer and perspiration was strong. A few of the men, like Walter, had downed a glass of ale too many and the song was getting more lewd and the laughter more raucous.

A cry went up for someone else to do a song and then the cry rose for 'Jack Bateman – Jack, give us a turn.' Jack let the clamour build a little before he stood with a show of reluctance as was the custom before launching into one's piece. He waited for silence. 'All right, but it isn't mucky, so you can shut your mouths and listen to some proper stirring stuff.' He found it easy to learn narrative verse and had several dramatic poems in his repertoire. He liked the rhythm of the words, the slap of the rhyme at the end of each line and the skill in varying his tone of voice according to the requirements of the poem – which in this case was melancholy, morbid even, about a girl who drowned herself because of the loss of her lover. The story suited Jack's mood of pessimism and his audience was as eager to shed a few tears over a bit of poetry as to laugh at a good song. He did not see Gerald Clough standing at the entrance to the marquee, but he heard him when the recitation was over. The vigorous clap of Gerald's hands sounded above the applause inside the tent.

Heads turned to regard the interlopers in the entrance. 'What are they buggers up to? They've got their own do,' muttered Walter.

The newcomers smiled and nodded and Gerald Clough called, 'Don't mind us lads, carry on.' There was a moment of hostility among the men, intensifying as it lengthened, then it gave way to a universal shrug of indifference and one of the railway workers got up and began another song.

Gerald intercepted Jack as he came out from the marquee. 'I followed your performance in there with great interest, Jack.'

'It was nobbut a party piece, sir.'

'It moved me to tears, my hearty. Have you had a thought or two about coming up to the house for an audition?'

Jack thrust his hands into his pockets. Clough had heard him recite the dramatic poem 'Griseley Fair' the previous Christmas, since when he had not ceased pestering him to have a go at 'treading the boards'. He could imagine what Matt and Walter would have to say to an audition, his father too – 'getting ideas above his station.' He could no more envisage entering the rarefied world which lay behind the doors of Gerald and Olive Clough's home than he could flying. People told strange stories about that household, where all were welcome – freaks and side-shows, dancing bears and a trained monkey if Gerald Clough thought they could act. Apparently, it was where Charles Clough had met Tessa O'Leary and put her in the family way. He watched her, unseemly in her condition, strolling back to the house arm in arm with her husband and Olive Clough.

Jack did not want to get caught up in that menagerie. 'Thanks Mister Gerald, I have thought on, but I should feel a bit of a twerp in a pair of tights to be straight with you.'

'Nonsense, my hearty. The stage would do you a power

of good.' Gerald's hand was firmer on his shoulder and he compelled his attention with his intense look and booming voice. 'I know you could act.' He released him and stepped away. 'I'll not give up, Jack. I'm still convinced you could move a wider audience. And you'd be an asset to us.'

At that instant Sarah came out from the tent. Gerald said, 'Ah! Here comes the girl who won my heart this afternoon in her haymaking bonnet. Pretty as a painting.' He waited until she was near. 'I've told your Jack he should try for a part in our next production. He would make a fine actor. See what you can do to persuade him and I shall get my sister Phoebe to talk to him.'

'Will he indeed?' murmured Sarah, blushing at Gerald's attention. 'I reckon Miss Phoebe would have her own thoughts about that.'

Jack saw Walter watching them from one of the benches inside the tent. His brother struggled from his seat and pushed his way towards them, keeping his eye fixed on Gerald as a landmark as he drew closer.

'Is he pestering you, lass? I heard he were making free with you this afternoon.'

Sarah's large eyes grew larger in the light from the tent. 'Walt! Think on what you're saying!'

'We're not in t' foundry now. And if he touches you, I'll break his neck.'

Sarah seized his arm. 'Walter! Shut up! You're talking to one of the masters! It's the drink, sir. You mustn't mind him.'

'Now look here, my hearty—' Gerald laughed good-naturedly.

'Clear off!' Walter stood in front of him. 'Who do you bloody think you are? You've got your own do and your own women.'

Some of the men came out from the tent to see what was

happening. 'Go on, Walt,' someone laughed. 'You have your say.'

Gerald laid a restraining hand on Walter's shoulder. 'I think you should sleep off all that beer, my hearty, before you say anything at all.'

Jack saw Walter's hand clench, foresaw the consequences of his brother's solid fist meeting the soft jaw of the manager of the works and slipped between them, pushing Walter aside.

'I'm sorry, Mister Gerald. My brother's had too much ale, sir. He doesn't really know what he's on about.'

One of the men shouted, 'Walt knows right enough. Tell him you want more in your pay an' all, Walt. Tell him to have a word in the ear of his dear old papa.'

Jack pressed his forearm against Walter's chest and felt the full weight of him as he strained towards Gerald. 'Please, Mister Gerald. Just go back to your own party. Walter'll be right enough when he's sobered up.' He watched Gerald walk away.

Walter continued to lean his weight on Jack's arm, then slumped forward on to the grass as Jack let his arm drop.

'Bloody loudmouth,' said one of the foundrymen. 'He's nobbut a troublemaker, your Walt.' He came towards Jack and aimed a boot at the recumbent figure.

Matt, who had left the tent after the others, signalled to Sarah to get out of the way. He strolled forward at a leisurely pace, easing his shoulders from his jacket and handing it to one of the bystanders. At the same time, Jack caught the man who had spoken by the shirt collar. 'That's our brother you're calling a loudmouth.'

Matt hit the man under his chin, felling him to the floor.

Within seconds the battle had spread. There were those who supported Walter and those who thought they were having a go at putting down troublemakers, there were those who were fighting for their rights – more pay, more say and down with the gentry – and those who did not care what the fight was about, no celebration was worth its salt unless it ended in a scrap.

Jack landed a few blows while his blood was up, then helped Matt drag Walter away from the centre of the brawl. He watched as his father with a gang of the Chillingdale staff weighed in and broke up the fight.

'We'll get thrown off the estate,' laughed Matt, rubbing at a splash of blood on his waistcoat.

Jack looked at the house. 'Mister Gerald's not one to make a fuss, and they're creating too much of a din themselves to know what's going on.'

The moon was out and a glittering stream of light silvered the meadow. Jack watched Matt and his father carry Walter into the marquee. Someone started up with a song again. He wandered towards the empty beer-cart in the darkness and could smell the horses and hear them scrunching at the grass. Faint strains of music and laughter drifted from the house, which was lit from end to end like a palace, its terrace a stage with figures moving against the colour of the windows.

The celebrations in the marquee had slowed to a few maudlin ditties and choruses with no energy left in them; they would soon be coming to an end, for the scrap had sobered everyone a little and the Chillingdale servants had an early start the next morning. Jack was thankful for a day of rest before getting back to the foundry on Monday.

Gerald Clough's words were still with him and his enthusiasm for the stage had been catching. Jack had been tempted. There was a kind of theatricality in his recitations when everyone listened and sat so still – as if he held them in his hands and could do what he wanted with them by a pause or sigh or the inflection of his voice; and when it was over and they clapped and shouted and the noise filled his head, it was like being all fired up with happiness.

Jack leaned against the cart, glad to be alone, aware of a rare sense of contentment which was edged with a lingering excitement from the brawl. He tipped his head back against the canvas and noticed a figure detach itself from the scene by the house. A woman had sped down the steps of the terrace and was running across the lawn. His heart began to pound and he straightened and stepped forward straining his eyes to be sure that he was not mistaken. The figure reached the marquee and halted, looking from right to left, and then veered quickly towards him.

Phoebe gave a little cry of fright, when she saw the cart was not deserted. She stood, her hand pressed against her ribs beneath her breast.

'Can I help, Miss Clough?' Jack stepped into the stream of light from the marquee.

'Oh – Jack, it's you.' She looked back to the house and gave a second cry, more in exasperation than alarm as she caught sight of the figure of a man starting across the lawn. 'It's Mr Underwood.' She stood, breathing quickly, watching the figure draw closer. She turned in desperation. 'If he asks – you haven't seen me,' and hitching up her flounced skirts she scrambled over the back of the cart and into its depths.

Phoebe crouched in the warm beery-smelling darkness of the cart, her heart beating and fluttering against her ribs. The monstrous indignity of what she had done crept over her and she knew that she should be mortified, but the adventure of her escape made her want to laugh.

They had danced a 'Sir Roger de Coverley' and she had afterwards declined Philip's offer to engage her for the next dance, pretending her card was already marked. She had hidden on the terrace, but he had soon followed her. 'Phoebe – I thought you would be dancing. You said you had a partner.' She had been embarrassed at being caught out and by the look of desperation on his face as he at last spilled out his love for her. She should have pitied him but she found his declaration faintly ridiculous as at length he came to it: 'Phoebe, my love, will you do me the honour of becoming my wife?'

He had not believed her when she said, 'No Philip, I will not.' He had actually laughed. And so she had said more emphatically, 'I cannot.'

'You love someone else?'

'No.' She had instantly regretted her honesty for he took her denial as a sign of hope.

'Then I shall ask you again until you give way.' He was almost jocular in his relief. 'I shall ask you after every dance until you say yes.'

Phoebe shivered, listening for the sound of voices, sure that by now Philip must have scoured the marquee and be approaching the beer-cart. She imagined him searching it, discovering her in her corner and dragging her out. *Now my girl, what's your answer?*

She held her breath as she heard voices outside, hearing Philip's, 'Bateman – have you seen Miss Clough here-abouts?' and then Jack's answer, 'That I have, sir.'

Phoebe clamped a hand against her mouth. She remembered her pleasure that afternoon in discovering Jack close beside her, the way he had thrown her slipper. Tears started to her eyes as she foresaw the shame of being discovered. How could he betray her!

And then she heard him, talking politely, as he would perhaps to Philip at work, heard him lie brazenly: 'She was here nigh on half a minute since – you've only just missed her – she's gone on up to the house.'

'Well now, there's a rum do. Just missed her.' Phoebe heard the note of disappointment in Philip's voice.

'Aye, sir. A proper will-o'-the-wisp. If you look sharp you might just about catch up with her.'

Phoebe waited as the darkness fell silent. Jack's voice startled her. 'You can come out now.'

He helped her from the cart and she was conscious of the heat of his body and the firmness of his arm and then he said with a trace of belligerence, 'You shouldn't have done that. It's not the way of a lady to go arse over tip like that into a cart.'

'And that's not a very gentlemanly way to talk to a lady.'

'Tha can't have it both ways.'

'Why are you so uppity?' she said crossly.

He did not answer. Jack knew that they had, by his complicity in her behaviour, come quite suddenly upon a situation for which there were no guiding rules.

'I expect you're wondering why I was hiding.'

He sought safety in formality: 'It's not my place to wonder.'

'Well, I'll tell you. Mr Underwood wants to marry me. Do you think I should? Do you have opinions, Mr Bateman? Or is that not your place either? Tell me – have I no more to do now that all of my brothers are married than become dependent on Mr Underwood? And what is there for me if I stay single? Like most women – nothing at all, prevented from doing anything by the accident of being born a female.'

'I don't know why you're telling me this,' Jack said uneasily.

'Because I thought I could talk freely with you. Because I felt that you and Sarah and your mother have become my friends.' Phoebe recalled her first visits to the Batemans' house when Kitty Bateman had been ill and when Jack and his brothers had confided the foundrymen's resentment over the lions. Jack had surprised her by the measured tone of his argument that the project would impose extra duties on the

82

men; his disparagement of the project had been guarded, his manner pleasant in contrast to Walter's, and their childhood animosity had seemed relegated to the past. She recalled Sarah's embarrassed, 'You mun' take no offence, Miss Clough, by their talk. They mean no disrespect,' and their mother's, 'Stop it, lads. Miss Clough don't want to hear your opinions.'

Jack had grown very strange of late when she called, almost as if he did not welcome her visits; he would make an excuse to leave if he was there when she arrived and his colour would deepen in her presence as it deepened now, his manner awkward. He stepped away from her in the darkness, and his face fell into shadow from the beer-cart. Phoebe remembered how, when they were children, he had chased her and pulled her hair. 'I think you should go back to the house now, Miss Clough, 'fore they send out a search party. It's a bit rough for a lady to be on her own down here.'

Phoebe sighed. 'Yes. You're right. Please forget what happened this evening.'

'I'll tell you something for nothing though,' Jack said as she walked away. 'You deserve better than Underwood.'

Five

Oh! the chap without brass! as a thousand fooak knahs,
Is as helpless in t' world as a cat without claws;
Though he's nayther deficient i' talent or pluck,
He mun stand on yan side or be trodden i' t' muck.

Tom Twisleton, 1845-1917

The labouring men and women of Griseley were on the move. The mill hands came down the streets from their houses and joined the stream of workers heading for the factories and railway yards in the valley bottom. A faint mist hung over the town and mingled with the permanent smoke haze. The streets were quiet except for the clatter of clogs and boots on the cobbles and a low babble of conversation with the occasional shout from one group to another.

Jack let his dinner can bang against his leg as he walked, keeping a steady rhythm in time with the tune of 'Sweet Lass of Richmond Hill' running in his head. Each time he came to 'Richmond Hill' he substituted the phrase 'Griseley Bank', less poetic, but to Jack's mind accuracy was more important. He reached Clough's yard – *I'd crowns resign to call thee mine* – and the clamour of the foundry works drowned the end of the song. He hung his coat and dinner

85

can on his peg and entered the foundry.

Matt and Walter had arrived before him and were already breaking open the moulds to clean up the previous day's castings. The low roof and dirty walls, the thick layer of black sand covering the floor, the loud conversation of the men and clank of tools and background roar of the furnaces were oppressive. Jack began loading a crucible and thought about his fight with Walter that morning. His knuckles still felt stiff and bruised where they had twice come into contact with his brother's solid jaw. He swore silently that he would swing for Walter one day.

They had been reminiscing about the wedding celebrations as he and Walter washed in the pub yard. It had been worth some brass for the pub – all that ale and spirits for the men at the works and the railway company, on top of all the wine and champagne for the gentry. 'The great grafting of the Underwoods and the Cloughs,' Walter had called the wedding. 'The question is – will Miss Phoebe be next? Master Philip Underwood can't wait to get his hands up her skirts. And wouldn't we all like a chance at it?'

Jack had straightened up from the pump and said, 'Stop your filthy talk.'

He recalled his brother's slow look of surprise, then the sly smile. 'Fancy a crack at Miss Phoebe ourself, do we?'

Jack had said nothing, knowing Walter's superior strength, telling himself there was dignity in silence. Then as he bent to wash in the tub, Walter had pushed his head under the water saying, 'Our little brother's cock-a-doodle-doo is hot for the lovely Miss Phoebe.' He had come up spluttering from the water and lunged as Walter laughed and danced away crowing, 'Cock-a-doodle-doo!' even as he hit him.

He swung the lid on to the furnace savagely. There was not a mark on Walter's vain, meaty face beyond a small cut at the corner of his mouth; he was used to taking heavier poundings than Jack could deliver and had shaken his head from the blows and laughed.

Matt passed close by him and said in his ear, 'Take no notice. Whatever it was – he meant no harm.'

'He shouldn't have said it.'

'You're too bloody sensitive.' Matt cuffed his brother's ear with his leather and chain-mail glove, grazing his cheek. He lowered his voice. 'And if it's what I think it's about – you'll not even think about it. Miss Phoebe's not for tykes like you.'

'She's not for that gret soft-head neither,' Jack said, seeing Philip Underwood talking to the foreman at the far end of the foundry.

Matt shrugged, losing interest.

Jack watched Walter who was loading the crucible at the next furnace. Beads of sweat glistened on his forehead; it was going to be a hot day. He repeated to himself through gritted teeth, 'He should never have said it.' His brother met his glance and moving to pick up fresh ingots jerked his head and strutted in imitation of a cockerel; the incident was not over yet. Jack vowed that if Walter let on to the other men that he was sweet on Phoebe Clough he would kill him. He could see Charles and Gerald Clough in the yard by the doorway. Outside, construction had begun on a new shed where the model for the lions was to be made. A lot of fuss and bother that was going to be – just to give 'young Bertie' something to do. Jack had no opinion about the appropriateness of lions in Griseley, but like those who were agitating for extra pay when it came to the moulding and casting, he resented the prospect of the extra work so that another of the Cloughs earned a good living and the buggers on the town council could decorate the town hall. One day – he told himself, pushing the metal down into the melt and stepping back as the blast of heat from the furnace seared his face – one day he would get out from all this. In the end, what did it matter if it was railway parts or lions? There was the same filth and dust and stink.

Jack ate his dinner of bread and cheese in a patch of shade outside, watching the carpenters knock up timbers for the new shed, enjoying the relative cool of the yard and the strong taste of cheese on his tongue and warm flat beer in his throat. He saw Gerald Clough come out from his office and down the wooden stair towards him as if with some fixed purpose.

Gerald sat on the saw-horse beside him, twitching the fabric of his trouser over his knee and swinging his leg. Jack looked at the striped worsted fabric next to his own fustian trousers and Gerald's neat leather boot against his clog shoe and shifted along the bench in order not to soil those fine clothes. He braced himself for another pestering as Gerald laid a hand on his shoulder.

'Had any more thoughts on what we were talking about, Jack?'

Jack looked away and broke off a piece of cheese, chewing on it thoughtfully. 'I know what it is you keep saying, Mr Gerald. But why me? I'm a foundryman, a plain bloke who doesn't know the first thing about acting.'

'But I do, lad. I know about casting bronze and I know all about casting actors. Now bronze glows brightly when it's hot but when it cools it's dull, there's no excitement left in it. The theatre is just the opposite. Dull enough at first – no wages, the drudgery of learning lines and rehearsals – but the excitement of a performance, Jack! You can't beat it. The smell of it, the thrill of making an audience laugh, making them weep. The glow from a performance which is well done can't ever grow cold; it stays bright in your heart for ever.' It was one of Gerald's better speeches and he felt rather pleased with it. He made a note to remember some of the phrases and incorporate them in one of his compositions.

'I don't know, Mr Gerald,' Jack said with the irresolution of a man who was already half won over.

'We'll be putting on a Shakespeare play next.' Gerald, seeing Jack's alarmed expression, patted his shoulder. 'I'll explain it all when the time comes. It will only be a middling sort of play, easy to learn, easier than your poems.'

Jack took a deep breath. He looked about him cautiously. His brothers were still in the foundry shed. 'All right, I'll give it a go.' Lord, what had he let himself in for? Clough was good with words – *the glow from a performance stays bright in your heart for ever* – Jack frowned at his own gullibility.

'Good man.'

'Only don't say owt about it when our Walter and Matt are around.'

Gerald nodded and tapped his finger against his nose. 'Fair enough. Not a word to a soul.'

Sarah came into the yard and saw Gerald. She blushed, remembering the fight at the wedding, and Gerald bowed to her with elaborate courtesy and with a sudden unexpected wink walked away.

'Miss Phoebe came down to the pub this morning,' Sarah volunteered, still blushing as she approached Jack.

He suppressed his immediate interest. 'Is Mother bad again?' He knew he had left his mother that morning in the best of health – fit enough to beat him and Walter about the head with a towel after their fight.

'No. She just looked in, friendly like.' Sarah saw Walter come out from the foundry and she flushed a deeper red with anxiety. 'I've got his dinner – he left so quick this morning.'

'You should let him go without. You're not his slavey.'

'You try telling our Walter that.' Sarah gave Jack a sidelong look. 'You went for him this morning, didn't you? Mam wants to know what it was all about.'

'It wasn't anything.' Jack watched his brother approach and squeeze Sarah's waist.

'You took your time. I'm fair starved.' Walter unwrapped the bread and bit into it greedily.

Sarah was full of her recent encounter with Phoebe. 'Guess what, Walt? Mr Underwood's right pleased with Father for doing the drink for the big wedding. Miss Clough said so.'

Walter glanced at Jack at Phoebe's name; he grinned and Jack clenched his fist as he waited for him to repeat his 'cock-a-doodle-doo' in front of Sarah, but his brother continued to eat his dinner and nodded slowly. 'Good. That'll be good news at home for when the next big wedding comes up.' Jack saw with satisfaction that the cut on his mouth had reopened.

'Well, I can't stand round here gassing.' Sarah, having disposed of Walter's dinner, was anxious to be gone.

Walter sat on the saw-horse beside Jack and watched her go. They ate in silence. 'Still mad at me?' he said after a while.

Jack did not reply. It would take more than a half-hearted apology, he thought sourly. His dinner finished, he walked back to the foundry and heard Walter shout after him: 'No need to go off the deep end, tha' daft bugger!'

The accident happened towards the end of the afternoon. Mishaps were not uncommon in the foundry – a loss of concentration, a fall too close to the row of unguarded furnaces or a lapse of caution when making additions to the molten metal in the crucibles. Burns were facts of foundry life.

Matt and Walter had removed a crucible of molten bronze from the furnace at the furthest end of the foundry where there was the greatest clutter of moulding boxes and piles of scrap metal. They transferred the crucible from the two-man tongs to a hand-shank for pouring, Walter taking the double handles on one side, Matt the single one on the other to steady it. The apprentice went forward ready to push back the slag when the men began to pour. Jack turned from ramming a mould with sand and watched them cross to the raised casting-bed filled with its rows of prepared moulds. Walter jerked his head briefly to shout at the boy to get a move on and shifted towards a spare moulding box left at the corner of the trench.

'Watch out!' Jack shouted in the same instant as Walter's foot caught the heavy iron box. He heard Matt swear, struggling to steady the single handle as Walter's end dropped, saw the bright splash of metal and the crucible discharge its load and heard the boy scream as the molten bronze hit his feet and splashed under his heavy apron. Then he was running with the other men, hearing the boy continue to scream; the sound filling his head and turning his stomach cold.

'Eh, lad. Eh, lad,' Walter crooned, on his knees and with the boy cradled in his arms. Tears poured down his face making black channels in the dust.

Men gave conflicting orders, until out of the confusion a makeshift stretcher of boarding was brought, a cart was harnessed and they carried the apprentice out into the sunlit yard. Jack accompanied the small group of workers who crowded round the cart. No matter how many times you saw the same sort of thing it still turned your guts to water. The

91

gaffer and the masters had arrived, like carrion crows in their black coats. Jack watched Edwin Clough, anger twitching at the man's cheek, and his sons who talked together in low voices. Gerald was grave-faced as he mounted the cart to accompany the boy to the infirmary. Walter, still in his foundry apron, climbed into the cart beside the injured apprentice.

'Where do you think you're off to?' shouted Edwin Clough. 'Who do you think's going to clear up the mess in the foundry?'

'I'm going with him to the infirmary.' Walter's face was white beneath the grime.

Edwin scowled. 'You can forget that for a start.'

'It were my fault.'

'Aye. And it's you who'll get back in there if you want a job tomorrow.' For a moment it seemed as if Walter would defy him. Edwin shouted, 'Or do I have to fetch you down myself?'

Jack pushed his way past the men. 'He fell over a drag, sir. It was my fault as much as anyone's. I was on moulding.'

Edwin turned on him and the muscle twitched again in his face. 'I don't like stupidity. And I don't like injuries.' He turned to Philip Underwood. 'Make sure both these men's wages are docked for a month.' He looked at Jack with contempt. 'And think yourself lucky you're not both out on your ear.'

Jack returned with the men to the heat of the foundry, hearing the rumble of the cart as it pulled away and the continuing sound of the lad's cries. Matt and Walter began to clear up the spilled metal. No one spoke of the accident and Jack continued to pack moulds. It didn't do to dwell on these things. He filled them mechanically, pressing down the black damp sand with his hands then beating it down with the rammer. He thought of the heat and dirt and the long hours and how the boy's family would manage, and his anger travelled through his arm with each thump until the mould was full and he had levelled it off smooth and flat.

The men raised a subscription for the injured boy. Edwin Clough put in five pounds and said the men should pray for the lad in chapel.

'*Pray* for him!' Walter counted up the money the next Saturday to take round to the boy's mother. 'That's what the old devil said. *I've not seen you men at the Ebenezer in a long time.*'

'Nor he shall, the old hypocrite.' Jack watched him sweep the coins into a bag.

'Are you coming to the meeting?' Walter stood up and pulled on his jacket. The accident had sobered him these days and he looked heavy and depressed; his shoulders were hunched under the jacket. The truth was the boy's injuries had shaken them all.

Their mother was preparing a meal for the inn customers, her sleeves rolled to her reddened elbows, her bony, red-veined face shining with the kitchen heat. The smell of cooking and the reek of beer which always lingered in the house were suffocating. 'I'll have no trouble from you boys,' she said sharply as she shifted pots of steaming vegetables on the stove.

Jack watched her, wondering about going to the meeting. The men had agreed that afternoon to ask for more pay for the extra work making the lions. Walter had been chosen as spokesman and Jack had been among the deputation of men who had gone to Edwin Clough's office. Clough had listened to the request with an amazement which quickly turned to indignation. 'More money, you greedy beggars! And straight after young Mundy being laid up in the infirmary!'

It was true the deputation had picked a bad time, thought

93

Jack, but the men were angry since the accident. The lad would not be able to work for months, if indeed he ever worked again, and it could happen to any of them. The labour was hard and there were dangers; he knew the men deserved better. But Jack's sense of justice was mixed with other resentments. There was Bertrand Clough going to model a daft lion so that everyone might marvel at the family's generosity to the town; there was the wedding where the Underwoods and the Cloughs had lorded it over everyone, and his own father chuffed to death to be delivering them drink; there was his mother working her hands red raw, cooking for an inn full of customers, while Phoebe Clough could play at cooking when she felt like it or leave it to her father's servants when she didn't. 'Do you know how much making them lions is going to cost me?' Clough had said. 'You should be proud to do it for nowt!' He had told them to think of the honour to the works and the testimony it would be to their skills when everyone read *Clough's Foundry* on the statues. A couple of the men had shuffled their feet at that, but others had grumbled on after work. News of a protest meeting – 'seven o'clock sharp' – had travelled swiftly.

The notion of ranting and shouting in the municipal park seemed pointless. 'Reckon I'll give it a miss,' Jack said and Walter shrugged and went out into the yard.

'If you're not going to the meeting,' said his mother, 'you can walk to your aunty's with our Sarah after tea, instead of hanging round the house looking miserable.'

Phoebe had been helping Beatrice address the bride's cards; these stated Christina and Bertrand's new address and the precise date in September when the newly married couple would be 'at home' on their return from honeymoon. There had been over a hundred of them and Phoebe's hand was cramped with writing. The house was quiet when she returned. Her father was at the foundry. The servants' chatter, a low murmur of sound, drifted along the corridor from the kitchen and the smell of sweet peas was evocative of the wedding. She remembered Philip's proposal on the terrace and, above all, the beer-cart and her encounter with Jack. Phoebe threw her gloves and hat on the table and declared to the empty hall that she never wanted to have anything to do with weddings again.

She thought about the men's grievances at the works and the apprentice who had been injured and went to the kitchen to ask Ellen to pack up a basket with foodstuffs. She would visit the boy's family.

Phoebe walked through the market where the stalls were arranged in straggling lines across the square. The smell of cheese, fish and meat, mingling with that of the ordure from sheep and cattle in the nearby market pens and the stench of the running drain down the edge of the street, was a heady concoction in the late afternoon sun. Children played round the traders' feet, scavenging in the dust and dirt for the last of the fallen fruit and vegetables before they were trodden into the cobbles. Phoebe hitched her basket more firmly on her arm, using it as a lever to push her way through the jostling crowd. The din of market-stall holders was punctuated by the bellow of protesting cattle and the whining cries of children begging for pennies.

She bought a leg of lamb for the injured boy's mother and tucked the bloody parcel into her basket, moving towards the edge of the market where she came in full view of the town hall. It was a plain, four-square Georgian building with a clock tower and dainty cupola. Phoebe halted, trying to picture how the lions would look. Charles drew sketch after sketch, ready for Bertrand to approve when he came home; he came up to the house sometimes in the evenings and discussed them with Father – how would it be, if they were to reduce the head a little? Where would they set the mould split lines? Here – or here? Filling his head with work on the statues to save worrying about Tessa, for the baby was almost due. Phoebe pitied Charles his infatuation with Tessa. Why did men and women become so obsessed with one another? How much simpler life would be if they all lived independently and remained spinsters and bachelors.

One of the lions at least would have a nice view over the park, she reflected. Oh, but it was too silly. Griseley people did not need lions. Lions were for people in cities – sophisticated, worldly people with big ideas. Most public monuments were a waste of money, but to place four great lions round that plain building was ludicrous, and if it was for nothing else but the glorification of her father's foundry it was an ignoble scheme.

Phoebe reached the municipal park gates, where a crowd had gathered round a photographer's cart, a canvas-covered hut on wheels, stuck all over with framed photographs to advertise its owner's trade. The photographer, a man with waxed moustaches and dressed in a frock coat and embroidered beret, was urging members of his audience to a sitting. She recalled sitting for a photograph once in Leeds. The photographer had invited her to look into the ground-glass screen behind his camera, a polished wooden box fitted with a brass-mounted lens and an enormous brass screw with which the man adjusted the focusing. He had draped a cloth over her head and she had been alone in the darkness with the coloured scene in front of her; the studio setting had been magical, beautiful, like a lantern slide, appearing upside down on the fuzzy glass screen with a mystical, unreal quality, the hazy blue of the scenery sky at the bottom, the luminous green of painted grass and leaves above.

A sign on the photographer's cart read: *Portraits executed within minutes. Likenesses recorded for posterity. Any number of copies.*

Why was everyone so concerned with posterity? Phoebe was aware of the discontent which had troubled her since the wedding, a longing for something to happen here and now.

She reached the far side of the park and entered a labyrinth of alleys, close to the railway and the canal. The canal was thick and black with the outspillings of the various factories; the noise of activity from the high red-brick buildings on its further side filled the air with the constant drone and heavy clank of machinery. Phoebe entered a court where the houses were crammed closely together, their front doors separated from the street by a stone step and thin strip of pavement, the windows narrow and regimented, some broken or boarded. Women stood gossiping against doorjambs and barefoot children played in the gutter. A few of the women paused to nod to her or stared to watch her pass.

After some yards she turned into a narrower path between high dark walls which cut out the low rays of the sun; it smelt of privies and dust-heaps. A channel of foul water ran a sluggish course down its centre and Phoebe lifted her skirts and stepped carefully over the cobbles, avoiding the worst of the dirt, while a cloud of flies buzzed over the meat in her basket.

The Mundy home was at the far end of the alley, directly under the railway arch. A train shook the air with a roar of sound as Phoebe rapped on the door panel and she stepped back against the bricks of the house wall, covering her mouth against the blast of steam and sooty smoke which swirled down from the railway line. The door opened and a woman of thirty or so stood in the entrance. She was heavily pregnant and wore a sacking apron over a plain dark frock, tightly buttoned at the neck.

'Mrs Mundy?'

The woman stared at her .

'Aye.'

'I'm Mr Clough's daughter.' Phoebe faltered a little, daunted by the blank indifference in the other woman's eyes. 'I called to see how your son is.'

The woman said without emotion, 'He died this afternoon, Miss.'

Phoebe stared. 'I'm sorry—' she looked down at the basket over her arm and the parcel of lamb, the blood drying where it had oozed through the paper. She flapped at the flies and her eyes filled with tears. 'I've brought you a few things.'

'Thank you for taking pains in coming. But there was no need,' the woman said stiffly. She too glanced at the basket and her face crumpled suddenly. Sobs came from her throat with a frightening sound. She fell against the door, her hand pressed to her mouth to stifle her cries.

Phoebe took her by the arm and led her into the house where she set the basket on the table and helped her to a chair. Two small children, a girl and boy, stood by the wall and watched Phoebe's attempt to stem their mother's grief.

At last the woman's sobs lessened. 'It were the sight of the meat, miss.' She dried her face on her apron and her earlier reserve had gone from her eyes as she seized Phoebe's hand. 'Eh, it's right kind of you. You're a good Christian girl.'

Phoebe was conscious of her own inadequacy as the woman continued to pour out her gratitude: 'Everybody's been that good. And your father, Miss – he's such a Christian man. Our William was always right pleased to be working at Clough's Foundry. They collected for him. Did you know? We knew it wasn't likely William would get over it. They warned us at the infirmary.' Her face crumpled again. 'But he was all we had. The others, the older ones, don't earn more than a child's wage at the mill. How are we going to live? Lord, it was little enough, but we just about got by.'

'Can't your husband provide for you?' said Phoebe in dismay.

'My man's poorly with his lungs, miss, and with me the way I am I can't work full stretch at the mill until after the baby's come.'

The children had crept forward as Phoebe unloaded the contents of the basket on to the table. She felt constrained by the woman's exclamations and the children's sudden animated chatter to protest that the food did not represent a fortune in victuals. Phoebe looked for somewhere to put the butter, cheese and other items in the hot little house, but the scullery to the rear was bare of cupboards. The front room was dark, for the railway arch prevented most of the daylight from reaching the window; there were few articles of furniture except for an unlit stove, a battered dresser which contained a few meagre items of crockery, a table and hard-backed chairs, and a picture of a woman cut from a calendar fastened to the wall above the dresser.

She persuaded the girl to help her stow the food on the shelves inside the dresser and sat for a while longer, chatting to the woman, advising her to take plenty of rest as befitted her condition and the children to learn their lessons. 'My father will send money each week until you or your husband are able to work again,' she promised, considering briefly how she would convince her father that to continue the dead boy's wage would be a charity which merited his support. And with the woman's praise still in her ears Phoebe left the house.

She felt a helpless anger rise in her throat as she hurried past the canal, hating the sound of the machinery which brought prosperity to the men who owned the factories. She saw how the woman must have despised her for her charity, for advising her to 'rest up' and for offering condolences – she who could not know what it was like to lose a son and means of support all in one, and who had never needed to do a stroke of real work in her life. And yet the woman had shown neither hatred nor envy. Did she believe, as Phoebe's own class believed, that it was God's will for her to belong to the ranks of the less deserving, while others merited a life of plenty?

Phoebe felt, as she always did when charity visiting, as if she had crossed a tangible boundary between Griseley's squalor and its respectability as once more she entered the park. She could see a crowd of workmen clustered under the trees. They stood in a large knot, directly in the path she had chosen to make her way back to Griseley Bank. Phoebe hesitated as she drew near, for the group was noisy and she recognised several of the workers from her father's foundry. She turned, ashamed of her instinct to retreat, and caught sight of Sarah Bateman and her brother Jack coming towards her.

'It's Miss Clough,' Sarah said excitedly. 'Jack, here's Miss Clough. Doesn't she look lovely?'

Jack frowned with embarrassment, for he had seen Phoebe's slim figure the moment she had entered the park. 'Miss Clough.' He removed his cap and held it in both hands against his waistcoat, gripping it very firmly. His heart beat against his ribs so that he was sure she must be able to hear it. How lovely she looked, her face flushed with the heat, her eyes luminous in the evening sunlight; they swam almost as if with tears.

'I wanted our Jack to have his picture taken,' said Sarah, and Phoebe saw that the photographer was packing up his cart.

Jack muttered, 'You'll not catch me making a monkey of myself.'

'You'd take a fine picture, Jack,' said his sister. 'Wouldn't he, Miss Clough? Lord, aren't brothers such gret babies.'

I should like to capture that face if I were a photographer, thought Phoebe. She was surprised by the strength with which she was drawn to the idea. The memory of the Mundy family, their bereavement and the meanness of the house under the railway arch faded in contrast to the vitality of the man before her. 'Sarah's right,' she said quietly. 'You would take a fine picture.'

Jack flushed. 'Get away wi' you.'

They fell silent.

'William Mundy's dead,' said Phoebe. 'I called on the mother this afternoon—'

Jack relived the incident in the foundry – the glare of heat and the boy's cries. He thought of the Mundys' home: the father on the sick club, the mother who had given birth to nine children, four of which survived now with William gone. Death was commonplace in that household. The pity was that it was one of the breadwinners, not the hungry mouths which had perished.

Phoebe prepared to move off but, glancing at the group of foundry workers, she was uncertain which direction to take. Jack saw her hesitation and saw too that the news of the boy's death had moved her and his heart swelled with sentiment at the notion of her feminine need for protection against the harsher aspects of life.

'I was walking Sarah home from our aunty's,' he said. 'If you care to, we could all three walk along together.' He crammed his cap on his head and marched quickly across the park with the women hurrying along beside him. He narrowed his eyes as they passed the meeting, searching for Walter and Matt among the noisy crowd. Walter would take it badly about Mundy's death, for he had held himself to blame for the boy's injury.

'Are the men angry?' said Phoebe, giving the meeting under the trees a final glance.

'They don't like the notion of doing something for nothing,' Jack said. They walked in a threesome through the park gates and along the cobbled streets past shops and houses.

'You mean my father's lions.'

He looked at her and remembered the wedding and his hostility towards her when all he had wanted that night was to sweep her into his arms. 'Aye. Something of the sort.'

Phoebe looked at him sharply. 'Don't you feel strongly about the statues as well then?' She was startled by what she had said, implying criticism because he was not with the others at the meeting.

'There's some as like hollering and shouting for the sound of their own voice.' Jack's face was red as he tailed off into silence. He slowed his pace as they reached the bottom of Griseley Bank and the road twisted sharply to climb the hill. Sarah chattered about Phoebe's family. When were the newlyweds coming home? And for once Jack was glad of her gossip for it disguised his own silence. He was conscious of the soft swing of Phoebe's skirt by his side and of the darn in his coat at the left shoulder, on a level with her eyes. He wished his sister would not talk so broad and would not play up so in front of Phoebe about how generous she was and how grateful his mother was after her sickness. Easy enough to be generous when you had money and time on your hands, Jack thought, remembering Phoebe in his father's pub and his mother's dark steamy kitchen. And all that nonsense about him having his photograph taken. How silly Phoebe must think his sister and what a gormless idiot she must think him, stomping along there beside her with nothing to say for himself, except to complain about his workmates hollering in the park. He was confused by the inconsistency of his feelings, one moment thrilled by the exquisite chance of meeting Phoebe and the next angry against her for the differences between them. He went over again how, when he had thrown the slipper at the wedding, she had turned to him with a breathtaking recognition in her lovely eyes and how, when she had hidden in his father's beer-cart, she had trusted him to save her from Underwood. He recalled his blundering response to that trust and his spirits were plunged into deeper gloom over the hopelessness of his adoration.

They reached the Nag's Head, a large, flat-fronted building with a badly painted sign depicting a horse's head, and he saw how inferior his home must seem compared with Phoebe's fine house at the top of Griseley Bank.

They halted and Sarah said goodbye. Jack hesitated, watching his sister enter the inn yard, knowing he must follow her but loath to relinquish Phoebe's company. 'Shall I carry your basket?' he said in sudden desperation.

Phoebe was startled, for the basket was plainly empty and not at all heavy. She blushed. 'Why, yes, Jack. If you'd be so kind.' She handed the basket to him as if it had been the bulkiest of shopping loads.

Jack was lightheaded with triumph. He swung her basket by his side. She had let him walk with her when clearly she should have refused.

'You know I am not a *lady* in the way you implied the other day,' Phoebe said after they had gone some way. 'I wish we could forget that my father owns the foundry.'

'No chance of that. With my own brothers beefing that Edwin Clough should be paying us more wages. You're the boss's daughter, Miss Phoebe, and that's all there is to it.'

They walked in silence for a little way. 'I wish we could

be better friends, Jack,' Phoebe burst out at last. She blushed, recognising how her words might be misconstrued and clearly wishing they had not been said.

Jack did not answer at first. Was she playing with his feelings? There were women who thought it sport to egg on a man and liked the danger of flirting out of their class. He had known a few: girls in the chapel choir who acted up and led a man on and then pretended to be indignant when you tried to kiss them. They were not worth the bother compared with the mill girls he had known, who were at least honest and honoured their invitations to a bit of fun and a cuddle. Phoebe Clough was no different from other women, he told himself. Oh, but she was. She was pure and tender and true. He saw again the blush on her face and was instantly ashamed and knew that he was not worthy even to carry her basket. He said, 'I should like you and me to be friends, Miss Clough. In fact I wish it with all my heart.'

They walked again in silence, each trying to make what they could of the other's behaviour until they came at last to the gateposts of Belle Vue.

Jack halted. 'What do *you* think about yon lions, Miss Clough?' He nodded towards the house, as if the lions resided inside.

'I would rather my father had never thought up the idea.' She was aware of the indiscretion of the remark. Yet Jack seemed to warm to her honesty and she saw that he would not try to profit from her disloyalty.

'I'll tell you this much. Some of the men won't stand for it, you know.'

'What else can they do but shout at one another in the park? Stage a revolt?'

He laughed for the first time. 'I reckon you're right. Who ever heard of a Griseley man starting off a revolution?'

* * *

'Have you heard? Young Mundy's dead,' Jack said over supper that evening.

'That's a bad do,' said his mother. They looked at Walter.

'Edwin Clough will be sorry to hear it too, I reckon,' said Joseph, drinking his tea.

'That bugger?' Walter exploded. 'He cares about nowt but his works and making bloody lions.' He stood up. 'That's all he cares about.'

His father gave Jack a searching look. They watched Walter march from the kitchen.

'Give him time. He'll be right,' said his mother philosophically. 'He had to know sooner or later.'

Kitty remembered when she had been a young barmaid and Edwin Clough a young engineer and the pride with which he had raised himself and his family to the level of prosperity which now made him one of the gentry. She recalled that Edwin had seen many accidents like Mundy's and worse as a young man. She reflected on time passing and the way people changed, remembering when she and Joseph had been green and in love and the passion with which Edwin Clough had courted his French wife. If it was true now that Edwin cared only for his foundry and making lions it had not always been so.

The Underwoods had announced to Phoebe that they wanted to buy her a gift. 'Because you have been such a support to us all, Phoebe love.' The wonders Phoebe had worked in getting Christina to the altar, where maternal affection had failed, were still fresh in Beatrice's mind. 'We thought something fairly substantial – say at a cost of ten pounds?'

This directness encouraged Phoebe to respond with equal candour. 'Then I should like a camera.'

The idea of owning a camera had caught her imagination since seeing the photographer and meeting Jack in the park.

She had not the faintest idea how to use one, nor what was involved in the operation of processing a photograph.

Beatrice said, 'A camera?' as if she had asked for something quite bizarre – and so it was, Phoebe supposed. The idea was a little mad, a product of her recent unsettled mood.

Beatrice recovered her composure quickly. 'How unusual. How modern. Alfred will see what he can do.'

'I should like to learn photography. It will be something to fill in the days.'

'Oh, I don't think you will be very long trying to fill your days.' Beatrice wagged a knowing finger.

Phoebe prayed that her acceptance of the Underwoods' offering did not presuppose her consent to a less agreeable proposal.

Six

What say you, Hermia? be advis'd, fair maid:
To you your father should be as a god;
One that compos'd your beauties; yea, and one
To whom you are but as a form in wax.

A Midsummer Night's Dream, Act I, Scene I

The door to Bertrand's room was ajar; its abandoned air with the bed stripped to the flock mattress reminded Phoebe of the time when he had been in France. She pushed the door a little. She had missed her brother then and she would miss him now that he was married, even though he would be living at the lodge with Christina when he returned from his honeymoon. The room was in darkness and had already taken on the smell of vacated furniture, closed windows and stale hair oil.

She crossed the floor and opened the window to the evening air, pulling back the curtains which had been drawn by the servants as if out of respect for someone who had died. Perhaps marriage was a bit like being dead; she was sure that marriage to Philip would be a kind of entombment. Phoebe was perturbed by a remark from her father that morning, an assumption he had made concerning herself and Philip. She saw that the Underwoods made the same

107

assumptions. Poor Philip. She wondered how she was going to let him down lightly. She certainly did not *dislike* him and she had a strong sense of duty: her Christianity was based on self-sacrifice – one took upon oneself acts of kindness to others whatever the inconvenience; she had employed that very argument when persuading her father to pay the Mundy family an apprentice wage for the next two months – but did her duty lie also in pleasing her father by marrying a man because he seemed suitable and because her father had chosen him for her? Philip had smiled at her with a forgiving tenderness the last time they met, as if to say that he knew all was not lost. She would never get married, she decided. She would never be interested enough in one man for that. She would live at home and look after Father. There would be the two of them left in that great gloomy house. The prospect was not a cheerful one.

The servants had gathered together a few scraps of Bertrand's belongings and laid them out on his dressing stand. There was a pair of cuff links, a comb and two folded sheets of paper, one a bill for two pairs of gloves, the other a letter. She unfolded it and then, more curious for it was written in French, she began to read:

Paris, June 10th, 1869

My dear Bertrand,
My reflections on your predicament at this late stage are that a rich wife can only be an asset to you and you may always take a mistress later. Madeleine, they say, has threatened to cut her throat because of your inconstancy and has gone off instead with a policeman (uncouth lackey of the bourgeoisie). She spits on your name. How fickle women can be!

Maurice is roaring from his cell, swearing to put himself forward in the elections, about which we must wait and see. Meanwhile one cannot fail to be aware of the electoral placards posted up everywhere, red, pink, blue, yellow – every colour but white, which is reserved in its purity for the Prefecture of Police. The Empire seeks to bolster its prestige as ever with splendid parades on the boulevards, with gilt and braid and Napoleonic eagles and promises of reform.

We have drunk Maurice's health and intend to make him fat again when he is released. We drank your health too, Bertrand. You see, we have not forgotten you.

And so, next the English lions! What a clever fellow you are. Maurice scorns your town hall and says the money should go to the workers. He is full of talk, but he is not alone. One hears everywhere these days the shout 'Long live the Republic!' even close to the imperial palaces, and the political meetings take place in spite of the vigilance of the police. I think we may see the glorious day before long.

Good luck, Bertrand. Take heed – marry for money, but never abandon love.

Your friend,

Antoine Latrasse

Phoebe sat on the mattress and held the letter in her lap. She should destroy it, or else return it to Bertrand. The servants could not have understood it, but what if Christina had discovered such a letter? Phoebe looked at it again. Antoine Latrasse talked of political unrest, but the time of social upheavals in France as in England was surely long years past: people were more reasonable now and did not rise against their masters. Maurice did not sound like a reasonable man, it seemed from the letter as if he was in prison. And who was Madeleine? She wondered whether

109

Bertrand could have been in love with such an unpleasant girl. Phoebe tucked the letter in the pocket of her frock and went on to the landing. One of the servants was crossing the hall and on seeing Phoebe, she called up the stairs to her with an air of agitation, 'Oh, Miss Phoebe – you mun go at once!'

'Go where, Ellen?' Phoebe hurried down the stairs and saw a second figure poised in the kitchen corridor. She recognised Charles's housemaid in a shawl and bonnet. The woman was short of breath. 'It's Mister Charles's missus – the midwife is there and she says, please would you go as soon as you can?'

'Where is Mr Charles?'

'The mistress says not to send for him. She says you're the nearest and she'll have no one else.'

Edwin did not understand his men's grievance. He knew he was not a bad master, he had put his hand deep in his own pocket to compensate the family over the death of young Mundy, he had paid for extra coal for the men the previous winter with the weather being so harsh and he cared about their moral welfare and urged them to go to chapel. As to wanting more wages – the foundrymen's pay was higher than most in Griseley, higher than Wormauld paid his mill workers – if they looked down on twenty-two shilling it was a poor do. It took character and hard work to better oneself, not badgering the boss for more pay. 'Keep an eye out,' Edwin had told Philip Underwood. 'Any more talk of meetings or owt of that sort I want to hear about it.'

Charles had finished the sketches of the lions and brought them to show him that afternoon. 'When Bertrand gets back off his wedding tour he can get started,' Charles had said.

'*When* he gets back,' grumbled Edwin. 'Two months to get married – did you ever hear the like? When I was wed it was back to work the same day.'

'I had no wedding trip either,' Charles reminded him.

'You didn't deserve one. You'd had your honeymoon already – putting the cart before the horse like that.'

Charles sighed. 'Tessa will shape up, Father. She's a strong character. You could like her if you'd only give her a chance, and there'll be a grandchild for you any day now.'

Edwin jabbed a finger at him and Charles rolled up the sketches protectively. 'I've told you. I'll forgive you, because it's a father's duty to forgive, but I'll not have your wife and her child in my house.' Edwin looked at his son and softened a little. 'Eh, but they're good drawings, lad. I'm right proud of you there, and I know you truly repent being led into temptation by that Jezebel. *When the wicked man turneth away from his wickedness that he hath committed, and doeth that which is lawful and right, he shall save his soul alive.* Chapter and verse?'

'Ezekiel 18, verse 27,' said Charles.

The trouble with young people these days, thought Edwin, was they had lost all respect for authority. It was the same with the working man. He climbed into the waiting carriage and drove out from the foundry yard some half an hour before the close of the works. He did not head up Griseley Bank but towards the town for he was due at a town-council meeting. He felt a sense of civic pride as the town hall with its columns and its bell tower came into view and a more personal pride as he pictured the lions standing at each corner. The trouble with working men these days was they didn't know when they were well off. Griseley men had a fine town to live in, railway, gas and water and drains laid on, not to mention the schools and infirmary and the fact there was work for everyone who wanted to put his back into it. There was no one starving these days in the town,

111

and all thanks to men like himself.

He nodded to Wormauld as the carriage came to a halt and he stepped down on to the pavement. 'How do, Harold. Plenty of smoke from the mill tonight.' The twin chimneys of the fulling mill spewed out a steady thick grey stream into the blue sky.

'Plenty of smoke means plenty of work.'

'Aye, right enough.' Edwin glanced in the direction of his own chimneys at the works as if to compare these tokens of productivity. They entered the cool vestibule of the town hall from which twin staircases curved in symmetrical half-moons to a railed gallery above. The two men began to climb the stairs with frequent pauses for breath, for both were overweight and used to being conveyed everywhere by carriage. Their feet echoed on the stone treads and their voices floated hollowly up to the ceiling.

'Heard you've been having a spot of bother again, Edwin.' Wormauld's concern concealed the happy malice of a man who was confident of his own ability to control his work-force. 'The men still not taking kindly to making lions on top of all else?'

'A storm in a teacup, Harold. You know what these fellows are like – they don't take easily to change. They'll come round to the idea right enough.'

'I hope so.' Murgatroyd, coming up behind them, a younger, more sprightly man, wiry like the brushes he manufactured, had mounted the stairs at a swifter pace than his fellow councillors. 'We don't want word getting round that you've got trouble. That sort of thing tends to spread. We have to keep up standards of order in our men, Edwin, just like we would with our own family.' Edwin glanced at him swiftly and confirmed from Murgatroyd's expression that the comment had been a well-aimed jibe.

'What right has the working man to hold meetings, I'd

112

like to know?' said Wormauld. 'He should be looking to his family, going to chapel, living decently, not holding meetings.'

'They've got the vote now, what more do they want?' said Murgatroyd.

'Aye – and look at the *meetings* there were about that. No, mark my word we don't want trouble.'

'What was it about – more holidays?' A fourth councillor had joined them. 'My clerks are always chuntering about holidays. What do they want more leisure for? They don't know what to do with it when they've got it. Look at Wakes weeks – nowt but drinking, gambling and fighting. There's no merit in being idle, I tell them.'

'There's no discipline these days,' said Murgatroyd.

'Aye,' Edwin agreed gloomily, 'times have certainly changed.'

They entered the council chamber where the other council members were already seated round the huge oval table. 'How have times changed?' Alfred Underwood said pleasantly. He was feeling mellow since the wedding party at Chillingdale and felt that his position had been more firmly established as a kind of honorary squire in the area.

'We were talking of the ingratitude of the lower orders,' Murgatroyd told him.

'And Edwin's spot of bother,' added Wormauld.

'A storm in a teacup,' echoed Alfred, and Edwin, who was beginning to feel that his 'spot of bother' was becoming a millstone, was grateful to his old friend.

They had discussed the drainage problem around the slaughter yard, the new housing to the east of the town and other items on the agenda and at last the council reached the moment for which Edwin had been waiting.

Alfred said, 'Now then, the town-hall lions—' Edwin

pulled Charles's sketches from his bag '—we've met today to officially authorise the erection of four magnificent bronze lions in our town, one at each corner of the town hall.' There were murmurs of general satisfaction and Edwin passed the sketches round the table for approval.

It was hot in the chamber. Edwin mopped his brow with a handkerchief as he waited for their comments. The sketches were good, lifelike, or so he imagined for he had never seen a real lion; he had never had time for frivolous pursuits like visiting zoological gardens.

Murgatroyd said, 'You say these lions are to be like the ones in London and Leeds. How big do you reckon they'll be?'

'Not so big as Leeds lions – that stands to reason,' said Edwin. 'Market-place wouldn't take lions that size and our town hall isn't so elaborate.'

'But big enough to give weight to the town?' prompted Larkin the bank manager, for whom 'weight' was synonymous with 'prestige'; prestige meant more investment. He held the sketch in his hand. 'He looks a sturdy enough beast.'

'I reckon ten feet nose to tail.'

They all agreed this was a 'fair size'.

'And when will the statues be ready?' someone asked. Edwin mentally overrode Bertrand's cautious estimation and said, 'I should say about a year.'

'We'll show 'em.' Alfred rubbed his hands. 'We'll show them Leeds and Bradford councillors a thing or two.'

'We should have to have a ceremony,' said Larkin, 'draw up a list who to invite from round about.'

'Well, Edwin,' Alfred beamed. 'Looks like we're all agreed.'

'Just one moment.' Murgatroyd raised a hand and heads turned expectantly. 'You weren't thinking of giving these lions a mark by any chance?'

'Marking them?' said Edwin.

'Aye, stamping them with a great "Clough's Foundry", that sort of thing.' He appealed to fellow manufacturers on the committee. 'I mean we can't have the foundry using this as an opportunity to advertise its trade.'

There was an uncertain silence followed by murmurs of agreement: the boost to Edwin's own prestige as a consequence of erecting the lions had been a subject weighing on several minds.

'I mark all my big castings,' bridled Edwin.

'But this is hardly the same thing as your general run of castings,' countered Alfred easily. 'We're all obliged to you for what you're doing, Edwin, but it must be seen as a gesture of pride in *all* Griseley's trade and industry – not just in Clough's Foundry.'

'Where had you thought of putting your mark?' said Wormauld. 'Emblazoned on their foreheads – "Made at Clough's Foundry"?'

'You make a woolly lion if you like! I shan't object to you stamping "Wormauld's Mill" all over it,' Edwin blustered.

'Now then, gentlemen. Now then. No need for any rancour,' Alfred coaxed.

'Well, what's wrong with the foundry's stamp? I'm paying for the statues, aren't I? And they're not going to come cheap, I can tell you.'

The others looked uncomfortable, divided between their professional jealousy and the knowledge that Edwin's scheme was a generous one.

'Where *had* you thought of putting it?' someone pressed.

'On its paw. Very discreet,' muttered Edwin.

'Wouldn't that spoil the natural look of the animal?' suggested Murgatroyd.

Wormauld, sensing victory over the point, added, 'I think we should vote on whether it would look right for the King of the Beasts to have "Made at Clough's" on it.'

The motion for the erection of the lions was carried officially, but with the proviso that there should be no foundry mark. Edwin left the town hall feeling out of sorts. He was annoyed that Alfred had backed the others against him. Murgatroyd was as daft as one of his own brushes, he told himself: '. . . spoil the natural look'! All the same, a word from Alfred in favour of the foundry's stamp might have swung the decision his way.

It was dusk and lights were coming on over the town as he drove up Griseley Bank. Henstridge, as always, quickened the horse's pace as they neared the terrace where Charles lived, but Edwin called out to him to halt, for he had caught sight of Phoebe emerging from her brother's house.

Phoebe approached the carriage and stood on the pavement beside it. 'It's Tessa.'

In spite of himself Edwin felt a twinge of concern. 'The child?'

'It's a boy. Charles is with them now.'

A boy, thought Edwin. The first grandchild. If only his Annette had lived to see it. He hardened his heart. Why did it have to be that harlot who had brought the infant into the world? 'Is it healthy?' he said coldly.

Phoebe smiled. 'He's a fine strapping lad, and Tessa is well enough. But it all happened too quickly. It's not good like that, the midwife said.'

'Justice!' said Edwin. 'God brings retribution on the sinner.'

Phoebe turned away wearily. 'Oh, Father.'

'Are you not coming on up to the house?' Edwin felt a sense of loss as Phoebe turned from him. He had hoped they would travel home together.

Phoebe pulled her shawl round her shoulders. 'I thought I'd go and tell Gerald and Olive.'

The rooms at the front of Gerald's house were in darkness. 'They're all up at the back, miss,' Gerald's housemaid told Phoebe with an expression of disapproval on her round face, 'up at the back' signifying that part of the house which was reserved for what Gerald's staff called the master's 'goings-on'. That these activities were innocent play-readings and rehearsals did nothing to affect the servants' title for them. 'Goings-on' they had always been and besides – they knew what they knew. There was more to some of that lot than met the eye.

Phoebe followed the girl along the stone-flagged corridor to a flight of shallow stairs which led up to the theatre annexe. A crack of dim light showed under the broad unpainted door. The girl knew better than to enter while rehearsals were in progress; she stepped aside, pressing her body against the wall for Phoebe to pass, and scuttled back along the corridor as soon as she had done so. Phoebe opened the door quietly and slipped inside.

The room was arranged like a small provincial theatre with whitewashed walls and a wooden stage lit on either side by gas mantles. Benches filled the pit for the threepenny spectators and chairs were placed in rows in the raked auditorium for the sixpence and shilling audiences. This was no fleapit however, nor was it a 'blood tub', for Gerald favoured Shakespeare and his own compositions for the most part, and attracted a cross-section of Griseley's population – though, had they admitted it, even the polite members of his regular but small audiences might have preferred a bit of blood and thunder to some of Gerald's attempts at high art.

Here, among his actors as nowhere else, Gerald was at ease and free from the control which his father still exerted outside the theatre walls. The world of fantasy and drama was life to him in a way that the foundry could never be. His father knew how to impose the dictates of one man on his work-force and his family, but at the heart of Gerald's success was an ability to inspire co-operation, perhaps even love.

Phoebe recognised none of this as she stood in the darkness. She watched her brother and Olive at the centre of the stage in earnest conversation with a man dressed like a grotesque child in a kind of sailor suit, whom she recognised as Victor the dwarf. Olive, her hair dressed loosely, wore a severe dark frock. Gerald was in full evening dress, which he wore in the theatre for performances and rehearsals alike. His golden yellow waistcoat and tie made a splash of colour in the light and a large red handkerchief formed another at his breast pocket. Their faces were lit eerily by the gaslight and Phoebe viewed the tableau with a feeling of unease, for it was as if the three figures were foreign to her.

The rest of the company, who numbered less than a dozen, sat about the benches in the gloom of the pit chatting lightly. Their gifts were diverse and they constituted an eccentric rather than a serious body of enthusiasts. A few were local amateurs – a butcher with a forte for comic parts, a few female shop assistants blinded by the glamour of the theatre, and a curate who specialised in presenting travel lectures with stereoscopic pictures at Griseley's Working Men's Institute, who was also skilled as a waggish raconteur. There was, besides, a nucleus of regulars to whom Gerald gave free board and the opportunity to act in return for odd jobs about the house. These were the dedicated players – Lulu, a former acrobat, Victor the sailor-suited dwarf, Lamplugh Dare, a faded tragedy actor, and Ben Dunn, a comic singer and dancer who had migrated with

Tessa from one of the shadier Leeds halls.

Phoebe waited impatiently at the rear of the theatre while Gerald continued his discussion with Victor and Olive. She remembered the last few hours. What a struggle it had been, almost as if the child were fighting its way from Tessa and she had fought to be rid of it. It was the only childbirth Phoebe had witnessed and she had been frightened by the blood; it was all so messy and brutal and Tessa strangely savage and primitive.

She recognised that the company was in the very early stages of a production for there were no props on the stage nor scenery and, discounting Victor, none of the players were in costume. The proceedings seemed to be taking the form of an audition. The dwarf beckoned to one of the players seated in the pit and Gerald held out a playscript. Phoebe watched a man from the front bench make his way to the stage and she caught her breath sharply for she saw that it was Jack.

Her first impulse was to leave. She had one hand to the door before she halted and considered the irrationality of her action. Her second instinct was one of curiosity. Jack was neither freak nor fop, nor an eccentric like Gerald. What was he doing here with her brother's friends? She moved away from the door and sat at the end of a row of chairs, watching as he mounted the stage.

He wore a cloth jacket and fustian breeches as if he had come straight from the foundry. His nailed boots were loud as they scuffed the boards and a murmur of amused anticipation rose from the other players. Jack stood with the playscript, searching for his starting point, and Gerald raised his hand in an elaborate gesture for silence. Phoebe smoothed her hands in her lap, strangely moved for him, willing him to show them that he was not the boorish fellow they imagined.

His voice when he spoke in his broad accent was unexpectedly authoritative. Phoebe felt an immediate thrill of surprise at the strength and confidence with which his words reached the back of the hall.

'*How now, my love? Why is your cheek so pale? How chance the roses there do fade so fast?*' The question hung in the silence of the theatre, awaiting an answer. It was as if he had spoken directly to her.

Olive, taking the female part, responded, '*Belike for want of rain . . .*'

Phoebe waited with her hands clenched unconsciously against her knees for Jack to speak again.

'*Ah me! for owt that ever I could read, could ever hear by tale or history, the course of true love never did run smooth—*'

The small audience of players were attentive now, beguiled like Phoebe by the spontaneity with which Jack read the part. He paused, turning to Gerald who explained some point in the text and then continued with the same conviction.

'We'll try some earlier lines,' said Gerald, apparently not satisfied.

'Jack *must* play Lysander,' thought Phoebe. He was so obviously right for the part.

They began again, Jack as the young lover pleading his case – '*I am belov'd of beauteous Hermia: why should not I then prosecute my right?*' – until Gerald, interrupting him, turned to his audience with a flourish of his arm and boomed, 'Was I not correct? Is he a natural? Shall he join us?' There was a clamour of assent and the players in the pit hurried to the stage and gathered round to shake Jack by the hand.

Phoebe felt herself an outsider, a lone witness to that lighted scene. She saw that there was a comradeship among the theatre players and a generosity in the admiration on the faces of the people round Jack. She felt strangely isolated and a little envious.

Only as the players dispersed and he left the stage did Jack catch sight of Phoebe. He halted, intoxicated by his success, the praise of Gerald's players still hot in his ears. He wondered how much she had seen and heard. He was sweating from the effort of the audition and ashamed of his work clothes but he wanted her to have seen his triumph and heard him say the words, *Why should not I then prosecute my right?* for it was of Phoebe he had been thinking when he spoke them.

Jack stood in the pit and she came towards him down the slope of the auditorium. 'Well done! I shall look forward to seeing the finished performance.' So she had been there all along.

Gerald joined them. 'Well Jack, you'll have achieved something if you've persuaded my sister to come and watch a play in this den of iniquity.'

'How nice to see you here, Phoebe.' Olive's voice had an uncharacteristic edge of sarcasm; she leaned a forearm on Lamplugh Dare's shoulder with an easy intimacy and an amused expression, and the actor, a man of fifty or more with a fleshy face and flamboyant side-whiskers like Gerald's, turned his head and said something to her which Phoebe did not hear.

Phoebe felt that her sister-in-law and even her brother had shifted from her perception of them as mere eccentrics; their authority in the theatre was strong and a little daunting. And then she remembered why she had come. 'Tessa's had a boy. I thought you would want to know.'

Gerald turned to the rest of the players. 'Do you hear that, my friends? Our Tessa has a son.' Phoebe was again aware of the comradeship which excluded her as they applauded the news and Gerald added, 'We shall go round

at the end of the evening; we must help them celebrate.'
Phoebe turned to go but Gerald placed a hand on her arm.
'Stay a while, Phoebe. It's so good to see you here.'

She recognised the faint reproach in his voice, the
unspoken accusation that she had by her poor support of his
plays sided with her father against him. She sat down on
one of the benches. Gerald touched her shoulder tenderly
and returned to the stage with Olive and after a moment's
hesitation Jack sat beside Phoebe.

Phoebe watched the butcher mount the steps of the
platform followed by Lamplugh Dare and Ben Dunn and
after a brief discussion they took it in turns to read for the
part of Bottom the weaver. She could not shake off her
strange mood: the memory of Tessa's ordeal, the air of
unreality in the theatre and the fact of Jack by her side in the
darkness contributed to her sense of alienation. Yet, how
peculiarly democratic it was to be sitting next to one of her
father's foundrymen. And they were all so at ease with one
another, Mr Bartholomew the curate chatting with the dwarf
and the shop assistants, Digby the butcher addressing Gerald
as if they were old friends and with none of the
obsequiousness he showed behind his butcher's counter
when he was recommending the best cuts from a side of
beef. Olive was laughing at something with Lamplugh Dare,
looking gay and flirtatious with none of her usual grave
reserve.

Jack concentrated his attention on the stage. Phoebe
watched him covertly, seeing his strong profile, his eyes
tense with interest, a slight frown on his brow and his
mouth parting in a smile now and then, pulling back over
slightly uneven teeth and, once, laughing out loud. He could
have been so many things, she thought – an artist, a poet, or
even a scholar; yet, just as she was prevented from achieving
any worthwhile goal in life by being born a woman, so must

Jack suffer the fate of all intelligent men born into the wrong class.

Ben Dunn was given the role of Bottom. 'I reckoned he was the best,' said Jack with satisfaction. 'I never knew Shakespeare were so funny.' He turned to her and said seriously, 'Why did Mr Gerald seem to say you disapproved of it all?'

'My father has always told Gerald he is frittering away his time here. I believed it in a way. It seemed a good thing when he was younger – he used to write plays when we were children and my mother was alive – but not for a grown man.'

'But it's so lively – so real.'

She was puzzled, for his conception of the theatre contrasted strongly with her own.

The players were preparing to visit Tessa and her baby.

'I must be getting off home,' said Phoebe.

'Should I walk with you, Miss Clough? It's dark,' Jack said.

She hesitated. 'There's no need. It isn't far.'

Gerald called, 'Are you coming with us, Jack?'

Jack, caught between the attraction of his new friends and the uncertain bliss of being alone with Phoebe, did not know what to do. 'I should only be in the way and babies bring me out in goose-bumps.' He looked at Phoebe. 'I'll walk you,' he said with sudden confidence.

They followed the noisy crowd of players through the house and out into the street. They continued to walk side by side at the rear of the group not speaking until the little assembly reached Tessa and Charles's house on Griseley Bank. Charles would be ill-pleased to see Gerald's strange family, thought Phoebe, and Tessa too tired. They said farewell and walked on, the sound of the players' voices growing faint behind them.

The night was full of constellations of stars. Their footsteps on the pavement fell into an even rhythm. 'Do you ever feel that they're watching you?' Jack said, looking up at the sky. He seemed happy and pleased with his success and Phoebe's heart beat swiftly with pleasure because they were so at ease with one another.

'Jack, you mustn't let anyone persuade you against the play-acting,' she said after a while. 'You would make a good Lysander and you would benefit so much by it.' She saw that the remark had been patronising, as if the diversion from his labours might help him better himself a little.

'And what do you gain benefit from, Miss Clough?' The old hostility in his voice confirmed that he had been quick to take offence.

'From looking at God's Heaven,' she said, gazing at the stars. 'From looking to do good to folk, but not from *pretending*. Not from charades,' she added decisively.

He laughed. 'You mean you reckon you live in more of a real world than they do?'

'I think so.'

'In your fine house, with no cares and no real work to make your lovely hands all raw.' He fell silent. He had not meant to let slip about her hands, not to call them lovely like that, nor to speak so disrespectfully with her.

'I do know how hard people like your mother and sister work and what it's like for you men in the foundry; my father and brothers earn their living by it, remember.'

'Aye—' Jack said angrily. 'Drawing pictures of lions and giving us men our orders. It's us gets cooked at furnaces and chucks hot metal about. A lad died the other week. Remember?'

'Why, Jack, do you and I always begin to quarrel?' protested Phoebe. 'We seem almost to reach a point of friendship and then—' she looked at him with a sense of desperation and felt an inexplicable urge to knock the chip off his shoulder by force, to seize him by both arms and shake him.

'Perhaps there is nowt else but quarrelling for you and me,' Jack said. He should not have spoken so freely and the *you and me* further implied a familiarity between them which was impertinent.

It was in that moment that Phoebe understood that her preoccupation with Jack was more than a womanly interest in the welfare of one of her father's workers. She felt a strange lightheadedness as she said, 'Would you have it any different if you could?'

'What's the use? That's how things are. It's how God wills it.'

'The rich man in his castle?' They had reached Belle Vue and the lights of the house were clearly visible through the trees.

He stepped back from the gateway for her to enter and said ironically, 'Aye – and the poor man at the gate.'

She did not want him to leave. 'I too have arranged a kind of interest for myself, Jack,' she said.

He did not know what she was talking about, but she seemed to want him to hear it.

'I am going to have a camera. What do you think?'

'I think it sounds a strange kind of interest for a female.'

'Perhaps it's a bit like my brother's plays, after all – constructing pictures, redesigning the world to suit ourselves?'

'Well then, by what you said earlier, you should look down on it,' he said coolly.

'But I shall take photographs of *real* people – like Sarah – and you, Jack. Would you sit for a portrait?'

He could not say no. She was the mistress again, condescending to him. She would put him in a collection for her friends to gawp at. An authentic labouring man. *Oh, isn't he real! How did you get him to sit so still?* 'Of course, Miss Clough. If you wish it,' he said stiffly.

She frowned, hurt by his coldness, feeling she had offended him, but not understanding what was wrong. 'Anyway,' she said. 'I enjoyed hearing your audition this evening.'

'Thank you.' He took a further step away from the gate. 'Please forgive me, Miss Clough, for making so free with my talk tonight. I was a bit carried away with your brother picking me out for the part.'

Phoebe's camera arrived a few days later. She took it from its box on the dining-room table, lifting it from the straw packing. The main section of the camera was made of rosewood; it gleamed a rich red brown. The lens, encased in a polished brass mount, was like a huge unwinking eye with reflection upon reflection in its depths.

'What piece of devil's own amusement is that?' said her father.

'It came from the Underwoods.' Phoebe saw that she must gain his approval quickly if her scheme was to be a success.

'Whatever put it into their heads to give you a camera?'

She said airily, telling herself it was only a white lie, 'I must have mentioned seeing one. It's a very *useful* gift, don't you think?'

'Useful? For what?'

She tucked her arm in his. 'For keeping me occupied. There's so little for me to do nowadays, with the wedding over and done with and no one but you and me to look after.'

'You will have your new sister-in-law to visit when she gets back,' he said and added with disapproval, 'And look at the time you spend with Charles and the child.'

'I can photograph the baby,' she said with cunning. 'And then you can see what he looks like.'

'That's a job for a tradesman,' Edwin said indignantly.

Phoebe was too clever for him. 'Would the Underwoods have given me a gift which was lowering, Father?' She turned the camera on the table and twiddled the brass lens screw experimentally. The large glass screen reflected the garden outside, a hazy image of light and colour, criss-crossed with the bars of the window.

Edwin watched her for a moment, defeated by her logic. At last he said, 'If it keeps you happy.' He was a little unsettled by her enthusiasm for the contraption, yet pleased in a way for her. He liked to see his lamb happy.

'I shall need to buy chemicals and various other things,' she called.

He waved a hand dismissively. 'Get what you need.'

Phoebe went every few days to the park with Ellen as chaperon and sworn to secrecy. After a week she was rewarded by the sight of the photographer's cart. It was a dull day, cold for August, and there were few people taking the air. The man in the frock coat and fancy beret was alone.

Phoebe moved nearer to the tripod. A sign over the cart read: *P. Macdermott. Photographer*. 'I have been given a camera,' she said.

The man looked suspicious. 'You don't want your likeness taken?' He glanced at Ellen. 'The girl does not want her likeness taken?'

'Mr Macdermott, I should like you to tell me what chemicals to buy, so that I might take photographs.'

Macdermott laughed. 'You want to take away all my trade in Griseley?'

'No,' she hastily assured him. 'I should only want to do

127

it for my own amusement. My father wouldn't let me set up in trade.'

This seemed to satisfy him. In his own world a father's word was law. 'So, you wish to learn how to take photographs. You think it's a suitable occupation for female dabblers and amateurs.'

She was quick to assure him again that she did not mean to attack his position as a travelling professional in his field. She added that of course, if he were to agree to instruct her, there would be a fee.

The man's eyes narrowed. 'How much?'

'Three pounds?'

This sum clearly struck Macdermott as phenomenal – as it had Phoebe, and Ellen too. His eyes widened and bulged. It was more than he could earn in a good fortnight – and nearly as much as Ellen earned in six months, thought Phoebe – but as she had guessed, the offer was tempting enough to turn him in her favour. Macdermott smiled, the points of his moustaches rising stiffly against his cheeks, a breath of onions wafting on the air. 'Come. I will show you from the start to the finish, the great mysteries of the photographer's art.'

Phoebe was not sure afterwards whether she had received her three pounds' worth, so cloaked in wizardry would Macdermott have it all seem. The technicalities of lens and shutter and interaction of chemicals were mixed up with 'beams of light' and the 'capture of magical images' and 'phantoms thrown off from the subject.' Ellen was enroled as a model, sitting rigidly to attention in front of the camera lens as Macdermott retired with Phoebe into his hut and the developing process was explained. The smell of onions in the cramped space of the darkroom overpowered that of the chemicals but at last she emerged, three pounds poorer and ready to embark on making 'representations of true life'.

* * *

Having discovered that she was in love with Jack, Phoebe had decided she must avoid him. She preoccupied herself with home and chapel, with preparing a studio in the conservatory at Belle Vue, and with doing good works. She visited the Mundy family until the mother returned to work at Wormauld's mill. And she went to Chillingdale frequently – though she took the precaution of visiting when Philip was not there.

Phoebe's relationship with Beatrice Underwood had altered subtly. She had felt intimidated by the older woman's ebullience in the past: there had been an arrogance in her manner, an understanding that Phoebe and her chapel ways were a little unfashionable in Chillingdale company. Yet since the wedding Phoebe had felt equal to Beatrice and her domain. She reacted to this new-found confidence with an outspokenness to which Beatrice responded with a strong almost maternal affection, as if in Christina's absence she had sought and found a surprisingly agreeable surrogate daughter. Phoebe, in the absence of a more appropriate mother, found Beatrice's attachment pleasing. Yet she regarded the friendship with considerable caution, for an increased affection towards Beatrice must not imply a more favourable attitude to her son.

The grounds at Chillingdale were picturesque in late summer. The lodge where Christina and Phoebe's brother were to live looked pleasant, with its garden filled with flowers and – one afternoon towards the end of August – with smoke curling from the chimney. The significance of the smoke did not strike Phoebe at first, for Bertrand and Christina were not expected for another week. Then she saw the carriage outside the door of Chillingdale and boxes piled in the hallway and her heart leaped with excitement.

'Phoebe!' Christina clung to her and pressed her cheek

with fervent emotion against her own.

Beatrice fussed about them all. 'What a shock, Phoebe! If only Alfred were here. If only Philip – would you believe it? The love-birds have only just this hour arrived!'

Bertrand, for a love-bird, was curiously reserved. He hugged Phoebe with none of his old exuberance and when she said, 'Have you had a good trip? Was Scotland beautiful?' he merely smiled and nodded and gently pressed her hand.

'But why so soon?' said Phoebe when they were settled in the over-stuffed drawing room.

Christina said lightly, 'Oh, you know – Bertie was anxious to begin again on the lions.'

Phoebe glanced at her brother who looked not at all anxious to begin on anything but rotated his teacup in its saucer and stared about with a weary and uncharacteristic expression of strain.

'They have brought some stereoscopic pictures with them, Phoebe,' enthused Beatrice. She turned to Bertrand. 'Phoebe has a camera now. She has become quite a bluestocking and interested in photography.'

Phoebe wondered at Beatrice's sudden admiration and concluded that whereas 'bluestocking' might have been a condemnation in other young ladies, it was clearly meant as a recommendation in her own case.

Bertrand smiled and said, 'A camera, eh?' tolerantly but without great interest.

'Christina's parents gave it to me. They've been very kind. Father says I may use the conservatory for a studio.'

'The light will be good,' Bertrand agreed and fell silent.

Beatrice pressed her hands together. 'It will be such fun to pose for a likeness.' She turned to Christina. 'Now then, poppet – we must get your luggage sent over to the gatehouse.'

Christina interrupted quickly, 'Come upstairs Phoebe and see what souvenirs we've brought you. Such buying sprees we've had. I thought I might have my old room tonight, Mama. It will save the servants going to too much bother.' Beatrice looked astonished and Christina flushed and looked away.

'Not sleeping in your own house on your first night back? The servants are over there now getting it ready.' She turned to Bertrand with a light laugh. 'What a funny oddity-boddity you've married.'

'I really don't mind what we arrange,' said Bertrand. 'Christina must please herself.' He set his teacup on the table and offered Beatrice a tight smile.

Phoebe sensed the tension in the silence which followed, knowing that something was wrong. Christina jumped up from her chair. 'Come on Phoebe, I want to show you everything we've bought.' She went to the door and Phoebe followed her upstairs. A heaviness settled on her as she remembered the fraught hours of the wedding day, a peculiar foreboding as she saw dresses and tartans and boxes spread about the room and watched Christina cross to the dressing table and pick up a small jewel-box.

Christina handed the box to her. 'This is for you. Bertie helped to choose it. He said it would match your eyes.'

Phoebe took the gift. She stared at the lid, engraved with the jeweller's name. 'Bertrand seems strange. Has something happened? Have you had a quarrel?'

'We don't quarrel,' Christina said distantly, flashing Phoebe a smile. She looked well and confident, almost pretty in a flatteringly cut green velvet frock. 'Come on Phoebe, look at your present.'

'But something *has* happened,' Phoebe persisted.

'No, Phoebe.' Christina laughed and the sound was brittle and false. 'I suppose you can say that nothing at all has happened.' Her appearance was odd now, her expression hovering between a smile and a kind of distaste.

Phoebe stared at her, the box unopened in her hand. Then she flushed scarlet as she understood the meaning behind her sister-in-law's words.

Christina tapped her foot. 'I do wish you would open your present.'

Phoebe's heart pounded against her ribs with the implications of that 'nothing at all'. She lifted the lid of the box, recalling the wretched expression on her brother's face. Phoebe did not understand exactly the nature of sexual behaviour but she knew that when people married something had to happen. If nothing happened there were no children. If nothing happened the relationship was unnatural, for a man and woman were not complete together unless they fulfilled their biological functions. Something had happened between Tessa and Charles which had resulted in that bloody and barbarous birth of a child. A thought occurred to her. Could it be that the thing which happened beforehand was bloody and barbarous as well?

She looked up from the silver brooch, a claymore set with a violet stone. 'It's beautiful,' she said automatically and wanted to cry. 'Perhaps later on things will be better,' she ventured.

Christina said harshly, 'You don't understand, Phoebe. Things are better as they are now.' She began to straighten the clothes on the bed. 'And Bertie agrees with me. We get along very well as we are.'

At that moment Beatrice came into the room, a look of determination on her puffy features. 'Right, my girl. I want to know what this is all about.'

Christina blanched; it was one thing confiding in Phoebe, her mother was a different matter. She held a tartan shawl against her breast. 'I don't know what you mean—'

Beatrice caught her by the arm and pushed her roughly to sit on the bed in front of her. 'I want to know why your husband is downstairs with a face as long as a fiddle and why you are wanting to sleep in your old room? You know very well what I mean. Things aren't right.'

'I think I should go.' Phoebe started for the door.

'No—' Christina cried in alarm. Her eyes pleaded with her not to leave her alone with her mother.

Phoebe stood with her hand poised on the door handle as Beatrice said with cold fury, 'You haven't damn well done it! Have you!'

'No!' Christina shouted with her last vestige of courage. 'We haven't. And we never shall.'

Beatrice hit her daughter hard across the cheek with the flat of her hand. 'How are you going to keep a man if you don't give in to him?' Phoebe flinched, seeing the tears start to Christina's eyes and a red weal flush her cheek.

'Bertie understands,' Christina whimpered.

'Don't you know what it means, you gormless girl!'

Christina shook her head.

'No babies! No grandchildren! What sort of scandal do you think that will be? Do you want them all gossiping about you – the servants whispering in corners – the whole town agog with it? You get him into your bed, my girl, and do what has to be done.'

Christina began to cry; great sobs convulsed her face with misery. 'But I don't know what has to be done,' she hiccuped, for indeed Beatrice had never thought it necessary to inform her in so many words, telling her only to 'submit to her marriage duties' and other such enigmatic advice.

Phoebe stared at her friend. So Christina did not know what was supposed to happen, either. But she was a married woman! Surely when a woman married she would know what to do. With a sense of penetrating some forbidden secret Phoebe allowed herself to speculate on how this change from a state of ignorance to one of awareness might come about, and Jack's broad and muscled image came unbidden and with an extraordinary intensity into her mind.

Beatrice's expression had softened as her rage abated. She sat beside Christina and drew her daughter to her bosom. Who knew what impulse had produced her fury – disappointment in Christina's lack of grit, genuine fear of a scandal, or resentment that her daughter might escape the fate all women had to bear? 'Come here my chicken, come to Mama.'

'It's so – nasty,' Christina sobbed.

'I know it's nasty, but we all have to do it and then once you've got it over with there's no end of excuses. You've got to be clever, you see. You let him visit you now and then, just enough to keep him happy, and once you are pregnant he'll leave you alone for a while. You tell him that sort of thing is dangerous in those circumstances.'

'What sort of excuses?' Christina dried her eyes.

'One's female complaint, headaches, appeal to his consideration, bring up the differences in your religion – Underwoods have always been High Church.'

Phoebe wondered vaguely what church edicts there could be on the matter. She released her hold on the door handle. There seemed something more subtly distasteful in the women's collusion than in the thing of which Christina was so afraid. She pitied Bertrand, remembering how bright and loving he had been on his return from France, contrasting the memory with the morose figure downstairs.

Christina was thoughtful, as though her mother had dropped pearls of wisdom in her ear, though as far as Phoebe could tell Beatrice had said nothing at all which might be of any use to anyone. Only now did the women seem to remember Phoebe's presence. Mother and daughter looked at her in surprise.

'Of course, none of this must go beyond these four walls,' Beatrice said sternly. 'I hope you have taken notice too, Phoebe. Not having your own dear mama to advise you on these matters.' And Phoebe, not having her own dear mama to advise her, wondered whether her real mother might not have handled the situation a little better.

A letter had arrived from France. Phoebe took it from the postman and seeing that it was addressed to Bertrand was struck by a fleeting sense of guilt, for she had lost the earlier letter which she had found in her brother's room. She looked at the scrawled address, recognising the handwriting. What if Antoine Latrasse had written as carelessly as before? Should she not forewarn Bertie? The letter was only lightly sealed and could with little trouble be opened, read and resealed; besides which Phoebe was curious about her brother's friends in Paris.

Paris, August 17th, 1869

My dear Bertrand,

So – the Republican victories show us how far the popularity of this glorious government has fallen. Three million votes, my friend. Three times as many Republican seats in the new Assembly and Gambetta elected to Belleville. Though, if the truth be known, much of Paris would vote for anyone who was opposed to the government. Maurice is sulking from his cell because he has failed as a candidate, though his votes among the old café fraternity were loyal you may be sure. I make light of his defeat and his imprisonment, but the working population needs more of his sort. The strikers at Saint-Etienne and Aubin have been

135

put down brutally by the police and they say the captain who gave the order to fire has been decorated. So much for Napoleon's greater liberalism. Haven't we always known that the State and the capitalists will ever remain hand in glove? We need a revolution, Bertrand. We need to cleanse the nation. The Empire has been a well-organised police state for too many years. It seems to me that the greatest iniquity of any government is the subjection of the masses for the comfort and prosperity of a few. But enough of France's troubles.

How is life in more liberal England? My regards to your good wife. I trust married life has turned you into a sober fellow.

I remain your good friend,

Antoine Latrasse

Phoebe resealed the letter carefully.

Disturbing enough news if one were a Parisian, but no mention of Madeleine. She could give it to Bertrand without fear.

Seven

... fixed you have your shadow here,
So that it cannot disappear.
This portrait as it is will last
And when some twice ten years have passed,
Will show you what you were;
How elegant, how fresh and fair.

Verses from *Punch*, 1862

Bertrand followed Charles into the drawing office of the pattern shop. A large sloping desk stood close to the window, a plan rack filled with long metal cases beside it; the surface of the desk was polished and empty, but a table in the opposite corner of the office was stacked high with ledgers, pens, callipers, rulers, sketches and rolls of drawing paper. Bertrand swept a space among the clutter with his forearm and sat in the swivel chair, unfurling a sheet of paper before him. On it were a number of scribbled designs for a lion, some of which were heavily scored through with ink.

Charles watched him with a look of fastidious distaste. 'This office was once an agreeable place to work. You've been back here a week and look at it.'

Bertrand looked up in surprise and followed his gaze to

the muddle of drawing materials. 'All artists are untidy. It's part of the creative process.'

'I'm not,' said Charles emphatically. 'I am very careful. I take a pride in what I do.'

'You always were an old woman.' Bertrand began sketching the head of a lion impatiently. After a while he said, 'You weren't very careful nine months back it seems.'

Charles crossed to Bertrand's table and removed three pens and a pair of callipers, transferring them in silence to his drawing desk. He opened a drawer and took out a notebook in which were amassed a series of neat sketches and calculations, then sat on a high stool at the desk and studied the figures with close attention.

A little ashamed, Bertrand said, 'Anyway – you'll have plenty of space to work when the shed's finished.'

'I dare say you'll make a pig's ear of that as well,' Charles commented without looking up.

'I suppose your brother is taking over the lion project now he's back,' Tessa said against Charles's ear as they lay together in bed the next morning. The sun cast a pale dawn light through the lace curtains; the rumble of traffic on Griseley Bank and the sound of distant factory hooters grew in strength outside and in the neighbouring room the baby's cries were insistent.

Charles refused to be provoked into saying anything against Bertrand to Tessa. 'At least we shall get a shift on with them now.'

'I'll tell you this much, you'd get on better without young Bertrand's help for all he's done so far.'

'Bertrand's the sculptor.' Charles rolled over and climbed out of bed. He wished she did not take such a delight in stirring up trouble. He wished he could pour out to her his resentment over Bertrand's involvement with the lions and the misery of hearing his father's repeated 'We must ask Bertrand . . . Bertie's the sculptor.' But Tessa would only mock, or else make use of his bitterness in some sort of scheme to her own advantage.

His father had never shown any artistic bent when their mother was alive, Charles remembered. Why had he let Bertie go to France, when it had always been clear that he was the better artist? Why did his father despise him and yet he loved Bertie, a talentless wastrel? He knew that his brother would take the project off his hands, using the drawings, the calculations and recently the more detailed designs on which he had spent hours during Bertrand's absence. He had thought that the day his father presented his drawings of the lions to the town-hall committee would mark a turning point, for he had seemed so proud of them. The lions were no longer merely to be a symbol of Clough's prestige, nor even a sign of his generosity to the town; they were a manifestation of his pride in his family and his new persona as an art-lover. Now that Bertrand was back it was clear that this was a role which he relied on his favourite son to fulfil.

Charles did not want to relinquish the lions; he could see the finished sculptures in his mind's eye, he knew the physical dimensions intimately, the weight, the solidity and the massive contours of the beasts – no tame recumbent lions these but animals taut with vitality.

Tessa got up from the bed and stood beside him, smoothing her hands over her stomach, pulling the night-dress flat as she examined her outline in the dressing-table mirror. Charles put his arms round her, locking his hands over hers. Her warmth was always a comfort. He needed her earthy lack of refinement. She drove out his fears of death, eased the memory of the prolonged years of bereavement over his mother and the pain of his father's rejection. 'You would never know it was less than a month since you had the child.' He felt the weight of her body as she leaned against him.

'I wish that were true.' She pressed her hands more firmly against her sluggish flesh. The demanding cries from the next room, though they triggered the automatic flow of milk which soaked her night-dress, drew no emotional response from her and she was reluctant to go to the child. 'How am I going to play Titania looking like this?' she complained.

'You look beautiful. But I wish you weren't going to do it.' Charles moved away to wash in the bowl on the window table. 'You're my wife now. You can put all that sort of thing behind you.' He pulled off his night-shirt and splashed water on his neck and chest. His body was broad but slack. The muscle would soon turn to fat, like Gerald and his father, reflected Tessa. The sound of the baby's urgent cries halted him. 'Aren't you going to feed William?'

'In a minute. It does him good to wait.' He returned to her and she pulled him close, responding to the immediacy of his cool damp body, stroking the solid arch of his back and curling her fingers in the dark hair at the nape of his neck.

'Do you really want to join that rabble of Gerald's again?' he said. 'Look at the rumpus they caused the day William was born, with no regard for how you might feel. And Gerald is such a perfectionist; he won't understand how Titania would tire you.'

'They're my friends,' she pushed him away, 'and I don't tire easily. Besides, I want to do it. You work so late at the foundry. Do you just want me to sit around the house all day waiting for the baby to cry?'

'Is that too much to ask?'

'Is it too much to ask, you take more notice of me instead

140

of fussing all the time about those lions?'

Charles pounced on her inconsistency. 'A minute ago you wanted me to take on the sculpting as well.'

'Well now I don't. I think your brother should do it. Bertrand's the sculptor. He learned how to do it in Paris.'

Sculpting was not all Bertrand had learned in Paris, thought Tessa when Charles had left for the foundry. She went into the adjoining room and lifted the child from his crib; he was wet and smelled sour but his screams stopped as she unfastened her night-dress and pushed his mouth against her breast. She returned to the bedroom with the baby sucking the milk from her, alleviating the needling pains. She opened the drawer of the dressing table with one hand; under a pile of linen lay the letter which Phoebe had let fall from her pocket almost a month ago.

Tessa sat on the bed holding the page on her knee. She should have returned it of course, though she could not imagine why his sister had such a letter in her possession. She was familiar by now with its content, though her grasp of the language was not good. The knowledge that Bertrand had a mistress in France had not surprised her but the evidence of it, here in her lap, the supplying of a name, made her brother-in-law seem more intriguing. You could be sure 'Madeleine' was no chilly Christina.

Her memory of Bertrand had faded recently, eclipsed by the appalling experience of giving birth. 'Never again,' she said aloud to the child at her breast. 'I shall make Charlie promise, no more babies.' She remembered the tension of Bertrand's body against hers, the boldness with which she had kissed him and his voice when he told her he wanted her. You might feel differently when I get back, he had said. Well, it was true, she had almost forgotten what he looked like, and what was one flirtation among all the rest? And yet, she *had* promised that he would have her.

141

She shifted the child to her other breast and folded the letter which seemed now to have a special significance. These things did not happen by chance: Madeleine had been sent to her as a challenge. She glanced down at the child against her breast. 'Why not?' she said. The baby had no knowledge yet of morality or sin, his eyes were closing, the cheeks flushed with sucking, the lips moving spasmodically but slackening with fatigue and the head starting to loll. She carried the child to the next room and washed him and changed the soiled garments. She pitied her son, for no child asked to be born, but she could not love him she thought as she laid him again in the crib. She did not know what love was. That spasm of awareness when you took a man's body into your own or a flicker of sentimentality over a sleeping infant?

Tessa returned Bertrand's letter to Phoebe later that day. She was aware of the depression which Griseley always drew over her spirits as she climbed Griseley Bank. Leeds was dirty and smoky too, but it had its theatres and music halls to enliven it. Griseley had nothing to offer but a few dreary public houses, its factories and its churches and chapels. The pubs, factories and chapels were inextricably associated – the pubs were the refuge of the workers, the factory owners were pillars of church and chapel, sober, hard-working and God-fearing; they gave Griseley's muck a sanctimonious edge.

She was faint from the exertion of walking uphill when she reached Belle Vue.

'Tessa, you should have sent for me!' Phoebe said with concern.

'I wanted to walk.' Tessa leaned against the doorpost. 'Are you going to let me in? Or are you too frightened of your papa?'

Phoebe opened the door wider as if to prove her charity.

Tessa stepped into the hall and sank on to a chair. 'Here, you dropped this.' She pulled Bertrand's letter from her pocket. 'I was that far gone at the time I never told you.'

Phoebe was startled as she recognised the letter; she had searched for it, apprehensive about where it might have fallen. 'I found it in my brother's room,' she looked at Tessa, wondering if she could have read it, and saw from her expression that she had. She flushed at their shared knowledge. 'I didn't really know what to do with it.'

'I should burn it if I were you. He won't want reminding now.' Tessa laid her head back against the rail of the chair and smiled weakly as she handed the letter over. 'Eh – it's a fair pull up that hill.'

'You shouldn't tire yourself.' Phoebe knew only a little about these things but was sure that most people would have considered walking up the hill a few weeks after giving birth was little short of madness. Beatrice Underwood would have had plenty to say on the matter. Phoebe found it difficult to dismiss some of Beatrice's more recently revealed opinions. The sexual union of men and women was clearly disagreeable or Christina would not have been so frightened by it and Beatrice so strange; and yet – she glanced at her more robust sister-in-law – Tessa could not have been frightened or she and Charles would never have done whatever they had done together. Tessa had not even been afraid when the baby came. She had sworn and shouted and made terrible animal noises but she had seemed angry and fierce, not afraid. Phoebe glanced at the letter which Tessa had handed to her – and then there was Madeleine, who had been Bertrand's mistress, a woman who did that sort of thing for pleasure. She would have liked to ask Tessa about it but could not; it was not decent for women to talk about these things. Instead she said, 'How is the baby?'

'Fast asleep with our housemaid fussing over him. She's

143

soft over babies, which is more than I can say I am.'

'Oh, Tessa—' Phoebe said in reproach.

'Why pretend? Why do we have to act up for everyone if we don't want to? I'm neither a good mother nor a good wife. And what's more I don't want to be.'

'We've a duty as women to try.'

'Get on with you! You don't believe that.'

'The Bible says—'

'Oh, the Bible! Can't you Cloughs ever think for yourselves?'

Phoebe said nothing, stung by Tessa's challenging stare and her opinions. She had avoided her company before the child was born and had barred her from Belle Vue in accordance with the wishes of her father. She saw now that it was cowardice had made her do so. Was it cowardice too which had made her connive in dragging Bertrand from France into a disastrous marriage?

'I'd best be off before *he* gets home,' Tessa said.

Phoebe smoothed her hands on her skirt. 'No, stay. I *want* you to stay. It doesn't matter what my father says.'

Tessa stared. 'Phoebe – your hands!'

Phoebe looked down at her fingers, blackened with silver nitrate from her photographic experiments that morning. 'It's from the chemicals,' she said and told Tess about her camera.

'Well I never. You're a rebel, and I never guessed it.' She smiled and Phoebe felt strangely pleased, for she was sure it was a compliment of sorts to be called a rebel by someone like Tessa. She felt that her new activity was indeed slightly anarchic, with its pungent ungenteel smells from the chemicals, the rows of glass-stoppered bottles arranged on a shelf in the half light of her curtained-off darkroom, and the proprietorship of a 'studio' where she could arrange the props and settings to suit herself.

'You will stay, won't you?' Phoebe repeated.

Tessa smiled. 'To tell the truth, I'm fair gasping for a cup of tea.'

Phoebe led the way through the house, calling to Ellen to fetch tea and cakes, and conducted Tessa into the conservatory. She opened the door to the garden, letting a cool breeze dispel the cloying smell of geraniums mingled with photographic chemicals. 'Gerald says you're going to play Titania. Do you think that's wise?'

'Probably not. Charlie's against it so there'll be a row, but I shall go mad else for nothing to do.'

A pile of net curtains, pulled down from the conservatory windows to let in more light, lay folded on one of the chairs. Tessa picked one up and held it against her chin, letting its folds tumble to the ground and cover her frock with a sea of dingy white lace. She turned to Phoebe. 'We're short on costumes. Do you want these? Titania needs something a bit flimsy and gauzy.'

Phoebe shook her head and it occurred to her that in a small way she might make amends to Gerald for her past neglect by the contribution.

Ellen brought the tea and set it on the table, glancing at Tessa with disapproval before leaving.

'You should come and see the play, Phoebe. It would please Gerald no end. One of the foundrymen has just joined Gerald's troupe. He's very good by all accounts.' Tessa bit into a slice of cake hungrily.

'Yes – he is.' Phoebe thought of Jack with a leap of pleasure. 'I saw them auditioning.'

'You ought to take a photograph of him.' Tessa set down the cake and looked at her, smiling and shaking her head. 'Fancy you doing something like that.'

'I'm not very good yet.' Her first efforts, of Ellen who would not sit still and even of a stuffed owl, had been

145

blurred and the developing had left blobs and streaks which were all very disappointing.

'You need to practise.'

'Would you sit for me?' Phoebe said suddenly.

'You bet. What a lark. We'll do it now,' Tessa said.

'How long do I have to sit here?'

'The plate takes a few minutes. Don't go away.' Phoebe, behind the curtained enclosure of her darkroom, was nervous, recalling Ellen's reluctance to pose. It was important all at once that the picture of Tessa should be a success. She tilted the plate from side to side, letting the treacle-like mixture coat its surface. She trembled a little with concentration; it was difficult to get an even layer and one had to complete the whole process, including taking the photograph, before the collodion hardened into a skin. The plate covered, she dipped it into the bowl of silver nitrate then slotted it into its holder and hurried out to the studio.

Tessa was sitting in a wicker garden chair, where Phoebe had placed her some minutes earlier. Her bonnet was still firmly tied under her chin so that only a fringe of her golden hair showed; her hands lay demurely folded in her lap. She grinned. 'Do I look respectable enough, Miss Clough?'

'You look *very* respectable, *Mrs* Clough,' Phoebe responded. Too respectable, she thought. The pose was stilted, but there was no time to change it. Phoebe pulled the black camera cloth over her head and focused Tessa's image on the screen.

'Don't move,' she ordered fiercely and counted the very long seconds of the exposure, seeing Tessa's immobile figure frozen in front of her.

At last she darted back into her darkroom with the plate in its holder. As she processed the negative, she could hear Tessa moving about the studio and singing softly to herself.

At length Phoebe came out from the curtains, drying her hands on a towel.

'You should take one of me as Titania,' Tessa said. She had removed her bonnet and had draped one of the net curtains round her body. With a fluid dexterous movement she unfastened her hair, shaking it with a pride in its abundance. She laughed. *What angel wakes me from my flowery bed?'* Her yellow mass of thick elfin curls and the grey-white drapery made her look ethereal.

'The nets need washing,' said Phoebe.

'Lulu sees to all the costumes, and Olive has a sewing-machine.'

'You are all very self-sufficient.'

'I suppose that's one word for it. They're a rum lot.'

Phoebe smiled, for Tessa clearly did not include herself in this definition.

'Olive's a good sort, for all her little weaknesses.' Tessa reached for the slice of cake again and bit into it, still draped in the net curtain. 'She's not all she seems. None of them are.' She looked at Phoebe knowingly. And there's more about your brother Gerald than meets the eye, she might have added, but even she knew that some things could not be said.

Phoebe puzzled only a little over Olive's supposed deficiencies, for Tessa had set down her plate and began to remove her frock. 'Might I? I just want to see—' and she stripped to her petticoats before Phoebe could reply. She folded and arranged the net into a costume which was less Shakespearean than oriental as she looped her petticoats between her knees converting them into a semblance of pantaloons. 'What do you reckon?' She draped one of the curtains from her shoulders. The effect, barely decent, succeeded in looking fanciful, perhaps even magical, thought Phoebe, as Tessa stepped among the plant pots and draped herself against a wicker chaise-longue. The transformation was remarkable. The simple drapery at once lent a naturalness to the pose which had been absent before.

'It must be in a fairy glade,' Phoebe said. 'The garden would give a better light.' She was already dragging her camera and its tripod on to the lawn. Tessa followed her, stepping barefoot across the grass, and leaned against a tree. Phoebe reset the camera and sped inside to prepare a plate.

She became absorbed by the notion of the photograph. Dissatisfied when the exposure was completed, she insisted that they repeat the procedure, placing Tessa's hands in artistic poses, rearranging the lace and tucking Michaelmas daisies from the border into her hair and bosom. The effect was puckish. She was enchanted by the camera's image. 'You look the part already,' she said when she was satisfied, and recalled too late that Shakespeare's Titania was more a malevolent queen of the sprites than a good fairy.

Edwin had decided to return early from the works that afternoon. He suggested that Bertrand come up to Belle Vue where they could discuss in his study the details of planning the lions. He was annoyed on reaching home to see that Phoebe did not come to the hall to greet him and ask what sort of a day he had spent and whether he would like her to order some tea.

'Perhaps she's in her studio.' Bertrand followed his father through the house. His first impression was of some gauzy fairy creature which had taken possession of the conservatory, his second was that the half-naked vision was none other than the woman who for the past weeks had haunted his dreams.

In Edwin's mind the semi-nakedness of the vision was second only in its flagrancy to the fact that his daughter was casually laughing and talking with the phenomenon and therefore condoned its behaviour. He stepped back from the doorway, averting his eyes. 'What's that Jezebel doing here!'

Bertrand saw Tessa's startled glance in his direction. Phoebe had swung round and stood in an attitude of distraction, her hands twisting against her skirt.

'My own daughter! That *my* daughter—'

The vision spoke: 'Now just a minute – if you want to shout at anybody, shout at me.'

Edwin complied with a bellow of rage. 'Hold your tongue, you harlot!'

Phoebe smoothed her skirts, her face very red. 'I think you're being a bit unnecessary, Father. Tessa was trying out her costume and I have been taking her likeness. Gerald's players are doing *A Midsummer Night's Dream*.'

'Over my dead body!' shouted Edwin.

·'The play or the photographs?'

There was a stunned silence. Never before had Phoebe been anything but contrite when their father ranted and raved. She even looked different; her hair was dishevelled instead of fastened neatly in its chignon and her hands were quite black with dirt.

Edwin was the first to recover. 'That harlot is denied foot in my house and you know it!'

Phoebe, on the point of answering him as sharply as before, changed her mind and said, 'I'm sorry, Father. You did say I might use the conservatory with complete freedom.'

'That harlot is in my house! Get rid of her!' Edwin turned swiftly and strode away.

Bertrand glanced at Phoebe with a rueful conspiratorial smile, remembering how when they were children they had exchanged secret looks and signals behind their father's back, magic signs which had protected them against the full force of his fury. But she was not looking at him and did not seem in need of an ally.

He left with a final reluctant glance at Tessa. She was magnificent, a fairy creature, a rebel. His father called from the study and he followed, acquiescent.

Eight

Think kindly of the erring one –
Ye know not of the power
With which the dark temptation came
In some unguarded hour.
Forget not thou hast often sinned
And sinful yet may be;
Deal gently with the erring one,
As God has dealt with thee.

Valentine message, 1864

Bertrand sat at his father's desk and heard the measured tick of the clock on the mantel and the murmur of his father's voice. The surrounding shelves and tables were filled with heavy bronze ornaments, castings made at the foundry, various ink-stands and pen pots, hunting dogs, a horse, and a cat which Bertrand himself had modelled – his first attempt at sculpture. The glass-fronted bookcases which flanked the empty fireplace were filled with improving titles – *The Seeds of Faith, A Methodist Message, The Ways of Truth* – and stacked on the floor were copies of the *Christian World*. Bertrand remembered the times when he had been summoned here to stand by the green-topped desk while his father read the riot act and invoked biblical condemnation over some misdeed or other. Edwin had never beaten any of his children but they had feared a summons across the hall to the study none the less for that.

Tessa's image in the exotic costume was still vivid. He thought of his wife, on the buttoned sofa, patterned in pink damask to match the curtains, the sun lighting her hair from behind as if she wore a golden halo. He had been willing enough at first to accept the analogy: she *was* an angel to have waited for him so long.

'I don't want to fail at this, Christina. If I could succeed it would prove to my father once and for all that sculpting is worthwhile. He might forget all about wanting me to be involved in managing the foundry.'

'You would have me to help you,' she had said shyly. 'Not with the sculpting of course – that's heavy, man's work, and *very* skilled – but you could tell me about it in the evenings when you come home and I'd listen and . . .' she had hesitated, 'I *do* want to be a good wife, Bertrand.' The sun lit her blushing face. He had reached for her, feeling an unexpected but encouraging surge of lust. Heartened, he told himself that their difficulties had been no more than honeymoon teething troubles. He could love Christina as well as any other woman and she, with a little encouragement, would perform the normal duties of a wife. He saw again the revulsion on her face as she shrank from his fingers before submitting to his embrace.

His bedroom held a single wooden bed with plain rails, an oak chest, dressing mirror and shaving-stand. Hers was a pretty room: the brass bedstead was light and graceful, the blue counterpane, the curtains and wallpaper were sprigged with flowers; a wash-stand with patterned ewers and a bowl stood in one corner; a dressing table set out with china pots and ornaments, a wardrobe and chest of drawers and dainty chairs were placed around the walls. Chillingdale was clearly visible through the window. It was also visible from the bed.

Don't touch me like that! A sentence of misery, endured from the first night of their married life. *Don't touch me!* And then the silent hysteria, the rigid body and the violent shivering which frightened him into compliance. He thought of the fairy creature in the conservatory; her whole demeanour invited – *come, touch me, come, touch me.* He imagined holding the gossamer vision in his arms, the contact of flesh, and folds of lace falling from silken shoulders.

Phoebe's transgressions were laid aside as the lions took precedence, though Bertrand knew as they discussed the lion project that his father, still agitated, was remembering the scene in the conservatory.

'I've promised the council a year,' he said after a while. 'Do you think it's possible?'

'Charles thinks so, but it'll take at least six months to construct the clay model even with Charles helping.'

'What do you think of his drawings? Pretty good? The council seemed impressed.'

'Not bad at all.' Bertrand knew that his brother's lions were far superior to anything he could have produced. 'I shall make a few amendments, then get to work.'

'How's married life?' His father attempted a kind of geniality.

'Well enough.'

Edwin stood up. 'You'll be wanting to get home to your missus. I expect Christina—'

Bertrand stood too. 'Yes. Christina will be expecting me.'

In the hall Phoebe came to meet him. She pushed some letters into his hand, saying she had discovered one of them after his wedding. 'What's going on in France, Bertie? Will there really be another revolution?'

153

Bertrand laughed and said he doubted it. He murmured reassurances as he left the house, but he was too pre-occupied with thoughts of Tessa to care what happened in France.

Edwin called for Phoebe and she went into his study. He felt keenly the burden of chastising her, for rarely had she disobeyed him so blatantly. He wondered briefly what Annette would have made of the situation and with a slight distaste suspected she might have found it amusing.

He recalled with extraordinary vividness the smell of his wife's perfume, the smoky haze of an oil lamp and Annette's low murmuring laugh. She had been able to extract a delight in unseemliness from him in those days. But all that had been in the privacy of a bedchamber. The harlot's display of flesh in the conservatory, in broad daylight, in the presence of his daughter and where the servants might see was unforgivable.

Edwin sought the best method of approach. 'It's one thing going to a woman in her travail, Phoebe, quite another to bring her into the house. When I allowed you to accept a camera from the Underwoods I never dreamed you might put it to an immoral use. I still cannot believe my lamb would do such a thing. I must only assume it was through ignorance and that you do not fully understand the ways of the world.'

'I'm sorry to have displeased you so much.' Phoebe's manner was meek. She seemed genuinely chastened because she had caused him pain.

Edwin decided that she had indeed acted in ignorance, out of sentimentality because of her brother's child. Babies brought out the softness in women. It was a fine-looking boy according to Phoebe. She had tried to persuade him to see the child, and he was curious, there was no doubt of that. But he would not weaken. He had said he would have nothing to do with the marriage and he would stand by his word. What a fool Charles was to have let the whore trap him. What a fool he had always been. 'Let him draw,' Annette had coaxed. 'He'll surprise you yet.' Well, Charles had surprised him right enough. In any case, what sort of occupation was drawing for a lad as dull-witted as Charles? Much better to channel his talents into the business. He had respected Annette's wishes over Bertrand by letting him study sculpting and had been forced by the circumstances of her legacy to respect them over Gerald; he had proved that he was not the philistine she supposed. He would prove it further. Wouldn't the lion project testify to it? Wouldn't it combine the talents of Charles's drawing and Bertie as a sculptor and himself as a master of industry?

'Father?' Phoebe prompted. Her voice was calm. It occurred to him that she was not afraid of him. How like Annette she was growing now she was reaching full womanhood. 'Don't be so rigid with them,' Annette had said when they were children. 'You frighten them when you are fierce.' And yet it was only through love he had ever chastised them. He had wanted so much from them and for them to be worthy in the eyes of the Lord.

'I am very disappointed in you, lass.'

Phoebe's gaze wavered. It was a form of attack which had always defeated her and did so now with its implications of failure, of a standard of perfection to which she had not effectively aspired.

'I am in two minds whether to let you continue with your pastime.' Her father tapped his fingers on the great Bible which lay as always on the study table and her heart sank lest he should decide to consult the Scriptures over the issue. Biblical texts had a way of adapting themselves to the most unlikely circumstance. She would defy him, she thought. She *must* defy him if he forbade her to use the camera.

'I had thought to photograph Mr and Mrs Underwood, also Bertrand and Christina,' she said. 'Would it not be churlish now to say I may not do so?'

This posed Edwin with a problem. He could not be seen openly to snub Alfred and Beatrice's gift. He frowned at the Bible, bound in leather with brass clasps and gilded edges, as if seeking the answer to this delicate social question.

'Perhaps it could serve as a test?' suggested Phoebe. 'If you approve of the likenesses of Bertie and Christina and the Underwoods, perhaps I might continue with the pastime.'

Edwin deliberated on this means of saving face and said, 'Very well. On condition that woman never comes here to be photographed again.'

Phoebe promised and the incident was over.

'We will say a prayer together,' Edwin decided.

Phoebe bowed her head and clasped her hands, the image of the dutiful daughter, and Edwin prayed fervently for the restoration of Phoebe's soul to its former immaculate condition.

Phoebe prayed half-heartedly for her soul and it occurred to her that her father had not forbidden her to process the pictures. She resolved to remain a dutiful daughter, if God would please not remind her father about the negatives.

Bertrand did not go straight to Chillingdale but stopped the carriage near the bottom of Griseley Bank. He waited outside the little house with the neat white curtains before stepping down. Tessa herself opened the door, dressed respectably again in a loose-fitting frock, her mass of hair fastened neatly.

'I thought you might come.'

'Is Charles at home?'

'He's not back from the foundry.'

'I have to see you. I've thought of nothing else. I shall go mad if you say no.'

'Not here.' She hesitated. 'There's a place on the road to Chillingdale – near the river by the pump house.'

'I know it.' He wondered jealously if it was where she had in the past met Charles.

'I'll meet you there shortly.'

She closed the door and Bertrand returned to the carriage wary of curtains twitching on Griseley Bank, but he saw nothing move at the windows as the carriage drove on – for who would think ill of a man visiting his brother's house to see his sister-in-law and young nephew?

He called to the driver to halt the carriage as they neared the river a short distance from the town. 'I shall walk from here.' He watched until the vehicle had turned a bend in the road before he entered the trees. A stone building, an old pump house, stood close to the riverbank. Bertrand reached it and leaned against the wall, calculating that it would take Tessa several minutes to walk from Griseley. He unfolded the pages of one of the letters Phoebe had handed him. Antoine's news of the elections and talk of revolution revived memories of Paris which tugged at his heart; it seemed as if he had aged several years instead of months since leaving France.

Why had he come home? he asked himself again, as he had asked repeatedly that summer. Why had he let duty and his father's will overrule his own judgement? He read the letter and, folding it, placed it in his pocket. He saw a figure on the road and stepped away from the shelter of the wall. 'Over here.' His voice carried above the rush of water.

Tessa looked fit and desirable as she walked along the path through the trees. She hurried towards him and they stood a little awkwardly and she smiled, as if she were shy,

157

though Bertrand suspected she was not. His heart raced as he reminded himself that, though she was his brother's wife she was at best a whore like Madeleine. 'Will you be missed?'

She shook her head. 'Charlie often works later than the rest of you on a Friday night. He's becoming obsessed by the foundry.'

'You looked splendid this afternoon – like an elfin spirit. My father was furious.'

'I hope he doesn't tell Charlie.' She fell silent and Bertrand wished that she had not mentioned his brother. The ripple of the river over the stones below them sounded loud in his ears. Dusk was falling and the air was damp. She shivered and pulled her shawl round her shoulders. 'It's the lions that have a hold on him. He says you're the sculptor but I think he'd like to do it all himself.'

'I'd let him get on with it if I could, but I've got to earn my crust of bread. I'm a married man, everyone expects it.' He gave a bitter laugh. 'She won't let me into her bed, you know.' He looked at her, tears of self-pity starting unexpectedly to his eyes.

'I could have guessed.'

'If you've changed your mind – I don't want you to feel obliged about anything.'

'A bit late for that.' She reached up to stroke his neck. 'Would I have walked all out here if I'd changed my mind?'

The touch of her fingers sent a shiver through him. He seized her hand and kissed it fervently.

'We must be very careful,' she said. 'I'm fond of Charlie in a way. I wouldn't want him to find out.'

He kissed her lips chastely, then as his fingers touched her throat and breast Tessa threw back her head and leaned against the wall with a sigh. He felt the taut flesh of her

158

breast and she helped him unfasten her bodice and pull back her chemise.

Tessa had thought up a few regrets coming along the road, but not now. For what harm did it do anyone so long as they were careful? She lifted her skirts for him and he felt for the gap in her drawers and parted the soft moist flesh between her legs. His fingers found the place and made her surge with the familiar pleasure. Why did they call this exquisite hunger a sin? People like his father and his wife. Even Charles, for guilt had always lent an edge to their love-making before their marriage. But Bertrand did not seem ashamed, he was self-indulgent in his enjoyment of her as if it was his right. He called her his love and his water sprite, pulling her skirts up to her waist and lifting her high against the wall, and she wrapped her legs round him and urged him into her, savouring each pulse of pleasure.

They leaned against the pump house afterwards, looking into one another's eyes in the questioning way one did the first time, wary of commitment. It was already growing dark along the riverbank. The water flowed noisily unseen. Bertrand was the first to speak. 'We've got to meet again. We can't stop now.' He looked away, and she knew he was afraid she would refuse.

'I'll tell you when. I'll let you know somehow,' she promised.

He kissed her and she clung to him a little for warmth before pushing him away. He watched her walk along the path to the road, but she did not look back more than once and hastened on towards Griseley.

The next day dawned fair and cool. Phoebe hurried down to her studio as soon as the morning chores were over and the house was quiet with her father at the foundry.

She worked until the afternoon, processing the pictures

159

she had taken. They were pleasing: the first, of Tessa in a dark frock and bonnet, was sharp with only a few flaws and scratches from her haste in developing the plate. Those taken in the garden were blurred: she had been less accurate with the focusing. There was a carelessness about them and a spontaneity in the poses which was absent in the first portrait.

Phoebe laid the dried and finished prints side by side on the floor of her studio and sat on the drugget by the conservatory door with her back against the door-jamb. The afternoon sun was barely warm: already a scent of autumn was in the air. She picked up two of the pictures – the very first she had taken, and one posed in costume in the garden. She had assumed that the camera recorded the truth, that whatever was in the camera's range would appear as an exact rendering of the subject in the finished picture. Yet, it was hard to believe that the two images were truthful representations of the same woman. Which was more accurate? The woman stiffly frozen, a half smile on her pleasant face? Or the wild-haired, elfin creature of Shakespeare's play. Clearly, the real woman sat in frock and bonnet with a direct stare into the camera. And yet, there was a sense of seeing into the soul of the beautiful, strange creature with the dreaming, sensual gaze in the garden, which was absent from the more conventional picture. Which then was the real Tessa? Could photographs record images which told lies?

Jack sat beside his sister with Matt and his wife in the gallery of the Ebenezer chapel. His starched collar rubbed his neck and he eased it with his fingers. Phoebe sat at the harmonium by the choir stalls and the music of the anthem swelled to fill the small chapel hall, rising to the gallery and making the air tremble with sound. From there Jack could look at her without being observed: she wore a dark blue frock and plain black bonnet – very sober, nothing la-di-da.

The sermon was lengthier than Jack had expected, but it was a while since he had sat through a chapel service. The man was a visiting preacher, full of long words and with a bee in his bonnet about the interpretation of miracles. Edwin Clough, with grey head bared and looking like one of the ancient prophets, stared straight ahead and nodded from time to time in agreement with the preacher's opinions. The man's voice flowed in an almost unbroken stream, light and pleasant at first, rising to stridency – *the fate of man's immortal soul . . . the fiery furnace . . . salvation through the blood of Christ.*

Jack fell to a further contemplation of Phoebe. He knew what would be a miracle – if he were to come into a fortune and be able to say, *Phoebe, my love, marry me.* He watched her strike up a hymn, the hymn-book open on the stand in front of her, her small hands confident in their touch on the keyboard.

Phoebe had noticed that Jack was in chapel; she was aware of him seated in the gallery and the knowledge that he had a clear view of her made her nervous, fearful of making a mistake in her playing. When the service was over he raised his cap outside and said, 'Good evening, Miss Clough,' just as if they had never spoken to one another more intimately. And then he was moving off; she watched him head on up Griseley Bank, handsome in his Sunday clothes, not waiting for Sarah.

The preacher had urged honour and obedience to one's parents; Phoebe had bowed her head and promised compliance, yet she was aware of a mutinous anger against the conformities of her upbringing. Seditious questions posed themselves. Where had been the immorality in photographing Tessa, when her father had sanctioned her photographs of

161

Bertrand and Christina, himself arranging for Henstridge to transport her equipment to Chillingdale that week and asking her solicitously afterwards how the session had gone? And what was so terrible anyway about receiving Tessa at Belle Vue? Another question rose as she watched Jack's departing figure. What was inappropriate about a friendship with one of her father's workers? Suddenly she was hurrying after him. 'Mr Bateman – please wait!' She was unnecessarily formal and cold with him. 'I believe the theatre company is short of costumes.'

He stared at her as if he could see through her subterfuge but answered politely, 'Aye, that's so.'

'I wonder, Jack, if you would like to collect some old curtains and bedspreads for Olive and Lulu to make into costumes. They're parcelled up but they're rather heavy.'

'No trouble, Miss Phoebe,' he said with a solid, unresponsive expression. 'Should I fetch them now?'

She said that she would be grateful and he walked up the hill beside her.

'Your father's not driving you home in the carriage then,' he said after a while.

'He has an elders' meeting.'

He nodded and Phoebe's heart beat quickly. Her father's absence made her request seem like an assignation. She knew that one of the servants could have taken the parcel and that Jack would know it too. She should not have asked him, she should not have provoked another encounter when her feelings towards him were so confused. They were silent as they passed the Nag's Head and climbed the Bank until they reached the house. 'The materials are in the conservatory,' she said. 'We may as well go by the garden.'

The sound of their feet was loud on the gravel drive and they walked, awkward with one another, across the grass and along the side of the house.

The conservatory was quiet, the scent of pot plants heavy and stale. 'Here we are,' she said very brightly and indicated the parcel on the wicker table.

'Is this where you do your photographing?' He looked at the curtained darkroom and the heavy camera on its tripod. He imagined sitting in front of the lens. Every shade of expression would be revealed to her through that clean cold eye, while he would see nothing of what she was thinking.

She said breathlessly, 'Jack, it would please me if you would sit for me one day.'

'Not me. You'll not make a monkey of me.' Was that all she wanted? To use him as a dummy? He felt angry with her and disenchanted. He walked to the table, on the point of stooping to pick up the parcel. 'Will that be all, miss?'

Phoebe nodded and said miserably, 'Oh, Jack – I wish we could be easier with one another.' How hot he looked in his Sunday-best jacket and how unbearably fine. He straightened and glanced at her with a strange expression, as if about to speak, but then with a look of desperation in his dark eyes said nothing.

'Don't you wish it too?' Phoebe said faintly.

At last he said, exasperation making his voice harsh, 'I can't tell you what I wish.'

'Try, Jack. Just say what comes into your head.' She knew she had spoken as she might to the Sunday-school class when coaxing an opinion from them. She felt awkward and her misery deepened for things seemed to be going wrong.

'Oh, Phoebe—' He took an involuntary step towards her and in an instant she was in his arms, not knowing which of them had made the move which welded their bodies together. The violence of the action knocked back her bonnet and she clung to the coarse cloth of his jacket. He kissed her on and on so that she could not breathe but kissed him back,

163

wanting never to stop as Jack held her even closer. His body seemed to melt against her until she felt as if she was on fire, and then a sound from the house broke into her consciousness and at last he let her go.

'Tell me. Tell me what you wish,' she whispered.

Jack waited, tense with listening, but no one approached the conservatory. His voice was abrupt in the silence, almost as if he wanted to hurt her. 'Woman, if you're too stupid to see.'

Phoebe looked at him, at his face flushed with kissing and the look in his eyes and responded with a surge of anger greater than his own. 'Don't call me woman like that!' It was not at all what she had meant to say. Her words launched the moment into a corkscrewing of all the old tensions and misunderstandings and she felt the flowering of happiness between them fly at once from her grasp. 'Don't "woman" me, like your father and brothers talk!' If only he had said, 'I love you,' if he had not been so thick-headed and rigid and true to his class. Phoebe pressed her hands against her skirt. 'I won't be talked down to and I won't have you taking liberties.'

He gave her a twisted smile. 'No, but you'll talk down to me, Miss Clough. You'll be content to talk down to me to the end of your days.' He picked up the parcel from the table and walked from the conservatory.

She watched him cross the garden towards the front of the house with it pressed against his chest.

Phoebe curbed a strong urge to run after him, to call out, 'Hold me again and it will be all right, don't run away.' Was there no hope for them of ever understanding one another except on a level of half-acknowledged truths and evasions?

She stood until he had turned the corner of the house and then she ran up the stairs to her room. She drew aside the curtain and looked down upon the front garden, watching him go along the drive, longing to touch him again, to feel the weight of his arms around her and the heat of his body, as she clung with white-knuckled fingers to the curtains.

Another letter from France came by the following afternoon's post. Phoebe decided to take it to Bertrand at the foundry to avoid giving it to him when he was with Christina. She arrived at the gates and came upon the newly constructed shed, a long low building with several windows along its length. Philip and Gerald were in the yard with a group of men in foundry breeches and aprons who were loading castings on to a wagon. Jack and his brothers were among them. Gerald came across the yard. 'How's my favourite sister?' Phoebe saw Jack glance in her direction and for an instant their eyes met before he looked away.

'Thank you for the costume material, Phoebe.' Gerald took her hand. 'It was a kind thought and much appreciated.' He turned to view the yard and seeing Jack still stacking castings by the wagon he said, 'Our new theatre recruit is shaping up well. You must sit in on another rehearsal.' She answered that she did not know if she would and then, afraid of meeting Jack's glance again or that Philip, his hair slicked back and his face pink and eager, would come over to speak to her, she hurried into the workshop.

Bertrand and Charles were together, leaning over a table on which were spread several rolls of paper. She stood for a moment, forgetting the scene in the yard, gratified by this image of her brothers working in co-operation; it reminded her of when they were children, when there had been no responsibilities of marriage dividing them nor rivalry over their father's project.

Charles, glancing up and catching sight of her, said, 'Phoebe! Come and see the latest drawings.' Only then did she sense the strain between her brothers which had not been evident on a first observance. She looked at Bertrand who shrugged as Charles led her by the elbow to a table on which were spread sheets of draughtsman's paper. He feigned a disinterest as she looked at Charles's work.

She saw a reclining lion, its head alert, the mane tossed back and all beautifully modelled and shaded to give a three-dimensional effect; the drawing was repeated over and over with lines and measurements, cross-sections and calculations scribbled on every page. For the first time she saw the lion as Charles saw it, a rather magnificent creature.

'Is it really going to work, Charlie?'

Bertrand had come to stand beside her. 'If he and Father have their way all four of them will be roaring their heads off outside the town hall before this time next year.'

'Doesn't that rather depend on you?' said Charles.

'And on the clay arriving,' countered Bertrand, explaining, 'Charles delayed ordering the clay. Without the clay, no lion. I can't model it out of thin air.'

Charles rolled up the drawings and took his pocket watch from his waistcoat. He glanced at it ostentatiously. 'I thought you said you had to get home early.'

Bertrand remarked with apparent nonchalance, 'So I did.' Phoebe gave him the letter from Antoine in silence. She watched him saunter from the shed, his hands in the pockets of his checked trousers, and saw Charles's look of hatred.

'He does as little as he can get away with,' he complained. 'Why can't Father see through him, Phoebe?'

'How is Tessa?' she said gently. 'You know I would visit more often if Father didn't make it all so difficult.'

Charles continued rolling up his drawings and seemed disinclined to talk.

* * *

166

Jack watched Phoebe covertly as she left the foundry, Walter saying in his ear, 'There's your ladylove again, our Jack. Say hello to your sweetheart.'

Matt with a warning hand on his arm said, 'Not here, Jack. Don't clobber him here,' for fighting on the works' premises meant instant dismissal.

Jack closed his mind to Walter's jibes and to the memory of Phoebe's kiss. He stared at a point on the boiler-house wall so that he would not have to look at her. It was cold in the yard, welcome after the heat of the furnaces, but it would soon be November. Six months since he had first fallen in love, and still in love Jack thought miserably as he saw Phoebe turn her lovely face to him and then walk away. He watched her straight back and her pert backside, and her gloved hands clasped together. Who would guess now that those dainty hands had held him close not twenty-four hours since?

Christina examined Phoebe's set of cartes de visite and spread them out on the table in her sitting room. 'Don't you think they're just grand, Phoebe! I shall take them to show Mama and Papa this evening.'

Phoebe pulled off her gloves and sat on the pink damask sofa beside Christina. 'Don't tell me I'm a clever girl. My father says it all the time.'

Christina smiled with a perplexed frown. 'But of course you're a clever girl. Why shouldn't he be proud of you? You're much cleverer than me.'

Phoebe's glance took in the array of fancywork articles in the room, the embroideries and water-colours, the arrangements of cushions, screens, handmade knick-knacks and mausoleums of dried flowers, and finally the photographs on the table in front of her. She had taken them on the terrace at Chillingdale, out of doors on an autumn day, when the weather gave an extra dimension of frigidity to the chilly poses. Christina was seated and Bertrand stood with a proprietary hand on her shoulder. The picture presented an image of middle-class respectability. The eyes looked directly at the observer and disclosed nothing of the lives within. There were no revelations in the poses, some taken separately, of Christina, sweetly sentimental, and Bertrand, handsome and sober, the devoted husband.

Christina met Phoebe's glance and looked away. 'I wish you would marry Philip soon, then we could spend so much more time together, you and I.'

Phoebe looked at her in alarm. 'Who says I'm going to marry him at all!'

'Oh, get on with you, Phoebe. I'm his sister. We've always shared confidences. He has *told* me,' she said meaningfully.

Phoebe ignored this evidence of Philip's certainty. She was more curious about Bertrand: Charles had said that he wanted to leave the foundry early, but clearly he had not come home. She turned to Christina and on impulse took her friend's pale hands in her own dark-stained fingers. 'Are you happier now?'

'Oh, yes,' Christina said brightly. 'Mama was wrong – though you mustn't breathe a word. I tell her Bertie comes to my bed.' She blushed. 'And he has – at least once or twice – but Bertie actually agrees with me that companionship is much more important in marriage than those other things.' Christina wished more fervently than Phoebe supposed that she would marry her brother, for closer female companionship would, she was sure, take her mind off her marital difficulties. Her mother had told her that by service and submission, asking for nothing, she would gain power over Bertrand. Yet Christina asked for nothing and got precisely that. She knew she did not deserve

168

to be treated as she was. The way Bertie had imposed himself that 'once or twice', so aggressive and brutal, had made her almost dislike him. She sighed with the satisfaction of a woman whose life is well ordered. 'Bertie *has* become very much more considerate. And he works so late at the foundry. He seems really to have taken an interest in making the lions at last. He says he will begin on the modelling soon.'

'I have just been at the foundry,' said Phoebe, remembering the animosity between the brothers, and wondered, where *was* Bertrand?

The air on the moor was cool and still, full of the autumn scent of heather. A dry-stone wall ran along the edge of the escarpment, the same limestone scar which overlooked Griseley and lower down the valley formed Griseley Bank. Tessa lay with her back to the heather and her skirts up to her waist. Her fingers gripped Bertrand's naked buttocks. They had taken a risk, out in the open, but the danger of it all was part of the excitement, that and the haste and the subterfuges; she enjoyed lying to Charles, she had always enjoyed lying; it gave her a sense of power. She checked Bertrand for a moment, hearing the high piping notes of a skylark, and then he shifted again and she was immersed in pleasure and could not hold him off any longer, crying, 'Now! now!' as he began to ejaculate.

'Did you hear the skylark?'

He rolled away from her and lay on his back with his hands behind his head. The sound had stopped. Tessa listened intently but heard nothing. She glanced down at him. Sweat dampened the hair on his forehead, his clothes were all unbuttoned and his shirt clung to his chest. He looked very vulnerable and she was swamped by a feeling which was new to her, a sudden tenderness.

'I must be the happiest man in the world,' Bertrand said.

She gave him a little push. 'Don't be soft. We just like it a lot, that's all. We're the same kind you and me.' She leaned forward and bit him gently on the nose. 'Bad, through and through.'

'If you're so bad, why do you make me so happy?'

'Because you're a bad lot too.' She began to dress, fastening the buttons of her bodice. 'Living with Frenchies all that time has turned you rotten, Mr Clough. Else why would you be fucking your own brother's wife?'

He was quiet.

'Now what's got into you – a guilty conscience?'

'I was thinking about France. Phoebe gave me another letter from my old friend Antoine. I can't bring myself to read it, it will make me want the old life in Paris again.'

She was instantly serious. 'You wouldn't go off and leave me now, would you?'

He looked at her for a moment, considering the idea. He was not tired of her yet and he did not doubt that he loved her, but women like Tessa were so easy to love; the moment would come when she was no longer unique and her attraction was reduced to this mere exchange of pleasure.

'No, I won't leave you,' he said and kissed her.

Dusk was falling. Tessa stood up and straightened her frock, then tied on a bonnet and flung a shawl round her shoulders; she did not wait for him to dress but set off alone for Griseley. Bertrand watched her for a while before opening the letter.

Paris, October 12th, 1869

My dear Bertrand,

Who in his right mind would not sympathise with a request for greater civil liberties, for freely elected mayors and local control, for fair wages, decent houses and an end to envy and greed? Who would not move heaven and earth to create an ideal world in which men smile upon one another as brothers, and a fellow need think of nothing but wine and women and painting pictures? This bloody police state! You either have to be hand in glove with a local police inspector or else so innocuous as to be beyond suspicion these days. No one is allowed to say anything at all controversial. The Press is stifled. The police can imprison whom they like on a charge merely of being hostile to the Empire.

Maurice at least has been freed at last and talks of little else but the social revolution. It is true that feeling is growing in strength against the Empire. If only it could be done without bloodshed. My heart is heavy, I confess it. I am not the gay dog you left behind, Bertrand, and am in sore need of your excellent company . . .

There was more – about his painting, about his mistress who had left him – yet all in the same vein as if the joy and colour of the boulevards had gone for ever. Bertrand folded the letter, Antoine's depression stealing over him. He followed the direction Tessa had taken as if out for a stroll in the evening air.

Nine

This lass so neat, with smile so sweet,
Has won my right good will
I'd crowns resign to call her mine . . .

Leonard McNally,
The Lass of Richmond Hill, 1789

Edwin left a chapel prayer meeting with Murgatroyd and his wife.

'I understand your Phoebe is getting quite a reputation for herself as a photographer,' said Mrs Murgatroyd.

Edwin responded with a touch of pride, for Alfred Underwood's reaction to Phoebe's photographs had been very gratifying. So much had he praised them in fact, that Wormauld had asked her to take photographs of his own family, and other members of the town council were now clamouring for Phoebe's attentions. Edwin congratulated himself on the fact that Phoebe had learned quickly what did and did not constitute an appropriate subject for photography.

'I see your Gerald is putting on a Shakespeare play next, Edwin,' remarked Murgatroyd with a critical jerk of the head. He did not share his wife's approval of Phoebe's new diversion, nor for that matter Griseley's enthusiasm for Gerald's plays.

They had paused in front of a poster as they walked to their separate carriages: it advertised Gerald's latest production, *A Midsummer Night's Dream*. A queer cove was Gerald, reflected Murgatroyd, but what else could you expect when the mother had been so indulgent and Edwin that soft on his wife when she was alive that he had let the children do just what they liked?

'Shakespeare helps encourage the working classes to raise their sights above the cockpit and the public house,' said Edwin defensively. The noise of revelry from the Nag's Head spilled out into the street from up the hill.

'Oh, I quite agree,' approved Murgatroyd's wife, thereby drawing the disapproval of her husband.

'And Shakespeare is hardly the music hall,' added Edwin.

'It's hardly godly neither,' murmured Murgatroyd.

'Your Gerald is helping to wean the minds of the lower classes from more vicious and sensual indulgences,' said Murgatroyd's wife, a benign-faced woman, with thin lips and cheekbones like her husband, which in her own case gave her an undernourished rather than an uncharitable look.

Edwin smiled at her, feeling grateful for support from an unexpected quarter. He took his leave of the Murgatroyds and basked a little in this novel reputation of his multi-talented family as he drove in his carriage up the hill.

'The Cloughs are an unusual lot,' continued Mrs Murgatroyd as she climbed into her husband's carriage.

'They're a lot of reprobates if you want my opinion,' scowled Murgatroyd. 'Edwin's missus spoiled them when she was alive. And Edwin's been too indulgent with them ever since.'

'Annette Clough's heart was in the right place,' said his wife placidly. 'And so was Edwin's once upon a time. It's

174

overwork has been to blame, if you ask me. No time to watch what was going on at home while they were growing up. Poor motherless creatures. Poor Edwin has suffered for his sons' youthful mistakes and there's no gainsaying these days that his children don't aim to bring credit on their father. Gerald putting on Shakespeare, Bertrand making a right good marriage with Underwood's daughter and Phoebe likely to marry into the same family. And look at young Charles. He's keeping his wife respectable these days. Aye, and making amends for past transgressions by working on the town-hall lions. The Lord forgives and so must we. Everyone in chapel is talking about the lions. I wonder if, when he's finished, Edwin couldn't work on something for the Ebenezer . . .'

Murgatroyd leaned his hands on his walking-cane, digging the end into the floor of the carriage. He interrupted her. 'Shut up, Emma. You talk a lot of foolishness at times.'

Edwin reflected on the one cloud which had appeared on an increasingly serene horizon as he drove past the lights and noise of the Nag's Head and up the hill. The thought of Phoebe, settling down to her needlework for the evening by a blazing fire, alone in the great house except for the servants, would have been cheering, if it had not been accompanied by a niggling doubt. It did not occur to Edwin to wonder whether such a fireside image ought to be as cheering to Phoebe. If he had considered the idea he would have supposed that it ought, on the assumption that women were by nature fireside creatures. The doubt arose from an observation that Phoebe, his lamb, once so modest, was becoming on the whole less lamblike since her foray into photography, less accommodating, less *womanly*.

Take his wishes over Philip. He had made them clear enough and yet she seemed to avoid the poor fellow. She had thrown herself into a thorough autumn cleaning which tied her to Belle Vue and necessitated a declining of invitations to visit Chillingdale. This was followed by a meticulous visiting of other families in the town, so that when Philip called to ask if she was 'at home' the servants were forced to say that they never knew where Miss Phoebe might be from one moment to the next. And – with regard to her photographs – there *had* been the irregularity over 'that woman'. Phoebe had in the end shown a proper remorse, yet her strange defiance that day had set the tone for other incidents: an insistence on visiting Charles 'for the sake of the child' for instance, a sudden strong interest in Gerald's theatricals and a defence all at once of his own workers' plea for recompense for the work on the lions.

'You'll be telling me you sympathise with the working man's claim for a regular half-day Saturday next,' Edwin had said, his good humour severely tested.

'But I do. And for a nine-hour working day and all.'

Edwin had shaken his head at the softheartedness of women. 'You sound just like your mother. The foundry business and Underwood's railway would never have been built that way.'

Edwin reached Belle Vue in the pony carriage and his spirits lifted a little as he saw smoke curl from the chimneys. He walked into the parlour and saw Phoebe's empty chair and a note pinned to her needlework: *Have gone to see a dress rehearsal of the play.*

Joseph Bateman closed the windows of the tap room and saw Clough's carriage drive past. He shook his head, pitying the hunched, overcoated figure. There went a lonely man. Only his daughter left to comfort Clough in that big house at the top of the Bank, and her likely to be marrying before a year or two was out, if all the gossip one heard was right.

He was glad young Sarah had no ideas on that score yet. Any would-be follower would have to be a stout-hearted lad to get past her brothers. He turned back to the bar. The inn customers sat at dark-stained tables with their glasses or tankards of ale and porter, one or two with a dog squatting between their feet. The room was clouded with tobacco smoke. The company was mostly local men, mill and factory workers, and a couple of commercial travellers who were lodging at the inn. In a corner a group of four men sat round a game of dominoes with an air of intense concentration. In the corner by the window a heated discussion was taking place among a group of foundry workers which included Walter and Matt.

'I reckon we should nail the bugger now. Demand a fair wage for all.'

Joseph frowned a little. What was eating into Walter these days, making him stir them all up? He didn't mind him bringing the lads here to drink, he was glad of their custom. But didn't Walt know how men suffered in a strike? His own brother there with a wife to support and soon to become a family man?

'If Mundy had taken home a proper wage, his mam could have put some by for *eventualities*.' Walter pronounced the word carefully for the beer in his head got in the way of his tongue.

'It could happen to any of us,' said one of the other men morosely. 'What do men like Clough care that we've wives and families to support?'

Walter laid a tender hand on Matt's shoulder. 'There's my brother here with a new missus, and before long there'll be nippers on the way. What if he kicks the bucket tomorrow? What then? Tell me that?'

'If we're laid off, or get injured or fall sick, it's our wives and nippers that suffer,' nodded Matt.

'Aye. And if you strike your wives suffer an' all,' said Joseph tersely. He was tempted to say that if most of them did less drinking they'd have more to take home in their pay, but he was not a man to thwart his own livelihood.

'What we need is a plan of action,' said one of the men. 'Someone to speak for us and have it out with Clough.'

'Where's Jack?' said Matt. 'He's right secretive these days.'

'Reckon he's got a lass.' Joseph gathered up the empty glasses, relieved to see one of the men fetch a cribbage board to the table.

Walter looked at Matt and winked. 'Reckon there's a lass our Jack would like to have, given half a chance.'

Jack wore a flat-crowned black velvet hat and a ruff round his neck and was uneasy about the rehearsal. He plucked at the ruff as he waited at the front of the pit and wondered what Walter and Matt would say if they could see him in green tights. Olive had designed many of the costumes, a curious medley of styles, from coloured hose and long padded doublets made from Belle Vue counterpanes, to full crinolines salvaged from wardrobes of a decade earlier – the company's budget did not run to Elizabethan authenticity. Jack sweated under the doublet and thought with terror of the day fast approaching when the secret of his disappearances from the Nag's Head would be granted the exposure of a public performance.

'Where is Tessa?' hissed Olive from the stage. 'She knew she had to be here on time.'

'I expect she's otherwise engaged,' said Gerald with a strangely significant look, and Olive flushed and looked quickly away.

Gerald bore Olive no malice as he recalled that afternoon's revelation. He had come home a little early from the foundry

178

to begin on preparations for the evening's rehearsal and had opened the door to the props cupboard to confront a spectacle which he had often imagined but to which he had never yet been witness. He did not know which of them had been the more embarrassed – himself, or Lamplugh – certainly not Olive. She had carried the scene with her customary aplomb, saying, 'Gerald, dear. Do close the door.' He had closed it. It was her right to seek elsewhere what he could not offer.

Jack saw the look which passed between Gerald and his wife. He considered its meaning and the significance of that 'otherwise engaged'. He knew nothing of course about the props cupboard, nor Olive's adventures, but neither had he any cause to think ill of Tessa, who was loyal to Gerald's troupe, rarely missed a rehearsal and made a striking Titania.

'How are you, Jack?' said Phoebe, coming towards him, driving thoughts of Tessa from his mind. He had not supposed she would come to the rehearsal. He coloured and answered awkwardly, 'Fair enough, Miss Clough, thank you.' What did she mean by her, *How are you, Jack?* and, *it would please me to take your photograph*, as if she were the lady of the manor? I have kissed you my lady, he thought savagely. I have tasted you, aye and could have tasted more, for you'd have let me. He watched her make her way to a bench on the second row of the pit. She was no different to any of the women in Griseley, nor Tessa Clough – if Tessa was playing that game – nor the easy women up the back of Griseley Bank. No different, Miss high-and-mighty Clough, Miss prissy chapel-faced Phoebe. And then he saw her expression as she continued to look at him and his heart lurched, for she did not seem proud, she looked sorry.

They began the rehearsal. After a while there was a commotion at the back of the theatre. A door banged and Gerald, squinting into the darkness, called from the stage,

'Who's that! Make less noise. Can't you see we've already commenced!'

Olive said, 'It's Titania—' and heads turned as Tessa came through the auditorium. A murmur of interest rose from the players for she was followed closely by Bertrand.

Gerald frowned and Jack saw again a quick exchange of looks between Gerald and Olive as they left the stage and went to meet the new arrivals. All four talked together in an agitated manner. Phoebe in the row behind Jack stood up as the impassioned discussion grew more heated. And then Gerald turned from Bertrand with a wild cry of, 'You fool! You damned fool!'

Phoebe said in fright, 'Jack, what do you think has happened?'

They sat in the sitting room of Gerald's house, Phoebe, as if turned to stone with her hands in her lap, Olive, her head back against the sofa, her eyes closed with Gerald beside her, and Tessa and Bertrand holding hands like a pair of sweethearts. Jack, who had been sent to fetch a glass of water for Tessa, handed it to her and felt awkward and out of place, for the other players had faded discreetly away.

'What are we going to do?' Bertrand kept repeating. 'Father will kill me.' He looked at his older brother as if he might rescue him.

'You and your selfishness.' Gerald spoke quietly in a tone quite unlike his usual hearty good humour. 'You'll drag us all down with you this time. Where were you seen? And why Murgatroyd of all people?'

Tessa's voice was husky but calm, as if she had not yet grasped the gravity of the situation. 'He was walking his dog by the river. Hardly anyone ever goes there.'

'Except Murgatroyd and his dog!' said Bertrand bitterly.

'You fool!' repeated Gerald.

Olive spoke for the first time. 'Perhaps the man will decide not to tell anyone. Perhaps he will be discreet.'

'Can you believe that?' Gerald snorted.

Phoebe looked up and her gaze met Jack's as if seeking his opinion on their dilemma. 'It was Murgatroyd who stood up in chapel and denounced Charles as a libertine,' she explained. She turned to Bertrand. 'How could you, Bertie? Don't you know what this will do to Father?'

'Your precious father!' said Tessa. 'I've had to live with hearing about your father until I'm sick of it.'

Gerald ignored her and addressed Bertrand. 'Where will you go?'

'Leeds. Tessa's mother will put us up for a while.'

He nodded. 'Perhaps it will give you time to come to your senses.'

'We're not coming back,' said Tessa.

'You must. You have a duty—' Phoebe tailed off, unsure about where Bertrand and Tessa's duty lay.

Jack knew he should not have been party to such disclosures. 'I must go,' he said, edging to the door.

'Do you have anything to offer?' Olive spoke with faint sarcasm and she, of all of them, seemed amused by what had happened.

Jack was startled that anyone should ask for his opinion. He said, looking at Phoebe, 'I reckon both should go back to their spouses.'

'Is that all?' prompted Olive.

'No.' Jack felt a surge of righteous disgust at them all, remembering the grand wedding, Edwin Clough's lecturing the men about morality, Phoebe's *How are you, Jack?* as if love was something that could be tossed lightly about. He said, 'I used to look up to people like you Cloughs but you're none of you any different to anyone else.'

* * *

By Sunday morning news of Murgatroyd's discovery had spread through all of Griseley. An air of prurient excitement accompanied the separate groups of worshippers on their way to church and chapel. Bonnets quivered with the constraints which decorum imposed upon the imparting of morsels of gossip; heads wagged knowingly; little gasps of horror issued from those most recently informed.

In the parish church the congregation told one another they were not surprised to see a dearth of Underwoods in the family pew. They expressed sympathy for the injured party, spiced with the satisfaction of seeing Alfred Underwood temporarily deposed from a position of lofty superiority.

Within the Ebenezer chapel the attention of the congregation rested upon Edwin, on Phoebe in her usual place at the harmonium with a white face and straight back, and on Charles, the cuckolded husband, whose appearance caused an extra whisper of sensation. They had grit, those Cloughs, one had to say that for them. Less respectful comments were exchanged in an undertone. Of course, no one was really surprised about what had happened. For all their chapel-going, looseness was ingrained in the family.

Murgatroyd affected an austere dignity and refrained from standing up and making a public statement of condemnation. The facts spoke for themselves. He pretended he did not want to discuss the matter; indeed, he had no need to discuss it, having already imparted the gist of what he had seen to enough of Griseley to ensure that it was adequately discussed elsewhere. The visiting preacher, the only one present who had not been informed about the scandal, delivered a lengthy sermon on 'Love thy neighbour' with fire and vigour and in happy ignorance of its particular relevance.

Having seen Edwin so thoroughly and publicly

humiliated, his friends and fellow men of business rallied in a body outside the chapel after the service. They murmured words of sympathy, 'A bad do that, Edwin', 'You carry a great burden in your children', and 'Trust in the Lord'. Murgatroyd went away with an uplifted heart and the knowledge that Edwin could not have been laid more low.

There was some discussion among the chapel-going members of the town council as to whether it was fitting for Clough's Foundry still to manufacture the statues for the town hall. Yet the decision had been carried; a motion took some revoking once it had been passed at a meeting and undertakings had to be honoured.

'Clough's fresh disgrace could reflect badly on the town,' was Murgatroyd's opinion.

There was a genuine fear that Griseley might be made a laughing-stock.

'We shall consult with Underwood,' suggested Wormauld, 'since he is the injured party.'

The possibility that the lion project could not in any case proceed in the absence of its principal architect was a consideration which had not occurred to them. It was a possibility which alarmed Edwin however and with sufficient energy to obscure his feelings about Bertrand. He had set such store by the statues and by the permanence they would add to the family name. Better not to think about Bertrand's wickedness, for it hurt his heart to consider his favourite son's repeated waywardness. His prayers were not for Bertrand's errant soul, nor even for a thunderbolt to strike 'that woman' dead – though on first hearing the news of his son's behaviour he had suggested that such an act of God would not be unwelcome. He prayed earnestly instead for the continuation of the lion project. To lose it because of a woman was unjust, he appealed to his Maker. He saw now, only too clearly, how wrong he had been to indulge Annette as he had over the children, for what did women know about anything? Look how things had turned out because of her influence.

'Bertie will come back,' Phoebe said, handing Edwin his hat and cane as he left for the foundry on the Monday morning. 'They will see they've done wrong and come back to ask Charles's and Christina's forgiveness.' Phoebe had been subdued since the breaking of the scandal. She bridled still at Jack's condemnation of her family.

'He'll come home and get on with that lion for me,' Edwin said gruffly; but the bravado was false and he left for the foundry with a heavy heart.

The men were already well informed about the scandal. Though the works was as busy as usual and they went about their tasks as on any other Monday morning there was a difference: a hush settled over the general foundry clamour as Edwin walked in from the yard and the work seemed to pause as he went to meet Philip Underwood.

'How is Christina taking it?'

Philip was grateful for once for Edwin's blunt manner. The situation was delicate, poised between his liking for Edwin Clough and undiminished regard for Phoebe, and the injury to his family's honour which necessitated a certain hostility. 'She's hysterical.' He recalled the terrible scenes, the shrieks and moans and the furious shouting of his mother.

Edwin laid a hand on Philip's shoulder sadly. 'I'm sorry, lad.' Only then did Edwin notice that the door to the new work-shed was open and that from within came sounds of movement. He looked at Philip questioningly. 'Has Charles come in this morning?' He had given little thought or sympathy to Charles, whom he considered had brought his misfortune on himself by getting mixed up with that Jezebel in the first place.

He went to the door of the shed and felt an upward leap of his spirits. His prayers for the lions had been answered, for Charles stood before a rough framework of wood with a hammer and nails. He had begun on the model.

Gerald's production of *A Midsummer Night's Dream* was swelled by the morbidly curious. Clough's theatre was where the infamous Tessa had begun her career in Griseley and gossip had it that the theatre itself, tucked away behind the house, was where the lovers had met and conducted their illicit affair. Some of Gerald's regular patrons, seriously disturbed by the family scandal, were reluctant to attend lest the stain of immorality might be seen to rub off on themselves. But the theatre nevertheless was filled to capacity.

The audience included customers of the Nag's Head. Among them were Walter and Matt, who had joined a group of rowdies which invaded the threepenny seats and crowded the benches right up against the stage. The men hooted and cat-called and stamped their feet for the performance to begin but with the opening flourish of the curtain the audience fell silent, instantly fascinated by the lighted scene and the heady smell of costumes and paint.

Walter and Matt were fascinated by a discovery which was closer to home. After an initial 'It's our Jack!' upon the entrance of Lysander, they uttered not another word until the end of the scene, mesmerised by the spectacle of their bother posing in doublet and tights, uncomfortably aware of the nudges and stares and whispered comments of their fellows. 'The silly bugger,' muttered Walter and the two sat in a moody silence which grew more heavy with resentment. They left before the second act.

Phoebe had taken Ellen and a couple of the other maids to see the play; they sat with a fanatical concentration on the stage. The darkness of the theatre hid Phoebe's own attention and she was grateful for its anonymity, for she could barely restrain an exclamation of pleasure at Jack's entrance. How different he seemed, how rarefied and dazzling, and when he spoke – *'You have her father's love, Demetrius; Let me have Hermia's'* – she did indeed gasp out loud. Olive had taken on Tessa's role in the play, but those who had come for the sake of titillation were disappointed, for Tessa's sensually promiscuous fairy had become an austere queen. Phoebe was captivated by them all; her mood of dejection lifted. Bertrand and Tessa were forgotten and she thrilled to Gerald's oration, to Victor's Puck, leaping and posturing, to Bottom in his ass's head, but bewitched most of all by Jack's performance, possessed by the swagger of his doublet, the tilt of his black velvet hat and the brilliant green tights.

The final applause was intoxicating. The cast stood blinking and smiling at the audience and Phoebe clapped her hands together until they hurt.

Gerald had arranged a party after the performance and Phoebe, who had declined his invitation to attend, now reversed her decision and sent Ellen and the other women home. She moved among the theatre players, offering congratulations, smiling a little at their delight in their success and looking for Jack in Gerald's sitting room. Ben Dunn wandered past her wearing his ass's head still and crying, *'Let him roar again, let him roar again.'* Victor, costumed as Puck in a leafy suit, sat cross-legged on the sofa. Olive, leaning over him from behind was pressing a glass of champagne against his mouth which he drank with his arms folded, letting it dribble down his chin.

Phoebe approached Gerald. 'Where is Jack?'

'I've sent him for more champagne. Phoebe love—' he

put his arm round her and squeezed her waist and his eyes were moist with emotion '—my cup overflows. My own sister, my dear sister here among us.'

Phoebe wandered into the corridor. Laughter and conversation drifted from the open door of the sitting room in short bursts of sound but the rest of the house was dim and silent. She saw Jack come towards her, carrying bottles of champagne in his arms. He had changed from his stage costume into shirt and breeches and a waistcoat and held the bottles close against his chest. He halted momentarily when he saw her, then came on. 'So you were there to see us all.' Jack was affected still by the success of the play; he was also drunk on champagne and feeling self-congratulatory. He saw the admiration in Phoebe's eyes and it occurred to him that his performance as Lysander had been little short of splendid. Instinctively he recognised the adulation of the fluttering female heart for a romantic hero.

Phoebe pressed her hands against her skirts. 'Jack, couldn't we forget all that has happened of late? I do wish we could still be friends.'

'I've never felt owt else but friendship for you, Miss Phoebe,' he said in a lordly sort of way.

'Nor I for you.'

They both lied. A 'friendship' – the very word was safe, it wiped out all notions of romance.

'Could we walk out on Sunday?' he suggested. 'Would you come with me on to the moor?'

She nodded and he said, forgetting that he had once thought himself less than dust beneath her feet, 'I'll meet you then, shall I? Two o'clock. Top of the Bank.'

That was the beauty of acting, Jack told himself, full of a blinding confidence as he walked home that night. It did away with class and made him Phoebe's equal – nay her better, for struck low by family scandal she should be grateful that a Bateman, whose family had never been touched by a breath of dishonour, was deigning to walk out with her. He remembered how he had once worshipped Phoebe. What had changed him? A kiss? Her family's besmirched reputation? His own metamorphosis from foundryman to theatre player? The theatre had made the pub and the foundry vanish, it rendered the opinions of his brothers irrelevant – he had seen Walter and Matt in the front row of the pit. He smiled, recalling their open-mouthed consternation. The moment he had dreaded, when it came, had affected him hardly at all.

He thought of the whole hour or perhaps more walking with Phoebe on Sunday afternoon . . . *whose charms all other maids surpass, a rose without a thorn*. An unworthy picture, seductive, carnal, invaded his thoughts as he swung into the pub yard and came to an abrupt halt.

They were waiting for him in the yard. Matt and Walter came towards him slowly into the light from the streetlamp, one either side, so there was no escape unless he were to run back down the street. Walter's expression was mean and Matt looked nearly as ugly.

'Our brother!' hissed Matt. 'Making a mockery of us. I can hear them now at the foundry.'

'Now wait on.' Jack flinched in anticipation of the first smack from a fist and burst of pain. 'It were a good performance. You should have stayed, Matt. Some of it was right funny—'

Walter, a man of fewer words, swung his fists and hit Jack below his left eye and again, with a clout like that from a crowbar, into his ribs. 'Tha' gret Margery!'

Jack caught his breath, blinded by the hurt to his cheekbone, and felt Matt's fist come up into his stomach. The blow was solid and his legs went from under him, his mouth filled with the acid taste of sour champagne. He reached for the wall and hauled himself to his feet, feeling the bricks against his back. The pain from Matt's fist made him retch.

Walter's face loomed in front of him, vain and scornful. 'Fight, won't you, Margery!'

Jack tasted with the bile in his mouth all the humiliations he had suffered at the hands of his brother and the past bitterness of loving hopelessly. Walter's taunt seemed to embody all his other jibes – *cock-a-doodle-doo, Say hello to your sweetheart* . . . Jack recalled Matt's warnings at the foundry, 'Not here Jack – don't go for him here.' Clenching his hand he thrust it with all his force into Walter's throat. He went for him blindly then, jerking his fists at his brother's face until Matt was pulling him clear.

A window opened and he heard his father shout, 'What's bloody going on down there!'

Walter, taking advantage of the pause, hit Jack with a blow which felled him.

The pavement came up hard against his knees and he saw the road and the lamps up the hill spin away from him. The smell of the gutter was in his nose and the stones icy against his face. Jack heard his brothers move off as he rolled away from the streetlamp into the shelter of the wall. The window closed with a clatter and the silence steadied the sky. He lay there, conscious of the moon floating in and out of grey clouds like a great silver coin. He guessed Matt and Walter would not return and put his hand to his face locating a bruise. He swore silently, feeling the sting of a cut on his lip and the stickiness of blood. How was he going to play Lysander with a cut face and a swelled eye?

News that Bertrand and Tessa had run away to France reached Chillingdale some weeks later. The letter, a brief

189

unworthy apology for 'causing you pain', revived Christina's talent for histrionics and her mother's sense of outrage.

Christina knew in her heart that she was merely performing the role demanded of her. There were indeed days when she felt extremely lighthearted at the thought that Bertrand might not return. True, it was humiliating to have one's husband run off with another woman, to have a great tragedy in one's life turned into a subject for gossip; but there were compensations in being the injured party – there was much personal attention and friends bringing ready sympathy and nobody even hinting that there might have been anything at fault with her side of the marriage bargain.

One sadness troubled Christina more than Bertrand's adultery; for, since the lovers had absconded, the Underwoods no longer consorted with the Cloughs. Philip, his loyalties torn, still worked for Phoebe's father, but Alfred's railway company had dropped all association with the foundry. Worse was her mother's insistence that Phoebe was no longer a welcome visitor at Chillingdale. Christina longed for friendship, for some emotional attachment to another human being. So it was that when she met Charles Clough one Sunday afternoon before Christmas while walking her spaniel she was sensitive to the notion that a common bond of misfortune might unite them. She overlooked their initial awkwardness as Charles raised his hat.

'I hope you are well,' he said gravely. 'I heard you've been much indisposed.'

'I'm well enough,' she replied. 'You'll have discovered too that people expect one to hide one's tears after a while.'

He nodded. 'To be continually heart-broken does seem to be an embarrassment to others.'

'Are you heart-broken?' Christina asked curiously, wondering how any man could mind being abandoned by a woman like Tessa. She knew little about Charles. Being so much older than Phoebe and Bertrand, he had always seemed aloof and, though handsome, a little dull, and seemed even older than his years when they were growing up. She had always linked him with Gerald and his father.

Charles was startled to be asked whether he were heart-broken, for the question seemed inordinately blunt. He had not yet considered the possibility that he might one day cease to be anguished by his situation. He saw himself as a man who had suffered greatly from the knowledge of being cuckolded by his brother and by the departure of his wife. He had masked his grief at first by continuing with the business of living, but it occurred to him suddenly that the business of living was perhaps more relevant than his pain. 'I suppose one puts one's energies to other uses,' he said. 'I avoid feeling sorry for myself by immersing myself in work.'

'You're very brave.'

Charles blushed for it was a word which he might in private have also applied to himself. 'You too are brave,' he said awkwardly.

'One has to continue the best one can.' She gave a plucky smile and prepared to walk on, then remembered, 'How is William? Is the little one well?'

Charles nodded but could not speak. One thing for which he would never forgive Tessa was leaving him alone with the child.

Christina paused. 'Poor Charles. You must let me see him one day.'

Edwin, like Charles, had sublimated his pain with work but the withdrawal of orders from Underwood's railway company had hit the foundry hard. Edwin did not blame his old friend for avenging the dishonour to his family. He even understood the need for some such public gesture, though it had made

191

communication between the two men difficult and there was a pronounced embarrassment at committee meetings, where everyone understood and enjoyed what was going on.

Edwin admired Charles's determination over the town-hall lions; he desired their completion himself, with all his heart, for the lions would restore his ruined reputation. But he had to admit that his son did not seem to have much idea of sculpture, wasting all his time reading and visiting zoological gardens and art galleries.

Shortly after Christmas Charles had decided on a trip to London. Edwin shook his head at his son's time-wasting as he drove through the foundry gates. It was a fine cold morning, the kind of day he liked, with a dusting of white on the hills.

Philip met him in the yard where some of the men were standing around a wagon. They had been told to unload clay and shift it into the studio shed, but they stood with surly expressions instead of getting on with the work.

'They say the work's too time-consuming and takes them away from the casting,' Philip said, taking Edwin aside. A deputation came forward from the group, which included Walter Bateman.

'Sir, Mr Charles not being here today, we thowt we'd be better employed in the foundry works,' said Walter.

'You thought—?' echoed Edwin. 'Since when did I pay the likes of you to think?'

The other men remained silent, they dropped their gaze, and all might have been well; Edwin might even have agreed with them on reflection that they would be more gainfully employed in the foundry if Walter had not spoken up again.

'You pay us to make castings, not shift clay for fancy statues. We reckon we should be paid extra for doing work like this.' Had Walter been a man of more perception he might have curbed his tongue. The recent loss of orders, the handicapped progress of the lions, not to mention Edwin's recent personal misfortune might have warned him that the hour was not right for the men's request for an increased wage. 'It's special work. It's going to need some skill—'

'Get back to unloading!' Edwin bellowed. 'Special work! You think you're special do you? Aye, you're that special I'll have you out on the street looking for work!'

One of the older men, William Burns, a man whom Edwin respected, said quickly, 'Walter meant no harm, sir. He's not speaking for himself, only putting the views of all the men. As you must know, there's been some talk—'

'And there'll be no more. I'll not have troublemakers working for me.'

The men returned to the wagon and started moving the clay. They worked in silence, stubborn, resentful; but they worked at it until it was done.

Jack like many of the other men feared that there would be dismissals at the foundry. The diminished volume of work indicated that Clough's warning of throwing out Walter had not been an idle threat.

Jack's beating had compensated Matt and Walter for the indignity they had suffered over his stage appearance. His embarrassment at playing Lysander with a swollen face had made them equal as it were. He was ragged a little at the foundry by the other men, and his brothers were still hostile; his father called him a 'daft beggar' and his mother and sister worried about his consorting with 'actresses'; but as the play ran its course the intensity of interest had died.

Jack avoided coming too sharply to the attention of Edwin, aware that he would come down heavily on his Sunday walks with Phoebe, not wanting to add unnecessary complications and seeking a quiet life. He blushed now to remember the arrogance with which he had asked Phoebe to walk with him, as if she were any Griseley lass instead of his 'lass of Griseley Bank'. He valued their walks more than anything, more even than the theatre, and he loved everything there was to love about that – the raw gaslights, the fusty smell of the costumes and the stage curtains, the smell of sweat, of paint and of fear. The terror of stage nerves had been new to him. But the intoxication when it was all over and the audience stamped and cheered was better than being drunk on champagne.

The Sunday after Walter's confrontation with her father, Jack met Phoebe on the moor as usual. They walked to the top of the scar and sat on a rock overlooking the valley. The acres of heather were almost hidden with snow; the air was cold enough to hurt, sharp in one's chest but clean, and the sky a pure deep blue. He told her about the incident over the clay.

'Perhaps the men are right to want more money,' she said, 'but you should not provoke my father, he's had so many troubles this winter.'

Jack was silent. He could not sympathise with her for he would never see Edwin Clough as a man like any other. Clough was the master, an employer, one of the enemy.

She sighed. 'Bertrand's running off to Paris with Tessa was a dreadful blow.'

'Of course.' Her family's disgrace still imposed restraints on their conversations. He wished he had not talked about the foundry; it always emphasised the differences between them.

'I've had a letter from Bertrand,' Phoebe said. 'Though I dare not tell Father.' She pulled it from her pocket but did not open it. 'Can you honestly say your life is hard? Do you know they have police on the streets everywhere in Paris, waiting to arrest people for speaking their mind?'

Jack said quietly, 'There are different kinds of repression,' and watched her return the letter to her pocket.

'And there are different kinds of revolution.' She rubbed her hands together to warm them. Her fingers were pale with the cold. Jack glanced at their delicate tapering form, spoiled by stains from the chemicals she used, but beautiful. Without considering what he was doing Jack placed his hands over hers, enclosing them completely.

Phoebe shivered. 'How bleak it is on the moor in the winter. It's so hard to believe there'll ever be another spring with rabbits everywhere and gorse blossom and the hedges down the valley full of may.'

'I always think you're like mayflower,' said Jack. 'It's that delicate and pretty, yet it's tough and spiky an' all.'

She laughed and her eyes met his.

'I kissed you once,' he said.

'And I scolded you for taking liberties.'

'Seems like it was a long time ago. We always talked of being friends like this. It looks as if it's come about.'

She smiled, and yet it was almost as if she were disappointed. He felt an impulse to kiss her again, remembering the intoxication of holding her close in the conservatory, the scent of potted geraniums, the hospital smell of her photography and the womanly smell of Phoebe herself. He knew that their acknowledged 'friendship' had imposed a restraint on their meetings. They talked and walked and cultivated a seriousness between them and avoided touching on their walks. He had learned to smother the heady sense of being in love with which he had lived all the previous summer. He leaned a little towards her and pressed his lips on hers, but their mouths were stiff and cold with the wind and he too felt a sense of disappointment.

She withdrew her hands from his and pulled on her woollen gloves. 'You don't have to oppose my father. If you want to change things, you could discuss it with him, you know.'

'Discuss things with Edwin Clough? Do you know what he told Walt the other day? He said he didn't pay us to think. We're no better than animals to him.'

'My father isn't like that. He's a civilised, reasonable man.'

'Aye, and so are we in the foundry civilised men and all we want is a fair do.'

'Well, you'll not help the situation by trying to squeeze more money out of the works. You should be thinking of its future.'

'Would he stand up for us?' he said and she could not look him in the eye. 'No thanks. We'd rather look out for ourselves.'

'Can't you see I must defend him?' Phoebe protested. 'I know he has his faults, but he's my father.'

He looked away. 'He'll always be your father and I'll always be one of his foundrymen.' He felt that they had progressed not at all from their first awareness of one another and as they turned for home, though Jack could not say that this had been a quarrel, he felt that she had driven an old wedge between them.

It was some weeks later that Edwin announced a drop in wages to counteract the foundry's diminished trade.

This time Jack and Phoebe quarrelled heatedly.

'Has Mr Philip Underwood offered to drop his salary?' said Jack. 'Has Mister Charles or Gerald? Have they called a stop to that waste of money over the lions? It's all they can think about.'

'And all you men care about is money.'

'When you're living on next to nothing there isn't much else to worry over.'

'You don't live on next to nothing,' she said scathingly.

'Your family live very well. And Clough's foundrymen are the best paid in Griseley.'

'*Were* best paid – if that's what you call it. Though God help the rest. And how about when us foundrymen are laid off because there's no work except making bloody lions, who's going to be the best paid in Griseley then?'

He saw her turn petulant. 'Can't you see my father has enough problems without upsetting him by complaining?'

He was condescending, gratified because he had bettered her. 'His problems have nowt to do with us. There's other families have problems all the time – sickness, bad houses to live in and too many mouths to feed. It's worse than some fellow running off with his brother's wife. My dad would have taken a stick to them both if they'd been our business.'

'Oh, yes, that's all you know. Beat it out of them.'

'Yes, because you and me are different.'

'It doesn't have to be like that,' she protested.

'Equal in the sight of God. Is that right?'

'I should like it to be so.'

'Which is why the gentry sit in a row in the front box-pew in chapel I suppose while my ilk are perched up near the roof. Why me and Matt and Walter sweat all week, taking orders from the likes of Philip Underwood. Why you live at the top of the Bank out of the smoke of the town and with a view over the moor, while we share our home with commercial travellers and have a view of rhubarb fields and mill chimneys. Why the gentry gave the working man a holiday to celebrate the marriage of the masters' son and daughter, and we're all supposed to turn a blind eye when the master's son takes a fancy to his brother's missus.'

'I think you've said enough.' Phoebe's voice was cold, her blue eyes burned with anger.

'I haven't said half enough. I've kept my mouth shut too long, but I'll tell you this much – if your father treats his men like muck under his feet much longer, there'll be war to pay.'

Phoebe watched him go. How could she ever have imagined she saw anything fine in him? He would never be anything but a foundryman.

To Phoebe's surprise, her father suggested one day that she photograph the foundry workers. She set up her camera and tripod in the yard, conscious of the men's and in particular Jack's critical attention.

Jack walked to the back row of the group to stand shoulder to shoulder with Matt and Walter. He could have sworn Phoebe had arranged the whole business on purpose, just to humiliate him. Some of the men, Walter for one, had said they would refuse to pose for the photograph. 'Parading us in front of his daughter to play with her camera! Whoever heard of a woman taking pictures! She should be at home, minding her drawing room.' But when it came to it, they had lost courage, mindful of Clough's recent threat of dismissals. In any case, the chance of a break from the heat of the foundry was not one to be passed up.

'Wouldn't be surprised if the old bugger doesn't dock the time off our wages,' Walter muttered as they waited for Phoebe to emerge from the store which had been converted into a temporary darkroom.

Jack saw Phoebe raise her hand for stillness and the men obeyed her, struck by her air of authority. She knew what she was doing, Jack realised. This was no 'playing with a camera'.

Phoebe developed the prints of the foundry photographs. The group of figures emerged from the empty print – grey shapes sharpening to outlines: grey caps, stiff necks above white kerchiefs, buttoned waistcoats and bare arms in rolled shirt-sleeves, some gloved and wearing heavy aprons, and the frozen hostile stares. She searched for one face among them and Jack looked back at her, grim and unsmiling, the surface of the chemical stirring with her breath as she leaned closer in the dim orange light.

Why had she agreed to take the men? This had not been her aim, she thought, this row of stolid figures. If it was Jack she had wanted to capture, she had not wanted him like this.

Her father said the pictures were a credit to her. He would have the best one framed and hang it up on his office wall. But Phoebe was disappointed. She flicked disconsolately through her collection of finished prints: the foundry workers, a few studies of Belle Vue and the garden, genteel poses of the Underwoods, and Mr Wormauld, like a surprised puppet, with a bristling moustache. Where was the reality in these carefully staged figures? She had hoped once to make discoveries, to evoke magic, to reveal truth. And yet, except for her pictures of Tessa as Titania, she had achieved nothing remarkable at all.

Ten

At no time has the maintenance of peace been better
assured than today.

Émile Ollivier,
speech in the Legislative Chamber, 1870

'By Christmas we shall be in Paris,' Bertrand had told
Tessa, and she said that she did not care whether they were
in Paris or Leeds or Timbuctoo, so long as she did not go
back to Charles and Griseley. By Christmas they were
living in an apartment near the Rue Rambuteau, close enough
to the markets to hear the rumble of carts, and in the
evening to breathe the smell of rotting vegetables. The
buildings in that street wore dignified façades yet they
seemed to hide a seediness, their appearance fell just short
of respectability or even charm. The house was washed with
the yellow paint which gave so much of Paris a shabby
faded look; it was six storeys high, Bertrand and Tessa's
apartment forming the third floor. The apartment consisted
of a kitchen and furnished sitting room with two large and
draughty bedrooms, entered by double doors and each with
its iron balcony. This delighted Tessa for she could look
down upon the street below and northwards to the Rue
Rambuteau.

'Can you believe that in England we were afraid of everyone in Griseley?' Bertrand stood beside her on the balcony. It was early morning and she wore a night-dress still, with a black shawl draped across her shoulders.

Tessa shivered and snuggled her body against him. 'I wasn't afraid of them.' She puffed out her lips in a derisory sound as she had seen French women do. 'I don't give that for Griseley.'

In the distance a clock struck seven and other churches took up the chime and the cry of voices carried on the air. At the end of the street a stream of traffic pushed on towards Les Halles, processions of massed greeny-white cabbages, a flash of bright carrots against the dark green of spinach and white of leeks and turnips and swedes, an opulent moving mountain of food.

'We shan't starve,' Tessa said. 'There'll be stuff going cheap at the end of the day.' They had brought little to live on, a few clothes and some money drawn in haste from Bertrand's bank.

'I shall get work. Antoine will know someone who can help, perhaps at a studio,' Bertrand said confidently. 'You have a good figure. Perhaps you could model.'

She laughed and stretched out her arms as if to embrace the scene before her. 'You're that different to Charles, Bertie. He'd have been shocked by the very idea.'

Bertrand shrugged. 'Why not? You'll get bored doing nothing at all.'

Tessa leaned on the balcony: here in Paris it was so easy to slip into the relaxed attitude of the Parisians. And yet, seeing a woman carrying an infant along the street below, she was suddenly hurt by Bertrand's nonchalance. Against all her expectations, Tessa missed her child.

Antoine called to see them regularly, delighted to be in the

202

company of his old friend. He was a little older than Bertrand, an elegant and amiable young man, who had come to radicalism late, Bertrand had always suspected, in a mood of rebellion against his aristocratic background of country squires and clergy, stolid bourgeois and docile peasants. Antoine was opposed to the present regime because he hated what the Empire had done to France, but he was not a die-hard, banner-waving Republican.

'You will find things have changed,' he told Bertrand that evening. 'Besides the strikes and all the old hostility against the Empire there is a belief that France will declare war with Prussia before long.'

Tessa could not understand the talk between Bertrand and Antoine; her knowledge of French was limited almost exclusively to the vocabulary of food and drink and love. Bertrand translated for her laboriously after each exchange of conversation. 'Don't take Antoine's talk of war too seriously,' he said in response to Tessa's look of alarm. 'They're always getting worked up over something or other.'

'Feeling against the regime is mounting,' said Antoine, accepting with a shrug this definition of his fellow countrymen. 'Ollivier's new *liberal* government is a farce. And now there is uproar everywhere over the latest scandal.' He explained that the Emperor's cousin had insulted a journalist on the dissident newspaper the *Marseillaise*; the journalist had reacted in true French tradition with a challenge to a duel. There had been a scuffle during the delivery of the challenge in which the Prince Pierre Napoleon shot the man's second in the chest.

'Murdered him?' said Tessa with a delighted shudder in response to Bertrand's translation. 'It's like one of Gerald's plays.'

'The noble prince will get off with a fine,' sneered Antoine. 'Only a special court may try a member of the imperial family. There's to be a demonstration at the funeral and the editor of the *Marseillaise* will speak. You should come. Maurice is sure to be there.'

Antoine came to call for them the next day. The streets were thronged with people and troops and the crowds grew thicker, making it difficult to move as they approached the Place de la Concorde and the Champs-Elysées. Bertrand gripped Tessa's hand and pulled her close to his side keeping sight of Antoine ahead. A group of hussars cantered by and the crowd parted before them. Someone in the crowd shouted, *'Mort à Bonaparte!'* and one of the soldiers swung round in his saddle. A sullen murmur rose from the moving mass of people. Antoine signalled to Bertrand to show that he had found a quieter space under the trees and Bertrand struggled through the mass of bodies, pulling Tessa after him.

They could not see the funeral bier nor the editor Rochefort, who was supposed to make a speech. Bertrand felt out of sorts and unhappy and knew that they had been foolish to join the demonstration, but Tessa's eyes were bright with the exhilaration of the shouting crowd. She called in imitation of the man beside her, *'Vive la Révolution sociale!'* not fully comprehending the meaning of the words and excited by their foreign ring.

A group of armed men were arguing with the police in the road. 'Blanquists,' said Antoine. 'It was understood the Blanquists would lead the procession from the Champs across Paris to the Père Lachaise cemetery, but it would be senseless in this crush. Besides, the troops are waiting. They expect an attack on the Tuileries or the Hôtel de Ville.'

In the distance where the crowd was thickest a man was being carried shoulder high. There were cries of *'Vive la République!'* and again, *'Mort à Bonaparte!'* and a great roar of *'Vive Rochefort!'* and at last they saw the funeral bier as the man, above the heads of the crowd, waved his arms and shouted.

Word went round among the crowd that the procession was to make for a different cemetery. But the change of plan had caused confusion. The shouts grew louder and soldiers pushed through the mob so that the mass of bodies pressed to and fro. Bertrand clutched at Tessa, afraid for her safety, afraid of the soldiers and that at any moment they would begin shooting. He pulled her away. 'Come on, we're leaving.' He called to Antoine that they were going.

Tessa protested, 'But we've not seen anything yet.'

'We've seen enough.' He held her hand in a strong grip and forced a pathway with his elbows until they had reached the Rue St-Honoré. Even here the streets were thronged with people who were saying with a kind of wonder that it was the biggest demonstration Paris had seen for years.

'What about your friend?' said Tessa sulking. 'Don't you care what happens to him?'

Bertrand, exasperated by the incident and furious with Antoine said, 'He's well able to take care of himself.'

Some days later Antoine came again to see them. This time he was not alone. Bertrand felt himself clasped in a rough embrace and Maurice seized his hand. 'Bertrand, my friend! It's good to call on you. You see how the revolution is advancing!'

As they parted and he let the other man's hand fall, Bertrand saw the scar which formed a thick white line across his wrist. He instructed Tessa to fetch wine and biscuits. 'You were there at the funeral?' he said to Maurice.

'But of course, and there too when they arrested Rochefort in La Villette, his own constituency.'

'But Rochefort is a Paris Deputy.'

'Rochefort hates the Empire,' said Maurice. 'His

newspaper speaks for the workers' societies. Oh yes, the Imperialist murderer's days are numbered.'

Bertrand was tempted to question Maurice's logic, since it seemed that it was the champion of the social revolution rather than the Imperialist murderer who was to go to prison. He cast an involuntary glance at the scar on Maurice's wrist and said instead, 'Haven't you had enough of demonstrations?'

Maurice looked at him coldly and Antoine threw Bertrand a warning glance, then Maurice smiled, while his eyes, as Bertrand remembered them of old, remained unemotional. 'I was told in gaol that I should not be so full of hatred for society. I was told I should take heart from the fact that many simple workers had advanced themselves under the Empire.' He paused. 'Where are they, these rich and simple workers? Do they live in Belleville? Do they work on the building sites or in the factories? Have they really shared so amazingly well in the riches of the Second Empire?'

'I suppose not,' said Bertrand lamely.

'Then you may suppose that I shall not tire of revolutionary action until this stinking regime is overthrown.' Maurice said nothing more while Tessa stared from one to the other.

Antoine made hasty conversation, reminiscing about their old association, and after a while Tessa announced that she was going to bed, and Maurice recovered a little of his humour. They talked into the night of the old times and life on the boulevards and laughed about the way Maurice had spilled blood all over his studio and about Madeleine who had married a policeman. Maurice told Antoine the anecdote of how Bertrand had discovered him 'screwing the whore single-handed' and Bertrand laughed too, yet, as he toasted Maurice's health and wished him long life, he knew that he felt little joy in this renewal of an old acquaintance.

Bertrand might have gained even less pleasure had he known that towards the end of the winter Christina had discovered that she was expecting a child. It was a bitter irony to her that her obedience to her mother's injunction to let Bertrand into her bed might now be the instrument of his return.

Phoebe was surprised by a summons to Chillingdale in April.

'We have decided Bertrand should come back to her,' Beatrice said calmly. Christina said nothing. She sat in the window-seat gazing out across the lawns. Her mother stood by the fireplace; Christina's pregnancy had revived the hostility between the two families and she stared at Phoebe without welcome. 'It's the only thing to do and Christina is prepared to forgive. A child must have a father. We think you can persuade him, Phoebe.'

'But how can I do that?'

'By going to France.' Beatrice pressed her lips together as if she had said something quite logical.

Phoebe stared. 'Why me?'

'Who else? Christina would never manage the journey and it would be risky in her condition – she isn't a strong girl like you are. And I couldn't go. I must stay with her.'

'I think it's a good plan,' Edwin said when Phoebe told him of Beatrice's suggestion and Phoebe saw at once that he already knew – that the matter had already been decided. 'Underwood is prepared to let bygones be bygones if you can carry this off. I can't spare time from the works and nor can Philip nor Charles, and they would be useless anyhow.' He took her hands in his. 'Phoebe, if Underwood were to place orders with the works again, it would mean security for the foundry, secure jobs for the men – and certain success with the lions.'

Phoebe snatched her hands away and said scornfully,

'Those lions! That's all you think about. Not the men. Not their jobs, but making your gesture to the town hall.' She was shocked that she had defied him and to discover too that she was no longer sure whose side she was on. She remembered Jack's words and how she had argued for her father against him. She wished now she had not been so rigid, for she missed their walks on Sundays.

'You're upset at the thought of leaving your poor old father.' Edwin felt a sudden misgiving about letting her go, for Belle Vue would seem a hollow place without her. He reminded himself how important it was to restore relations with Alfred Underwood. 'We'll manage well enough lass, for a week or so. And you were always the closest to Bertrand. He'll take heed of you. Will you go?'

Phoebe felt herself cornered. She was swamped by a sense of paranoia. They all wanted to get rid of her, as if everything were her fault. And wasn't it? she wondered. Hadn't she encouraged Bertrand's marriage? Wasn't it fitting it should be she who made reparation? She looked out into the garden, remembering Jack walking down the drive with a parcel of curtains in his arms. But even Jack hated her since their quarrel on the moor.

The winter was over, yet a sprinkling of snow covered the gravel drive. She thought of Paris in the spring – people said it was blossomy and balmy. She considered not so much what was being asked of her as what she was being offered. Had she not longed for something to do? She could leave Griseley's poverty and grime, its respectability and its small concerns, forget her father's problems for a while and forget all about Jack. When she returned she would be a heroine, she would have saved the foundry from ruin and Christina's baby from being fatherless.

'We will pray about it,' said Edwin. 'The Lord will show us the way.'

The matter was settled, reflected Phoebe, for the Lord had a knack of showing Edwin Clough's way when He was consulted.

Bertrand had found work teaching English at a school in the Rue de Rome. The school accommodated about fifty pupils, boys from the middle-class areas north of the Champs-Elysées. It had been a building of some distinction during the days of the Bourbons, with ornate ceilings and high windows. Now the whistle of trains heading into the Gare St-Lazare to the south added an anachronistic touch to the still, almost religious atmosphere of the building.

'You must not let them know you associate with socialists,' Antoine laughed. 'Better also not to tell our revolutionary friends that you are instructing the sons of the bourgeoisie.' Antoine had mocked the notion of his friend's educating the flower of France's youth, yet Bertrand had discovered an unexpected competence in himself: the boys liked him and his superiors respected him. And in a few months he would have earned enough by teaching to begin sculpting again.

Bertrand had no deep interest in the country's political disharmony. To Bertrand France was Paris, and Paris was the wonderful city which had freed him twice now from the oppression of Griseley. This time, with Tessa beside him, he would find success, he would sell his work for enormous sums of money and together they would build a new life.

One day early in May however Bertrand's reflections were on the past rather than the future as he considered the implications of Phoebe's recent letter. He left the school in the early evening and walked along the familiar streets below the Butte of Montmartre. She had not said why she was coming, only . . . *meet me at the Gare du Nord*. In

209

Griseley memories tended to be long and it was too much to hope, even after six months, that people would have forgotten the scandal; the visit from his sister could not have been undertaken without good reason. Yet the thought of Phoebe coming to Paris was also rather splendid. He could show her the sights; it would be an adventure for her.

The shops were putting up their shutters and the restaurants and cafés preparing for the evening's customers. The marble tables, the gleam of heavy cutlery and glasses and globe lamps were reflected brilliantly in the mirrors as waiters lit the gas lamps, flooding the individual cafés with colour. The smell of soup and coffee, of coarse tobacco and the odour of absinthe was heavy in the air. The streetlamps of the boulevard gave a bright-green cast to the undersides of the plane trees which stood out against the darkening sky and the wet pavements reflected the light.

A thin procession of white-faced girls with painted mouths and eyes moved past him on a tide of cloying scent, heading for the more fashionable boulevards, and from a side-street came the melancholy sound of a violin playing in a back room.

This was the Paris he knew: it was impossible on such evenings to believe that France stood on the brink of a civil or national war. Yet his return had not been the joyous reunion with the city he had imagined. Paris had changed; there was a tangible unrest and the police made frequent arrests. In a few days there was to be a plebiscite: the people of France had been asked to vote their approval of the Empire's liberalisation. The result, according to the Bonapartists, would prove once and for all that the electorate still supported Louis-Napoleon.

The vast front of the railway station with its glass roofs came into view, solid against the evening sky. Bertrand quickened his step, anticipating the moment when he would see Phoebe. A flower-seller sat in the station courtyard with a few faded sprays of almond blossom in a bucket beside her and Bertrand's mind was cast instantly back to a distant memory of Phoebe, running towards him along the station platform at Griseley with bunches of may blossom in her arms. On an impulse he paid for all the flowers in the bucket. He brushed off the woman's thanks with an air of bountiful magnanimity.

He saw Phoebe before she saw him: she looked small and very much alone in the station atrium but her head was lifted with her familiar air of determination. She clutched a valise and stood close to her box trunk, endeavouring to look like a seasoned traveller. Bertrand marched towards her with the flowers, in his stylishly cut mulberry coat and fancy waistcoat, feeling knowledgeable about dealing with railway stations and life in a great metropolis.

They embraced with a constraint imposed by the memory of Bertrand's disgrace. He gave her the blossom and saw that Phoebe's eyes glistened with tears. He wanted to say, Do you remember? You forgave me for going away the first time, perhaps you can forgive me again?

She took the flowers and dabbed at her eyes with her glove leaving a smudge of soot on her cheek. 'What a daft thing I am.'

'I expect you're tired,' he said as if her sentimentality needed excusing.

'It's been such a journey. I was seasick and it took an age on the train.'

'We'll soon restore you to your old self again.'

He hailed a cab with an air of superiority and they headed south into the city, Bertrand sustaining his mood of affable know-how by pointing out landmarks as they passed. Griseley's obsession with respectability seemed very parochial and far away: this was Paris, where virtue, though worthy, took second place to *l'amour*.

At last the cab came to a halt outside the apartment building. The driver handed down Phoebe's luggage and she said with an air of surprise, 'But I can't stay here with you and Tessa. It wouldn't be proper. I expected you to find me a hotel.' She sat with her hands folded neatly in her lap; her face was flushed, her eyes bright with anger. She clearly did not intend to move from the carriage. 'Bertie – just why do you think I am here?'

Bertrand's opinion of himself as an excellent fellow toppled. He remembered how obstinate his sister could be, but a hotel would mean paying the driver for a further journey and a heavier tip besides. He was loath to explain to Phoebe that he had spent nearly all his spare cash on the flowers. He opened the cab door. 'You're tired. You can stay here tonight and in the morning we'll find you a hotel.' He saw her hesitation and gained confidence from it. 'You needn't tell them at home.'

After a moment she climbed down and stood on the pavement, looking up at the building with its tiers of balconies and windows. The darkness hid the shabbiness of the paint, the house's apparent grandeur was reassuring, and with a 'just for tonight then,' Phoebe followed him into the dimly lit vestibule and up the echoing stairs.

They reached the third floor and Bertrand said, deciding to get it over with, 'Well, why have you come?'

Phoebe paused for breath, leaning on the bannister. 'Christina's going to have a baby. They've sent me to fetch you home.' He stared at her and she looked away, for she had not meant to tell him so abruptly.

The shock of Phoebe's revelation hit Bertrand hard, yet his first desire was to laugh. He understood at once their predicament at home but he had no immediate perception of his own. Antoine would have joked, he thought wryly; he would have said it was a proof of his manhood. Bertrand said nothing. He opened the pair of double doors which led from the landing into a corridor. Paint flaked from the walls lined on either side with pairs of scuffed maroon-coloured doors. The floor was uncarpeted, the passage lit by a translucent globed oil lamp which stood on a table halfway along its length. With a somewhat desperate flourish Bertrand threw open the first pair of doors and they entered a small red-carpeted sitting room where Tessa rose from a low sofa to greet them.

'Phoebe wants us to go home. It seems all is forgiven if I return to my wife,' Bertrand said in a harsh voice.

Tessa wore a loosely fitting blue-and-grey striped frock and her golden hair fell softly about her full face. She smiled with that challenging mockery which Phoebe remembered. 'Eh, Phoebe – did you really think he would?' and Phoebe saw at once that she was pregnant.

They embraced a little awkwardly and Phoebe, recalling the fairy Titania, reminded herself that Tessa was a wicked woman.

Tessa sprang to activity. 'You must be famished. I'll get you something to eat.'

She left the room and Bertrand's expression was one of wry amusement. 'You see the dilemma? Would you still have me go back to Chillingdale?' He sat on the sofa and his dark-fringed eyes grew instantly serious. 'Don't say anything about Christina to Tessa. I must be the one to tell her.'

Phoebe sat down suddenly beside him. 'I feel so incredibly tired. What am I going to tell them at home?'

'It seems simple enough to me. You go back and say I'm not coming.'

'She's your wife, Bertie. You married her.' She lowered her voice. 'She's going to have your *child*. And what about poor Charles and little William? Doesn't Tessa care about them at all?'

'Tessa loves me and I love her.' Bertrand tried to sustain the belief that it was all that mattered.

Phoebe looked at him, helpless with exasperation. 'Oh, Bertie!'

Tessa returned with a tray of bread and wine and cold sausage. 'How are you feeling?'

Phoebe with a glance at Bertrand said, 'Everything is rather muddled.'

Tessa poured the wine. 'A good night's sleep is what you need.'

Phoebe woke the next morning in a feather bed with vast pillows and a high oak headboard. The room was softly lit by the pale light which shone through a gap in the heavy curtains. Beyond the foot of the bed a gilt-framed mirror, reaching almost to the high ceiling, hung above the marble fireplace; it was ornamented with vines and cherubs and reflected a painting of ladies and gentlemen in old-fashioned dress from the wall over the bed. Between the windows stood a huge dressing table, painted white and gold. Except for the bed and a plain wooden chest against the wall, on which rested her own trunk and valise, this ornate table was the only furniture in the room.

Phoebe threw back the sheets and heavy braided counterpane and tiptoed across the carpet to open the curtains fully. She saw then that the windows on either side of the dressing table were in fact glass doors which gave on to a long narrow balcony. She flung a robe over her night-dress and stepped outside.

The rumble of traffic was loud from the top end of the street, where wagons piled with vegetables were passing. The houses opposite were blank and silent, their balconies empty, every window curtained or shuttered and with a row of grey canopies shading the topmost floors. The anonymous traffic and the empty street gave Phoebe a sense of being entirely alone. The feeling was vaguely exciting, for never had she been anywhere that did not have some connection with Griseley or her father. She hurried to wash and pulled a dress from her trunk, wishing she had hung out the creases the night before. She remembered the revelations of the previous evening, and the fact that her mission was no longer clear made her feel strangely carefree rather than despondent.

Tessa greeted her in the sitting room with a breakfast of fried eggs and hard French bread. She looked happy and cheerful. 'Bertrand had to leave early. He teaches at a boys' school and it's a long walk. He said to apologise.'

'Bertrand has become a teacher?' Another revelation. Phoebe saw that nothing about her trip to Paris was going to be predictable.

'He teaches the boys English. He's clever. He's been teaching me French.' Tessa broke off. 'It's right good to see you, Phoebe. You don't know how lonely I've been.'

Phoebe reflected drily that the purpose of her mission had not been to keep Tessa company, nevertheless she felt at home in Tessa's sitting room. She remembered saying she would go to a hotel but was loath now to do so. She tried, from a sense of duty, to straighten the confusion of her feelings and knew that she was no longer convinced that the lovers should return home. Where was the line to be drawn between libertinism and the liberty to live with the person one loved? Was Bertrand and Tessa's escape self-indulgence, or was it justified by their feelings for one another? And there was the added complication of Tessa's pregnancy. Why should Bertrand return to be father to one child and leave another child fatherless? Or Tessa return to her husband

215

and son with a child fathered by another man? She wondered how Jack would now defend his simplistic view of the affair and felt a strong desire to talk to him.

'Bertie has all these strange friends,' Tessa was saying. 'Students and revolutionaries and anarchists and one of them has been in prison. They jabber away in French all night and I sit in a corner or clear off to bed. I might as well not be here. I expect you'll meet them later.' She paused. 'You will stay? You'll not be going off to a hotel?' Phoebe did not answer and Tessa began to clear away the remains of their meal. After a while she said, 'He's told me Christina's pregnant too. God only knows how it happened. But I'm sorry for her. I really am.'

'You must see that Bertrand is obliged to consider going back to her.' Phoebe helped her carry the plates into the kitchen which smelled of cigarettes and cabbage water.

'Not really. Christina's got her family and her money. I've got nothing now except Bertie.'

'You've got Charles. He would forgive you. And there's William,' she added more gently.

Tessa turned away and said with a false brightness, 'You will stay, won't you? We've got plenty of room.'

'For a little while,' conceded Phoebe, and Tessa turned swiftly and hugged her.

'I need time to think what I'm going to tell them,' Phoebe said after a while. 'Tessa, I know things can't be easy and Father made me come well provided—' her father had in fact furnished her with more than a hundred pounds which when converted into francs seemed to Phoebe an enormous sum '—I'll pay for my board and anything else while I'm here.'

Tessa shrugged, disconcertingly casual. 'Thanks – that'll help.' She looked at Phoebe with a sudden air of mischief. 'Might as well make the most of it. We'll have some fun.'

* * *

'There's increasing talk of war,' Bertrand told Phoebe that evening. 'People say it's inevitable. The Germans want a war to avenge their defeat by the first Napoleon. The French want compensation for losing territories on the Rhine. They've been threatening for years to rectify the frontier, and besides all that, feeling is growing for another revolution.'

Phoebe remembered Bertrand's letters from Antoine Latrasse. 'Paris is too sleepy for a revolution,' she said lightly. 'I've hardly heard or seen anyone all day.'

'Wait until you meet Maurice and his friends,' Tessa told her darkly.

An hour or so later there came a knock at the outer doors of the apartment. 'That will be Antoine,' said Bertrand.

Tessa looked at Phoebe and rolled her eyes. 'The anarchists.'

Bertrand left the room and returned with two strangers, one in a workman's blue smock, the other dressed in a fashionable frock coat, wearing a large soft hat and sporting a small pointed beard. Phoebe guessed that this elegant youth was Bertrand's friend Antoine.

'May I introduce my sister Phoebe.'

Each of the men bowed low over Phoebe's hand and kissed it with rigid ceremony. They had an arrogance about them, she thought, but the most condescending was the one called Maurice. He regarded her intently, then smiled with cold dark eyes and a sensual mouth which drew one's attention to the scar on the side of his face. Phoebe felt a little thrill of horror remembering that it was Maurice who had been in prison. Bertrand said that Maurice was a socialist leader – he and his friends had been largely responsible for three strikes in the past six months at the foundry where he worked.

217

A foundry worker. Phoebe felt an immediate hostility to the man. She could not be bothered with all that again – the injustice of the employers, the subordination of the workers – she prepared herself to dislike him. '*Three* strikes? Is that not a little excessive?' she said.

Maurice looked at her with narrowed eyes. 'At Le Creusot in January the steel manufacturer Schneider brought forty police and two infantry regiments against his workers. In March a brigade and two generals were summoned to put down the miners to defend "order, property and respect for the law" with bayonets. These are the sort of acts which to me seem excessive, Miss Clough.'

'My sister is something of a revolutionary too,' Bertrand said, 'for she has come to fetch me home.' He smiled a little bitterly and Phoebe saw that he had not yet forgiven her.

'What admirable sisterly devotion,' declared Maurice, and Phoebe at once flushed scarlet. 'Would that I had such a sister. Alas, I have neither sister nor brother, nor father nor mother, Miss Clough.' He looked at her with a soulful expression which made her blush a deeper red.

'Never mind all that.' Bertrand recovered his humour. 'How about some eatables, Tessa?'

Phoebe followed Tessa into the kitchen from where they could hear the murmur of voices rise and fall in the sitting room. 'Anarchists!' Tessa repeated, breaking a baguette into small pieces and tossing them into a basket. 'What did I tell you?'

Phoebe found a corkscrew and uncorked a bottle of wine. 'I find Maurice rather disagreeable.' The arrival of Bertrand's friends had unsettled her, though she could not quite tell why. She uncorked a second bottle pensively.

Tessa noticed her silence. 'Don't you listen to them,' she warned. 'They're mostly talk but all Frenchmen are irresponsible. Bertrand said so and I believe him.'

Phoebe laughed, for who could be more irresponsible than her brother?

'Do you know old Jean Tissier?' Maurice was saying when they returned to the sitting room.

Bertrand shook his head.

'He has a bullet from forty-eight which missed him and hit a factory gatepost. He keeps it as a souvenir. He will never forget how the government closed the National Workshops. A hundred thousand workers rose in a three-day battle. The revenge by the army and reservists was terrible. But Jean escaped to fight again: he was opposed to the *coup d'état* of Louis-Napoleon, when people were arrested in their hundreds; and now he talks of the next time, the final uprising. "Next time", he says, "we shall win".'

'You all seem very sure of it,' said Bertrand.

'We *must* win,' said Maurice. 'All men with any fire in their guts believe it. The State is the declared enemy of the people.'

Bertrand felt constrained to remain silent and swallowed a glass of red wine with a swift concentration. But Phoebe was engaged by Maurice's rhetoric. She had never, except perhaps from the Ebenezer chapel rostrum, heard anyone speak with such fervour.

'You are disconcerting the young lady,' said Antoine with an ironic expression.

Maurice flashed her an unexpected smile. 'Of course. What does she know of our troubles, coming as she has straight from England? Will you stay until your brother weakens and goes home with you, Miss Clough?'

Phoebe glanced at Bertrand. 'I regret, I must leave without him,' she said stiffly.

Antoine laughed and winked at Tessa to whom it was clear he had taken a fancy and Phoebe felt that they were all four united in their disordered way of life and enjoying her embarrassment.

Maurice turned suddenly to Bertrand. 'You must allow us to help you show Paris to your sister.'

Bertrand and Tessa took Phoebe to the noisy Halles Centrales, with the manner of magnanimous conjurors revealing a secret land to which only they had hitherto had access. The streets all around Les Halles were slippery with old cabbage leaves and filled with horse buses and carts disgorging their produce – rich black aubergines, tomatoes and pale-green salad crops and piles of golden cheeses. Tessa haggled among the hardened market traders in her bad French with unabashed vigour while Phoebe and Bertrand looked on in admiration. They were jostled by men and women carrying huge baskets on their arms and porters tumbling sackfuls of potatoes into subterranean chutes like coal down coal-holes. The cries of shrill foreign voices filled Phoebe's ears, the reek of vegetables, of meat carcases, of fish and garlic and cheese was pungent and unrelenting until at last they emerged from the misty light of the glass-roofed pavilions to the relative quiet of the street.

It was the weekend and they hired a carriage and drove to the Bois-de-Boulogne, dressed in Parisian style or as near an approximation to it as their finances and notions of fashion could manage. Phoebe wore a dress of red-and-purple striped silk with the fullness directed extravagantly to the rear and a tiny veiled hat perched high on her chignon. 'Exactly right for the Continent,' the Griseley seamstress had assured her when Phoebe had expressed doubts as to the costume's dignity, but here in Paris she felt very chic.

They joined the promenading society in the Bois. Carriages jostled on either side with a creaking of harness, the colourful trappings of coachmen and trotting horses with gleaming coats – an endless display of vehicles which bowled along by the lake. Women with dyed hair and in extravagant clothes and jewellery trailed their furs over the edge of polished and satin-upholstered carriages. There was an impression of lightness, of flying manes, flying dust and veils floating about animated or bored faces, and a hot acrid scent of horses mingling with the faint perfume of expensively maintained feminine radiance.

They returned to the Arc de Triomphe and Bertrand, feeling the first chill of late afternoon strike the open carriage, announced, 'Let's dine out.'

Phoebe pressed her gloved hands together in a kind of ecstasy and said, 'Oh, yes! Do let's!' and Tessa, her fair curls topped by a straw bonnet tipped forward and decorated with ribbons, said, 'Eh yes! Let's spend some more of the old skinflint's money!'

The cafés in the Boulevard des Italiens overflowed already on to the pavements. People lounged at little tables, sipping drinks and watching the passers-by and one another, though it was not yet the fashionable hour to dine. The three entered the discreet, pillared interior of a restaurant which Bertrand said was 'rather a decent place for grub', and Phoebe saw from the white-and-gold decor that Bertrand's idea of 'decent' meant 'expensive'. The only sounds were the intermittent chatter of diners, the tinkle of cutlery and the muted murmur of traffic as they were shown by a waiter to one of the tables. Bertrand ordered iced soup and champagne. He told them about the private room where there was a mirror scored all over by diamond rings on which women had written their names and the names of their lovers or had inscribed risqué verses and promises of love.

Phoebe sat very upright, thrilled by her first real taste of Parisian luxury, but sensing that it was all perhaps rather

221

wicked to be spending her father's money in that way. Phoebe's chapel upbringing had in fact begun to trouble her. She wondered what her father would have made of it all, and the more she wondered, the more she sipped at her champagne. The more champagne Phoebe drank the more she became convinced that Griseley and her father were outdated and really rather absurd. Disconnected thoughts flitted through her mind, a mix of biblical texts – *the wages of sin and he that is without sin among you . . .* and Jack's *my dad would have taken a stick to them both if they'd been our business*, which now seemed so foolish and narrow.

The lights of the restaurant danced and dazzled and Phoebe said after they had eaten, watching Tessa as she laughed and joked with Bertrand, 'Tessa – don't you ever miss little William?' And Tessa who like Phoebe had drunk too much champagne suddenly began to cry.

Bertrand jerked up his head at Phoebe's question. In his cutaway coat and yellow checked waistcoat he had said that he felt like the Emperor himself with a princess on either arm. But the coat was getting shabby, thought Phoebe, and with the pregnant weeping Tessa and his country bumpkin sister they must seem a peculiar trio. She stared at Tessa helplessly, until Bertrand said, 'Come on, we'd better leave.'

They reached the apartment and Phoebe, sobered by the night air, said, 'I'm sorry, Bertie. I'll go home at the end of the week.'

Tessa began to cry afresh, saying, 'Don't leave yet, Phoebe. I get so lonely.'

Bertrand, exasperated with them both, said bitterly, 'You must have been mad to think I'd be going to England with you.'

The result of the plebiscite was known. The day had been declared a public holiday in celebration of the nation's declared confidence in its Emperor. Was this the city which stood on the brink of a revolution? Bertrand remembered the scenes he had witnessed in January and the cries of *'Mort à Bonaparte!'* How could anyone believe in the working-class opposition to the Empire when the city was so clearly ablaze with confidence and when it was that very working populace which were now cheering over the plebiscite and shouting *'Vive l'Empereur'*?

The streets were crammed with people, the distant boom of cannon could be heard above the traffic and he was drawn outside to join the crowds with Phoebe and Tessa. A mass of people surged in the Rue de Rivoli. The police and soldiers were all in good humour and exchanged banter with individual revellers. They neared the Tuileries and all at once the cheers of the crowd rose to a fever-pitch of excitement. *'L'Empereur . . .'* was passed from mouth to mouth and a number of glittering carriages swept from under an archway and moved in majestic procession in the direction of the Champs-Elysées. The Place du Carrousel was brilliant with the colour of military and civil uniforms, footmen in green and gold and scarlet, the green and silver of outriders and equerries, detachments of cavalry jingling and sparkling from their spurs to their helmets and plumes and fluttering banners embroidered with imperial eagles.

Phoebe, standing on tiptoe, caught a glimpse of a man in a general's uniform, a kindly, sad-faced man with a waxed moustache, waving to the crowd. Beside him sat a woman, radiant in a pale-gold silk dress, with red-gold hair and a hat trimmed with feathers which sparkled with diamonds. 'He is the Emperor and she is the Empress,' said Tessa, and Phoebe, who had never even seen the Queen of England, reflected on the splendour of the procession and the fact that she had observed the Emperor and Empress of France pass by.

They wandered out of doors in the evening for it was hot in the apartment. Phoebe was conscious of a desire for more of the spectacle she had witnessed; she wanted to experience everything of magnificence there was to see in this city which was Paris. Walking north from street to street, for Bertrand said he wanted to show Phoebe his old haunts, they turned a corner and came all at once upon Maurice, strolling with a companion along the edge of the pavement.

Maurice clasped Bertrand in his arms as if he was a blood brother and introduced his companion, a man of forty or more with a grizzled beard and greasy moustache, as Georges Marin, a stonemason. The two men talked excitedly about the plebiscite and after a few moments Phoebe realised that both were a little drunk. Maurice smoked a cigarette. He narrowed his eyes against the smoke and talked with it joggling between his lips.

They walked in an untidy group along the street and after some distance Maurice dragged them all into the smoky interior of a lighted café bar. The brilliant illumination of globed gas lamps lent the mirrors in their gilt frames a glamour which was contradicted by the scent of coarse cigarettes, strong coffee and an underlying odour of cooked cabbage.

They sat at a marble-topped table and Maurice ordered wine and absinthe, waving aside Bertrand's protests that they should be heading for home.

Bertrand was thoughtful, for the parade had left him with a sense of unease. He had felt alienated from the jubilation as the last rumble of carriage wheels died away and had sensed a note of hysteria in all that shouting. Could the frantic celebration over the plebiscite be the Emperor's last desperate blaze of glory?

Maurice was convinced of it. He drank his absinthe morosely. 'Our time will come, the Imperialists' days are numbered,' he declaimed, but with less vigour, Phoebe noticed, than at their previous meeting.

He turned to her with that flash of charm which she guessed he reserved for the company of women. 'And what do you think of Paris?'

'It is very beautiful – the river, the palaces and the blossom on the trees. We drove the other day along the Champs-Elysées, past the fountains of the Place de la Concorde and the obelisk, where Bertrand said once stood the guillotine.' Phoebe's violet-blue eyes sparkled, for she was utterly seduced by the city, with its buildings reaching seven or even eight storeys high and everything so different, so superior in elegance and style to Griseley.

'You must allow *me* to show you the city.' Maurice repeated his previous invitation.

'I have already shown Phoebe the sights,' said Bertrand, and Phoebe detected the note of hostility in his voice.

'Ah, but you have shown her the Paris of the Second Empire – the splendid buildings, the glorious Étoile under whose arch our splendid Emperor rode with the Spanish woman today. I am talking of the real Paris, the city of the people who live in Belleville, La Villette and Ménilmontant.'

A man entered the café, dressed like Maurice and Georges Marin in a faded blue workman's blouse. He was followed closely by Antoine, both men looking downcast. Maurice and his companion went to join them and all four embraced with a display of emotion, ignoring Bertrand, Tessa and Phoebe.

'This has been a crushing defeat for the Republicans,' said Antoine, slouching against the bar.

'We will recover,' murmured Georges Marin. 'France will throw off the yoke of tyranny.'

Tessa glanced at Phoebe and shrugged in an exaggerated French style. 'I can't understand,' she said provocatively, 'if everyone hates the Emperor and Empress, why they were cheering for them so noisily.'

'That's the enigma which is the Parisian,' Bertrand said with a wry smile. 'He clasps you to his bosom one moment and would cut your throat the next.'

'Let me clasp you to my bosom, my dear Tessa,' said Antoine, coming forward to bend low over Tessa's hand. 'Though heaven forbid that I should ever contemplate cutting that lovely throat. And how is the little one?'

'He has begun to kick,' said Tessa in French.

Antoine turned to his companions and laughed. 'A revolutionary in the making.'

'We must all kick against the chains of tyranny,' said Georges Marin. The men drew up chairs to the table.

'The workers were loyal,' said the other newcomer. 'It was the provincial vote, those country sheep who granted that evil swine his majority.'

'The Emperor did not have the appearance of an evil man,' ventured Phoebe, remembering the sad-faced figure in military uniform.

Maurice gave her a scathing look. 'And how must a wicked man appear? Like the devil himself?'

Antoine said, 'Louis-Napoleon is weak rather than evil, and that in a leader amounts to the same thing, for he's allowed the greed of the bourgeoisie to outweigh his one-time promises of reform.'

'Let me tell you something about this not-so-evil man,' said Georges Marin. 'When he came to power in fifty-one he inherited a republic, which we workers had helped to create by the revolutions of 1789, of 1830 and 1848. It was Louis-Napoleon who unleashed a terrible vengeance on those who had opposed him. Twenty-six thousand workers who had been resistant to the *coup d'état* were arrested and transported on prison ships. We shall never forgive him for betraying us and for destroying our Republic.'

Maurice was watching Phoebe closely as the older man spoke. He leaned forward and said confidentially, as if they were alone, 'I should like you to see the workers' Paris, Miss Clough, before you go home. Our cause demands that the people in England know how things really are in France.'

'I know nothing about your "cause", Monsieur Chaudet.' Phoebe felt her cheeks colour.

He leaned back and raised his glass to her. 'Then you owe yourself an education.'

Phoebe lay that night in her feather bed, dazed by the revolutionary talk of Bertrand's friends. She saw that she was constantly being required to revise her impressions of Paris and its inhabitants – from the elegant men and women on the Champs-Elysées and in the Café Riche to Maurice and the other 'anarchists' with their revolutionary talk, abrupt manner and sudden flashes of charm. She stared at the cherub-and-vine encrusted mirror, a relic of the *ancien régime*, and fell asleep to distant shouts and the noise of traffic from the Rue Rambuteau. The contemplation of Griseley seemed a poor thing to tempt her home.

Eleven

The main thing is to be moved, to love, to hope, to tremble, to live. Be a man before being an artist.

Auguste Rodin

It was almost July when Edwin received yet another letter from Phoebe in which she put off returning with Bertrand to Yorkshire. *It will take time*, she had written in June, and now . . . *the circumstances are more complicated than it might seem.*

'What does she mean – more complicated?' Edwin demanded to know, showing Charles Phoebe's letter. 'The situation couldn't be more simple. Bertrand has a wife who will from the size of her bear him an heir at any minute. His duty to them both is to come home.'

And I have a wife whose duty is to her husband and son, thought Charles wryly, for Edwin always avoided mentioning Tessa. Yet as the months passed Tessa's departure seemed less of a tragedy. William was thriving under the care of a nursemaid and he too was flourishing; he would never have achieved so much work if she had returned. He stepped back from the sculpture of the lion.

'It's good,' said Edwin grudgingly. 'I'll say this much, you've surprised me, lad. You've done the foundry proud.'

Now that the clay model was finished, it did have the look of a very respectable lion, thought Charles. More than that, the beast was as good as anything his brother could have accomplished, and in half the time. It was approximately ten feet long and six feet high. The head was turned quizzically towards the onlooker, the jaws and eyes alert as if the animal was about to spring from its reclining position. The front legs were outstretched, the back legs curled under the haunches with the tail resting on one of the large out-turned back paws. The mane, sculpted in intricate detail, flowed and curled like human tresses on the animal's shoulders.

Charles felt a little empty. The sheer physical effort of the work had drained him, yet he did not want to rest and would have liked the work to have gone on. He did not resent Bertrand's abandoning of the project but was glad that his brother would get no credit for the sculpture. A good sculptor could create an illusion of life, Bertrand had once told him with an air of disparagement. This lion would be more than an illusion, it would live as a testimony to his own greater skill.

Philip came into the workshop. 'Is it done?'

'It is that.' Edwin rubbed his hands together, his cheek twitching into a smile. 'Now we'll get the men working on the moulds and Charles can get back to his proper work.'

Philip fingered one of the boxwood sculpting tools. 'The men have heard that the lion is nearly ready. There's been some of the old talk about wanting more money.'

'They can talk till they're blue in the face.' Edwin walked to the door. 'Much good may it do them.'

'I think you should take it seriously this time,' Philip called after him.

'Are you telling me how I should run my business, lad?'

Philip coloured. He stood for a moment after Edwin had

gone, plucking at his sandy moustache. With a swift embarrassed glance at Charles he left the shed and went into the yard.

Philip's unease with the family since Phoebe's departure for France had become more pronounced as the weeks passed. The promise had been that she would return with Bertrand in tow and save Christina's baby from being born fatherless. Phoebe would be the heroine of the hour and he could resume his courtship of her with a clear conscience. He knew that Edwin shared in this happy vision of Phoebe's success, and not only because it would save the foundry from its present financial embarrassments. Edwin had made it clear that he fully supported his pursuit of his daughter. Yet as the weeks became months Philip's own difficulties had multiplied. His mother enquired frequently for news about Phoebe and when there was none called down curses upon the Cloughs. His father wanted him out of Clough's works and was threatening to find him a desk position in the railway company. And his sister was increasing in size with awesome speed. In some ways it would have been a relief to abandon the Cloughs altogether and let them stew in their own troubles; but a job at the railway company office was a prospect of being buried alive. He liked his work at the foundry, he even liked the Cloughs – for all their shortcomings. He missed Bertrand, his closest friend since childhood, and then there was Phoebe: he would not abandon all hopes of winning her. He could not think why she did not come home. Even if Bertrand refused to come with her, there was no shame in returning empty-handed.

'The lion is ready for moulding,' he told Gerald who was directing a delivery wagon into the yard. They stood for a few seconds watching the cart roll past.

'Well, my hearty,' said Gerald, 'we thought we had difficulties. I should imagine they've only just begun.'

231

'I don't think your father understands the strength of the men's feelings. Since they took a drop in wages they've been looking for an excuse for a row.' Philip's long face puckered anxiously.

'All he had to do was win them over from the start – a bit of explanation, a bit of flannelling, a bit of reasoning and, yes, consideration – but his way is *we are the masters*. If they don't like what we tell them they can find work elsewhere.' Gerald mimicked Edwin's bluff voice and Philip allowed himself a smile.

His smile faded as a carriage drove up the street and halted outside the foundry. Recognising the vehicle and his sister inside it, Philip went out of the yard to greet her. 'Have you come to see me?' She smiled and shook her head.

Like many angular women Christina's figure was subtly enhanced by her pregnancy. The fullness counterbalanced her sharp features, and the plumping of her face and bosom gave her the appearance of a flower come into full bloom. She allowed Philip to help her from the carriage. 'Didn't Charles tell you? He has invited me to view the finished lion.' The astonishment on her brother's face made her occupy herself suddenly with her gloves and parasol, for Philip did not hide the fact that he thought the invitation strange. She supposed that under the circumstances her developing friendship with Charles was faintly shocking: Charles was her wayward husband's brother, his wife the woman who had stolen Bertrand from her, the associations should have been too painful for friendship. And yet the more she sought his company, the more Charles seemed to offer her solace.

Philip walked with her to the workshop. He drew her aside. 'Do you know what you are doing?'

'Yes. I'm going to inspect Charles's lion.'

Charles was alone with the sculpture, consulting a half unfurled sheet of paper. He rolled it up when he saw Christina and came to meet her, tapping the paper against one hand. 'I'm so glad you decided to come.' He spoke casually though he felt strangely gratified that she had remembered his invitation.

Christina blushed at the pleasure in his expression. 'Philip seems afraid we might invite gossip.'

He looked down at the roll of paper in his hands. 'Well, let's ignore all that, shall we? We've better things to think about.'

'Such as this!' Christina walked the length of the lion's body and examined it from all sides. Charles watched her anxiously, surprised at how much store he set by her opinion. After a complete circuit of the sculpture she turned to him with shining eyes. 'Do you realise this could bring you fame?'

He laughed. 'Don't tell Father. He wants me back at a desk.' But the notion caught his imagination. Griseley's famous sculptor with a string of commissions to his name.

'*My* father knows all sorts of useful people. You could get hundreds of commissions,' Christina said as if she had read his mind.

Charles looked at her and wondered how he could have overlooked her all these years and how his brother could have deserted such a fine selfless creature. It occurred to him that there were several reasons why he hoped that Bertrand would not return. He said, careful not to reveal any more of his thoughts, 'I've a feeling your father would not go out of his way these days to help a Clough.'

William Burns had taken pains to win Jack's friendship since the foundry workers had been forced to take a drop in wages, for Burns was anxious about the Bateman brothers' influence over the men and, in particular, about Walter's increasing belligerence. So it was that he encouraged Jack to visit his home on Sunday afternoons.

Mrs Burns was in the kitchen, dozing by the stove with a worked rug on her lap one Sunday soon after the lion was ready for moulding. She jumped up when she heard her husband and Jack come in, letting the half-finished rug slip from her knee. 'Eh – I must have dropped off for five minutes.' She hurried to clear a pile of clippings from the chair on the opposite side of the fire. 'Eh, dear! Whatever must you think! There, Jack, sit you down,' wiping it clean with a towel.

Jack helped to gather up the long clippings of tailors' waste which littered the brick floor and handed them to her. The meanness of the house – a back-to-back on the canal side of the town – was countered by the scrubbed appearance of the small, overheated living room. A kettle whistled on the polished hob, a coal fire flickered in the grate and the stove doors on either side were perfectly black-leaded. There was a sofa on the further wall, on which sat three of Burns's daughters. The youngest girl, a child of six or seven, worked in silence at a rag rug like her mother, taking strips of red worsted and pushing them through the sack backing of the rug. Next to her was a girl of his sister Sarah's age, her head craned to the wall, smiling at nothing and rocking herself to and fro. The third girl, as pretty and slight as the eldest was ungainly, braided her sister's thick red hair.

Jack greeted these three and they blushed and watched him slyly when he sat by the fire as he was bidden.

'Have you been walking on the moor this afternoon, Jack?' Mrs Burns filled a large brown teapot from the kettle. She was referring to the fact that he spent most Sunday afternoons on the scar above Griseley Bank. He used the moor to rehearse his part for Gerald's next theatre production, following the paths he had taken with Phoebe and composing the things he would say to her when she came home: how he was going to leave foundry work for good and become an actor, how the difference of class between them signified nothing. *If* she ever came home, he reminded himself. It was midsummer now and no sign of her in Griseley. If only they had not squabbled so much, perhaps she might never have gone to France.

'Aye, I've been on t' moor today, Mrs Burns. I'm right glad to get off out of it to be honest, with our Sarah and Mam fretting all the time over Rebecca's confinement.'

'Eh, so Matt's to be a father.' Mrs Burns sighed and shook her head. 'Well, he'll have to mend his ways from now on and no mistake with Rebecca and a new baby to look to.'

William Burns stood by the mantel, staring into the fire, remembering his own wife's hard confinements. The fact that she had borne him no sons was one for which he reproached himself every day of his life. Seven daughters and Hetty a half-wit had surely been a judgement on him. True, the Lord had tempered His punishment by taking three children from them in infancy, and one girl had married, but a house full of females was a vigorous drain on a man's wage.

Jack pulled a newspaper-wrapped parcel from inside his jacket and handed it to Mrs Burns. 'My mam wondered if you could use a bit of bacon.'

Mrs Burns took the parcel without any pretence of polite protest and went with it into the kitchen. Jack's household had suffered only a little because of the reduction of wages at the foundry, supported as it was by two grown men on top of the income from the inn: both families understood that the gift of a pound of bacon or a chicken occasionally was a fair exchange for Jack's Sunday afternoon cups of tea.

'Time you were courting a lass, Jack.' Mrs Burns, returning from the kitchen, settled herself on the sofa beside her daughters.

'It's time your Walter settled down,' muttered William. 'A wife and family would soon put a stop to all his talk of strikes and suchlike.'

'I'm surprised Matt listens to him like he does,' commented Mrs Burns, who while acknowledging that a woman's place was at the back of the room when her husband entertained his friends, did not hold with the notion that a woman should always keep silent. 'I'm surprised Rebecca doesn't say her piece and stop him agitating and causing trouble.'

Rebecca was too soft to stand up to Matt, thought Jack, remembering Phoebe, who looked so soft and tender but who could spark up a row with her sharp tongue. Matt was weak: he went whichever way the wind blew, or whichever way Walter beckoned. 'All the men were upset by what happened to young Mundy, Mrs Burns,' he said. 'Walter's not been at peace with himself since. Nor me and Matt neither.'

'But Walter goes at everything like a bull at a gate,' said Burns shaking his head sadly. He reached for his pipe on the mantelshelf, removing a wooden spill from a pot beside it and lighting it in the fire.

'We're all mad at the notion of Clough wasting profits on statues, when there's men not knowing these days where their next meal's coming from,' said Jack.

'But we have to be canny about this.' Burns put the spill to the pipe, bending close to the fire and sucking on the pipe to make it draw. 'Clough's an obstinate so and so. He's setting his reputation on these lions and he's not a man to

236

back down easily once summat's said and done.'

'Seems to me we ask for more and all we get is being told to work harder for less,' said Jack.

'Aye. And maybe we should have kicked against it sooner.' William spoke with uncharacteristic bitterness. 'But we thowt of the good of the works like we was asked. Times are hard for Edwin Clough, I'll grant you that, but I don't see him and his sons sacrificing owt.'

'If we could persuade him somehow. Appeal to his reason. Show him that folk are pleased to labour if they could feel some benefit from it.' Jack remembered Phoebe's insistence that her father was a reasonable man.

'The working man's labour will always be to the benefit of the rich,' said Mrs Burns. 'Bronze lions for the town hall! Did you ever hear the like!' She fell silent at a frown from her husband, aware that she had overstepped the bounds of his tolerance.

'In times when trade was good, Clough squeezed big profits from our labour,' said William slowly. ''Tis only right that in hard times those profits should have been put by for the benefit of the workers, instead of going to make fancy lions.'

'So, shall we appeal to him?' persisted Jack. 'Get him to see reason? Walter's called a meeting of the men tonight and he's dead set on causing trouble.'

William drew on his pipe slowly. 'I think you and I should be thinking about organising things, Jack. I've been in touch with union men at Bradford and Leeds and they reckon it's time we did summat.'

Jack wandered up the back hall to the public bars which smelled of beer and stale tobacco smoke. Walter and Matt had shifted tables to make more space but the tap room was hot and close. The open windows admitted little relief, for it was one of those sultry July evenings when no air stirred. The room was crowded to overflowing, with people still trying to squeeze their way in through the doors. The news that the lion was ready for the foundry had been like a red rag to Walter and he was in a lively humour over the good turn-out, anticipating some fun from the meeting.

Jack stood near the window, remembering William Burns's talk of unions and action, yet feeling he had no connection with his plans, nor seeing how a lot of talk could change things. He watched the procession of people returning from chapel and church who stared curiously as they passed the Nag's Head on their way up Griseley Bank. They murmured to one another, slightly anxious because something was going on and they were not party to it, not sure whether it might not spell trouble for someone. He turned back to the room. His father stood beside him. 'Likely Edwin Clough will get an earful when he rides up the hill from chapel.'

The speaker who had been given first turn to stand on a chair by the bar, out of respect for his seniority, was William Burns. It occurred to Jack that William, fifty or sixty to look at, may well have been younger, for after twenty years or more at foundry work most of the hands looked like old men. The room fell silent as he began to speak in a quiet, measured way. 'Now sithee. Tha' knows what this is all about. The question is do we make these lions, now Clough's gone and cut our wages, or do we stand fast for our rights?'

'Stand fast,' someone said and one or two others echoed the cry. 'Speak for yourself lad,' muttered one of the older men.

'Penny an hour more for working on t' lions or we don't do it!' shouted Walter.

There were murmurs of uncertainty from around the room, for everyone knew how set Walter was on striking and the notion was one which frightened many.

Burns continued in his slow manner: 'Well then, let's see how 'tis. The master is asking us to go on working for a reduced wage – and we've hardly a man of us balked up to now—' he looked at Walter as if daring him to contradict '—for we thowt it was for the good of the foundry and the prosperity of all in the end.'

Walter pushed his way to the front. 'Can't you see, Will, how we've played all along into Clough's hands?'

A few cries of agreement made William hold up his hands for silence. Jack saw his father at the opposite corner of the window throw Walter a warning look but his brother did not notice for he was eager to take his turn at the chair.

At that moment Sarah came to the door of the tap room. She searched the sea of faces uncertainly and a respectful silence settled among the men. At last, locating her brothers, she called out, 'Matt – it's Rebecca – Mam thinks you should go.'

Matt stood up uneasily and pushed his way to the door amid murmurs of concern and good wishes for his wife's confinement. Anxiety was etched on Matt's pleasant features and embarrassment too at being called away from the meeting on woman's business.

Walter was quick to seize his advantage. 'There's my own brother. Soon to become a father. How's a family man supposed to manage on the wage Clough's paying us?'

There were cries of agreement, full of fellow-feeling and not a little sentimentality, among those who had wives and children.

'I say we put an end to the masters' taking the *lion's* share of the profits!'

A louder cry greeted this suggestion. William tried to speak, to calm the mood of the meeting, but Walter was encouraged by his reception. There were cries of 'Get down, Will. Let Walter have a say,' so that William Burns was forced to concede his place as speaker.

Walter surveyed his audience. 'Are we to work like slaves for ever more – everything going to the masters and bugger all to the working man?'

A cry of 'No!' filled the room.

He lowered his voice and the men fell quiet in obedience to it. 'Well, lads, Edwin Clough's going to get what's due to him before long.'

At that moment Edwin himself drove by and Jack said involuntarily, 'There he goes.'

The word went round. 'The master's just gone by.'

Walter shouted, 'Look at Clough there in his fine carriage, off to his big house with his fine furniture. He tells us all to act like decent family men and go to chapel like God-fearing men – and if we do, well, that's our business, and if we can on the wage he pays good luck to us – but I reckon it's time someone spoke up and told him to put his own house in order.'

William Burns raised a hand. 'We'd all like that, Walter. But there's ways and means.'

'You old men are all talk!' shouted Walter. 'How about the family men among you, with nippers to support like my brother Matt? Shall you go on letting Clough tread you into the dust?'

The men, asking themselves why they had tolerated Edwin Clough's tyranny for so long, shouted, 'No!'

'We ought to go now and tell Clough what we think.'

Some of the men fell quiet at this, but others shouted there and then what they thought of Edwin Clough, and others, stirred by the opinions of their fellows and Walter's flushed face and waving fist, began to stamp with their boots on the wooden floor.

Walter jumped down from his chair. 'Are you with me, lads!' Carried away by his first taste as a leader of the populace, he thrust his way through the crowd by the door. A clamour of approval accompanied his passage. Men slapped him on the back not clear as to where he was going, nor the nature of the task before them, but prepared to carry it out with relish. A tide of men followed him, some picking up bar stools and others bottles as they made their way to the door.

Joseph shouted at Walter not to be a 'bloody idiot'. He tried to push his way into the crowd jamming the door and turned to Jack in exasperation, prepared to break a few heads. 'They'll not wreck my bloody pub.'

'Never mind that,' said Jack. 'If they get up the top of the Bank in the mood our Walt's in they'll wreck Clough's house. There'll be worse than a few bent stools and bottles.'

It was impossible to reach Walter through the pub. Jack climbed through the open window on to the outside ledge, dropped to the pavement and ran to the front of the deputation, holding out his arms as if he would physically hold them back as the first of the men came out from the yard. A sea of pale faces and dark bodies rose before him and Jack felt a sudden swell of fear. *What are you up to, tha' daft bugger, they'll run you down*, he told himself.

'Get out of the way, Jack,' said one of the men in an amiable way.

He drew a breath. 'No – wait. Think what it is you're doing.'

Walter at the front said, 'We're going to teach Clough a lesson.'

Jack ignored him. He raised his voice and shouted, 'This business isn't going to be settled by violence.'

'You tell us how then,' muttered one of the others.

The tail of men coming out of the pub wanted to know what was going on. 'It's Jack,' someone told them. 'He wants to have his say.'

Jack stepped back a little to get the measure of his audience. 'We're all agreed. The way Clough's ignored our grievances, as if we're no better than savages, is the way the masters have always treated the workers.'

The men cheered, thinking him with them, and prepared to move off up the hill, but Jack did not shift his ground; he raised his hand and they were silent. He felt his throat close up with nerves but he had begun well and they were willing to listen to him; he must not lose them now.

'What are you going to do about it? Prove Clough right? Aren't we acting like savages, to go and break up a man's home?' They were silent; some looked at one another uncertainly.

'Tha' daft Margery.' Walter, turning to the others, cried, 'Are you going to listen to a bloke who prances about in tights in his time off? He's scared. Can't you tell?' He jabbed a fist at him. 'Look. He's scared.'

One or two of the others laughed as Jack jerked his head aside from his brother's arm. 'I'm not frightened of Walt, but I'm frightened of what harm you'll do if you invade a master's house on the sabbath and terrify his household. Is that the way to show we're more decent-living men than our employers?'

'How else do we make him listen to us?' shouted one of the foundrymen.

'We'll strike!' bellowed Walter. He caught Jack by the lapel of his coat collar, twisting it in his hand so that his fist pushed up under Jack's jaw. His face was close to Jack's own and furious. 'Shut your mouth, Jack, or I'll bloody shut it for you.'

Two of Walter's companions had come up on either

side. They stood with their hands in their pockets, waiting for a word from Walter.

'And if you strike how long could you last?' persisted Jack.

'Two days before the wife's nagging drives me back to work,' laughed one of Walter's cronies and was rewarded with a glowering look from Walter.

'Jack's right.' William Burns moved forward. 'We're right in our claim for better wages but we're ill prepared for a strike. We're too disorganised. We should form our own association of workers and get up a proper deputation. Show Clough our strength.'

Walter jerked Jack's collar. 'Aye, show him it now.'

But the mood for a riot was dissipating as quickly as it had begun. A few cries of support for Walter were suppressed among a growing murmur in favour of Jack and William Burns.

'I say, take heed of Jack's common sense,' called one of the men.

'Then all you who are with us come back inside.' William Burns laid a hand on Walter's, indicating that he should release Jack's collar, which he did reluctantly. 'Let's get together a committee and representatives. Let's show Clough we mean business.'

Jack eased his cramped neck and straightened his jacket. He turned back to the pub with William Burns and saw Walter's bitter expression as the way parted easily before them. He heard Walter's promise: 'I'll silence thee once and for all one of these days,' as he passed him and then Jack was leading the way back to the bar.

They decided on 'The Griseley Bronze-Founders' and Metal-Workers' Society' for their title. A meeting was conducted in an atmosphere of solemnity which contrasted markedly with their mood of an hour before. Their aims, after much consultation, taken down on paper by a hastily elected secretary, were to protect the interests of the working man against exploitation by their employer, to negotiate with their employer in regulating rates of pay and working hours according to the profits of the company, to assist fellow workers who were sick or otherwise prevented from working, to unite in federation with other similar associations in the West Riding and seek their advice in conducting their business properly, and lastly to negotiate a rate for the special work of casting Clough's lions.

Within a few days a delegate from one of the Bradford unions had come to advise them and under his approving eye William Burns was elected chairman. A committee was appointed and eager members of the society paid their subscriptions and cheered as their chairman and chief delegates were assigned to meet with their employer.

'Jack should be spokesman according to his experience on the stage and since he speaks least broad,' said William Burns. 'Clough will feel better disposed towards a more refined and mild-mannered man.'

Jack, elated by their success in forming the association, agreed to join the deputation. It was not so different from Gerald Clough's theatre, he reflected, except the lines had not been pre-set in his head that night outside the pub but had come as if from nowhere.

The delegate from Bradford, hearing how Jack had turned the men aside from violence by his eloquence, rested a hand soberly on his shoulder. 'Well now, lad. Tha's a great future ahead of thee.'

'Do you know the men have formed some sort of society?' Philip said to Edwin. 'They are demanding a meeting to talk about work on the lions.'

'I'll not meet with them,' burst out Edwin. 'Demands! Societies! Who do they think they are?'

Philip lowered his gaze uneasily. He had joined Gerald and Charles to consult Edwin, for all three had recognised the danger of the men's unification into a society.

'Father, I think you must,' Gerald said.

Charles cleared his throat. 'I heard that a mob of them were all fixed on tackling you about it last Sunday night. It was only Jack Bateman prevented them storming the house.'

'Drivel! They know I'd have the constables to them.'

'This latest isn't a mob.' Gerald moved away from the doorway and approached his father's desk. 'It's a proper deputation. I think you should hear them out.'

Edwin looked at Philip. 'And what have you got to say about all this?'

'I think you would be wise, sir.'

Edwin looked down at the ledger in front of him. The prospect of allowing workers into his office and hearing them out, men who should be taking orders not giving them, made him uneasy. At one time such a notion would have been laughable and yet here were two of his own sons advocating that very thing. The world was changing: his sons were turning against him, even his daughter had spoken up in favour of the men before she went away. And now Phoebe was in France, defying his wishes, turning mutinous like Bertrand before her. He wondered for a moment what Annette would have said about the trouble at the foundry. He had rarely asked her opinion on matters to do with the works, holding to the belief that a woman's domain was the home while a man must shoulder business cares alone. On the rare occasions when he had confided in her, she had offered an opinion forcefully. 'Let them have their say,' she would have told him. But Annette had been wrong over so many things, he reminded himself. Women relied on sentiment to form their opinions. Women did not understand how to handle a work-force and Annette had not even understood how to manage her own children. And yet, how he had worshipped her. And how the children had loved her. If she had been here now, would Charles ever have married that whore, or Bertrand have been in France, or Phoebe have deserted him as well?

After a moment he raised his head and his expression was strange: there was an element of indecision in it. To his sons and Philip the idea of Edwin's vulnerability was a novel one.

'Very well,' he said at last. 'Best get it over and put an end to all this nonsense.'

Gerald and Charles glanced at one another after Philip had left, while Edwin feigned an urgent interest in the figures in his ledger. It was hot in the cramped office. The clock on the wall above Edwin's head gave out its deep measured tick next to Phoebe's framed photograph of the works and a portrait of Queen Victoria.

Gerald contemplated the latter picture and the nature of the woman behind that queenly dignity and wondered incongruously what Olive was doing. Were all women equally unassailable in their self-possession? Christina, placid in spite of her predicament. Phoebe, marching off to France to do battle with Bertrand and deciding she preferred the Parisian way of life to defending family honour – for Gerald had no illusions about why Phoebe had not returned. And Olive. He felt an uncharacteristic stab of jealousy, for Olive had transferred her affections this summer from Lamplugh Dare to Victor. Victor was special. There had been an unspoken agreement between them that she would never poach on his own territory.

There was a clatter on the outside stair and the four society delegates filed in from the yard. Edwin continued writing for several seconds before he laid down his pen and eased back in his chair. He glanced at the clock on the wall. 'I'll give you five minutes to say what you've got to say and that's all.'

Gerald watched Jack as he began: 'Sir, we of the Griseley Bronze-Founders' and Metal-Workers' Society—'

'You can stop that for a start,' said Edwin. 'While you work for me you'll call yourselves Clough's foundrymen and nothing else.'

Jack looked uncertainly at the others and began again. 'Sir, the men feel it's unfair to be asked to do the extra work of the lions without reward so soon after taking a drop in wages.'

'You know the reduced wage was necessary. Better than throwing men out of work.'

'Better than that. But we don't agree it was necessary.'

Edwin bellowed, 'Who makes the decisions round here?'

Jack paused, then regained confidence and Gerald felt a surge of pride in his protégé and a lump of emotion filled his throat. 'Before all the upset at the foundry, before the works lost orders through no fault of us workers, the men were asking for a rise in wages—'

'They wouldn't be asking for rises if they employed more thrift and prudence in their daily lives and practised their moral duties,' interrupted Edwin.

'Sir, going to chapel might be good for the soul but the men know it doesn't fill bellies,' said Jack quickly. 'Some of the men are suffering because of the reduced wage.'

Gerald thrilled to the boy's eloquence. He had recognised his potential from the start – that fine flat voice with such power in it, the broad handsome figure, the delightful combination of muscle and sensitivity. He made a mental note of the phrase about going to chapel not filling bellies, for he was embarking on an idea for a new composition and Jack must play the lead.

Jack, unconscious of Gerald's admiration, was struggling with a rising anger. He continued levelly, 'Sir, if you'll just listen. We've agreed to hold back on asking for a rise on our old rate until the company's in profit again.'

'Very noble of you.' Edwin sat down and stared at the ledger. 'What are you asking?'

'We want a reinstatement of our rates of pay before we took the drop and a promise to review our hours and wages in six months' time.'

Edwin was thoughtful. 'You know I could sack you on the spot for what you're up to.'

'If you do there's others would leave with us,' said one of the men. 'You'd be left with precious few skilled workers.'

'And you'd get no more work here in Griseley. I'd see to that.'

Jack said, 'We're not up to anything, sir. We're for the foundry not against it – it's our livelihood.' He glanced at Gerald, remembering his promises. *There's a future for you in the theatre, Jack. Wait on and we'll turn our backs on the foundry for ever.* 'But there *is* a threat of a strike from the men.'

'Threat! You dare to use the word threat with me!'

'I was not meaning that we're threatening you.' The old devil was obstinate and determined to turn it into a scrap. 'But there's a danger of the men taking things into their own hands.' In an appeal for reason he turned to Gerald.

'As delegates of your society, you should have some control over whether the men strike or not,' Gerald said.

'It's difficult, Mister Gerald. They're impulsive men as you know and they feel strongly about the injustice.' Jack turned again to Edwin. 'Sir, it's a very reasonable request, just our old wage again and we do the work on the lions without grousing.'

Edwin looked at the clock. 'Your five minutes is up.'

The men filed out into the yard; they slowed their pace as they neared the foundry doors not knowing how to break the news of their failure to the men working inside. As they reached the foundry Walter came out to meet them. He saw the disappointment on their faces and rounded on Jack, smashing his fist into the palm of his hand.

'You and your talk! Where's it got you? What bloody use are your delegations and unions?'

'Where are you off?' shouted Burns as Walter marched into the foundry.

'I'm calling the men out on strike!'

The clock ticked on in the office. Edwin stared stubbornly at the ledger. He would not be beaten by his own workers, yet as Gerald, Philip and Charles stared at the floor their combined silence seemed to indicate that he was somehow in the wrong. At last Edwin looked up. 'There's three of you here. You're all grown men. Has none of you owt to say?'

'If they start a strike—' said Gerald.

'If they come out on strike I'll sack the lot of them. We'll see who breaks first over this.'

'They've got support from other unions in the area,' said Philip.

Edwin looked at him suspiciously. Why were they all against him? Was Philip playing a double game, put up to it by Alfred by way of some sort of devious revenge? 'How do you know so much? Whose side are you on?'

'I make it my business to know things, sir. And I'd say there's a strong chance you're making a mistake by not

249

giving way on this just a little bit.'

'You think I should put up their wage?'

'To be honest – yes. At least back to what it was.'

'You all think so?' Edwin looked at Charles and Gerald, voicing his suspicions: 'It seems even my sons are against me.'

'Not against you,' said Gerald soothingly. 'But if work were to stop for a strike we'd lose orders we can't afford to let go.'

'And there are the lions,' Charles reminded them. 'Who knows when that would get under way again.'

They were silent as Edwin contemplated the possible collapse of the lion project. The council had been clamouring for a completion date. Any more delays and it could all come to nothing. He could not bear the ignominy of its failure. He looked at his sons and felt a sense of defeat.

The men coming out from the foundry in a body met Gerald and Philip crossing the yard towards them. The workers came to a halt.

Gerald held out his arms in an appeasing gesture, thinking of all the great speeches he had performed – Mark Antony's funeral oration over Caesar, Henry V at Agincourt. 'You can hold your horses, my hearties.'

Walter stepped forward. 'You'll not make us go back to work.'

'Make you? I think you'll go back voluntarily.' Gerald raised his voice. 'Friends, fellow Yorkshiremen, foundrymen, my father has asked me to tell you that he has listened to the views of your delegates this morning and, in the interests of humanity and not wanting his men to suffer undue hardship, he has decided to reinstate your old rates of pay. The crisis in the company is not yet over and we hope you will go back to work with renewed efforts. But now, seeing as you are all so conveniently gathered together, let's give Mr Clough three rousing cheers.'

The men hesitated. This sudden reversal of their fortunes, not to say demand on their loyalties, was confusing, but in response to Gerald's genial 'Hip, hips' they produced three half-hearted 'hurrahs'.

Walter stared as the men returned to the foundry. The strike had lasted little more than two minutes. Some of the men acknowledged that they had won a victory, but it was Jack who was praised to the skies, and one or two were even saying what a generous master Mr Clough was.

Edwin drove up Griseley Bank that evening, if not exactly a defeated man, one who was much reduced in spirit. It occurred to him that his allies were gradually deserting him. Alfred Underwood, his oldest friend, would communicate these days only on committee business. Philip had sided with the rabble and so had Gerald and even Charles.

He entered the silent house. The murmur of servants from their quarters seemed to add to his alienation. Edwin went straight to his study and slumped at his desk without removing his coat. The evening sun cast its light on the polished furniture. A blackbird sang in the garden near the wall. Alone, he thought. Bertrand had confirmed his profligacy after the fiasco last Christmas and all but ruined him in the process, and Phoebe – his heart ached with a tight knot in his chest as he thought of his favourite child – Phoebe no longer wanted to comfort her father in his old age but made excuse after excuse to stay in Paris. He opened the Bible and turned slowly to the Gospels, badly in need of a friend.

Twelve

If a man persists for years in brandishing his fist in your face, telling you that he will thrash you some day and that you dare not fight him – a wise man will, like Germany, hold his tongue till he is actually struck; but he will, like Germany, take care to be ready for what will come.

Charles Kingsley, 3 July 1870

Phoebe could not believe she had been in Paris so long. She read her father's letter with a guilty conscience, yet the weeks had flown by and first Tessa, then Bertrand had asked her not to leave. The mood of eternal summer which had invaded the city since the plebiscite made her lazy and contented and loath to think about going home. The political intrigues had apparently died down, the possibility of revolution or war seemed so many fantasies of the imagination. She told herself that Maurice and his friends' revolutionary rhetoric was all empty bluster.

Phoebe spent the days in Tessa's company or sometimes alone, wandering under the plane trees by the Seine, watching the lively activity of the boats or browsing on the *quais* with their stalls and entertainments. She wandered the silent forgotten lanes of the Île St-Louis and the beautiful Île de la

253

Cité, enjoying the long evenings and glorious weather. 'How could anyone willingly exchange all this for Griseley?' she asked Tessa.

Phoebe was a tourist among hundreds of other tourists that summer, yet she felt that Paris was a city waiting to be discovered by no one but herself. One afternoon, walking along the Seine, past the towers of the Tuileries and the avenues of chestnut trees in the gardens to the fountains of the Place de la Concorde, she was surprised to see Maurice coming towards her from across the Pont de la Concorde. He seemed in a lighthearted mood and greeted her as if she were an old friend, with an affection which flattered her.

She beamed at him, feeling extraordinarily delighted. Maurice was unreliable according to Bertrand, a man who revelled in stirring up trouble. Her father would have been horrified to discover her alone with such a man. And yet he had a strong fascination, for Maurice belonged to the romance of her new life.

'Do you still maintain this is not the real Paris?' She swept her arm to indicate the fountains, the vast airy space of the Place de la Concorde, the dignified curve of the Seine with the sun glittering on its surface and, behind him, the sweep of the city and the roofs of the Left Bank.

'You are easily deceived,' he said mockingly.

He told her how the guillotine had once stood at the centre of the Place and how blood had flowed into the Seine. He said that the bridge had been built from the stones of the Bastille, so that the people of Paris might trample them underfoot. 'There will be another revolution,' he said. 'The Seine will again run red.'

Phoebe shivered, not knowing whether to take him seriously.

He was a lively talker and punctuated his sentences with gestures as all the Parisians did, yet his expression was rarely animated, Phoebe noticed, and his eyes showed little emotion. She did not know what to make of him as they walked back towards the vast grey expanse of the palace of the Louvre. Like Paris itself he was full of contradictions – charming or polite one moment, the next coldly mocking and superior. He spoke of injustice and said that half of Paris lived in poverty which bordered on destitution, yet Maurice himself did not seem poverty-stricken.

'I accept your challenge,' she said as they parted near Les Halles. 'I should like to see the other Paris you spoke of.'

He smiled and she was surprised to discover another inconsistency in him, for there lingered a flicker of warmth in his eyes. 'I am pleased.' And he added enigmatically, 'I knew when I saw your picture that I should not be disappointed in you.'

'Phoebe!' said Tessa in alarm when she told her that Maurice was to show her Belleville.

'What's wrong?' Phoebe, sceptical of Maurice's claim that anything in the splendid city could shock her, looked at Bertrand. 'Will you come?'

She sat in a crowded omnibus beside Bertrand one morning early in July, heading north. Belleville was one of the working-class districts created by what everyone called the *Haussmannisation* of Paris.

Haussmann, Maurice said, had been deprived of his office of Prefect of the Seine in January of that year for malpractices in his administration, namely corrupt speculation in land. His rebuilding programme for Paris during the Second Empire had brought the advantages of better sewerage and water supplies, employment in the vast reconstruction projects – twenty thousand slum properties demolished to make way for forty thousand new buildings –

but *Haussmannisation* had also meant that working-class families had to move away from the new but expensive apartments on the boulevards into the eastern districts where they lived in unfinished shanty towns, where the rents were lower but it might take an hour or more to get to work since they could not afford to use public transport.

All this Maurice told them as they walked with him from the omnibus stop through a honeycomb of narrow streets and sinister alleys near the Canal St-Martin with its towering warehouses.

Maurice said that the canal had been covered over by Haussmann; the boulevard thus created was named by the Emperor himself after a worker. 'But we are not fooled,' he said. 'Its purpose was to remove the line of defence of the workers and give the troops at the barracks a clear run to the Place de la Bastille.'

'I think you're being a little hard on Haussmann,' said Bertrand.

Maurice paused. 'You're an innocent Englishman, Bertrand. Has it not occurred to you what excellent opportunities are offered the army by those magnificent boulevards, what a clear field they open up for artillery fire and for troops to move in and outflank workers' barricades?'

Phoebe listened to his rhetoric, suspecting much of it to be repeated from the speeches at the workers' meetings in which he took part. They walked through dirty streets of one- and two-storey houses, shabby hotels and vegetable shops, a few cafés with rotting shutters, dingy factories and tumbledown workshops. Corners were blocked with rubbish and an unpleasant smell overhung the area, a mixture of garlic and drains, the distant slaughterhouse and the stench of the canal.

'The Second Empire was a period of expansionism,' said Maurice, 'but it has all been in favour of the propertied classes while the workers' wages have lagged behind. Besides, many workers are employed in the building trade. Though it's among the best paid, a man might be laid off for four months of the year.'

A crowd of children had begun to follow them begging for sous and pulling vigorously at Phoebe's silk skirts.

'Give them nothing,' said Maurice sharply as he saw Phoebe reach for her pocket. 'We don't want three times as many brats on our heels.' The children fell back as Maurice swore at them.

Here and there they passed a wine-shop with men standing inside at the bar who regarded them suspiciously as they passed and then, at a nod from Maurice, looked away. At length they entered a low building, one of a row of houses whose roofs were broken and where rats scuttled away from their approach, and it occurred to Phoebe that Maurice might be their only guarantee of safe passage in this bleak no man's land.

Inside the building, black after the sunlight of the street, the smell of unwashed bodies was strong. As Phoebe's eyes grew accustomed to the dark the place seemed to swarm with dirty children, like the rats which roamed the streets. On a straw mattress in one corner lay a woman, half clothed and in a drunken stupor.

'For goodness' sake,' said Bertrand to Maurice. 'Do you think this is a fit place to bring my sister?' He took Phoebe's arm angrily and pulled her to the door.

One of the children roused the woman as if to inform her that she had visitors and she shouted a stream of abuse telling them to get out of her home. Phoebe saw Maurice toss a coin on to the mattress casually before he followed them into the street.

He returned with them to the omnibus stop. 'Well, you have seen just a little of the other Paris.' He seemed rather

257

pleased with himself, detached from what they had witnessed rather than impassioned by a sense of injustice. Phoebe tried to understand him. What had been his motive? To shock them, to drop the scales from their eyes? Certainly he had done that for, though she was used to the poverty of Griseley, she had never witnessed a squalor in which people had let go so completely of all dignity or hope. She was subdued as they returned to the apartment. She knew that Bertrand was angry with Maurice and angry too because it was she who had insisted on the visit to Belleville.

'Their desire to reform is very understandable,' she said in response to Tessa's query as to how she had enjoyed her tour.

'I think we should avoid Maurice's company in future,' said Bertrand. 'He's a strange man. He has many vices.'

Phoebe told herself Bertrand was right. Maurice was not worthy of their friendship; and he was so clearly their inferior. Yet Maurice did not seem to believe that he was beneath her, she recalled from that afternoon. On the contrary, one would have thought that he was the superior quality of human being.

'Tomorrow we shall do something more pleasant,' Bertrand declared, sitting with his legs stretched out on the sofa.

It was the very next day that France declared war on Prussia.

Phoebe saw later that she should have gone home. Just as so many other things were to become clearer in retrospect, she saw that her delay had been due to the seduction of Paris. Yet in July she did not see that she could be in any particular danger. The war was being fought far away on the German borders and everyone said that the Prussians would never come this far. As to the reasons for the war, Phoebe understood them only vaguely – Prussia had put forward a candidate for the Spanish throne and France had protested, whereupon Prussia had withdrawn its candidacy. The King of Prussia had then snubbed the French ambassador by refusing him an audience. France demanded retribution for the insult.

'Of such trifles wars are made,' Antoine said with a shrug. 'If they did not go to war over this there would soon be some other excuse for it.'

Maurice said that the war was a madness. He said that the people of Paris were mad to cheer the troops being sent off to die. 'For what?' he stormed. 'Because the French ambassador suffers a small humiliation! Because Napoleon and the Right hope that a victorious war will win support for the Empire!'

It was true that Paris had gone mad. The crowds carried the national sense of outrage to a pitch of delirium which lasted for a week. There were illuminations, parades and outbreaks of patriotic waving of banners and tricolour flags, chants of *Vive la France! À Berlin!* and *À bas la Prusse!* The singing of the 'Marseillaise', banned during the past eighteen years of the Second Empire, was heard everywhere from the Opéra to the back streets and three thousand people danced round the obelisk in the Place de la Concorde shouting *'Vive l'Empereur!'*

Maurice dragged them all out to see the 'crazy celebrations'. Phoebe, losing sight of Tessa and Bertrand, found herself alone except for Maurice among the closely packed seething crowd in the Rue de Rivoli. She saw a man dragged from a café, beaten by the mob and punched to the ground. 'Someone help him!' she cried and Maurice, watching the scene impassively, turned her away and said, 'You don't understand. He's German.'

He was suddenly impatient with the feverish celebrations. 'We will go back.'

'But Bertrand will be anxious,' protested Phoebe.

'Bertrand knows you will be safe with me.'

They left the main thoroughfare, the crowds thinned and the cheering was muted by the tall buildings. Maurice talked about the great men of the revolutionary socialist and republican movement as they walked. He spoke in hushed tones of how the great Blanqui himself had once attended a workers' meeting and had embraced him saying he was a 'true son of the revolution'.

He was a strange companion, one of those people about whom it was said, he doesn't suffer fools gladly. Maurice was a man who suffered few fellow human beings at all, wise or foolish, decided Phoebe. He had been born in Belleville, he told her, and repeated the colourful histories of glorious deeds of heroism on the barricades in the 1830 and 1848 revolutions.

'Antoine is with us in spirit,' he said, 'but he is not one of us in the same way as Georges and Henri and old Jean Tissier who fought in forty-eight. Antoine's is a privileged family, he's neither a worker nor a Parisian; he's a Republican by persuasion but at heart he is one of the bourgeoisie.'

'And what is your opinion of my brother?' asked Phoebe.

'Your brother is a good fellow. He helped me once when I was in trouble.' He showed her the scar on his wrist. 'I shall always count him a friend; but he is a child when it comes to France's struggle. He does not understand. You English have no history of revolution. You cannot understand.'

Maurice liked impressing Phoebe with a series of adventures. His true background was a subject he confided to few people: he did not tell of the father who had died on a barricade because he had been too drunk to see the enemy coming, nor of the mother whom he scarcely remembered because she had run away when he was an infant. He rather disparaged the English for their gullibility, even the scornful Tessa had an admiration in her eyes when he and Georges Marin told their stories. But Phoebe had a special charm for him. He was captivated by her Englishness. Her accent, her correct, textbook French and her English looks lent her an air of romantic fascination. Though he had little time for women, Maurice was not a woman-hater and his attraction to Phoebe had been immediate upon their first meeting – perhaps before that, he reflected, remembering the occasion when he had first seen her photograph.

They reached the apartment and Phoebe said, 'Thank you, Monsieur Chaudet, for escorting me home.'

He stood for a moment surveying her. She noted the scar which curled his top lip, the dirty neckcloth and unshaven chin and wondered that she was not afraid of him as she sensed Bertrand and even Tessa were a little afraid.

'I will call for you again soon,' he said suddenly. 'You and I, we should dine together.'

She began to say that she did not think her brother would allow it, but with a little bow he had turned and walked away down the street.

'What were you thinking of?' said Bertrand, furious because he had spent an hour searching for her. 'To go off with him like that! I told you he's not reliable.'

Phoebe decided not to tell him that Maurice had asked her to dine with him. But Maurice did not come the next day, nor indeed the next and Phoebe, aware of a disappointment in him, decided that he had forgotten his invitation and that her brother was right: Maurice was not to be relied upon.

Early in August came the news of a French victory at Saarbrücken, the advance on Berlin was under way. Phoebe's instinctive sympathies, like those of most English patriots, lay with Prussia in the war. She was becoming irritated by these excitable Parisians with their cries of *'Vive la guerre!'* and *'À Berlin!'* She assumed that France would win, for had not the Napoleonic Empire conquered its neighbours in the past? Yet, even as Paris cheered over Saarbrücken, the first French defeats were taking place. More followed and the nature of the war began to change subtly: people started to contemplate the possibility of invasion.

Late one evening Maurice arrived at the apartment. He was alone and looked dirty and dishevelled. He strode past Bertrand into the sitting room. 'This war!' He went to the open balcony and shook his fist at the empty street. 'It will be death to the social movement.'

Tessa looked at Phoebe and shrugged and went to the kitchen to fetch a bottle of wine.

'Men are joining the army rather than strike.' Maurice flung himself upon the sofa. 'They think they will get better pay and the fools want to fight for the Empire alongside their Emperor.'

'It's only natural for your countrymen to be united by patriotic feeling when they feel that France itself is threatened,' said Bertrand.

Maurice swung round angrily. 'If we fight to defend France it must be with the Republic. Don't they see what is happening? The only purpose of this war is to cover up the iniquities of that despot Napoleon.'

Phoebe was angry with him. How dare he storm in at this hour and disturb their domestic tranquillity when he had ignored them all for weeks? She looked at Tessa, who had slammed glasses and a bottle heavily on the table and did little to hide her irritation; the heat bothered her and she tired easily these days.

'It's late,' Tessa said. 'I'm going to bed.' Phoebe watched her go.

Maurice poured himself a glass of wine and drank it quickly.

Bertrand said, 'Do you have to shout?' and Phoebe, exasperated, could not bear Maurice's rudeness nor the stifling heat any longer and went out on to the balcony.

The air was hot from the street. The night was full of the sound of distant traffic and drunken shouts from the direction of Les Halles. She leaned her arms on the iron rail and bowed her head over them, pressing the cool skin of her wrist against her forehead.

She sensed Maurice join her, smelling the wine on his breath. He spoke in English, his tone instantly engaging. 'Phoebe – don't be cross.'

She ignored him.

'Are you frightened by the war?'

'No, of course not.'

He held her by the shoulders and turned her to face him. 'I think you are just a little. But you must not worry. The Republicans are growing in strength. It is only a matter of time before the Empire falls and then Paris will be truly united. Already people are clamouring for the abdication of the Emperor.'

'And then what – when Paris is united?'

'Then comes the glorious day of the revolution. Ollivier has issued a proclamation urging everyone to be calm. His government and the Empress are panicking. They know that if there is not a complete rout of the enemy the citizens of Paris will rise against them.'

'You make it sound very simple.' She almost envied him his conviction.

'It is very simple. But it may be a dangerous time. Perhaps you should all go home to England.'

'I told you, we're not frightened,' she said and knew that she was not.

He laughed, then bent and kissed her hard on the mouth before drawing back to regard her critically. 'Perhaps *you* are not.'

Phoebe pressed the back of her hand to her lips and glanced towards the sitting room.

'He has gone to Tessa—' Maurice said, attempting to kiss her again, and she moved away swiftly, holding his gaze, her heart beating painfully in her chest as if she had been running.

She was angry, and yet he stirred other, more equivocal emotions. 'It's late. I think you should leave.' She felt the sting of his kiss still in her lips.

He nodded and left the balcony and Phoebe went with him to the door of the apartment, her heart still thumping in her chest.

'If the Prussians attack Paris we shall defend it to the last,' Maurice said as he swung nonchalantly down the stairs. His voice drifted up the stairwell. 'But there are battles nearer to hand which must be won when the population is fully armed.'

Phoebe took his talk for bluster. The truth was she did not believe it: she no more believed in Maurice's revolution than she did that the Prussians would attack Paris. She was not even sure now that she believed he had kissed her, so indifferent did he appear. She found herself contrasting the incident with another kiss exchanged with passion, fraught with guilt – how naive and absurd her behaviour with Jack now seemed.

The war was going badly. Reports revealed that the

mobilisation of troops had been frantic and chaotic. Reservists, told to report to regimental depots, were sent in search of their regiments and wandered the country, shunted from pillar to post on crowded trains while their commanders, no better informed, travelled in search of their men. At the front the chaos was apparently worse. Commanders and men lacked every requirement for conducting a war, from food and cooking pots to ammunition.

With each fresh report of disaster at the front the radical newspapers and Republican Opposition clamoured against the mismanagement of the campaign and the inadequacies of the regime. The hunt for scapegoats was on and the Legislature was recalled. Ollivier was replaced by Palikao who began preparations for the defence of Paris. More than three hundred thousand men were drawn from all areas of the city to join the National Guard. And meanwhile, all through August the Prussian armies were gaining more ground.

The individual battalions of the Guard ranged in character from bourgeois citizens loyal to the Empire to out-and-out revolutionaries from La Villette and Belleville who were stockpiling weapons for Maurice's 'battles nearer to hand'. And Maurice himself, casting aside his earlier pacifism, justifying his change of heart with stories of the revolutionary wars where Frenchmen had fought together to save the motherland, joined in the cry for a 'nation in arms' and took his turn at drilling and manning the fortifications. Antoine hinted at Maurice's participation in raids on arms stores for the coveted *chassepot* rifles. 'The Government think they are preparing for national defence,' he said. 'But the people are preparing for revolution.'

A rumour reached them one day that Maurice and Georges Marin had been arrested in an abortive uprising at La Villette. Bertrand said that Maurice was a lunatic and Tessa that it served him right. But Phoebe felt an overwhelming relief when Antoine arrived with the news that neither man had been involved in the affair.

Tessa's child was due in September. She was growing daily more nervous about her situation. She fretted about her confinement like a cat seeking a safe corner for its unborn kittens. 'What if the Prussians come?' she moaned. 'They've burned villages. They kill women and babies.'

Bertrand knew that they should leave, if only for Tessa's peace of mind, but he did not know where they could go. He refused to return to England. One thing was clear, Phoebe must go home at once. But Phoebe was obstinate and Tessa fell into a panic when she thought that she might leave her.

'Don't be silly,' Phoebe said when Bertrand again suggested her return to England. 'The Prussians aren't interested in Paris. We've more to fear from Maurice's lunatic friends. Besides, I have to stay with Tessa for her confinement.' And so the weeks dragged on and, though Paris made its preparations, Bertrand's little household made none.

Bertrand was returning from the school one Saturday at the beginning of September. His class of students had been reducing since August, for many bourgeois families had packed up their affairs and gone to the country or left France until the Prussian threat was over. It was a warm mellow afternoon; he was considering vague schemes for moving from Paris – Antoine had offered refuge at his family's country house to the north – but one could not make too many plans on such a day. The scent of autumn was barely discernible in the air, the streets were quiet and here and there *concierges* and shopkeepers gossiped on street corners. He had almost reached home when he saw the first newspaper placard which announced the collapse of Sedan. He stopped and lit a cigarette and saw that his hands were shaking. He pushed his way through the growing throng of people by the kiosk and bought a paper. *100,000 troops surrounded.* Panic-stricken soldiers had retreated on the town under a massive Prussian bombardment. Sedan burned. The streets and moat were filled with the dead. And the Emperor had surrendered his sword in person to the King of Prussia and was taken prisoner.

Bertrand hurried to the apartment through the aimless angry crowds and found it already filled with Maurice and his compatriots who sat and rested their boots on his chairs.

'Our hour has come!' said Maurice with a fury mixed with exhilaration. 'The Empire is done for!'

Tessa sat on the edge of the sofa. She held her knees tightly with her hands as if in pain and her eyes pleaded with him to get the men out of there.

Phoebe came in from the kitchen. She muttered as she passed by him, 'Thank goodness you're here. They're *your* friends. I wish you'd tell them they're not welcome.'

'Bertrand!' Antoine kissed him affectionately on both cheeks. 'Are you coming with us? We are gathering forces for the demonstration tomorrow.'

'I don't know anything about a demonstration,' Bertrand said uneasily.

'You soon will,' said Maurice. 'Tomorrow will see the dawn of a new republic.'

'I think you should leave,' said Phoebe. 'Tessa is unwell – it's near her time.'

Maurice glanced at Phoebe's face flushed with anger and then at Tessa sceptically. He stood up and obeying his signal the others stood with him. 'Very well. Stay here as if nothing is happening. But I promise you, history will be made tomorrow.'

'*Vive la République!*' Georges Marin cried and the others echoed '*Vive la République!*'

'What shall we do?' said Tessa when they had gone.

'I think we should leave Paris.' Bertrand sat down wearily. 'If only they weren't all so impulsive.'

'They have a cause to fight for,' said Phoebe with a trace of envy.

'You can't mean you're in sympathy with their glorious revolution?'

'Aren't you – just a little?'

Phoebe could not sleep that night. She could hear distant shouts as men roamed the streets and now and then came faintly through the open windows, *'Vive la République!'* and *'À bas l'Empire!'* She pictured the scenes the next day, the barricades like those of forty-eight, the troops with guns and sabres. She fell into a fitful sleep and dreamed of Jack, his arms outstretched, crying *'À bas l'Empire'* while blood poured in a fountain from his chest.

She woke late the next morning and lay for a moment, bathed in the luminous light from the window, fancying herself still dreaming as she heard the shrieks from the next room. Then she was tearing back the bedclothes. She met Bertrand in the corridor half clothed and pulling on his jacket.

'It's Tessa! Can you go to her? I must fetch a doctor.'

Bertrand forced his way through the barrier of hostile, jostling humanity. He had forgotten the events of the night before; the tide of demonstrators making for the centre of the city seemed to have deliberately set out to oppose him. At one time he thought he saw Antoine, but the face in the crowd was soon lost and as he turned into a side street the sea of singing, shouting figures swept by him and was gone.

The air was hushed away from the crowds. It was a gentle summer morning. Bertrand banged on the doors of the physician and the sound echoed in the quiet shade of the street. He prayed that the man had not, like so many others in that area, taken his family away. After a few seconds a shutter opened above and a voice called out sharply, 'Who is there?'

'My wife—' Bertrand called and realised that it was the first time he had spoken of Tessa as if they were man and wife. He shouted more clearly, more determinedly, 'My wife is having a baby. Tell the doctor he must come.'

'Just a moment, please.' The shutter closed. Slow steps sounded on the stairs and the outside door opened. The doctor, a small, long-nosed man with a pointed moustache, shuffled on to the step and squinted at him. 'I hope it isn't far.'

'Just a few streets. Please hurry.' Bertrand barely restrained himself from dragging the man by the arm as they made their way laboriously to the main thoroughfare.

'What a day to have a baby!' grumbled the doctor, eyeing the mob heading westward suspiciously; but this time the direction of the crowd was in Bertrand's favour and it bore them along at great speed.

Maurice, in his new uniform of the National Guard, thrust his way towards the Pont de la Concorde with his rifle over his shoulder. The plan had been to turn out without arms, but seeing several of the Blanquist-controlled battalions with their weapons he and Georges Marin and a few of the others had gone back for their rifles. He saw now that many other battalions had armed themselves.

All the way the crowd milled about the streets and streamed past the Tuileries towards the Palais Bourbon. He spat on the pavement. The Spanish woman's hours were numbered. Demands for dethronement of the imperial family were everywhere as the cry was repeated, *'Déchéance!'*

The National Guard were massed in the Place de la

Concorde along with the regular troops. Even the regulars were on their side now, for their hatred of the imperial family was as strong as that of the National Guard. The crowd pushed forward and Maurice with them. He joined Georges and his friend Henri and Jean Tissier on the bridge. The day was warming up in more ways than one, the sky overhead a clear blue, the sort of blue which made the blood rush to the head with a joy for living and the prospect of a fight. They would show those moderates of the Legislature just who it was controlled Paris. Not Palikao, the scourge of the workers, not the Empress Eugénie – they would do with her what the people of Paris did with that other, the hated Antoinette, and her blue Spanish blood would spill on to the cobbles. He raised his rifle, and his companions did the same. *'À bas l'Empire! Déchéance!'*

A regiment from the Left Bank quarters, a docile battalion, stood nervously in defence of the Palais Bourbon. The great iron gates which led to the forecourt were closed and a line of police confronted the crowd with their sabres drawn. Maurice felt a thrill of fear. He turned and urged his friends forward and came upon the uneasy gaze of a gendarme and the glint of a steel blade close to his face. Maurice smiled. 'Come now, would you cut down a comrade?' he said easily.

A group of Blanquists joined his side. 'What is it you would defend, my friend?' said one to the trembling officer. 'The Empire? It's finished. The troops won't come to your aid if you make a fight of it. They might be relied upon to put down the mob, but they will not fire on the National Guard.'

The man lowered his eyes. His hesitation was brief but it was enough; in a moment Maurice's portion of the crowd had shouldered their way through the gates. The police on all sides were turning away, the troops reversed their rifle butts to show that they would not fire on the crowd and within seconds they were in the Assembly building.

Maurice shouted to the others to stay close as they joined the excited flood of men and women which swarmed through the doors and invaded the corridors and stairways. Men were climbing in through the windows, and a roar of sound echoed through the building as the people surged towards the Assembly.

Within the chamber the din was exhilarating. The benches and galleries were packed with shouting, howling men and women, and Maurice added his *'Vive la République!'* to the cries of those around him. Gambetta was yelling, attempting to give some direction to the protest, but the clamour was too great and he was shouted down. The President of the Assembly's furious calls for silence were greeted with howls of derision until at last he was forced from his seat.

Two of the Blanquists had reached the presidential chair, and the first called out, 'The people of Paris have invaded this place to proclaim the Republic and the downfall of the Empire.'

Maurice's heart felt as if it would burst as he joined his voice to the cheer which rose from the galleries and the floor of the Assembly.

At that moment a roar from outside could be heard above the din.

'The mob has broken through the gates,' said Georges. 'Now we're in for some fun.'

People in greater numbers began pouring into the building. The Deputy Jules Favre shouted, 'It's not here you should proclaim the Republic! You must go to the Hôtel de Ville!' Maurice admired the man for his quick thinking as a roar of approval greeted his suggestion. Favre made for the doors, followed hastily by the other Deputies, and the crowd inside the Assembly streamed after them.

In the courtyard an impromptu procession was forming. Maurice pushed his way outside and a woman stuck a flower in the barrel of his rifle. He laughed and kissed her and then turned to the others. 'Let's get there first and see what's happening.'

They parted from the procession as it reached the Pont Solferino, hastening by the Left Bank, weaving in and out of the crowds to find a swifter route to the Hôtel de Ville. It was fitting that the Republic should be proclaimed from there, thought Maurice. It was the traditional gathering place for the creation of revolutionary governments. His heart sang with the triumph of the past few hours. The Empire was done for. The workers had conquered. The names of Blanqui, Delescluze, and Flourens were already flitting among the crowd as possible new leaders.

In the square in front of the Hôtel de Ville the crowds were even thicker. The men of the left had already set about proclaiming a government; lists of names of the candidates flew from the windows to the waiting crowds. Maurice caught one up and shouted: 'Rochefort! We want Rochefort!' and as if in response a message went round the crowd that Henri Rochefort had been sprung from gaol and was at that very moment entering the square. Maurice watched, his heart full of joy as the radical leader was carried shoulder high into the Hôtel de Ville.

Jules Favre and his procession had reached the building. He appeared at a window above, trying to call for some sort of order. He shouted to them that the new government would be composed of the existing Republican Deputies of Paris. The news was hailed with a shout in favour and Gambetta climbed out on to a windowsill. There was a pause which amounted almost to silence and then he announced, 'The Third French Republic!'

The crowd was delirious with joy. Maurice felt tears wet

272

his cheeks and a sob rose in his throat as Jean Tissier, the old man unashamedly weeping, grasped him in his arms. Antoine, whom Maurice had not seen all day, appeared by his side. He kissed him on both cheeks. 'Well, Maurice, France will at last be ruled by a government formed by and for the Parisians. Is this not a glorious day?'

Phoebe emerged from the house in the late afternoon. Bertrand had told her about the crowds that morning, but neither of them had stirred from the apartment all day and only now did she begin to consider what might have happened. Would she come upon bodies mown down by the troops, or brutally vengeful revolutionaries? She did not care, she needed to escape from that terrible room and to breathe fresh air. Escape – even if they had wanted to get away from Paris, they could not leave now, not with the child so small and likely to die and Tessa in her weakened state.

She reached the Rue de Rivoli, hearing the celebrations before she saw them. A man was standing on a ladder chipping away the word 'Imperial' from an official sign with a chisel and hammer. And then, as she neared the Hôtel de Ville a scene of exuberance opened out before her. She did not understand and stopped some passers-by. 'Excuse me. What has happened?' and they looked at her in amazement. 'My child, have you not heard? We have a republic.'

Phoebe walked on in a daze. No fighting? No bloodshed? The mood of joy seeped into her and she found herself smiling unconsciously as she reached the square in front of the Hôtel de Ville.

The afternoon sun struck the magnificent building and the scene was ablaze with gaiety. Hats flew in the air. A vast sea of black coats and blue and white smocks undulated before her eyes. Some carried flowers, others branches ripped from trees or wore leaves fixed in their hats. Some of the soldiers had tied flowers and leaves to the ends of their gun barrels. Men shouted and sang. Women laughed and hung with their arms round soldiers' necks or tossed bunches of leaves at one another. And then Phoebe saw Maurice. He was clinging to a lamppost above the heads of the crowd, waving a red banner. He saw her and cried, 'We have won! My lovely Phoebe, I told you! *Vive la République!*'

Thirteen

Not to be omitted are divers and terrible mishaps that
occur from time to time, and often bring to nought all
the poor master's pains.

Benvenuto Cellini,
Treatise on Sculpture, 1568

In England, it seemed impossible that the French Empire
could have suffered such a swift collapse. Popular support
for Prussia had changed to sympathy for the defeated armies
and to a consternation that Prussia's conquering arrogance
might now turn itself on Paris after the defeat at Sedan.

In Griseley, Edwin denounced the 'Republic'. He
remained staunch in his support of Prussia, approving of
Lutheran hymns and even 'Die Wacht am Rhein'. The
Germans were a masterful, pious people compared with the
French, who were ruined by a combination of Roman
Catholicism and a natural tendency to licentiousness. He
reminded himself that even his own Annette had inherited
the national want of discipline. Yet Edwin fretted for
Phoebe's return. 'Why doesn't she come away from it all?'
was his constant querulous cry.

And Jack too feared for Phoebe's safety, for everyone
had read in the newspapers how two hundred thousand

troops were burning French villages and shooting those who resisted their advance. In secrecy he asked himself the same question as Edwin. Why had Phoebe not come home? He knew that the answer must be that she had found a Frenchman. She had a lover.

The downfall of the Second Empire and proclamation of a republic meant nothing at all to Jack: he felt neither love nor hatred for either side and cared little about the country's social revolution. His prevailing feeling when he thought of France was one of personal jealousy because of Phoebe. And as for politics – the politics of the foundry were enough to be going on with. There were meetings of the newly formed society, meetings with the Leeds and Bradford delegates, minutes of meetings and speeches – he had begun to wish he had not started it all – and yet, he reminded himself, it was because of William Burns and himself that the workers had gained the upper hand. Edwin Clough was a changed man; he no longer walked and dressed with the strutting pride of ownership, nor looked a man straight in the eye when he talked; he had grown slovenly in his habits. People said he was grieving over Phoebe's leaving him so closely upon his son's disgrace – and there was something of that in his face. But Jack guessed that Edwin Clough's strangeness had more to do with lions.

It was the day of the casting of the first statue. Jack swung his dinner can against his leg as he trooped with the other men down Griseley Bank towards the foundry works. There was a touch of frost in the early morning air and a fog hung over the town, but by the feel of it the day was going to be a good one. The others seemed to sense it too, for there was a lightness in their step and a sense of excitement accompanied them as they neared the yard. Their spirits were high, their mood almost one of festivity, for, though none would have admitted it in so many words, they were all looking forward to the day's casting.

From the first time Jack had seen Charles's lion he had been taken aback at its realism. Not that he had seen a real lion in the flesh, but if he were to meet one face to face, he was sure it would look like Griseley's own lion. They had all grumbled over digging out the large casting bed, erecting frames and pulleys and getting every single furnace into working order. They had never before had to tackle a project as large as this, never had to co-ordinate their efforts so completely so that the content of every furnace might be poured into one gigantic mould. The men expressed an obligatory pessimism over the daftness of the scheme and had said that it was doomed to failure. Yet from the moment the clay model entered the foundry, from the making of the mould with its precisely measured core and precisely determined runners and risers, from the moment when the plan of campaign had begun to depend on the speed and skills of the foundrymen, the lion had become theirs. The scheme was out of the masters' hands and it was important that it should not fail.

Edwin put on his black coat to go to the foundry; Ellen handed him his hat and cane from the hall stand and bobbed a curtsey.

'We're casting the first lion today, Ellen. An important day for the family and for Griseley.'

'Yes, sir. May I take the liberty, sir, of saying all the indoor staff wish you well.'

Edwin was touched by the girl's words. He had not imagined that the servants concerned themselves with what went on beyond the kitchen of Belle Vue.

'That's very kind.' He cleared his throat. 'Tell Cook and the others that their good wishes are much appreciated.'

Henstridge was waiting on the drive with the carriage.

He too expressed good wishes for the success of the day's casting. Edwin thanked him gruffly. He sat stiffly upright at the centre of the leather seat as the carriage bowled down the hill towards the town. His servants' affection had moved him strangely, accentuating for him the fact that members of his own family did not care to wish him well that day. Oh, but Gerald and Charles were keen for the lions to succeed, he reminded himself. And had not his prayers in part been answered? For all that business of strikes and agitation among the men was over, the lions were uniting his eldest sons at last and the project had made them begin to take a pride in the business.

It was a fine day; the sun lit the far hills, touched with brown and purple. An uplifting day. He gave thanks to the Lord for all His works as he passed the Ebenezer chapel and offered a small prayer for his Maker to look kindly on his own works that morning. How proud Annette would have been, he thought, for it was she who had always urged him to make more at the foundry than railway and engineering parts.

Henstridge turned the sharp corner neatly at the bottom of the Bank and Edwin craned his neck to look back towards the town square and the town hall. He braced his feet on the carriage floor as the carriage rattled over the cobbles. His knees and haunches felt painful and heavy. He was getting old. He saw the shopkeepers unrolling and taking down their shutters and remembered when he was a young man, buying a pie for his dinner each day from the shop at the corner of the row. Plate glass and gilt lettering had replaced the small-paned bow windows in the street, though a few of those remained still. The smell of butcher's offal and drains – he twitched his nostrils with only mild distaste – had been mixed to a stronger brew in those days. Edwin reflected with satisfaction that he had done his share in putting the

278

town to rights and building it to its present level of prosperity. The lions would be a memorial to him one day. Edwin's naturally morbid turn of mind caused a sudden fear to overcome him. What if he should die before the project was finished? He reassured himself that Gerald and Charles would continue with the lions in his memory. People would pass the town hall and remember Edwin Clough not only as a benefactor to the town, but as an innovator, one of Griseley's men of vision.

Jack hung his cap and dinner can on its peg and put on the heavy leather foundry apron which reached to his neck and down to below the knees of his fustian trousers. The excitement could be felt more strongly now as the men marched into the foundry. The air was already hot and dusty for some of the men had come in early to fire up the furnaces and each one flared with an orange flame in the semi-darkness.

Philip Underwood and Charles stood together, conferring in low urgent voices over the waiting casting-bed. Jack placed some metal ingots to heat on the edge of the furnace to which he had been allocated. It was strange how one formed a preference for a particular furnace and crucible, though all of them were on the face of it the same. He was working today near to the entrance, where from the corner of his eye he could see the daylight of the yard and fancy sometimes that he was a degree or two cooler than the rest of the men.

'It's a big day for the master,' said Matt who was working with Jack at the first furnace. He jerked his head to indicate Edwin coming to stand at the entrance to the foundry. He lowered his voice. 'I hope the bugger's not going to watch us every inch of the way.'

'He's too jumpy for that.' Jack watched Edwin pace

along the row of furnaces then cross the floor to inspect the casting-bed, then return to the entrance and stand with Gerald.

'Reckon he's going to make a bloody speech,' muttered Walter, pushing ingots into the crucible of the adjacent furnace. All along the row the foundrymen were doing the same.

'You're right,' said Jack as Edwin walked to the casting-bed again and raised a hand for attention.

'Now I don't want to hold up the proceedings, lads,' he began, 'so I'll just say I'm relying on you to work together and get this right. I know you won't let me down.'

'Short and sweet,' said Matt approvingly.

'Why doesn't he just let us get on with it?' Jack pushed one of the ingots into the crucible. He was beginning to feel jittery himself, but as he turned and saw Edwin walk from the foundry he felt a sudden sympathy for the man, for the master set such store by this day's casting.

By mid-morning the melt in each crucible, charged to the brim, had reached the required temperature. The teams of casters stood by the furnaces and Philip Underwood and Charles moved away from the casting-bed. Gerald had returned to the foundry accompanied by his father.

Jack felt a surge of apprehension and gripped the handle of the crucible tongs. The men shouted brief words of encouragement to one another – 'Right lads', 'Don't tha' bugger it up now!' and 'Here goes then' – which increased rather than relieved the rising anxiety in the foundry. The first team of men moved their load of molten bronze from their furnace. Philip Underwood gave nervous instructions to William Burns who was co-ordinating the operation. The skill lay in keeping a steady action, one team overlapping with another, for if the flow of metal halted it would begin to solidify and ruin the casting. Burns nodded placidly and said, 'Easy, lads. Easy as you go.' Jack and Matt waited their turn, for they, with Walter and William, would be the last of the pairs to approach the casting.

The first of the casters had finished. They gave a shout of relief and retired to the task of scraping out the emptied crucible as the pouring continued. Steam rose from the vents in the mould as crucible after crucible was discharged. It was going well. Edwin rubbed his hands, admiring the precision of the operation, applauding the men's skill, perhaps even Philip's planning a little, but in the main congratulating himself on knowing how to run a company.

At last it was Jack's turn. He eyed Walter and William Burns who were already pouring into a feeder at the opposite side of the casting-bed. The brimming crucible swung from the ring of the two-man shank, Matt taking the weight of it and keeping the pot level, Jack steering and keyed up to pour. The skimmer came forward to hold back the slag and Jack guided the crucible close to the lip of the feeder-cup, concentrating on keeping the cup full so that the dross did not enter the mould.

They were less than halfway through the pour when Jack began to sense that something was wrong. He glanced at Walter and saw from his expression that he was anxious. Both crucibles were almost emptied yet no excess metal surged up the risers and vents and the feeder-cups still swallowed the diminishing metal. 'We're running out!' he shouted. The others crowded nearer.

Walter cursed, 'The bugger's used up!' and he and Burns swung away from the mould with the emptied crucible.

Jack watched the last of the molten bronze in the final crucible slip into the cup and disappear. The feeders and risers remained empty. He stepped back. 'That's the lot.'

There was a stunned silence.

Charles was the first to speak. 'I think we must have miscalculated.'

Philip shook his head with an air of bewildered disbelief.

'Miscalculated?' Edwin looked from one to the other. 'What do you mean? Miscalculated!'

'The mould hasn't filled.' Charles turned on his father angrily. 'That's plain enough, isn't it?'

Edwin walked round the bed inspecting each riser as if the swell of molten metal might at any moment appear. The men stood talking in hushed voices; they all knew that the blame was not in the casting, yet they felt responsible for the failure.

Charles was numb with disappointment. He did not look for a miracle like Edwin as he stared at the casting bed; he knew that what lay beneath could not be retrieved. They would have to start again.

Edwin rounded on Philip who had worked with Charles for weeks on the calculations. 'This is your doing.'

Philip was white-faced. 'I don't know what you mean.'

'You. Your family. You've been waiting to get your own back.'

Philip appealed to Charles, and Gerald said, 'Shouldn't we continue this conversation somewhere else?'

They retreated to the office in the yard. Edwin scarcely waited for the door to close before he attacked Philip once more. 'You Underwoods are trying to ruin me!'

'Father, we both worked on the estimation for the melt,' protested Charles, fearing at last for his father's sanity.

'Then he altered the figures!' Edwin sat down suddenly at his desk.

Charles glanced at Philip and for a moment he half believed his father's accusation, but Philip's ashen face was enough to convince him there was no truth in it.

'Everyone wanted it to fail,' Edwin said self-pityingly.

Was it true, he wondered, shocked by the notion that his sons had been in the plot as well. Must he accept once and for all that each of his children had turned against him – that Bertrand and Phoebe, Charles and Gerald, his four lions, had come to nothing?

At length Edwin looked up and said to Philip, 'I want you out of here.'

Philip said quietly, 'I couldn't work for you anyway after this.' He went to the door. 'I'm not surprised Phoebe hasn't returned to you. You don't merit anyone's loyalty.'

Gerald and Charles followed him, glancing uneasily at Edwin, who sat slumped at his desk and seemed not to notice as they left.

Edwin wanted to weep. All come to nothing. Oh, but did the statues have to fail him as well? Why was the Lord punishing him? Where had he failed Him? He had led a sober and godly life in his middle years, had done his best for his children and for the town which had nurtured him as a young man. Was he to be punished because his children had sinned? Or had the Lord been displeased because he had married a Frenchwoman? Was all this tribulation a punishment for loving profanely?

Charles began on another model. The statue would have to be smaller. The months of work had all been for nothing. He worried about the change in his father. 'It's as if his heart has gone out of everything,' he told Christina.

They stood on the terrace of the main house at Chillingdale. Since the birth of her child in August Christina had moved from the gatehouse to live again with her family. It was a fine afternoon in September; the trees in the water-meadow were already turning yellow – the same pale gold as Christina's hair, thought Charles. She wore a lilac frock with a full bustle and train; she looked very neat and calm t ease. All through the feud between the families Charles had been a welcome visitor at Chillingdale. Beatrice Underwood had called him 'dear Charles' and said what a comfort he had been to their daughter, 'quite a different kettle of fish to your brother. If only—' she had allowed herself to say one day in an unguarded moment.

If only, thought Charles as he looked at Christina, more fragile since the birth of her son, Christopher – a companion for William. The two lads would grow up together.

'Your father will be better when you get the next casting over,' Christina said. 'It will be all right next time. You'll see.' She turned to him and smiled with her soft limpid eyes. 'I feel so sorry for him, Charles. Oh – I know he shouldn't have attacked Philip and everyone's very angry, but he must miss Phoebe dreadfully. I miss her too.' She paused. 'Gerald has his theatre and you and I can forget our disappointments. We have – other things now, but your father has nothing.'

Sheep called from the meadow and the air was very soft and still and balmy with the last taste of summer. We have each other, thought Charles and knew that without Christina's friendship the failure of the statue would have crushed him just as hard as it was crushing his father.

Philip came out on to the terrace. His manner was stiff, for though he bore Charles no personal malice, his dismissal from the foundry had placed a strain on everyone. He marched forward and shook him by the hand as if to confirm that what he had to say had no relevance to his own particular feelings.

'Christina, Mama and Papa would like to talk to you.' He turned to Charles. 'They would like to talk to you both.'

Her mother and father were in the drawing room. Beatrice avoided looking at Charles and patted the seat beside her.

'Come to Mama, poppet. Tell me, have you spoken to Charles as I told you?'

Christina looked at Charles a little desperately, then moved obediently to sit beside her mother without speaking.

'You understand there's nothing against you, lad, in this,' said her father gruffly and with just a trace of embarrassment.

'I'm afraid I don't know what you mean.' Charles felt his throat constrict as he looked from one to another and then at Christina as Beatrice took her daughter's hand in her own and patted it against her knee a few times. 'I told Christina she must talk to you,' she said in a determined tone and looked for confirmation at her husband. 'Are you fond of our poppet, Charles dear?'

Charles sensed a struggle with that 'dear' and as Beatrice looked at him he was aware of the full resilience of her maternal armour.

'Charles has been a dear good friend,' said Christina before he could answer.

Her father cleared his throat. 'A good friend. Yes. And before young Christopher was born you were, no one would deny, in need of a friend.'

'What my husband means,' explained Beatrice, 'is that while Christina was in her *condition* no one would be likely to think ill of such a friendship.'

'We didn't discourage you from visiting, in spite of the differences between our two families,' said Alfred.

'Charles was in no way to blame,' said Beatrice hastily.

'Nor was his papa,' said Christina. 'I do wish you two could be friends again.'

Alfred looked down at his feet and Beatrice said stiffly, 'Our family has always had a great affection for Edwin Clough, but he is not the man he used to be.' She set her lips, implying with just a slight lift of the eyebrows that

285

Edwin's metamorphosis might border on derangement. 'Besides, Society's demands are important.'

'Which is why,' said Alfred, 'we want you both to consider whether it's wise to go on cultivating this friendship.'

'You do see, don't you, Charles?' Beatrice decided to employ tact.

Charles felt his eyes prick with emotion as Christina looked at him and her own lovely pale eyes swam with tears. He saw that the Underwoods had him cornered.

'But I like Charles,' whimpered Christina.

Beatrice rounded on her, forgetting her resolution for diplomacy. 'Sometimes I wonder whether you are being deliberately obtuse or whether you show a want of intellect. Don't you see that a woman who has a living husband, who pursues the friendship of a man who has a living wife lays herself open to public gossip?'

Charles cleared his throat, pulling himself together visibly, for hadn't he been used all his life to disappointments of one kind or another, and where was the use in fighting against them? 'It's true that people love to speculate,' he said stiffly.

'You forget that poor Charles was the injured party,' sobbed Christina, 'and that my *living* husband is now *living* with Charles's wife.'

Charles recognised with Beatrice that the Griseley gossips would overlook it too in the delight of finding something new to talk about. 'You asked me if I am fond of Christina,' he said. 'I must reply that I would die rather than harm her. She is a pure, good-hearted girl,' his voice wavered. 'Not for the world would I expose her to further public slander.'

Christina stared at him in dismay. An awareness that he was about to surrender made her desperate. 'Let them talk! I don't care.'

286

Beatrice was taken aback, and so was Charles, for his angel seemed almost to relish the prospect of scandal.

'You must understand,' Beatrice said fiercely. 'If you continue with the friendship nothing can come of it, absolutely nothing.'

Christina's rebellion was as of old short-lived. She looked at Charles in despair and Charles at her and they knew that there was no hope for them.

Charles's spirits were heavy as he left Christina weeping and drove away down the drive. How foolish he had been, how selfish too to believe that he would not harm that dear sweet girl by pursuing their friendship. His thoughts turned with a small sense of betrayal to consider his life without visits to Chillingdale and he discovered that the prospect did not seem so terrible on reflection as it had with Christina weeping before him. A light breeze touched his face and the horse whinnied and in spite of his disappointment and the emotional turmoil of the past hour Charles's heart lifted a little. Christina *did* weep abundantly, he recalled, and a woman's tears were of course very touching, yet the prospect of no more being faced with a weeping woman was not on the whole disheartening. It led him to consider what next? and his thoughts turned readily to the foundry. He had already gone over the calculations with Gerald. There was no reason why the next statue should not go well, for this time the foundrymen would be with them. He clicked to the horse and shook the reins as the gig bowled past the lodge and out through the gates.

'There's always got to be a scapegoat,' William Burns had murmured when they watched the masters leave the foundry.

Walter had shrugged. 'Sooner Underwood's job than ours.'

The foundrymen had covered their disappointment. They

had said they had known from the start that the lion was jinxed.

'We shouldn't fret over Underwood. His pa will have found him a position,' said Matt one Sunday evening. His wife, a small creature, little older than Sarah, with pointed features and a waxen complexion, jogged a contrastingly robust baby on her knee by the kitchen table.

The subject of the lions was still one for discussion among the foundrymen. 'What do you think the master will do now?' said Walter. 'We had all the furnaces working full tilt – he'll need more to melt enough metal, else make the bloody lions smaller.'

'Don't swear, our Walt. Not in front of your sister and Rebecca,' said Kitty, pouring tea from a vast black pot into his cup. She slapped Matt's hand as he reached for the dish of baked potatoes on the table. 'And *you'll* wait for grace.'

Jack was putting on a clean shirt by the stove. He stood in silence while his father said the grace and watched while his brothers dived for the dark brown potatoes. He buttoned the neck opening and tied on a clean kerchief, going to smooth his hair in the glass above the mantel. 'Clough won't give up the idea. They're an obstinate family.' He paused and thought of Phoebe, the most obstinate of them all. His face in the mirror looked back at him impassively.

'He'll have to bring his ideas down a peg then,' said Matt. 'It will have cost the firm a tidy sum.'

Jack pulled on his jacket and went to the door.

'No tea?' said his mother reprovingly.

'I'm not hungry. I'll have some supper after rehearsals.'

'Will you indeed?' Kitty set her mouth. 'You're mighty sure of yourself.'

His father glanced up from slurping his tea, holding the day's newspaper in one hand. He folded it and laid it on the table. 'You'll eat the tea your mother's made you.'

Jack sat down at the table, knowing his father's word was law. He glanced at the paper as he reached for the dish of baked potatoes and his heart lurched, his hand halting in mid-air. Then, as he saw his mother look at him curiously, he picked up a potato. He cut into it and buttered it, his heart still pounding, reading the headline again more slowly. Paris was under siege.

Fourteen

How odd, all the news and letters we get from Paris
now coming by balloons and carrier pigeons.

Frances Kilvert,
Diary, 3 October 1870

At first, spirits had been high. There were those who panicked
of course, and the railway stations were scenes of chaos as
people scrambled for the trains leaving the city. Yet among
those who remained there was an air of confidence. People
told one another that the danger would soon be over: Prussia
would give up and go home or else Britain and Russia
would come to their aid. The new Republican Government
led by General Trochu would order an uprising from the
provinces. Paris would not be left high and dry.

After Sedan the bedraggled army had begun to return, a
poor shadow of the glorious regiments which had marched
out one July day to the enthusiastic cries of *'À Berlin!'*
Meanwhile the authorities were preparing for the worst.
Before the Republic, Palikao's Government had begun
amassing foodstuffs: thousands of sheep and beef cattle
filled the Bois-de-Boulogne and Luxembourg Gardens, trees
had been felled for fuel. Now Trochu's Government of
National Defence continued the task of strengthening the

city's fortifications. A continuous railway line supplied arms to the ramparts manned by battalions of the National Guard. Outside the city walls and the moat, at a distance of a mile or two, a series of forts equipped with heavy guns, each within range of one another, provided Paris with its main hope of defence.

By the middle of September the city had become a fortress; its squares were parade grounds, the theatres and the Opéra, the public gardens and even the Louvre, its art treasures spirited to safety out of Paris, had closed and were turned into military depots and arsenals, billets and hospitals.

Bertrand no longer taught at the school. Most of the pupils had been evacuated from the city and the rest had been sent home, for the building was to be used as a hospital. He and Tessa relied on Phoebe's money again and Phoebe was uneasy about the rate at which it was dwindling. Already the price of food was rising in the markets, which were now guarded by soldiers. A few people had begun hoarding.

'We must begin thinking of the future too,' Phoebe told Tessa. 'We must buy more carefully.'

'What for?' Tessa replied. 'It will all be over soon and there's plenty of food in Paris. Bertrand has heard that there's fuel and flour and grain for at least eighty days.' She came in from the balcony where she had been sunning herself, for the summer weather seemed to be going on forever. 'Besides, we'll be gone before the Prussians come. Just as soon as the little one is well.'

Phoebe could not share Tessa's confidence. It seemed already as though Paris had always been under siege. In the early days they might perhaps have escaped along with everyone else had Tessa not been so ill. Now the gates were closed and no one might enter or leave without special permission. She looked at Tessa in her broken-down slippers and night-dress as she crooned over the sick baby in the cot. She remembered how once she had admired her for her individuality. Now she wanted to shake her and Bertrand too sometimes, for they seemed so unconcerned about everything except the child. Phoebe feared Tessa's obsession with her baby. Perhaps they all knew even then in their hearts that it would not survive. Phoebe refused to allow herself to form an attachment for the yellow scrawny infant which lay staring blankly at the ceiling in the Moses basket refusing even to cry; she heard her brother's assertions that little Thomas was getting fatter with an increased impatience and pity. How could willing something to live make any difference? Only by remaining detached could Phoebe bear to watch the child grow more sickly.

As September drew on and the pleasant summer weather held, the mood of confident patriotism continued, though as Phoebe said, 'There's a limit to how many times one can thrill to the sound of brass bands blaring out the "Marseillaise".' By now Paris and the surrounding countryside was encircled by Prussian forces. The investment had taken place with little opposition. 'Let them come!' people said to one another defiantly. 'They won't stay for long!'

It had become fashionable to visit the fortifications. Now that the Bois was cluttered with farm animals the smart set drove on sunny afternoons in their carriages along the circular road inside the ramparts instead of along the Champs-Elysées. The baby seemed less fretful one day. Bertrand said it was a turning point and all their spirits were high. 'You girls are looking pale,' he told them. 'Why don't you both go out for some fresh air? I can mind Thomas for an hour or two.'

'Let's go for a drive!' said Tessa at once. 'Oh, do let's, Phoebe! At least we shall see something happening.'

Reluctantly Phoebe paid for a carriage and they set off along the Rue St-Denis out towards the old city customs post. The inner circular road was full of activity: men were digging trenches behind the high wall, fetching and carrying sandbags and fascines and at one point unloading cannon-balls from a wagon with a great rumble and thud on the paving. The various battalions of the National Guard wore uniforms of all kinds and colours. 'Don't they look *theatrical*,' breathed Tessa. It all had the splendour of a larger-than-life spectacle, like the activity of an enormous dress rehearsal before the play. There were red stripes on military trousers, blue, black and white blouses, green tunics and brown. Nearly all the Guard wore peaked *képis* set at a jaunty angle.

There seemed no proper system to the way the work was going on along the railway line, round the powder magazines and petroleum stores or on the ramparts where gangs of dandies and roughs, obviously not used to handling artillery, were practising. Some of them leaned on their guns and with insolent stares and whistles watched the women in carriages pass.

'It almost makes me wish I wasn't spoken for.' Tessa tossed her head to show off her fine curls and laughed at Phoebe's shocked expression.

Tessa wondered sometimes about Phoebe. Did she never feel the need for a man? She had thought once that Phoebe had taken a fancy to Maurice. He had certainly taken one to her, for he had brought her a canary in a cage and she had hung it on her balcony where the damned thing never stopped singing. Tessa seized Phoebe's arm. 'Isn't it exciting? Did you ever think you'd get so close to a real live war?' The sound of cannon to the south of Paris, like the rumble of metal sheets in the wings to fake thunder, seemed a fitting background noise to their outing.

As they drove home the dull roar of the cannon continued; its intensity grew more ominous. People were out on the streets, asking one another what it could mean. Tessa heard someone shout that there had been a victory to the south and she and Phoebe looked at one another as a cheer went up from those gathered on the pavements which echoed behind them as they went by.

'Thank God,' said Phoebe. 'Perhaps it will soon end.'

They climbed down from the carriage, Tessa clinging still to Phoebe's arm. Bertrand called down to them from the balcony. 'There's been a battle.' His voice echoed in the narrow street.

'We heard,' called Tessa excitedly. 'A victory.'

Bertrand laughed and again the sound echoed but there was no mirth in it and Tessa's elation drained away. She had felt well for the first time that afternoon but now her lethargy returned.

The battle had taken place at a group of small French outposts situated on the Chatillon plateau to the south, manned by raw recruits, unaccustomed to battle conditions, whose heads were stuffed with tales of the barbarity of the Prussians. The outposts had been quickly captured, for at the first onset of hostilities the soldiers had deserted.

Maurice and Georges Marin arrived with Antoine that evening, incensed by what had happened. They said that three of the principal forts near the city, perhaps even Paris itself, would now be vulnerable to the batteries mounted on the plateau by the Prussians. They told them how the deserters had been spat on as they entered Montparnasse. Maurice himself had been among the Guard watching the battalions detailed to escort them into the city where they were arrested. 'We should have lynched the cowards there and then.'

'No matter,' said Antoine easily. 'They will be shot.'

'We should have strung them up! A bunch of us were

ready to do it, if our colonel hadn't come along and spoilt things.'

It occurred to Phoebe that the news of the supposed victory had strengthened her desire to leave Paris. Perhaps in a few days Tessa's baby would have been well enough to travel and they could have left for the country – perhaps even for England. She was weary and already frustrated by the siege. She thought of Griseley and its open moors with a peculiar longing.

Henri arrived. He looked grave. 'Have you heard? Favre has gone seeking peace negotiations with Bismarck.'

'Treachery! France won't accept terms!' said Georges.

'Treachery?' queried Antoine. 'Didn't we all once want peace? Weren't you shouting for Favre and the rest as loudly as anyone on the day of the Republic?'

'They're nothing but a load of lawyers when it comes down to it,' said Maurice and would have spat, thought Phoebe, had she not fixed him with a look, daring him to soil the carpet.

'Is it their fault they were forced to power so quickly after a lifetime of opposition?' Bertrand said mildly.

'They've got no stomach for a fight!' cried Maurice. 'All they care about is law and order.'

'They've no real plan, that's the trouble,' said Georges Marin, 'except to make sure the bourgeoisie stay on top.'

'Pigs!' said Maurice. 'They'd double-cross us at every turn, these liberals. They want peace! Whatever the price.'

Phoebe wanted to remind him how only weeks earlier he had called the war a madness. But the crisis had changed now, he would say. They were fighting for Paris, not an empire. Paris was the sacred city of revolution and must be defended to the last. Phoebe understood his patriotism; she understood his love for his city; but she did not understand the fickleness with which Maurice and the others could turn against their leaders – first *Down with the Empire*, then *Long live the Republic* and now *Down with the men at the Hôtel de Ville*.

Georges Marin said in his measured way, 'They will alienate themselves from the people if they accept terms.'

Maurice was pacing the floor with his arms folded across his chest. His face twitched with suppressed fury and Phoebe felt a shiver of disquiet. He swung round suddenly and jabbed his fist against the wall. 'They should let the National Guard fight. Endless drills but no proper training. We waste time doing nothing but gossip and stand watch. We're a laughing-stock because the government thinks it isn't safe to give us decent weapons in case we use them!'

'It's certainly a monotonous existence,' Antoine said. 'But the turn of the National Guard will come.'

Maurice rounded on him suddenly. 'You talk in platitudes like they do! Whose side are you on?'

Antoine had joined the National Guard that very week, 'for the hell of it', he had said, and because everyone else seemed to be in it. 'You should join,' he had told Bertrand. 'They are accepting foreign volunteers too.' Antoine's composure seemed shaken by Maurice's attack. He said gravely, 'Why my dear fellow, I hope we are all on the same side. Have you forgotten that it's the Prussians who are the enemy?'

'Come.' Bertrand poured wine for everyone and handed Maurice a glass. 'At least we are all friends here. And your government will never accept terms which would humiliate France.'

But Maurice was not convinced. 'Hear me,' he swallowed the wine quickly, 'it's only a matter of time before those pigs do a deal with the Prussians.'

The evening passed uneasily and, as if to emphasise the mood of discord, the baby cried fretfully from the bedroom.

At one point Bertrand repeated his belief that the Government of National Defence would not accept a peace on humiliating terms.

'What do you know about it? You're English!' Maurice snapped his fingers, including Tessa and Phoebe in the dismissive gesture. 'Why do you stay here? So many extra mouths for Paris to feed! Go, write to your government and tell Gladstone that France is in peril. See how much he cares. See how soon he sends your armies and your navy to help us!'

'The letter would have to go by balloon. You might consider that a waste of resources,' said Phoebe, stung by his bad temper. 'And we stay here only because we have a sick child.'

Antoine chided Maurice for his abuse of Bertrand's hospitality and soon afterwards all four men left.

'Why do they come here all the time?' Tessa plumped up the chair cushions viciously. 'That Maurice always upsets everybody.'

'Perhaps they think we might just be useful to them one day.' Bertrand was cynical, remembering that he had once provided Maurice with a hiding place from the authorities.

'I can't see how, seeing as they hate us so much.' Tessa went into the bedroom. They heard her begin to cry, an ugly sound made more disturbing by the knowledge that Tessa had once scorned tears.

'She's still weak.' Phoebe looked anxiously at the closed door. 'And she's frightened for the baby.'

'She's frightened that the Prussians might win,' admitted Bertrand. 'But she doesn't like Maurice and his friends either.' He regarded Phoebe soberly for a moment. His dark eyes were shadowed these days and his face thinner. His love of stylish dressing and extravagance had diminished and he rarely left the apartment. 'I wish you hadn't got trapped here because of me.'

Phoebe began clearing away the glasses. 'Don't be silly. I didn't have to come to Paris.' She paused. Had she really believed when she came that she might persuade Bertrand to return to Christina? She wondered briefly how Christina had coped and a mental picture of Beatrice dominating the nursery was faintly reassuring. How far away and secure in its own self-image Griseley seemed. 'And I didn't have to stay here,' she added.

'Phoebe, we must be wary of Maurice. He's such an unpredictable fellow. I don't think we can trust him.'

Phoebe too had been shocked by Maurice's outburst, but her brother's claim that Maurice and his companions might use them in some way was also shocking. 'You rescued him once,' she reminded him. 'He won't forget that. He said once that he would always count you a friend.' Yet Maurice's mood that evening contrasted sharply with his former opinions. And she remembered uneasily that when he had once told her Bertrand was a 'good fellow', he had almost in the same breath denounced Antoine as one of the bourgeoisie.

She left the glasses in the kitchen and went to bed. She could hear Tessa singing now to soothe the child; her misery was always short-lived, but it was disturbing, for Phoebe remembered that she had once been in awe of Tessa's vitality.

She was a little in awe of Maurice these days, she thought as she undressed. She went to the window in her chemise. The birdcage hung on the balcony, its shape silhouetted against the night sky, its tiny occupant hunched on its perch. 'An unpredictable fellow,' she murmured. Maurice was that, but more. He believed in a cause: he would fight, she was sure, to his last breath for his city. 'What can I say that I would fight for?' she asked the silent canary as she covered the cage with a cloth.

Maurice and the men he followed, the fiery orators of the cafés and clubs, were known as the Reds in more moderate circles. They were clamouring for a rebirth of a Commune of Paris to save France from the foreign invaders. For many of the left and for the newly formed Central Committee of the Twenty Arrondissements, the word 'Commune' signified justice for all, a right to elections, freedom of the Press and the freedom of the working man to form associations and affiliations. But for others the mystical Commune stood for violent revolution and the power of the mob. Some nights after Maurice's outburst against the Government of National Defence, Bertrand went with Antoine to one of the Red clubs in Montmartre, known for its seditious gossip and rhetoric and calling itself the Club de la Rectification. The clubs formed a source of amusement since the theatres had closed. Their lectures on free love, on the abolition of religion, on advice to the government on how to win the war – by releasing all the lions and tigers from the zoo or by killing the enemy with an onslaught of fireworks – were an alternative to the dull orators of the bigger public meetings.

Bertrand and Antoine sat in the smoky room of the club, each with a glass of beer, smiling now and then at the nonsense, until a man who had spoken more violently against the Government of National Defence began to compare the irresolution of 'Those idiots at the Hôtel de Ville' with the 'Clean decisions of the Terror'.

'Those traitors mean to join forces with the Prussians and squash the true Republicans of Paris,' the man shouted to hysterical applause. 'Arrest the men of the Hôtel de Ville!' was followed by cries of 'Down with Trochu! Down with Favre!' and even 'Down with Gambetta!'

'Arrest all the mayors of the arrondissements!' the man cried to more applause and there followed an outburst of names, thrown from the audience, of men who might more popularly take the place of the local mayors.

'Arrest all the priests!' was rewarded with shrieks of approval.

A member of the audience who clearly did not share this view, protested that Trochu and the others were 'Doing their best'.

Bertrand, tired of so much cant going unopposed, nodded and cried, 'Bravo!'

The president stood up from the front and began in a torrent of indignation to say that the club was not a public meeting where any supporter of the government might come in and say just what he pleased. Those who took part in the proceedings must declare themselves in favour of the principles of the Club de la Rectification. 'We don't oblige anyone to take part in our assemblies,' he shouted. 'But we are in control and if you are here, you had better be with us.'

'Arrest him!' someone shouted. 'If he's not with us, he must be a Prussian spy.'

The man who had spoken in favour of the government got up hurriedly and went outside. Cries of *'Vive la Commune!'* began. The chant became rhythmic. Bertrand turned in search of a face other than his own and Antoine's in which he might read a trace of sanity and saw Maurice at the door of the club, shouting with the rest, *'Vive la Commune!'*

Someone near Bertrand said, 'Didn't you speak against us as well as the other fellow?'

Before he could reply Antoine said in a relaxed way, 'What of it, friend? He is an Englishman. The English believe in free speech.' He spread his hands in a gesture which indicated that Bertrand was a little crazy.

301

'And who are you?' the man said. 'How do we know you're not both spies for the Prussians?'

Antoine continued to drink his beer steadily, but others near them had begun to take an interest. The man who had spoken laid a hand on Bertrand's collar and, tightening his grip, pulled him from his seat. Bertrand clung to the table and heard Antoine somewhere near him say sharply, 'I told you that you can trust him!' but hands seized on Antoine too and he was dragged to the floor.

They were bundled to the door and Bertrand, half choked by the hand twisting his collar, his knees and elbows banging against tables and chairs, looked wildly for Maurice – Maurice would vouch for them – but the figure in the doorway had vanished.

Someone hit him hard as he reached the street. The blow to the side of his head made him reel. A voice cried 'Not here! In the cemetery!' and he was dragged along the cobbles. The cool air revived him a little and he could see Antoine near him being hauled between two men like a sack of vegetables. Bertrand knew then that they were going to kill them. He thought of Tessa and Phoebe, who would wait for his return and not know what had happened – perhaps never discover the truth. He prayed that Tessa would not think he had abandoned her, that Phoebe would stay with her and the baby, and that his father and Christina – even Beatrice – would forgive him.

The street sloped steeply and every now and then his knees met the cobbles with a sickening jerk. He knew that they must soon reach one of the steep flights of steps which led to a lower street. They are going to throw us down there, he thought. First Antoine, then me and bury our bloodied bodies in the cemetery. Terror seized him as he realised that the little procession had stopped.

A figure had stepped forward from the shadows barring

302

the way with one hand against the wall, and Bertrand saw that it was Maurice.

'And where are you all going on this fine night?' He spoke with that strange humourless smile.

'We've found a couple of spies,' said one of the men eagerly. 'Get out of the way and we'll deal with them.'

'But this is Antoine Latrasse, a friend of mine, and my good friend Mr Clough from England, who hid me from the gendarmes last year.'

Bertrand felt the hand on his collar release its hold. Others heaved him upright and the men dusted him down and murmured vague apologies.

Antoine shook himself free of the solicitous attention. 'And where were you when you were most needed?'

Maurice began to laugh. 'Come, come. You are lucky I was passing. Come back up the hill and we'll have a drink and a laugh together.'

But Antoine, nursing a cut on his jaw, declined, and Bertrand walked away with him knowing that Maurice had seen the incident from the start.

By October the siege was no longer a novelty, and the mood in the city became one of grim resolve rather than optimism as people bomb-proofed their cellars with bags of earth and gathered stocks of tinned mutton and vegetables. One thing cheered the little family near the Rue Rambuteau, for the baby rallied and was putting on weight. Tessa, recovering her pride in her appearance and her old exuberance, nursed him in her arms and called him 'My little Thomas, my darling boy', and even Phoebe now allowed a flowering of love for the child. Cradling his soft trembling warmth, she felt the same fear for his fragility as she felt for the canary which sometimes let her hold it in her hands.

She went one day to the British Embassy with a vague

optimism that they all might now leave Paris, but was told that their chances were slight. The British Ambassador with most of his staff had left at the beginning of the siege, the British Consul had followed not long since. 'Don't you know there are four thousand British people in Paris?' said the minor official who came downstairs to speak to her in the lobby. 'They can't all be furnished with a *laissez-passer*.'

'They've not all asked for one,' retorted Phoebe. 'There are only three of us and a baby.'

'It's not in my power,' said the man. 'Only the other day a party was arrested on the Pont Neuilly. The French are getting very wary of foreigners.'

'The Americans are allowed through,' pressed Phoebe.

'The French feel better disposed to the Americans,' he told her. 'And there are not so many of them. Besides, the Government of National Defence doesn't want large numbers of foreigners to leave. It's discouraging for the army and the French citizens.'

And that was that. 'The British Embassy staff have bolted,' she told Bertrand angrily. 'If we try to leave too we'll be arrested by the French or else shot by the Prussians.'

Bertrand was silent. He felt his own helplessness deeply, yet the same mood of despair seemed now to be affecting everyone. The presence of armed soldiers everywhere, the distant sound of cannon and the rumours of battle and wild stories of possible rescue missions were all lowering to the spirit. There was a preoccupation with the price of food and a growing paranoia about spies so that Bertrand saw that he and Antoine had been lucky to escape at the club in Montmartre, even that he should perhaps be grateful to Maurice for rescuing them.

The worst was the lack of news, thought Phoebe, for though she had written home by balloon post, no letters or newspapers from outside reached them. Bertrand seized eagerly on information in the main thoroughfares and cafés, but most of the stories were built on rumour. No one could tell fact from fiction or how long they would be trapped or how the war might end.

'I shall look for work,' Phoebe said, anxious about their diminishing supply of money.

'It's not for you to look for work.' Bertrand was made acutely aware again of his inadequacy. 'You've done enough for us. I should be providing for us all.' The next day he joined Antoine's battalion of the National Guard. But the regular wage of one franc fifty a day eased their financial burden only a little and he knew that it would not be enough to sustain them with the prices of food rising so quickly.

Bertrand's duties as a soldier were few, though they took him away from home for days at a time: they comprised standing watch on the ramparts, attending drill twice a day and making the occasional arrest, which usually involved some innocent citizen who had been seen with a telescope or showing a light after curfew, cast under immediate suspicion of being a spy. The sense of uselessness which pervaded the Guard was as demoralising as that which already troubled Bertrand. The men whiled away their time smoking, drinking and playing cards, boredom and discontent affected everyone and the gossip echoed the exaggerated talk in the Red clubs and bistros. The captain of Antoine and Bertrand's company was a moderate man, but other battalions were run by fervent revolutionaries who had appropriated the senior ranks with few military qualifications. If Bertrand had imagined once that Maurice and his friends represented a minority of extremists, he saw now that the contempt for the government was more widespread. Why had Trochu and the others no plan? Why had they not proclaimed a mass rising throughout the whole of France? Why was the military potential of the Guard being wasted on endless drilling inside the city walls?

The battle for Paris had settled down to outpost skirmishes, a sort of half-hearted war where neither side would take a major initiative. Some of the men said that if the Prussians had known the true weakness of the city's defences they would have marched straight up the Champs-Elysées in September.

The Central Committee of the Twenty Arrondissements was constantly issuing manifestos. They defied the government to attempt any more peace missions: *Paris will be buried under its own ruins rather than surrender*, they proclaimed. *The Republic must not negotiate with an occupying enemy*, and again came the demands for the election of a Commune.

Phoebe had begun in secret to look for work. Most of the commercial and business life of the city had come to a halt and the entire industry of the capital was given over to the war: factories had been converted to munition plants and cannon foundries; men and women made weapons and uniforms in basement cellars; workshops with improvised equipment were turning out cartridges, shots and shells and converting ancient guns into modern ones, and subscriptions were raised among the ordinary people of Paris to fund the manufacture of yet more cannon.

Phoebe was taken on at a workshop across the river, where women worked at rows of sewing-machines installed in a former music hall in Montparnasse. There she learned to stitch the huge cotton balloons later to be taken for varnishing in the deserted Gare d'Orléans and the Gare du Nord. Accompanying a consignment of work one evening she saw the finished balloons, billowing like vast and airy eiderdowns. Grass was beginning to grow between the rusting railway lines. How strange it seemed, that trains could have once run in and out of the huge and eerie station.

A balloon was being prepared for flight. She walked to the end of the platforms and stood, hugging her shawl about her arms, fascinated by the immense difficulty of the operation. People had joked at first about this bizarre means of outwitting the Prussians, but to Phoebe the balloon was awesome and the task the men faced not crazy but courageous. Accidents and explosions were frequent for the balloons were inflated with coal gas; they were vulnerable to enemy rifle fire and went where the wind blew, and the Prussians had stepped up their vigilance since Gambetta had escaped to Tours to raise an army among the provinces.

The boom of cannon could be heard intermittently. The upper section of the balloon swayed and surged, straining at the ropes tied to stakes which creaked in the ground. Phoebe imagined the freedom of soaring above the draughty glass roof of the station and out beyond the walls of the city over the heads of the enemy.

The evening wore on and men lit oil lamps which shone on the underside of the balloon as it swelled, yellow and monstrous against the darkening sky. Beneath it the tethered basket with its occupants lifted and bounced a little and at last a cheer rose from the onlookers, the ropes were released and Phoebe, craning her neck upwards, heard again the dim boom of Prussian cannon as the balloon took off into the sky.

She walked home and offered up a prayer for the men who manned the balloon, recalling the expressions on the faces of the watching crowd. She passed people in the street and wanted to embrace them in sympathy, feeling a surge of love for the city which had so charmed her when she arrived and now seemed lost and leaderless. People felt betrayed by their so-called Government of National Defence who did nothing while others like Gambetta risked their lives. No wonder they went wild when there were rumours of the smallest victory. No wonder spirited men like Maurice, restricted to drills and time-wasting, were longing for a fight, if not against the Prussians, then against the politicians and the generals who frustrated every hope of success with their inactivity and bungling.

There had been a demonstration of the National Guard outside the Hôtel de Ville at the beginning of October. Several battalions from Belleville and Ménilmontant, headed by their hero Flourens, marched to the strains of the 'Marseillaise' and assembled on the square. Flourens demanded in the name of the whole of the Guard that an immediate sortie against the enemy should be made, that the Guard be issued with modern rifles instead of their ancient muskets and that there should be municipal elections. No one in the government had been very alarmed by the demonstration but a few days later there had been a more menacing march of Belleville battalions, led not by Flourens but the more fanatical Sapia and that time, Phoebe knew, Maurice had been present. Someone had tried to pull one of Trochu's staff officers down and spat in his face. Tamisier, the Commander-in-Chief of the National Guard, had shouted at the rebel battalions to disperse and the Guard shouted back, *'Vive la Commune!'* The atmosphere had been one of revolution.

She reached the apartment and Maurice and Georges Marin were there. They were talking still about the demonstration. It was all they talked about these days – how and when the Government of National Defence might be brought down.

Phoebe stood in the doorway and saw Bertrand and Tessa, seated close together on the sofa. Bertrand wore his Guard's uniform and looked unkempt and weary. Phoebe remembered a little sadly her debonair brother of the old days. Georges smoked his foul tobacco pipe and squatted by the barely smouldering fire warming his hands. Maurice was at the opposite corner of the fireplace, his arm resting casually on the marble mantelshelf.

'They were ready for us,' he complained. 'Trochu had his bourgeois battalions at his heels. Some coward turned on Sapia and handed him over. All it needed was for someone to make a speech and the rain to come down and everyone gave up and went home.' He spat deftly into the fire which sizzled as if it might threaten to expire altogether.

Phoebe walked briskly into the room. 'Surely you wouldn't want Frenchmen fighting Frenchmen?'

Maurice looked at her for a moment. 'True Frenchmen will kill anyone who is an enemy of victory.'

'They say Sapia is to be court-martialled,' murmured Georges.

Maurice laughed. 'They would like to arrest Flourens and Blanqui too, but no one will risk trying it – least of all the police.' He looked at Phoebe and winked suddenly. 'Kératry the Police Chief has resigned and left Paris by one of Phoebe's balloons.'

'Perhaps a Prussian sharpshooter will get him,' Bertrand said ironically and Phoebe saw Maurice fix him with a mistrustful stare.

Phoebe lay in bed that night and tried to picture the scenes at the Hôtel de Ville. She fell into a doze and the rebel soldiers were mixed up with the faces of the crowd at the Gare du Nord. She saw the balloon framed by the menacing structure of the station building. Bertrand stood beside her shouting 'Down with the Reds,' and then Maurice was marching towards her bearing a tricolour. He said, 'My lovely Phoebe, we have won!' and struck Bertrand to the ground.

Little knots of people stood in the rain one morning at the end of October when Phoebe went with her coupons to queue for bread and the daily meat ration. Indignation broke from the queue as everyone discussed the latest news. They were bitter about the fall of Metz a few days earlier in a humiliating surrender. General Bazaine, responsible for the capitulation of 150,000 men, was a traitor, they said, for how could such a calamity have happened without his treachery? Worse though was the rumour that General Thiers had taken an armistice proposal to the Prince of Prussia at Versailles and was urging the government to accept peace terms.

Phoebe returned to the apartment where from the balcony she could hear a clamour of drums and trumpets not far away.

'Don't go to the workshop this morning,' begged Tessa. 'Something's going to happen. Don't leave me with Thomas on my own.'

Phoebe leaned on the balcony and could see the uniforms of a detachment of the National Guard marching along the Rue Rambuteau. It was clear from the growing swell of sound in the distance that crowds were gathering and heading for the Hôtel de Ville. Further along the street the *concierges* stood outside their doors, conferring with one another; some were fastening up their shutters. The canary fluttered against the bars of its cage, sensing the excitement in the air.

Phoebe turned to Tessa who stood in her night-dress, cradling the snuffling Thomas against her breast. Tessa gave her a weak smile, half apologetic, as if she too recognised in her behaviour a poor shadow of her former self. 'I'm frightened for Bertrand.' Her eyes were reddened, as if she had been weeping.

How strange, thought Phoebe, that she had once considered Tessa spirited, and yet it was she who felt no fear at the movement of troops and crowds; the sound of drums to the south was even vaguely stirring.

'Bertrand will be safely tucked up in his battery,' she said. 'He's in more danger from a Prussian sniper than a demonstration.'

'Please don't leave us,' Tessa repeated.

Phoebe sighed. 'Very well, I'll stay at home this morning. But you know how they blow hot and cold. It will all be over by midday.'

But the drums and marching continued as they ate their meagre lunch. The tension and the noise made Phoebe choke on the dry bread and she gave her share to Tessa. She went to the balcony and tried to understand what was happening, but she could not tell whether the shouts were raised in anger or whether the crowd at the Hôtel de Ville were cheering. At last she put on a shawl and pulled a scarf over her hair. 'I shall go and investigate.' Promising that she would not be gone above an hour, she set out for the Hôtel de Ville.

The streets around echoed with a dull roar of sound from the thousands of people who crammed the square. Well-dressed men and women mingled with workers, top hats and umbrellas were dotted among the caps and *képis*: it was as if the whole city had boiled up at once, united by their frustration against the government. Men in the different military uniforms of the National Guard jostled close to the front of the building, some bearing tricolours and carrying their muskets with the butts raised in the air to show that they were in sympathy with the feelings of the crowd.

There were cries of *'À bas l'armistice!' 'La levée en masse!'* and *'Vive la Commune!'* which were drowned by the raucous blasts of bugles and the rattle of drums. Phoebe

311

could see someone at one of the windows of the Hôtel de Ville, waving his arms and trying to make himself heard. 'What's happening?' she asked a woman nearby.

'They are going to overthrow the government,' the woman said placidly. 'Let's just pray none of them starts shooting.' She turned to stare at her and Phoebe realised that her own worn hands, her style of dress and look of hunger distinguished her as a worker rather than a member of the bourgeoisie. 'Arago, the mayor, had a good old yell at everybody,' the woman laughed. 'Then he lost his nerve. He's called all the government together – Trochu done up with his sword and medals and all – we booed them good and proper. And now they've gone and locked themselves in a room upstairs.'

Phoebe now recognised the man at the window as Rochefort. He was clearly trying to calm the crowd. Phoebe recalled how not long ago he had been the darling of the Republicans – Maurice had spoken his name with a kind of awe – and yet this woman was smiling as she told how the mob had tried to pull him down, and even as the woman spoke there were angry shouts of *'À bas Rochefort!'* from the crowd.

'Trochu tried to give us one of his long-winded speeches,' said Phoebe's informer. 'We soon sent him off with a flea in his ear.' She broke off as a flurry of activity made people surge forward at the edge of the square. The crowd parted and a roar of approval went up as a posse of men on horseback appeared, led by a man in a magnificently embroidered uniform and carrying a scimitar.

An hysterical cry of 'Flourens!' was taken up and other shouts for Delescluze and Félix Pyat and the other Red leaders who followed. Phoebe stood on tiptoe to see these heroes of the Belleville battalions as the procession swept on towards the building and she stifled a cry of surprise, for in the wake of the mounted leaders marched Maurice and Georges Marin and Henri, all in their National Guard uniform. They paused for a moment silhouetted against the entrance before they were swept with their fellow soldiers into the Hôtel de Ville.

Maurice had been fired up with nervous energy all morning. The streets of Belleville were in an uproar with people yelling and shouting *'À bas l'armistice!'* Everyone knew that something was going on at the Hôtel de Ville and yet Flourens and the other leaders had wasted precious hours, arguing among themselves about what they should do. The fact was the demonstrations had caught everyone by surprise. Those that were closer to the centre of things said that the discussion between Blanqui, Delescluze, Pyat and Flourens had been a bit strong, with them all yelling one another down. Flourens and Blanqui did not get on and Delescluze and Pyat could not stand the sight of one another. But for the sake of the cause they had come to a decision: the Belleville battalions of the National Guard would march on the Hôtel de Ville, overthrow the government and replace it with one headed by the Reds.

Maurice fumed that he could have made that very decision for them hours ago and saved them a lot of breath.

'Never mind. We're at them at last,' said Jean Tissier as they marched along. The old man looked pale. He said he was getting too ancient for this sort of thing, but Maurice knew he would not have missed it for anything.

'Vive la Commune!' yelled Maurice, forgetting his impatience and feeling excitement churn through his veins as at last they met the vigorously applauding crowd in the square in front of the Hôtel de Ville. He gripped his loaded rifle. How magnificent Flourens looked in his fancy uniform

as he dismounted. How the crowd cheered them all as if they were heroes.

'Here we go,' laughed Georges as, to a fanfare of trumpets, the procession pushed on into the building. No one tried to stop them and they surged up the stairs, everyone pushing forward, eager not to miss anything. Someone said the Cabinet had shut themselves in. Mayor Arago appeared on the stairs and bellowed at everyone to get out but they just laughed at him and the leaders reached the room where Trochu and the other Ministers sat.

Everyone was jostling and yelling in the corridors and on the stairs and for a while Maurice could not tell what was going on. He pushed his way closer to the front where he could see into the room and catch glimpses of Flourens striding about on the table in front of the seated Government Ministers. Flourens waved his sword and issued orders to the bemused Cabinet, kicking over inkwells and treading all over the green baize.

The men behind Maurice started grumbling. Why didn't they just take over and get on with it? Snippets of information about what was happening were passed from one to another. Favre had apparently declined an invitation to resign, and Flourens was urged to arrest him, but Flourens said they did not have enough men.

'Not enough men,' fumed Maurice. 'We've enough fucking men to string up the lot of them.'

Throughout it all came the report that Trochu sat puffing on a cigar as if he hadn't a care in the world.

After a while Flourens and the others adjourned to various rooms to discuss the matter. It was the way it had happened in September when they had proclaimed the Republic: lists of names put forward for a Committee of Public Safety, with Flourens heading nearly every list, began flying from the windows to the crowd outside.

Maurice could hear the mob calling for Dorian, the Minister of Works, one of the popular members of the old Government of National Defence, but Dorian refused to head the Committee.

Minutes and then hours passed and everything was in confusion. Some of the Guard had been detailed to issue *laissez-passers* to regulate who might enter the building, but no one knew who was supposed to sign them or provide the obligatory blue stamp. No one seemed willing to enforce any sort of order and Flourens and the others were squabbling again. The crowd apparently believed that it was all over, that Dorian had replaced Trochu as they wanted and elections were assured; they began pouring into the building in triumph. The crowd surged up the great staircase past the heavy iron bannisters to reach the rooms above. Some stood on tables demanding their own hearing; men were sitting on the windowsills with their legs dangling outside, shouting to the people in the square below. Those downstairs began ransacking everything, looting the kitchens and smashing furniture. Someone incessantly blew a trumpet close to Maurice, another was beating a drum, and in a room off a corridor he could see the old man Blanqui being pushed about, obviously unrecognised by the mob as the greatest of all revolutionaries.

It's a rabble, thought Maurice, marvelling at the scene. but a rabble to no purpose. If only someone could channel all that energy into a single driving force, what power they would have. Henri and Georges and Jean, caught up in the confusion, wandered off to find food and drink. Why did no one do anything? Was this new leadership going to be as bad as the one before it? The only man there with any dignity was old Trochu. Maurice felt a grudging respect for his calm indifference. A sergeant of the Guard, echoing his thoughts said, 'Those sods have brought us here and now they haven't a clue what to do.'

'They have been holding the entire Government prisoner all afternoon,' Phoebe said to Tessa. 'It's all over. People are talking about a Commune being established as soon as the elections take place tomorrow.' She was shocked by what she had seen in the square, and yet it was rather magnificent.

'You're soaked!' said Tessa. 'And you've been gone for hours.'

Phoebe looked in surprise at her wet clothes. She had hardly noticed when it had begun raining but had watched the windows of the Hôtel de Ville looking for Maurice among the figures who appeared and disappeared, wondering what was happening inside. She had left when the crowd, saying it was all over and there were going to be elections, drifted away and it began to grow dark.

'Did you see Bertrand?' begged Tessa.

Phoebe, glad that she could reassure her, said, 'Don't worry. He wasn't taking part.'

Drummers had beaten out the rappel all over the city, calling the moderate battalions of the National Guard to arms. The Place Vendôme was crowded with battalions, among them Antoine and Bertrand. They had been met with rumour and counter-rumour as they waited for the order to march off. Some said there had been a revolution and there was now a Red republic with Flourens in charge. Before they knew it there would be hangings and killings and the Terror all over again.

Everyone asked one another why no one would give the order to free the Ministers and it soon became clear that there was no one with the authority to give such an order. General Tamisier, the Commander of the Guard, was trapped with the government in the Hôtel de Ville as was the new Prefect of Police.

Afternoon wore on into the evening. Some of the Guard, unhappy about what might lie ahead, drifted away. Then came news that Adam, the Prefect of Police, had been smuggled out of the building, Trochu too had escaped and the revolutionaries' hold was beginning to slip. It was raining heavily and pitch dark. Bertrand's uniform was sodden and men talked uneasily about the possibility that the regulars would be called out against the rebels. Antoine said that he would not fire on a fellow member of the Guard, he would disobey orders. Bertrand was silent, wondering why he stood there in the rain, blaming himself, blaming Tessa, blaming the French whose arrogance and inconsistencies and bad organisation had been responsible for everything that had gone wrong. Incongruously, he thought of Yorkshire and the blackened stone houses of Griseley, always made blacker by the rain. They were silent at night, the curtains drawn tightly at the windows on Griseley Bank, coal fires burning inside, the glow of gas lamps making wet pools of light on the pavement outside. He remembered his youth and childhood and was overwhelmed by a longing for the past.

It was ten o'clock before the signal came for them to march to the sound of drums and trumpets out of the Place Vendôme. They reached the Hôtel de Ville where several battalions of Guards were already in the square. The building was lit from end to end and its occupation seemed to consist of several hundreds, even thousands of rebel Guards, though the crowd outside was not as large as they had been led to expect.

'They've all gone home,' joked Antoine. 'And wouldn't I like to slip off too.'

They were ordered to take up a position among the men

317

surrounding the building. Word went round that a couple of battalions of the Mobiles led by the Prefect of Police were entering the building by a secret underground passage which led between the Hôtel de Ville and the barracks. They were going to pop up through a trap door in the cellars. Bertrand thought of Gerald's theatre and felt a sudden desire to laugh. 'Like the demon king,' he said, and Antoine, not knowing what he was talking about, shook his head and said, 'Which of us are the greater demons, Bertrand?'

Bertrand waited nervously. Antoine beside him looked pale. Bertrand knew as the tension mounted that they shared the same fears. What if Maurice and the others were among the rebels inside? What if he or Antoine were called upon to arrest them? The rescued Trochu had maintained that there would be no shooting and no repressive measures would be taken against the rebels, who had acted understandably out of disappointment over the capitulation at Metz. It would all be done with reason. Without this pledge Bertrand doubted the Guard would have followed orders this far; as it was there was a distinct sense of disquiet among those assembled outside. One or two shots were fired, though it was hard to tell who had fired first and no one was hurt. Many more of the men had fallen off on the way to the Hôtel de Ville, reluctant to confront their fellow soldiers.

News was passed among the lines that the Mobiles had succeeded in getting into the building and that the rebels had threatened to kill Jules Favre if they advanced beyond the stairs. The Mobiles were at the bottom of the grand staircase ready to fire if the rebels did not give up peaceably, the National Guards stood at the top.

'Deadlock,' murmured Antoine, looking up at the lighted windows where many shadows flitted to and fro. His voice bore none of its usual flippancy as he said, 'God, I wish we could get out of this rain.'

318

But they were to stand in the rain for more hours yet, while the men inside discussed how to resolve the situation. Rumours reached them now and then. The leaders were parleying; they had agreed to a bloodless evacuation; Dorian and Delescluze, men of reason, were doing all the talking.

And then, in the early hours of the morning, the march out from the building began: Tamisier escorting Blanqui, Dorian and Delescluze, and the rest of the government walking amicably with the rebel leaders, 'Almost as if they had all been to a party,' said Antoine.

Bertrand watched the rebel National Guards file out, shouldering their muskets, some looking abashed, others defiant.

'Hold up your heads. You've not been conquered,' said Adam the Prefect of Police, but they knew it was not true and Bertrand felt the resentment of the men who passed as they regarded the 'loyal' Guards with scorn. And then he saw him – Maurice walking with impatience, scanning the ranks of men outside. Bertrand lowered his gaze and prayed he would not see him. He heard someone, perhaps Maurice himself, shout, 'You pigs! With your assistance we could have won!'

Trochu and the government had promised immediate municipal elections and no reprisals against the rebels. The promise of elections was turned the next day into an offer of a plebiscite – a straight yes or no answer to a vote of confidence in the government – and faced with the uncertainty of an alternative, the majority of Parisians played safe and voted 'yes'. And then the government began rounding up the leaders and throwing them in the Mazas gaol.

Maurice, though not under arrest, did not come to see them any more; Antoine was the only visitor. He and Bertrand brooded over the consequences of the failed revolution of the 31st October knowing that it had marked a turning point. 'How could we have guessed the government were not to be trusted and would renege on their word?' said Antoine, and Bertrand talked of the necessity for law and order, a little shamefaced, for he knew the arrests had been inexcusable.

Phoebe shared the fierce anger of the people against the men at the Hôtel de Ville and understood their sense of betrayal. She felt estranged from Bertrand, who had taken the government's part against the rebels – not only Bertrand but Antoine, a Frenchman, a Republican. Maurice had been right, Antoine was a bourgeois at heart.

But, as the weather grew colder, the desire for revolution became less important: people turned their attention from politics to the business of survival, for the bread and meat rations had been reduced and gas supplies were running out.

Gambetta's recapture of Orléans after his escape by balloon had brought a restored confidence to the streets. People in food queues hugged and kissed one another and everyone at Phoebe's workshop knew that without their own efforts it could not have happened. People said, 'Surely this time the chain of bad luck is broken!' But Phoebe was sceptical, afraid that it would be the same old pattern again: people getting excited about the notion of victory only to have their hopes dashed later on.

News that there was to be a 'Great Sortie' to meet up with Gambetta produced a further flowering of optimism. The walls were plastered with heartening proclamations. There was going to be a tremendous battle – two hundred thousand French, half of them from the National Guard. Guns and supplies, pontoons and men and their equipment were shifted across Paris in preparation for an attack to the south-east, the strongest sector of the Prussian line.

Battalions of the National Guard drilled and assembled in squares all over the city and at last they marched out from the gates to the sound of regimental bands and the cheering crowds.

The sortie was Maurice's first taste of battle. He marched with Georges, Henri and Jean Tissier and his body was alive with a sense of comradeship. Even those turncoats Antoine and Bertrand were among the marching units. He could almost forgive Bertrand for his part in the Hôtel de Ville débâcle – he was an Englishman, the English had no revolutionary fire in their bellies – but he would never forgive Antoine for betraying his compatriots.

The weather was damp and cold and they had a fair way to go. Never mind the Hôtel de Ville and the 31st October. Here was a chance to get at the Prussians. This time they were united and faced a common enemy. The rank upon rank of National Guard were magnificent and everyone was longing for a fight.

Maurice's company was among the first to take one of the Prussian barricades and the men swarmed over and through it. Maurice was not there at the kill and, disappointed, contented himself with spitting on the body of a Prussian. At last, to come face to face with the enemy! He was filled with a wonderful murderous rage which made his head feel as if it was bursting. He rushed on up the hill, hearing a roaring in his ears, recognising his own voice, *'Allons! Allons!'*

He could remember little afterwards and had no idea where they were. He recalled hearing screams, seeing men fall on every side as he raced towards the distant stone walls beyond which the Prussians held their position, and then all around were the cries to retreat, while the guns shattered the air.

Bertrand, half a mile to the south, was to remember only

the fear: the terrible loosening of his bowels and the sweating which soaked his uniform through and turned his bones to ice as they neared the sound of battle.

The continual roar of sound, the shattering explosion of shells and the rattle and crack, crack of rifle fire drove a panic through him and he wanted to run as far from the din as he could go. He took cover behind a wall in one of the villages. He saw the bodies piled up in the lanes, men trampling on the wounded in the crush to get away, officers yelling themselves hoarse, ignoring the heaps of blue and scarlet figures as if the carnage was insignificant. He backed against the wall and there saw a man blown apart before his eyes. The image would be seared on his memory forever and he cried out in protest, wanting his childhood, the untainted air of the moors and an end to the nightmare of war.

Maurice bellowed in fury at those who yelled, 'We're beaten.' Men were running past him away from the enemy position and he wept with disappointment for he had believed victory was possible. 'Amateurs!' he shouted. 'Cowards!' And then he too joined the retreat. He wept again as he saw Jean Tissier spread-eagled in his path. He halted, recognising the grizzled head, the *képi* fallen from it in the grass and blood matting the hair.

He dried his face on his sleeve. Jean was old. He should not have marched with them, but better to meet a valiant end than die in his bed. It was then, as he came to his senses, that he saw the remnants of the glorious army streaming towards Paris in their thousands.

Bertrand returned after a few days, walking among the files of blood-stained carts, but he would not talk about what had happened. Tessa fussed over a flesh wound in his arm and Phoebe grew anxious about his depressed spirits. Antoine

322

told them how they had been trapped for hours by the confusion of the retreat.

It was several days before they learned that Georges and Henri and Jean Tissier were dead. All over Paris people mourned similar losses. The final blow came when they heard that the Prussians had recaptured Orléans.

Fifteen

... France will have to choose between a Peace which cannot be otherwise than humiliating and a continuance of the War under wholly new conditions.

The Times, 28 January 1871

Phoebe walked towards her usual food queue in the hour before dawn, banging her hands together to keep warm as she walked. The few people on the street were silent. The weather had turned much colder since November. The long Indian summer was now like some half-forgotten dream and Phoebe's life before coming to Paris seemed to have belonged to a different person.

Phoebe rarely thought of Griseley or her father and brothers, nor even of Jack except with a faint but rather rueful nostalgia. She worried about Tessa and the baby: Thomas had caught cold and was sickly again; an outbreak of smallpox had made Tessa timid and fearful for him and she stayed indoors in the apartment leaving Phoebe to join the lengthening food queues every morning before she set off for work.

She hurried her step a little. Often the traders put up their shutters early; the supplies ran out quickly these days, though in some cases it was more profitable to sell under the counter. Everyone despised the rich bourgeois who did not have to queue, and hated the butcher who kept the best for himself and his friends and was making a profit. The meat ration had been reduced again – if one could stomach it, for the salted stuff was almost inedible; the fishermen no longer found fish in the Seine; milk had run out, for the herds of cattle and sheep in the Bois had all vanished. The restaurants catered for more exotic tastes with animals from the zoo if one could afford to dine on bear or camel or elephant. The butchers had begun selling dogs and cats some weeks ago and now even the rats were in short supply.

Phoebe remembered Maurice had said all along that the government should have taken full control over the food stocks so that they would be fairly distributed. The only control now as to who got what seemed to lie in one's perseverance at queuing or an ability to pay the high prices. Not that she imagined Maurice did either. In the early days, before the October uprising, he would tap the side of his nose when asked where he had found the chicken he had brought them, its feathers still warm, or when he produced pâté and chocolate and bottles of fine cognac done up in a *boîte* with the label ripped from it. 'Don't worry for yourself,' he had once told her grandiosely. 'You shall not starve while Maurice is at hand.' But since the attack on the Hôtel de Ville Maurice had not been to see them. They heard that he had taken part in an attempt to recapture the outpost Le Bourget a few days ago, a second hopeless sortie which had resulted this time in a near mutiny amongst the troops. She guessed he no longer cared whether the three of them survived or starved.

She thought of the canary he had given her, which she had allowed to flutter free and take its chance on the streets of Paris. Hunger gnawed at her stomach as she shifted her feet in the queue. She wrapped the ends of her shawl more tightly round her waist. Everyone knew that famine could not be far away. She doubted that she would have had any qualms now about eating the canary, bones and all. She scanned the queue: the line of men and women this morning was already some forty or fifty strong, on some days there would be as many as a couple of hundred. As usual, armed National Guard were there to prevent any disputes. They stamped their feet and their breath made thin white clouds in the air as they laughed and joked among themselves.

Phoebe had been waiting for almost an hour, her feet numbed by the frosty pavement, when a familiar voice spoke quite close to her ear. 'What a sight for sore eyes on a freezing morning. A merry Christmas, my lovely Phoebe.'

Phoebe was startled to see Maurice when she had only that morning been thinking about him. 'Good morning,' she said, 'I am just waiting to collect my turkey.'

'Bon appétit.' He did not move away with his companions. The Guard on duty nodded to him pleasantly. 'I could get you further up the queue,' Maurice said in a low voice, but Phoebe shook her head; she had seen the hostility of the crowd towards anyone who was granted such 'favours'.

She looked at him sideways. He seemed fit compared with Bertrand and had not lost weight as the rest of them had; she doubted that he went hungry. His face was patched red with the cold and she noticed a darker weal near his temple, half hidden by his National Guard *képi*. 'It was bad to hear of the rout at Le Bourget,' she said. 'They say some of the men froze to death.'

'The Guard fought bravely,' he said, as if she had implied otherwise. He stood watching his companions continue up the street to a point where it curved away to the right.

'I'm sorry about your friends who were killed. You must miss them.'

He frowned. 'They died the deaths of heroes.' He turned

suddenly to look at her. 'I admire you, Phoebe, for the way you have kept a brave spirit through France's troubles.'

'I thought you resented our being here – so many useless mouths to feed,' she reminded him.

'You are different. I feel your sympathy for our cause.' After a while he said, as if remembering why she had stayed in Paris, 'Is the child well?'

She frowned. 'He's sick again and Tessa and Bertrand almost out of their minds with worry.'

'I'm sorry.' He paused. 'I feel sorry too that our close friendship came to such an abrupt end.' It was a reminder of the fact that he had once kissed her. 'The siege has altered many things. It has turned friend against friend. Perhaps even brother against sister.' He reached forward and took her cold gloved hand, covering it with his own hand, and she saw again the white scar on his wrist. 'I shall always be a friend to you, Phoebe. Closer than a friend. Closer than a brother.' He bent swiftly and kissed her. People in the queue near her, glad of a diversion from the tedium of waiting, laughed and someone cheered, *'Vive l'amour!'*

'Monsieur Chaudet – please!' She pulled her hand away and pressed it hard against her thigh. 'You haven't been near us for weeks and here you are, on the strength of a chance meeting, practically—' she had been going to say 'declaring yourself in love with me', but could not finish the sentence. She decided that he was drunk. He certainly smelled as if he had been drinking. All the Guard, even Bertrand, spent their money on alcohol; it was the only commodity which was not in short supply in this beleaguered city.

He stepped forward from the pavement and doffed his *képi* with a bow and she saw the extent of the wound, running from his temple into his hairline. *'Au revoir*, fair Phoebe. I shall rejoin my men.' Phoebe glanced up the street. The little group of National Guardsmen had

328

disappeared, but Maurice moved away quickly to catch up with them, walking with a spring in his step.

The woman in front of Phoebe had turned to watch her; she pursed her lips in a smile as if to say, 'Aren't you the lucky one to have such a fine handsome sergeant.' Phoebe bowed her head and pulled her shawl tighter, staring hard at a worn seam in her glove.

Maurice had been drinking but not to excess. He walked steadily toward the Rue St-Antoine as the dawn lightened the buildings and the sun shone on the frost-whitened pavement. He felt exhilarated by his encounter with Phoebe. To come upon her so unexpectedly had been a sign from God, he was sure of it. He recalled his glimpse of her in the queue of half-frozen women; he had not been sure at first that he recognised her in the faded shawl and carrying a wicker basket like any Parisienne, so patient and brave, like the spirit of Paris herself in this crippling siege. Phoebe was, it was true, a member of the bourgeoisie, like her brother and Antoine he reminded himself, but her birth was an accident of fate and her heart was with the workers. She had told him how she sympathised with the employees in her father's foundry. He remembered how moved she had been at the plight of the people of Belleville.

Maurice had cherished desirous thoughts of Phoebe from their earliest meetings, producing them in his mind at will to cheer bleak moments, discarding them when the revolution required his energies, and more recently rejecting his obsession altogether because of his disgust with Antoine and her brother. Yet a flame of his devotion had remained and now here it was entirely rekindled. He marvelled again at the coincidence of meeting her, his brave Englishwoman who had stayed on in Paris when so many of his own cowardly countrymen had deserted. He swung his rifle over his shoulder, recalling how nobly she had refused an advancement in the queue.

Maurice sustained this noble image of Phoebe when the long-expected bombardment started after Christmas; his first feelings were of elation, for at last something was happening and anything was better than the sense of inactivity which had for the past weeks infected the city. The first Prussian shells fell on the forts to the east: the attack continued for two days in a nerve-racking, searing bombardment. Then at the beginning of January the Prussians began on the southern forts and Paris itself with their 56-lb and 110-lb shells and Maurice began to fear for Phoebe's safety. The defence guns of Issy and Fort Vanves were soon silenced and the same day the bombardment of Paris proper began. Though the death toll at the forts was not particularly high, the first heavy shells to fall on Paris, slaughtering women and children in the heart of the Left Bank, had a terrifying effect on everyone. The cannonade could be heard all over the city; with it came the realisation that the enemy's fire power was greater than Paris's ability to defend herself.

Maurice, hearing one day that a balloon-factory workshop near the Gare d'Orléans had been hit, hurried there, his mind full of Phoebe. The building and cellar still stood but the workroom was stripped out by the explosion. The survivors wandered about in confusion. 'Some women were killed,' one of the bystanders said in answer to Maurice's frantic questions. Yes, they thought that an English worker may have been among them. He searched from street to street and went at last to the apartment near the Rue Rambuteau. There was no one there, the rooms were shut up and empty. A neighbour, weeping, for there were so many funerals these days, looked at him strangely and said, 'But sir, they have gone to the cemetery.'

* * *

This nightmare went on and on, thought Phoebe as she walked home with Bertrand and Tessa from the interment. All the way in the darkening streets half-starved women and children sat on their doorsteps. The distant boom of cannon accompanied their silent return from the cemetery. Bertrand, in civilian clothes instead of his uniform of the National Guard, was sunk in thought and distanced himself a little from the women. Thomas had died without any fuss, just slipped away from them as if the child was tired of struggling any longer. Bertrand shivered. The sky was a heavy slate colour and full of threatening snow and the air was damp and fiercely cold. He noticed how few trees were left on the outer boulevards, only the remains of where trees had stood with the protective iron railings torn away in the need to get at the source of firewood. The fuel which Bertrand brought home to the apartment was pillaged from a wood depot, but no one asked too many questions these days; the siege had turned even the most upright citizen into an opportunist who would steal wood from the nearest fence or railway station.

He glanced anxiously at Tessa who, since the child's death, had been as icy as the raw weather which touched their faces. She had not spoken all day. The cold froze their minds as well as their bodies, for Bertrand himself scarcely knew what day it was. He told himself it was for the best; the child would not have to endure whatever suffering was still to come. He had said so to Tessa, trying to comfort her, but she had shouted at him that he had no heart.

They reached the apartment as it was growing dark. The bombardment had already started up again. It was always heaviest at night. Several hundred shells fell each day with a regular pounding roll like the sound of approaching steam engines. There was a small reassurance in knowing that the Prussian guns could not reach this side of the Seine, though a shell had fallen on the Pont Notre-Dame which had frightened everyone out of their complacency. Bertrand opened the door and the women passed through and entered the almost pitch-dark vestibule below the apartment. As they started up the stairs a figure moved away from the wall and Tessa gave a little cry. Bertrand saw at once that the man was Maurice.

'What's *he* doing here!' Tessa clung to the bannister as if she had seen the devil himself.

Maurice gave a little bow, his *képi* in his hands. The gesture, thought Bertrand, was strangely touching for Maurice was not a man given to courtesy. He said that he knew of Thomas's death and wished to offer his condolences.

'Get out!' Tessa's voice was harsh from her long silence. 'You brought us bad luck right from the start. I don't want your bloody pity.'

She ran up the stairs and Bertrand stood for a moment. He said awkwardly, 'Thank you for your sympathy, Maurice,' and followed Tessa slowly, feeling close to tears to think that of all people Maurice should have come to see them.

'She blames herself,' Phoebe said when Bertrand and Tessa had gone, 'but it was the lack of milk – our diet has been so poor. It's very common among the infants.'

'It's better that the child should have perished now. Things can only get worse.'

'I know,' Phoebe sighed. 'And there are plenty of others as badly off but the knowledge is not much comfort tonight.'

'I came to look for you,' Maurice said as she hesitated on the stair. He told her about the shell which had destroyed the workshop.

'I must go to help them,' she said in alarm.

Maurice placed a restraining hand on her arm. 'The wounded have been taken to safety and you can do nothing there until the morning. The Prussians will soon see that they can't win by shelling the city,' he said confidently. 'The houses are too solid to be knocked down by a few shells and the more the people of Paris are bullied the more determined they will become not to surrender.'

'The people may not. But what about the government?'

'If they sign an armistice now they will be signing their own death warrant.' There was an echo in his words of his old rhetoric, yet Phoebe knew that many others shared the same view. Since the bombardment had begun the mood of resistance was increasing; red-dyed posters had appeared in the streets, signed by *the Delegates of the Twenty Arrondissements*, which called as they had in October for the government to be replaced by the Commune; and though the Red leaders were locked in the Mazas gaol the revolutionary newspapers had renewed their attacks on the government.

'There's going to be another sortie,' said Maurice.

Phoebe's heart sank, remembering the disasters of the previous sorties. 'Will your battalion take part?' She felt a sudden concern for Maurice, for so many had been killed the last time and hearing of the deaths of Georges and Henri had been a shock.

'Try keeping us away.' Maurice swung his rifle on his shoulder with some of his old swagger.

'But there have been so many calamities.'

'Not this time. This time it will be different.'

Phoebe crossed to the Left Bank the following morning. Many of the houses were damaged with shell-splinters. In one street a row of first-floor balconies was ripped away and hung over the pavement. She went to the workshop and found a few of her fellow workers picking over the debris. She set to work with the others, trying to create order out of the muddle. They swept away broken glass from the windows and shifted the rubble from the sewing-machines, talking in low voices about their comrades who had been hurt and Phoebe grieved a little for the two women who had been killed.

At midday everyone went home. Shells were falling again in the area and they had been told that the balloon production was to be moved to the north of the city at the Gare de l'Est where they should all begin work the next day.

People were flocking across the bridges as Phoebe made her way home, some pushing handcarts piled with their possessions, a thin exodus without panic, from the Left Bank districts towards the relative safety of the city centre. The crash of shells filled the air to the south. Resignation showed on most faces, but it was a resignation tinged with anger because the enemy had dared to strike at their city.

'This time it will be different,' Maurice had said of the sortie. And the crowds on the boulevards had thought so too as they cheered the troops marching out of Paris.

It was no different. Four thousand dead and wounded and more than a third of them from the National Guard. The Reds were blaming the leadership, but everyone knew that, whoever was to blame, there was nothing left now except capitulation. Trochu had called for a three-day armistice to bury the dead.

Bertrand had been spared the horror of another sortie: his commander had given him compassionate leave because of the child. But he heard about the confused marches in the slush and mud, the chaos of soldiers finding themselves separated from their companies and in the end men refusing to obey orders and firing against their own side. He thanked God he had not been there, for he knew he would have disgraced himself as a coward. Some said that the sortie had been a cynical ploy on the part of the government to allay the threat of revolution by reducing the numbers of the National Guard. But the Reds had demanded this sortie louder than anyone; they must take some of the blame.

Bertrand almost welcomed his return to the hours of Guard duty for he was at his wits' end how to comfort Tessa who seemed not to understand what was happening around her. She refused to eat the ingenious hot-water-and-wine soups Phoebe concocted from bones and meagre vegetables, which with black bread formed their staple diet. The bread, made of rice and oats, was heavy and tasted of sawdust with a smell of Paris gutters. Once, Phoebe had bought jam made from molasses and horse gelatine, but they had tried it and it had made them sick. The bread too made them ill. It was the poor food which had diminished Tessa's milk and made Thomas scour badly towards the end – if only Tessa would talk about the child. Her lovely features had grown sallow, her once-provocative body was thin and weak and her yellow hair in which she had taken such a pride was lifeless and unkempt.

She sat facing the balcony window in the sitting room and said little when he left for his battalion, asking only what day it was and, on being told that it was a Sunday and that he was to go back on Guard duty she said, 'But I can't hear the church bells.'

'We will have another death in the house if something doesn't happen soon,' Phoebe thought sadly. She stood on the balcony and waved as Bertrand walked away down the street. She let her hand drop when he had gone and stared across the street at the houses opposite. They were dreary in the grey light of morning; many of them had been abandoned by their occupants. She recalled how, when she had heard of the latest defeat she had begun to pray for miracles, like the women in the bread queues who called on Saint Geneviève, the patron saint of Paris, to help them. She wondered what her father would have said, had he known that she had indulged in such papist idolatry. But there was no way of knowing what he might have said, not even in response to the letters she sent each month, nor whether he had received them. The sense of isolation from the world outside had a peculiar effect on one's mind: it was as if everyone except the Prussians had forgotten them. It was a situation which made one jumpy and ready to get excited about anything.

People had taken to the boulevards again since the sortie, shouting that they were being betrayed. There must be no surrender; the people of Paris would fight on. Trochu had been forced to resign because of what had happened and his place as Governor of Paris was taken by Vinoy, but everyone knew that an armistice was inevitable.

Phoebe rubbed her arms to warm them and turned to the room where Tessa sat rocking herself a little in her chair.

'You've not been here much lately,' Tessa said suddenly.

Phoebe sighed, expecting her to be clinging and dependent today, as she had been when Thomas was ill. 'I've been at the workshop,' she said patiently. She was glad it was a Sunday for it was hard to drag herself from the apartment and walk to the Gare de l'Est each day to sit and stitch at her sewing-machine with half-frozen fingers.

'Perhaps I could go to a workshop too.'

Phoebe stared, startled by the practicality of Tessa's suggestion, but she was distracted by the sound of someone shouting in the street and, straining her ears to catch the latest news, heard a woman scream to her neighbour that some of the Reds had sprung Flourens from gaol.

Phoebe went to the small heap of firewood in the hearth to prepare the fire for lighting that evening. She wondered what would happen now that Flourens had escaped, and thought of Maurice. Antoine said he had returned unharmed from the latest sortie and she had felt a passionate thankfulness because he was safe. She bowed her head over her knees, overcome all at once with weariness, sickened by the siege and its trail of disasters.

'The mob will be flocking in their thousands to the Hôtel de Ville again,' Tessa said.

Phoebe looked at her, hope growing at the strength of Tessa's voice.

'I told you when I was with Charlie I wasn't a good wife and mother. You said we'd a duty as women to try.'

Phoebe said, her own voice trembling a little, 'I remember. I tried to quote the Bible and you said that thinking for yourself was more important than being dutiful.'

'So it is.' Tessa gave her a twisted smile. 'I suppose some of these Frenchies could teach us a thing or two about that.' Her voice held no trace of self-pity as she added, 'Looks like I've failed them both – Thomas and poor little William.' She stood up suddenly and came to the fireplace, crouching beside Phoebe on the carpet. She took the bundle of sticks from her and began to lay them neatly for the evening fire. 'So I'd best start trying harder.'

Phoebe rejoiced at the revival of Tessa's old spirit. She went the next morning to the workshop with a lighter heart than she had known for weeks. In the afternoon came news that there had been a demonstration at the Hôtel de Ville: the Guardes Mobiles and some extremists from the National Guard had been shooting at one another.

Phoebe hurried home that evening, afraid that the noise from the demonstration might have disturbed Tessa. She arrived at the apartment to find Maurice sitting on the stair in the darkness of the vestibule.

'I hoped you weren't there among the other hot-heads,' she said, sitting down suddenly beside him.

'It was a rabble, not a proper revolution.' Maurice was disparaging. 'Delescluze and Flourens would have nothing to do with it, nor Blanqui, though I expect the government will try to arrest them again and say they were behind it all.'

'Is it true women and children were killed?'

Maurice shrugged. 'Only a few. People shouldn't have panicked.'

'But shooting one another!'

'Does that go against your English sensibilities?'

She was shocked by his flippancy. 'No. It goes against all moral and Christian sensibilities.'

'Ah – that,' he said with a sneer.

'And what will happen now?' wondered Phoebe out loud.

He put his arm round her. 'There will be an armistice, and you will be able to go home.'

From the darkening street beyond the open entrance doors she could hear the faint boom of the bombardment. She let her head rest against Maurice's shoulder and felt a comfort in the weight of his arm round her. He smelled strongly of wine and cigarettes and garlic and his tunic was dirty, but even the pungency of him was reassuring.

'I have brought you something.' Maurice pulled a dead pigeon from inside his tunic, quickly followed by another, and dropped them in her lap. 'A peace offering.'

She touched the limp bodies of the birds in wonder for she had not seen fresh meat for two months. 'You must come up to the apartment,' she said. 'Bertrand will be here later. It will do him good to see you.' She remembered Tessa then, recalling her hostility, and Maurice, remembering it too, shook his head.

'Another day perhaps.' He smiled and she saw the gleam of his teeth in the darkness as he pulled her close with an unexpected tenderness; his lips were warm on hers and she felt the strength go from her and a longing for him to hold her until this terrible siege was over.

They read the newspapers avidly: Jules Favre had spent two days in discussions with Bismarck. There was to be a three-week armistice when France would be allowed to elect an Assembly which would either settle peace terms or decide to continue the war.

'It's capitulation. No one can be in any doubt about it,' said Antoine when he came to visit them. 'A war indemnity of two hundred million francs! The forts of Paris and the entire army to be surrendered! They have left us nothing!'

Tessa brought them wine. 'Something. The National Guard is to remain under arms.'

Phoebe went to the window. She could hear someone shouting drunkenly that 'Paris would never give in!', demanding another sortie against the Prussian devils, as if the poor man was still trapped in the fantasy of the unconquerable city. 'At least it will be an end to it all,' she said.

Antoine laughed, as if surprised by her naivety. 'My dear Phoebe, when the government signs the peace treaty it will be only the start of the shooting.'

Sixteen

The lion of freedom's let loose from his den,
And we'll rally around him again and again.

Chartist song

Edwin read the news of the capitulation of Paris from the newspaper. 'What a humiliation!'

Charles had formed a habit of spending the occasional evening at Belle Vue, begun when he and his father were discussing the remodelling of the lion and continuing out of habit. Their company with one another was an expedient, an acknowledgement that they were both alone and – since Charles's enforced segregation from Christina – lonely. They were bound by ties of family and by the lion project, but there was no warmth in their alliance; Charles remembered too well the years when his father had shunned his company. He waited for him to lay down the newspaper and turn the pages of the Bible to the text for the evening. He anticipated something on the wages of sin, for according to his father, that profligate nation France had brought all its suffering on itself – not to mention on his daughter. One day, Charles promised himself, one day I shall tell him I'm not going to listen to any more of his damned sermons.

'There's a moral in all this, lad.' Edwin folded the

newspaper carefully. 'Never start a fight you can't finish.' He stood, wheezing a little, and went to the study to fetch his Bible.

'At least Phoebe will be safe and might be able to come home now,' called Charles.

Edwin did not reply and Charles thought he had not heard, or else he had angered him. After a moment he heard his footsteps recross the hall.

His father opened the heavy book on his knees, looking pensive as he selected a suitable text in his mind. Perhaps thankfulness that Phoebe was now safe would prevail and they would have one of the Psalms instead of the anticipated thunderings on the wages of sin. But to Charles's surprise his father, with a catch in his voice, chose a passage from the book of Jeremiah about the regathering of the tribes of Israel.

He watched Edwin's lips move, '. . . *thy work shall be rewarded saith the Lord; and they shall come again from the land of the enemy . . .*' He studied the way the old man sat, hands folded precisely on the edge of the book, head lifted with an arrogant confidence in his right to use the Good Book to corroborate his moral thoughts for the day. The old man was fooling himself if he was cherishing ideas about the regathering of the Cloughs; even Gerald had been talking on the sly lately about getting away from Griseley and starting up a theatre company in Leeds. Did his father still think that Bertrand would return? Bertrand might, like himself, have been a fool over Tessa, but he was clever enough to have escaped. And I would get away too if I could, Charles thought sadly. If I had the courage I'd go far away from Griseley.

He thought of Christina with sadness. Their friendship had dwindled to the occasional chance meetings during the past months: social occasions arranged by mutual acquaintances, whist drives and parties, or the rare encounters in the town. Charles had stuck rigidly to the principle that he must preserve her from further scandal at all costs, but Christina seemed disappointed in him. She had said once that she regretted the fact that 'poor William' would not have a playfellow at Chillingdale and he had felt guilty for his son's sake, yet he sensed too that she concealed more in her 'regret' than she had disclosed. If only things had been different. If he had not been such an idiot over Tessa or if he had paid attention to Christina's virtues sooner.

He wondered as he listened to his father's voice whether Phoebe might never come back. She had been in France for the best part of a year. They had all of course worried about his sister's surviving a state of war and siege in a foreign country, and the thought that he might not see her again saddened him, though in all honesty, he had grown used to Griseley without her. His father too, though he had worried, and complained about managing without her, had employed a housekeeper just before Christmas to make his domestic life more comfortable, as if he had begun to accept Phoebe's absence as permanent. How easy it was to carry on as if she no longer existed.

'. . . *How long wilt thou go about, o thou backsliding daughter?*' read Edwin, his voice rising and booming, indicating a sudden self-pity.

Charles wanted to laugh. Why shouldn't Phoebe 'go about'? What if she *did* stay in France now all the danger was over? He wished her well.

Sarah sat at the kitchen table dreaming a little and plaiting the fringe of the tablecloth, for Sarah was in love.

Her mother tapped her wrist as she passed. 'Nothing better to do this morning?'

Sarah sighed, wishing it was Sunday, for she walked out

with her beau on Sundays. She began clearing the breakfast pots from the table.

'The Devil makes work for idle hands!' said Kitty.

'That old devil Clough would be quick enough to agree with you.' Jack was tying his neckcloth in the mirror. He bent and kissed his mother's cheek and Walter, taking his turn at the mirror, said, 'That old devil's got us poor devils working for nothing again on another go at a mould for Mister Charles's bloody lion next week.'

'Don't swear, and don't be disrespectful about Mr Clough,' said Sarah piously, for her beau, a clerk in Underwood's railway company and staunch chapel-goer and choir member, frowned heavily on swearing.

Kitty offered her cheek to Walter to kiss and followed them to the door. 'Edwin Clough's got more to think about than lions now the war in France looks like it's all over.'

'We shall give him summat else to think about an' all,' said Walter. 'He promised six months back to put up our wages come January. It's time someone reminded him.' He looked at Jack who did not respond.

Kitty watched them cross the yard. A hen with bedraggled feathers walked across their path, pecking at the cobbles near the yard pump, its rubbery wattle trembling at it moved its head. Walter aimed a kick at it and sent it squawking to the stable in a flurry of feathers. Jack turned to her with a little troubled smile at the edge of his mouth as they went under the arch and out on to the street.

Kitty returned to the kitchen where Sarah was still clearing pots. She was puzzled by the look behind that smile. Was there going to be trouble and Jack worrying about being made spokesman for the men again? He set such store by the Workers' Association's way of working things out.

* * *

Jack was silent as they joined the early morning march of workers on the hill.

'What do you reckon? Is Clough going to take notice of *negotiations* and *delegations* this time?' said Walter, trying to rile him. He was only echoing the talk which had been going on at the foundry for some days. There would be plenty more of it that morning, along with talk about the surrender of Paris. Jack kicked at a stone. He did not want to think about the possibility of Phoebe's coming home, yet Phoebe kept nudging herself unbidden into his thoughts.

'I reckon Clough might listen to us,' he said and continued down the hill, ignoring Walter's scepticism and banging his dinner can against his knee. He had no real heart for another confrontation with Edwin Clough. He thought of the new play which Gerald had written for the theatre company, but even the thought of rehearsals starting afresh made him feel unsettled. Jack knew people had started linking his name with Cissy, Gerald's new comedy actress. He wanted nothing more to do with women. Women were the cause of all the trouble in the world. Wasn't it the French Empress who had egged on the Emperor to start a fight with Prussia and now the poor fellow was a prisoner in Germany? And wasn't it that Tessa who was the cause of Edwin Clough's family troubles? They reached the foundry and saw Clough himself walk across the yard to the work-shed with a spring in his step. It was clearly lions not daughters Edwin Clough had on his mind that morning.

Edwin walked into the work-shed where Gerald was watching Charles put the final touches to the model for the lion. This second attempt, though somewhat decreased in size, was no less bold and fearsome in appearance. Edwin stood rubbing his hands, regarding the sculpture critically, a little disappointed it was true by the reduction, but he told himself it was hardly noticeable.

'Well, it seems it's all over,' Gerald said to his father.

'Over?' Edwin looked at the new lion which had obsessed his every waking thought for the past four months.

'The French. The capitulation. There's no going back on it now.'

'What about our foundrymen? I don't think *they've* capitulated from what I've been hearing,' Charles said ironically.

Edwin frowned for he too had heard that the men were agitating again for an increase in wages. 'They're only happy if they've got something to grumble over.'

'You did promise to review their hours and wages this year.'

'I promised no such thing.'

'Not in so many words perhaps, but it was understood, when you agreed to reinstate their old wages, that you'd review the situation six months on,' said Gerald.

'Not by me it wasn't.' Edwin wagged a finger. 'They're not ruining me just when trade's starting to pick up.'

Charles turned back to the sculpture. 'Casting the lion is bound to start them off again.'

'I thought we were talking about the war in France.' Edwin was irritated. He had not wanted to think of life's more disagreeable aspects this morning.

'Capitulation,' Gerald reminded him.

Edwin went to the door, deciding to ignore his son's strange sense of humour. 'I wonder how soon they'll let people leave the city.'

Charles began to consider the same question. If Phoebe did come home now, who was to say that Bertrand and Tessa might not come with her? He knew that Tessa would not come back to live with him, and the thought was repellent after all this time, but what if Bertrand should return to Christina?

Thus it was that when Charles drove to Chillingdale in the dogcart the following Sunday afternoon he was in an apprehensive state of mind, for Alfred Underwood had made a strange request: he had asked for a family conference between the Underwoods and the Cloughs.

Charles joined his father and Gerald in the drawing room where Beatrice Underwood in her Sunday best was making stilted small talk and Philip with a red face handed round biscuits.

'What's all this about?' Charles whispered to Gerald who twiddled his side-whiskers and stared thoughtfully at the Chinese carpet.

'Lord knows. Let's hope it's a thaw in the ice.'

Alfred began when they were all assembled; he cleared his throat, moved by his initiative in calling such a momentous meeting. 'Now, it's fitting, it being a sabbath, that we should all meet here in a mood of forbearance. As you'll appreciate, we Underwoods and Cloughs had been friends for many years before the unfortunate business last year—'

'When your libertine of a son deserted our daughter and ran off to France with that hussy!' Beatrice was less inclined to mince words.

Edwin, willing to show a united front at least this far, put in, 'That harlot! That Jezebel!'

Everyone looked at Charles as if expecting him to argue the point but he no longer cared what they said about Tessa. He glanced at Christina who had come last to the gathering and sat, very pale, her hair severely pulled back from her face, with her hands knotted together in her lap, and his mind leaped to its former anxiety that Bertrand had written to say that he was coming home.

'Whatever our feelings about the *female* party,' said Alfred, 'we all know that the war in France is over, and it's fitting that we too should put our own little disagreement behind us.'

There was a hearty cry of 'Hear! Hear! An armistice,' from Gerald followed by an uncomfortable silence in which Gerald beamed unperturbed.

Alfred attempted a smile. 'Fair enough – an armistice.'

Beatrice interrupted: 'The point is – Bertrand might well come home now. We must all decide what to do.'

'Why should one do anything?' Charles felt his face grow hot.

'Because it's been the lad's duty all along to come back to his wife,' Beatrice said, giving way to a surge of anger.

Christina spoke up clearly: 'I don't want him to come back.'

'Of course you do.' Alfred threw a nervous glance at his wife. He signalled to Philip to hand round more biscuits. 'You need a husband and young Christopher needs a father.'

'I'd pick a different husband and father for my child if I could choose again.' Christina looked at Charles swiftly and with a significance which made his colour deepen.

'Well, you chose the one you did eighteen months since,' declared Beatrice.

'I didn't choose him. *You* did. You *all* did!' Christina included Edwin in her accusation.

'No one has mentioned Phoebe,' said Philip. They stared at him. 'Perhaps she'll come home without Bertrand. It strikes me when all's said and done it would be for the best all round. Shouldn't we be planning a welcome party?'

Charles stared at him dumbfounded. The man really was a fool. Welcome parties? When his and Christina's futures were at stake? But the suggestion had apparently appealed

348

to Beatrice for she was dabbing at her eyes.

'She has been a good girl, to go all that way among foreigners for the sake of family relationships and then get herself nearly killed and starved to death by the Prussians.' She glared at Christina. 'You're a very ungrateful child.'

Christina, taken aback, sought refuge in tears.

Alfred greeted Edwin at the next town-council meeting as if there had never been the slightest animosity between them. The Sunday conference had not gone quite as he had intended but at least the families were on speaking terms again.

But Edwin sat in the council chamber with a heavy heart and a burden of guilt: the foundry was to cast the new lion in a week or so and he had not yet broken the news to the council that the finished statue did not conform to the original plan. He speculated as to whether the proposed size had been recorded in the minutes, and pictured Wormauld's and Murgatroyd's reactions to his announcement. He felt himself begin to sweat under his broadcloth coat.

The meeting reached the subject of the lions rather sooner than Edwin had hoped. In fact the subject of lions had risen with alarming regularity at council meetings since the failure of the casting the previous summer. He had disguised the miscalculation in the melt variously as 'a minor setback, inevitable considering the singular nature of the casting', and 'an unavoidable technical error'.

'When can we plan for the inauguration ceremony?' Larkin the bank manager voiced the question which recurred with the most monotonous predictability.

'We shall recast the first statue in a week or so,' said Edwin, 'and then there will be the other three, and the finishing touches – fettling and suchlike.'

'I heard you're having trouble with your workers again,' said Wormauld.

'Well, it isn't true,' said Edwin.

'We appreciate you've had a few difficulties,' said Alfred, 'but we were wondering when we might count for sure on the lions being finished.' His expression took into account a friendship recently restored to its former sympathy. Yet there was in his smile an awareness that his own part in healing the rift – not to mention his recollection of past injuries – made him morally the superior of the two. 'After all, there are arrangements to be made. Invitations to be sent out. We want to make a bit of a splash.'

'We can't do with indiscipline among the workers,' said Murgatroyd. 'We only need a few of them palavering on soapboxes, denouncing their masters, turning themselves into martyrs. Look at France. Revolution and riot, that's all that leads to. The rule of the mob!'

'There's no trouble,' insisted Edwin, feeling the sweat trickle down his back.

'I don't think there's much fear of mob rule in Griseley,' soothed Alfred.

'Don't you be so sure.' Murgatroyd looked at Edwin darkly. 'And if it comes we shall know where to look for the blame.'

'Well then – shall we fix on a date for the ceremony?' Alfred pressed. 'The king of beasts, nobly done by young Charles, will I'm sure justify the long wait.'

'How do we know it's going to be nobly done?' Wormauld was sceptical. 'No one's seen sight nor sound of it yet.'

'I promise you, gentlemen, that the council will be the first to view the finished casting.' Edwin sent a silent prayer heavenward. 'And if you're not satisfied—'

'Of course we shall be satisfied. We saw the drawings.

We've got great faith in Charles's skills,' said Alfred.

'You promised us it would take a year some eighteen months since,' grumbled Wormauld. 'Does your Charles know what he's about? He seems to work mighty slow.'

'These professional London sculptors have assistants to make up rough models for the sculptor to finish,' Edwin bridled. 'Our Charles has done it all by himself. There isn't a square inch that isn't the work of his own hands.'

'Aye – and those hands got it wrong first time.'

'Perhaps you shouldn't have been so ambitious,' suggested one of the other councillors.

'I might remind you who's bearing the cost of it all. Which, when all's said and done, will set me back a thousand pounds or more' – much more, Edwin thought grimly.

'We must be patient, gentlemen,' put in Alfred. He smiled again at Edwin. 'One day we shall behold the lions in their full glory. Meanwhile I'm sure it's only the council's enthusiasm for the project which prompts these anxieties.'

Larkin confirmed this sentiment. 'We're impatient, Edwin, to see the quartet grace our town hall, the four glorious beasts making it the central point of the municipality.'

'How about July?' pressed Murgatroyd.

Edwin threw up a second silent prayer for divine blessing and nodded, hearing Alfred say, 'July it is then.'

Edwin fell silent. How could he tell them now that the lions would not appear in quite the glory they expected? Three foot short of glory to be exact.

Gerald had begun rehearsals on the theatre company's next production. 'The last to be performed in Griseley!' he told Olive and the resident members of the cast who were seated round the table in the dining room.

Olive smiled tolerantly and wondered whether this time he meant it; she had heard him declare that he was leaving

Griseley and his father's foundry so many times before.

'Will you come with me, lads and lasses?' He turned to Victor and the others.

'Just say the word,' said Victor.

'*Lead on Macduff! And cursed be he who first cries "Hold! Enough!"*' declaimed Lamplugh Dare.

Olive yawned delicately, wondering how she could ever have found Lamplugh's way with words seductive.

'That's the spirit.' Gerald pulled his pocket-watch from his waistcoat. 'Time for rehearsal. The natives will be arriving.'

Olive linked her arm through Gerald's and they led the way to the theatre annexe. Victor and Lamplugh, Lulu and Ben Dunn crowded eagerly into the corridor. They would follow Gerald anywhere, thought Olive. They adored him, and so did she in her own way – when she was not adoring Victor with his solid and muscular child-man's body or Ben's multifaceted talent for amusement, but would he really ever find the courage to tell his father he was leaving?

'You realise that if we do go—' she paused, letting the significance of leaving Griseley hang in the air, 'none of the players except the family will come with us.'

Gerald lit the gas in the theatre. 'I am counting on one other.'

Olive turned to see Jack arrive and hang his coat over one of the front stall benches. His body was broad under his shirt and waistcoat and she felt a warm sense of pleasure to see him. Then, startled, she saw Gerald's tender gaze. Did he not guess that Jack was to be hers? Or was he going to get his own back over Victor? 'Are you sure?' she said lightly. 'Jack has got very wrapped up in trade-union business lately.'

'It has helped him. It's nurtured his self-respect, expanded his capacity for broader thinking, elevated him as an individual. Jack knows now there is a better life for him than that at Clough's Foundry.'

Olive smiled and she and Gerald shared a look, an expression of suspicion mixed with a long-standing tolerance, but in the main a look which suggested a drawing up of battle lines. 'I suspect the poor boy knows very little of what awaits him,' said Olive.

Jack no longer felt like an outsider among the theatre players. He treated Victor and the others and they him with the affection of old friends. He was to play the lead in the new play, yet none of the established members of the company resented the fact. At rehearsals each week the cast read through *And All That Makes a Man*, a tragedy of Gerald's own invention, inspired by events in France and set in a mythical land, a cross between a southern European principality and Macbeth's Scottish Highlands – a device which saved on scenery. Jack was to play a rebel leader who roused his followers to rise up against the tyranny of a despotic ruler. The despot was played with relish by Gerald, his beautiful queen by Olive. The plot was heightened by the rebel leader's love for the tyrant's beautiful wife whom he persuaded to their cause and was further complicated by the devotion to the rebel leader of a peasant girl, played by the new girl Cissy. The play reached a climax in a battle scene in which the hero died touchingly in the peasant girl's arms, followed by the tyrant's conversion to the ways of a beneficent monarch aided by his enlightened queen.

Jack thought it was going to be a splendid production. He knew many of his lines already. *True change is impossible without revolution . . . the rights of man know no boundaries of class or creed.* He was to be the archetypal rebel with a cause – a Latin Rob Roy, a kilted Garibaldi. He left rehearsals in the evenings knowing that there was no more satisfying world than that of make-believe.

Steeped in the doctrine of equality for the common man, he began to view the foundry in a different light. The week was fast approaching for the recasting of Clough's lion and the foundrymen had become more insistent in their opinion that it was time the Griseley Bronze-Founders' and Metal-Workers' Society did more for them than gobble up their twopence-a-week subscription. Jack, leaning towards the same opinion, agreed to attempt a negotiation for a rise in wages. The society had presented their request in the form of a petition, which had received no response from Clough. Jack said he would go alone, 'man to man', Clough wasn't a monster: the rights of man knew no boundaries of class and no one was entirely closed to reason.

William Burns clapped him on the back but his brothers declared little faith in his mission. 'He'll send thee packing,' said Walter sceptically. 'Clough won't budge through talking. He never has done yet.'

Jack was aware of a touch of stage fright as he mounted the steps to the office one day in February. Patches of ice adhered to the wooden steps and his breath froze upon the glass of the office door as he leaned forward to listen for an answer to his knock. At least Clough had not refused to see him, and he must know by now what it was all about, for there had been the petition and the men had been hollering again since January for more for the work on the lions; the whole town must know by now that there was a dispute on hand.

'Come in, Jack.' Gerald opened the door and drew him inside, his hand firm on his arm. A low coal fire burned in the grate and Edwin sat in his coat at his desk. He was reading a letter and ignored him until Gerald said, 'Father, Jack Bateman's here.'

Jack hoped that Gerald would stay, for he needed moral support and he was sure that after writing his play about revolution Gerald was firmly on the side of the men.

Edwin looked up. 'Is this another deputation?'

'The men have sent me, sir.'

'To beard the lion in his den,' Gerald said cheerfully, but his father did not smile.

'Perhaps he's the young lion out for his first kill.'

'I don't know about that, sir.' Jack wished Clough would not talk in figures of speech as well as his son; it had a way of disarming him.

Edwin leaned back in his chair and pressed the tips of his mittened fingers together. 'You know I disapprove of your society.'

'It was formed, sir, as a benefit society for the men and for the purpose of putting us on a fairer footing when it comes to bargaining for wages.'

'For the benefit of the men's greed more like.'

'That's not so. For long enough the men agreed to take a drop in wages and to work on your terms.'

'But I myself remember a controversy some months since, occasioned by the men's refusal to stick with the lower wage rate, a refusal which has cost the firm dear.'

'The society wasn't accountable for the loss of business.'

'You and your society attacked me when I was at my most low,' Edwin said angrily.

They were silent. Gerald stared out of the window and said nothing. Why did he not speak in his support? thought Jack. Surely he knew the men had been in the right?

'The men only want what's fair. We'll not agree that we've done any injury to trade. Or that we are in any way responsible for the management's blunders.' He saw Gerald blink. Had he gone too far?

'If you've come for more money, you're wasting your

time.' Edwin returned his attention to the letter on his desk.

'I've come because of the petition.'

'I know of no petition.'

'Sir, we hoped you'd read it and be prepared to discuss terms with us.'

'Well, you hoped wrong. And I don't discuss matters with my foundrymen, I *tell* them what to do.'

Jack felt his temper rise. 'I think you should know sir, the society regards your obstinate attitude as a great injustice to the men.'

'Does it indeed? Wasn't it your own obstinate attitude that forced me to an agreement to reinstate your old wage?'

'It was only fair. And it's only fair now that you reconsider our rates of pay, since six months in profit have passed.'

'You cheeky beggar!' Edwin banged his fist on the desk. 'You tell me what's right and fair! You cheeky beggar! You don't know when you're well off.'

'There's nowt wrong with expecting a fair day's pay for a fair day's work.' Jack felt his determination to keep the atmosphere reasonable begin to slip. *'The rights of man know no boundaries of class or creed,'* he said and saw Gerald flush a bright red at hearing his own words quoted. He knew then that he was alone and he would get no help from his mentor. He saw too that Clough was not going to give way an inch, was not even going to listen to his case. Matt and Walter were right, there was no sense in jawing about it. He attempted one last appeal to reason. 'I should warn you, sir, the society are prepared to strike – they are prepared *for* a strike and will have support of other unions in the area.'

'Unions!' shouted Clough. 'Societies! Associations! They should be declared unlawful. My foundry workers used to look to me for approval, they used to be proud to give satisfaction and stand well in their employer's eyes.'

'Aye and what you're talking about is slavery,' said Jack angrily. 'The worker shouldn't be subject to the master's rule over what's a fair deal – he wants to be able to defend his own rights.'

'Get out!'

'If you won't agree to even talk with us the men will quit work to a man.'

'Get out!'

Gerald opened the door. He whispered, 'Well done, my hearty,' but Jack ignored him as he pushed his way past him to the door.

Gerald stared out of the window. He watched Jack cross the yard with his hands thrust deep in his pockets, an angry swing to his step. How at ease the working man was with his own body when passion made him forget his inhibitions. He admired the breadth of Jack's back and shoulders and supple lower body. He must make sure that Olive devised a costume which would enhance that so-appealingly lusty physique. The dear boy had spoken up well. He would congratulate him properly later, but what a pity that things were going to get difficult again and life would be tiresome for a while. Oh, how pleasant it would be to walk out from the office for ever and take Jack with him, shaking the foundry dust from their heels.

There was a silence in the office.

'Phoebe is going to stay.'

Gerald turned from the window and looked at his father in surprise.

Edwin held the letter which he had been reading. There was a quieter note of fury in his voice and his hand was trembling. 'Read it!' He flapped the page on to his desk and jabbed at the neatly penned lines.

Tessa is very weak and needs me still—

357

Edwin interrupted. 'She's going to stay on because of that whore!'

'Phoebe always did feel a great sympathy for anyone in need,' suggested Gerald. 'Perhaps now things are returning to normal in Paris it won't be long before Tessa's well and doesn't rely on her any more.'

Edwin looked at him in amazement. '*She* rely on Phoebe! What about me? Her father!'

The committee was quick to propose strike action. Jack, who did not believe in strikes, who knew that differences with employers should be settled by discussion, found himself for once in agreement with Walter. The only way to make Clough see sense was through action.

'Call the men off work,' he told William Burns. 'We'll stand up to him this time.'

A cheer rose from the committee. Walter slapped him on the back. 'That's fighting talk, lad.'

'Nothing but trouble will come of this,' groaned Kitty when she heard. Joseph told her there were times when a man had to make a stand.

'The whole of the foundry is coming out,' said Walter with satisfaction. 'Even that cautious lot in the machine shop. Reckon we'll have most of the town behind us this time.'

The men from Clough's did not go to the foundry the following Monday but made their way to an open-air meeting in front of the town hall. Many had spent the weekend making placards, announcing their grievances to the world at large and inviting the workers of Griseley to show sympathy for their cause.

William Burns said they must begin by singing a hymn to put the townspeople's minds at ease and show they were a law-abiding gathering with God on their side. Jack stood on the town hall steps with the other delegates and wondered, as they sang a thin but energetic 'Fight the Good Fight', how God could be on Edwin Clough's side and that of the strikers at the same time.

The committee had decided that Jack must speak first, since he was at the centre of what might pass for negotiations with the master. 'You must begin by explaining your credentials,' said William Burns. 'Say how you're a God-fearing man and a good worker.'

'But they all know who I am,' protested Jack.

'Makes no matter. It's the way it's done.'

Jack climbed the steps near one of the pillars of the town hall in order to be seen and to view his audience. He looked to right and left and saw on all sides a sea of faces, for the workers' meeting had attracted a large crowd from the town. 'Friends and fellow workers—'

'Speak up Jack, there's a good lad,' someone shouted and the listeners, who were in a good-natured mood, cheered.

'You all know me and those with me. We're all of us honest-hearted men, not a few of us are teetotallers and chapel-goers.'

'Speak for yourself,' someone cried.

'Many of you have families to support and rent to pay. You know what a struggle it is to keep body and soul together and how it feels to see our masters ride about in fine carriages telling us we must be content to struggle, because that's how the world's ordained.'

There were cries of affirmation.

'Our employer, Mr Clough, has refused to listen to our request for mutual co-operation, and in consequence we are compelled to call a strike today. If Mr Clough wants to spend his money on statues to decorate this very nice town-hall building – which to my mind looks well enough as it is

– well, that's his own concern. But he'll not puff up his pride at our expense.'

A roar of approval rose from the foundry workers, but the rest of those present began to look uncertain and a few from the better end of town, among them men and women personally acquainted with Edwin Clough, turned away murmuring among themselves.

'We've been told we should be grateful for t' crumbs from the masters' tables for too long,' Matt cried, gaining courage from Jack's success.

'Down with Clough and his kind!' yelled Walter, and others took up the cry.

Out of the corner of his eye Jack saw women hurrying their children away. He raised his hands for silence. 'We don't wish harm to any man. Nor do we wish to injure Mr Clough by our actions. We only want our rights. It's the obligation of our employer to pay a fair day's wage for a fair day's work. We want no more than that – a modest enough request, you might say, and why not? We're modest men.' There was a ripple of laughter. 'Last July we were in no position to strike; this time we have our society and the area Trades' Association to back us so that none shall starve.'

'Except Clough – God willing!' shouted one of the men.

'Aye – we'll show him!' yelled Walter. 'See who gives in first!'

Jack had seen a posse of constables approaching from the corner of the square. There was an edging movement towards the steps of the town hall as others caught sight of the local force for law and order and Jack looked to William Burns to continue or close the meeting. 'Make it short,' he urged as Burns shouted, his voice hoarse from excitement, 'Fellow workers, we shall be receiving first subscriptions towards the strike fund from Sunday at the Nag's Head, where we shall also pay out weekly strike pay as of Monday next. I'll thank you please to disperse in an orderly fashion.'

The police constables stood at the corner of the square, affecting a cavalier indifference to the sudden peaceable break-up of the meeting as men filed past them and dispersed in various directions. The members of the strike committee moved to the park to stand in little knots with a wary eye on the uniformed men and talking amongst themselves. After a short hesitation the constables swung away and returned the way they had come.

'Do you reckon Clough called out the Constabulary?' said Walter.

'If he did, he'll be disappointed.' Jack watched the retreating police with a strong sense of having scored a moral victory. 'There'll be no reading the riot act while I've got anything to do with it.'

Edwin was baffled by his men's action. Men should be grateful to be in work, like he had been when he was an apprentice, not shouting, 'Down with the masters!'

'They should be looking to me, as the master, to tell them what's right,' he complained to Wormauld after a chapel prayer meeting one evening. He confided in his fellow councillor with reluctance, for he suspected that Wormauld and Murgatroyd, though keen enough on Christian brotherhood in chapel, lacked Christian charity outside the Ebenezer and that they were enjoying his discomfort.

'It's all unions and societies nowadays,' agreed Wormauld. 'And for no other reason than to injure us as employers.'

'And if they injure me, don't they in the end do harm to themselves?' Edwin's usual ebullience had sunk to a pitiable protest. 'Where do they think the work's going to come from, if not by my efforts?'

'What about the lions?' Murgatroyd, detecting a conversation to which he should be a party, had hurried down the steps of the chapel. 'You told us the new one was waiting for casting.'

Edwin stared up the street, unable to meet Murgatroyd's challenge. The lights of the Nag's Head seemed to wink at him insolently and he felt a surge of impotent fury against the Batemans, the source of all the trouble. 'The men will be back soon enough to get on wi' the casting. They'll soon break, with no regular wage.'

'Seems they've got money enough still for drinking,' remarked Murgatroyd, following his gaze.

Edwin bade his fellow councillors good evening and walked to his carriage with heavy dignity. Henstridge's respectful, 'Straight home, sir?' was reassuring. He did not look back as the carriage moved off up the hill, but he sensed that the other men were watching him, and that they were talking still about the fate of the lions. He did not look to right nor left as Henstridge drove past the Nag's Head. 'They'll soon break,' he murmured to himself, but his hunched figure and troubled frown demonstrated less certainty.

The strike committee relied heavily on subscriptions brought by delegates from the other local towns where sympathy among iron founders and engineering workers was strong. The queue of men which lined up in the tap room for their weekly strike pay was lighthearted at first. As the weeks drew on the mood grew more sombre.

Matt had said with the others that he would not break before Clough did, but as he looked at the few shillings in his hand each Monday, he felt a chill come over him. A wife and child were a drain on a man and no mistake. Gone were the days of roistering with Walter, when there had been only rent to pay to his father, not coal and food to find and, with Rebecca sick from a fever, things like doctors and medicine to square with. Marriage made a man of you all right.

Walter was still bruisingly cheerful, bragging about 'grinding Clough into the ground', but if they crushed Clough so hard the foundry went out of business – what then? What would become of his own and his brothers' livelihood? They knew nothing else but foundry work.

He scuffed his clogs on the pavement, passing the rows of shops in the dark. The open doors, inviting custom, the lighted windows, hung with beef and lamb carcases, or crammed with packets of groceries, seemed put there on purpose to taunt him. His mother occasionally pushed a wrapped piece of cheese or a few sausages into his pocket when he left the inn, but he knew she could scarcely afford to give him hand-outs with Jack and Walter to feed and takings gone down at the pub. Jack walked about with a worried look too these days, wondering how what he and William Burns had started was going to end. And Burns seemed to have shrunk, like an old man, Matt reflected, as he passed the end of the street where the other man lived. There would be little joy in that house for a while.

He turned into the alley, catching the stink of privies and the canal and the sooty smell from the railway all in one before he reached the back gate.

Rebecca was crouched in a chair by the smoky fire, wrapped in a shawl, her feet tucked under her for warmth. Her usual waxen complexion was cold against his lips when he bent to kiss her forehead. She began to struggle to her feet, saying she would get him some supper, but he held her firmly in the chair, reminding her that they had already eaten that day.

'Mam gave me some cheese.' He put the small parcel carefully on the table.

Relief flooded Rebecca's childlike face and she began to cry. 'Take no notice. It's nobbut a weakness from the fever,' she protested. 'I asked for Digby to put what I owed on the slate today. It was only for a bit of scrag end, but he said he wasn't subsidising strikers no more.'

Matt let her weep. He heard the child begin to whine in sympathy from the upstairs bedroom. There would be few except strikers' families cried with them, he thought. The initial support among mill and factory workers had already died in favour of rumblings of discontent in their own interests. Besides, not all of Griseley were in agreement that the statues for the town hall were a waste of time. Lions had a certain grandeur about them, they elevated a town above the common run. Among the respectable artisans and shopkeepers and others in work, opinion was growing in support of Edwin Clough, who had suffered a bad time of it lately, people said, yet had at his own expense offered to place Griseley squarely on the map.

For the first time, Matt began to doubt the soundness of the strike.

'We shall beat them,' murmured Edwin, beginning to believe it at last. The local paper, having as its editor a man who attended the Ebenezer chapel and had dined with Edwin occasionally, reported weekly to his intense satisfaction on the strike's downhill progress.

In a week or two the men would be back at work – he would be magnanimous about taking them back, he had decided. He could not do otherwise, he needed them more than they could guess. How would the lions ever see the light of day without their foundry skills? Edwin fretted about the lions. He lay awake at night, worrying, not about

364

disappointed customers, unfinished orders or the loss of new ones, but haunted by the thought that his gesture to the town would flounder. The stigma of failure made him sweat with fear. How could he face them in chapel, or sit on the town council, or drive down the street, knowing that the whole of Griseley had witnessed his final humiliation? And it would be final. Edwin had no illusions about his dwindling energies surviving such a blow. Yet, how could he face his Maker, after being brought so low?

He spread the newspaper on his knees and called Charles's attention from the opposite chair, where he was holding a crumpet on a toasting fork to the blazing fire. Edwin read aloud: *'The strikers say they have agitated in a businesslike manner with their Employer and that the result has been disappointing. Are they not, to be more truthful, disappointed by the refusal of their Employer, whom we all know as a most generous and much respected pillar of society, to be intimidated by their seditious behaviour?'* He turned to the following page, folding the paper carefully. He was cheered by the pleasing ring of the phrase, *generous and much respected pillar of society.* 'Well said. A good man that.'

Charles did not reply, concentrating on browning the crumpet evenly. He would be glad when the men gave in and the whole damn business was over.

Edwin turned to the news from France. He observed aloud that there had been more disturbances since the Prussians had performed their triumphal parade through Paris: *'Last night about ten o'clock, companies of National Guards carrying a red flag marched along the principal boulevards. In the neighbourhood of Montmartre there were encampments of National Guards with outpost sentries. Those men have artillery, small arms and abundance of ammunition. One company has threatened to hang its commander. They allege that their government has betrayed them and they are preserving the peace of Paris.'* Edwin shook his head. 'When will they learn it's all over?'

'People are suggesting there will be a revolution in France,' said Charles placidly.

Edwin frowned. Three hundred thousand Parisians taking to the streets in a protest which had lasted from morning until night, certainly smacked of a revolt. He had read in other news reports how the National Guard had marched with their standards draped in black in protest against the capitulation. Some of the National Guards had seized two hundred cannon and hauled them up the hill of Montmartre so that the Prussians should not have them. And the crowd had seized on one poor fellow for a government spy and stoned him and drowned him in the Seine.

He felt a chill of apprehension, in fear for Phoebe's safety, but he thought too of the strikers and their *Down with the masters! Down with Clough!*

Seventeen

What is happening is nothing less than the conquest
of France by the worker and the reduction to slavery
under his rule of the noble, the bourgeois, and the
peasant.

Edmond de Goncourt, 28 March 1871

Maurice ranted against Thiers's newly elected government
which had sentenced his heroes Blanqui and Flourens to
death for their part in the October revolution. His own
name, he bragged, was on a register of blacklisted National
Guards. 'But not yours, my fine friend,' he said to Antoine,
slapping him on the back with exaggerated *bonhomie*. 'Not
those who remained loyal to *law and order*.' Though
Maurice had forgiven Bertrand for his role in the October
uprising, the rift between Maurice and Antoine had not
healed.

Now that winter was turning to spring and food had
become plentiful again, there was no urgency to leave.
Bertrand's battalion of the National Guard had been
disbanded and he took up another teaching post. Tessa no
longer sat for hours by the balcony window or staring at the
empty cradle and Bertrand would pet her and make her
smile and forget the long weeks of misery. But Tessa was

weakened by the winter. Phoebe said she would not go home until she saw her plump and blooming again.

There were days when Phoebe longed for clean country air, to walk away from the apartment and board a train – she did not care where it went. And yet she stayed, not because of Tessa, but because the life of the turbulent city was like a drug to her. People talked of having been 'buried alive' during the siege but Phoebe knew that she had been entombed in Griseley, suffocated by chapel-going and dutiful behaviour, and that she had never felt so independent as since she had lived in Paris. She wanted to stay with this sense of a quickened existence.

The city's return to normality was deceptive. There had been demonstrations and isolated incidents of violence. Paris had divided itself into two factions – those who supported Thiers's Government and the peace with Prussia and those who vowed vengeance, a continuing of the fight to the death, *résistance à outrance*. In mid-March Thiers's Government had arrived from Bordeaux and the army tried to recover the cannon which the rebels had dragged to Montmartre. A mob had turned on them, the women screaming for blood and two of Thiers's generals were murdered.

Phoebe had shuddered, imagining the frenzied mob and the women, like the women round the guillotine years ago, howling for death.

Thiers and his men, taking fright, left for Versailles the same day. And now there was a red flag flying over the Hôtel de Ville, posters everywhere had summoned people to Communal elections and Paris was at last in the hands of the Commune.

Maurice was wild with elation. 'Paris is ours, my lovely Phoebe. At last we shall rule ourselves.'

Phoebe could not believe him. How could it have

happened so quickly? How could Thiers have been so afraid? Everyone had said he was a tough old bird. Yet Phoebe's heart quickened too with excitement as people cheered and sang to celebrate the inauguration of the new administration. She did not know why, seeing as so many people wanted it so much, Paris should not have its Commune with its red flags and banners and be self-governing. True, more of the bourgeois classes who had stayed on through the deprivations of the siege now began to leave. And there was the story that a crowd of citizens who had demonstrated against the Commune had been ambushed and shot by the National Guard in the Rue de la Paix. But Maurice said that no change could be brought about without some bloodshed. Besides, it was spring and the weather was warm and Paris beautiful. People were going about calling one another *citoyen*, and now Paris had a legally elected council surely there would be peace.

'The government will be gathering their forces,' Maurice said one evening when he came to visit them. He frowned to see that Antoine was at the apartment before him and decided to pretend he was not there. 'Thiers won't sit at Versailles doing nothing. He'll be getting ready to attack.'

According to Maurice, the Commune was dragging its feet; they should have ordered a march on Versailles straight away. The Commune consisted of too many intellectuals and members of the 'establishment'.

'We need men of action to lead us. All this lot do is argue among themselves and issue decrees.' He would know how to get them moving and put Paris in order, but the first thing to do was march on Versailles and execute Thiers for treason.

He was the typical know-it-all proletarian, thought Phoebe with amused resignation, watching him pace the floor, contrasting his wild mood with Antoine's serene, slightly condescending smile. He was not content unless he was agitating against something – against the masters in his former employment as a foundry worker, loud-mouthed among the ranks of the National Guard, and as soon as he had his longed-for Commune, complaining too about that.

Antoine, lounging on the sofa, said that the Commune should not rule out talking with Thiers's Government. 'Paris can't set herself against the whole of France.'

Maurice rounded on him coldly. 'Not for the first time I wonder whose side you are on.'

'Not the side of murder and anarchy,' Antoine said calmly.

'Then you'll have to make your choice soon. For it will come to that.'

'Oh, come. Why do you always have to be so extreme?' Phoebe laughed, handing Maurice a glass of wine. 'The two sides only have to talk with one another and let the mayors of the twenty arrondissements act as mediators and everyone can work together for justice and liberty' – she raised her own glass – 'and for a new France!'

'And then we can all have a quiet life,' murmured Tessa.

'Maurice would detest a quiet life,' Bertrand said bitterly.

'Phoebe is beginning to sound just like one of them,' he said to Tessa later as they lay in bed together. Bertrand was growing daily more exasperated with Phoebe and her enthusiasm for the Commune. He was uneasy about the split between Antoine and Maurice, which seemed to reflect the growing differences in Paris between the moderates and the extremists. 'I wish she wouldn't encourage Maurice to come to the apartment. If he's on a blacklist at Versailles, like he says, he's endangering us all by his visits.'

'I think she's fallen in love with him,' murmured Tessa, snuggling her body against him.

'Phoebe – in love with Maurice?'

Tessa did not answer. Already she was falling asleep.

Bertrand lay awake in the darkness, disturbed by the thought that Phoebe was in love with a madman.

The troops from Versailles attacked the following week, recapturing the bridge at Neuilly. At every cross-street marched battalions of National Guards and the throb of drums and sound of bugles called citizens to arms. Antoine, drafted by the Commune back into the National Guard, called to say goodbye. He looked very white, thought Phoebe as she kissed him, and he did not seem fired by a spirit for battle when he said, 'There's going to be a counter-attack. Everyone is getting ready to march.' He kissed Bertrand on both cheeks and then left them.

Maurice came to say goodbye an hour later. He was very formal and with his occasional flair for Parisian courtesy he had brought a bottle of wine with him.

'The government troops are going to liberate everyone from your wonderful Commune,' said Tessa mockingly.

Maurice ignored her. He bowed to Phoebe and said he had been charmed and honoured to know her and Phoebe felt a chill of fear at his solemn manner. 'If I die, will you remember your brave Communard when you return to England?'

She tried to laugh. 'Of course. But I'm sure there's no need to be so dramatic.' Though he looked dramatic, and every inch the revolutionary in his black trousers and boots, white shirt and red scarf and unshaven chin, and the scar from eye to mouth.

'Tomorrow will be a decisive day for the Commune.' He glanced scornfully at Tessa. 'We shall put those Versaillais to rout and save all of France.'

Phoebe refused to let herself believe he might die. She went with him to the stairs and down to the vestibule and he said, 'Do you remember when the balloon factory was hit and I waited here on the stairs for you? I was so afraid you had been killed.' But Phoebe was remembering another time, when he had brought her a brace of pigeons and kissed her.

'Will we meet again, Maurice?'

'Who knows?' He shrugged his shoulders with his old bravado.

'I will pray that you win. Your cause deserves to win,' she said with fervour.

He took her hand, turning it delicately, before stooping to kiss the palm. 'When I first saw your photograph, I thought how very English you looked.' He lifted his head to look at her and the expression in his eyes was tender. 'Now I wish you had been born a Parisienne.'

Maurice marched with the right-hand column of National Guards. Their orders were to attack the fort at Mont-Valerien, occupied by government troops, and make for the village of Rueil while the second and third columns attacked further south. There was a conquering spirit in Maurice's heart and he felt the anger among the men because of the justice of their mission. They sang the 'Marseillaise' as they marched and boasted how they would string the murdering old toad Thiers up from a chandelier in the palace of Versailles.

Maurice's section of the column was headed by Flourens, looking splendid in blue pantaloons and a belt stuffed full of pistols and brave as a lion though condemned to death by those bastards in the government.

As they reached the plateau with the fort in sight the guns of Mont-Valerien opened fire. For an instant the column paused, then shells burst among the ranks ahead, the dust was flying and men were shouting and panicking. Maurice saw the blue-and-white figure of Flourens with a small group of his Chasseurs head onwards as if oblivious of the general retreat.

'Cowards!' he shouted. 'Look at your leader!' He hit a man running past him with the butt of his rifle. 'Fucking cowards!'

The figures of Flourens and his men grew smaller in the distance. It was clear that their mission was suicidal. They must know they did not stand a chance. Maurice was seized by an urge to follow them; his heart pounded wildly and his head throbbed with an agony of intense excitement. He hesitated, then turned towards Paris. He was no coward, he told himself, but he was not the sort of chap to get himself killed for nothing.

Phoebe opened the door of the apartment and was shocked by Antoine's appearance. He said he had spent several days holed up, hiding from the Versaillais and had walked all the way from Meudon. He wore a workman's blouse and coarse trousers instead of his National Guard uniform. He was weak from a flesh wound and very pale.

Phoebe held him and kissed him, and Tessa with none of her former mockery said, 'We didn't know if you were alive.'

Antoine sank on to the sofa. 'Is Maurice safe?'

Phoebe nodded. She poured him a glass of wine which Maurice had brought them and Antoine drank it with shaking hands. He said that he had been with a column on the left flank under General Duval, which had reached the Chatillon plateau. 'But the Versailles troops were too many for us. They shot prisoners out of hand, I saw with my own eyes men I had fought with—' His voice shook. 'And Duval himself – executed by firing squad.'

The defeat of everyone's hopes was the worst, thought

Phoebe, for though the Communards now held the bridge at Neuilly, Paris was again under siege and this time from an army of their own countrymen.

'You must be prepared to leave in a few days,' Antoine said suddenly. 'The Commune are building barricades. It's only a matter of time before MacMahon's troops enter Paris and take it street by street.' He looked at them earnestly. 'We must face the fact that the Commune is lost. Believe me. When the Versaillais learn that you've sheltered rebels here, you too will be shot.'

Tessa went at once into the bedroom and began to pack. Phoebe sat with her hands tightly clasped in her lap.

'What about Maurice? What will happen to him?'

'If he has any sense he will leave too. The Commune has gone mad,' Antoine said bitterly. 'It's being taken over by men like Rigault who want a Committee of Public Safety and the old Terror all over again; they arrest and shoot anyone on the smallest suspicion of treachery. They are taking hostages and are threatening to execute them three at a time for every National Guardsman killed, while the men of reason sit in the Hôtel de Ville arguing and blaming one another for the mess we are in.'

Phoebe saw in her imagination how the Versailles troops would sweep through Paris, destroying everything in their path. The attack on the western suburbs where Maurice was fighting had been continuous for days, the cannonade and sound of artillery fire could be heard on the warm spring air even near the Rue Rambuteau. She saw at last how senseless it had been to delay so long.

'It will take a day or two to organise,' said Antoine. 'We may be safer if you're not conspicuously English. Rigault's arrests apparently know no logic. We will dress as peasants – I have friends, farming people who will lend us a market wagon and see us on our way to my mother's house. But we must move quickly, while traders are still allowed through the city.'

Maurice's hatred for Thiers and the Versailles government deepened. In the ruins of Neuilly whole streets of houses had been opened to the sky and shells whistled constantly overhead. The Communards' chief hope of success lay in the building of barricades and finding enough brave men to man them; that was how Paris had fought in the past. It was the traditional way and Maurice still believed that victory was possible. His pride in the Commune for which they had all struggled was his beacon of inspiration. People said that there had been excesses of violence and worried about Police Chief Rigault's taking of hostages, the Archbishop of Paris for one. But what did the death of a few priests matter in the struggle for liberty and equality? The Church had done worse in the name of Christianity in the past. And in any case, the government troops were dealing in wholesale slaughter.

Maurice felt like one of the 'old ones' who had fought in the streets to save Paris. The fate of Flourens troubled him a little. The Versaillais had taken him prisoner. Those pigs had dragged him to a riverbank where a captain of the Gendarmerie had split his skull with a sabre. It was a violent end, yet it had seemed to Maurice to be almost glorious, a martyr's death, until he learned that they had paraded Flourens's mutilated corpse through the streets of Versailles in a dust-cart. He had wept when he heard. He vowed eternal vengeance on the Versailles pigs. And yet a nagging thought recurred: if the splendid Flourens had met such an end, what chance was there for the rest of them?

He thought of Phoebe with a sudden burst of romantic feeling as he made his way to the apartment one afternoon, remembering how her lovely eyes always lit with pleasure when he called to see her. He had heard rumours that Antoine had escaped alive and rejoiced that they were again fighting on the same side. What brave fellows they all were and how these English were forced to admire them.

He ran up the stairs to the apartment and glimpsed the bags and boxes behind Phoebe in the open doorway. Phoebe threw her arms round him in the French manner and with none of her English reserve. 'Thank God you've come!' Even the bitch Tessa looked pleased to see him. He kissed them heartily, enjoying and prolonging for a moment the notion of his being a hero.

'Those Versailles pigs will have to shoot better if they want to catch me.' His glance fell again on the waiting luggage. But they were going away. He felt a terrible sense of disappointment. How could Phoebe think of leaving now, after all they had been through together?

Bertrand told him how Antoine was going to help them escape. They must disguise themselves as farmers and be ready when he came for them.

Phoebe seized his arm. 'Maurice, you must come too, while there's still time.' She repeated Antoine's opinion that the Commune could not survive, that it was being eaten up from the inside by malice and suspicion among its members.

'It's madness to stay on now,' Bertrand said. 'If the Versailles troops weaken at all the Germans are there to support them. But the point is they are not weakening. The troops will soon break through the western suburbs and then Thiers and the Commune between them will destroy your lovely city.'

'Then all Parisians must fight to prevent Thiers from winning,' he said angrily.

'Please, Maurice!' begged Phoebe. She had prayed that he would for once see reason and had set her heart on his escaping with them. 'Come with us. Come with Antoine.'

Maurice shrugged off her hand from his arm. He said coldly, 'Do you take me for a deserter?' They were trying to justify their escape but he was not fooled, he could see they were all shit-scared, and Antoine too by the sound of it. He looked at Phoebe and his anger turned to sadness. He had invested such faith in her and she had disappointed him. She continued to press him to go with them, her eyes filling with tears of frustration, but he steeled his heart and bowed to them and wished them well and went away.

He brooded for a long time on the little scene he had witnessed. He would miss Phoebe. Did she not know that she had been his inspiration? Why was she leaving now, just as they were about to face victory together? His disappointment made him bitter. Worse almost than Phoebe's leaving him was the fact that Antoine should give in when things started to look bad. It was a side to the business which troubled him profoundly. The Commune needed all the fit men it could get. Had Antoine lost his nerve just because he had seen a few men beaten up and shot? The Commune would shoot three times as many of the enemy in retaliation. One battalion had caught a government soldier and nailed him to a stake. That was the sort of thing to strike fear into Thiers's men. The more he thought about it, the more he saw that Phoebe must not leave and that Antoine, who was no better than a deserter, must be punished. The National Guard was an army and deserters from regular armies were put to death – the Versailles lot did not hesitate to put traitors to the firing squad. Once the idea was formed it became the inevitable consequence of Antoine's cowardice; it was the only fitting solution.

It was not difficult for Maurice to force an entry into one of the empty houses opposite Bertrand's apartment. The rooms were covered with dust-sheets and his feet echoed as he walked through them, selecting a window which looked down on to the street. He took food for a week and kept watch on the apartment, impatient for the matter to be over and done with now the judgement had been made and sentence passed.

He woke one morning as usual and took up his position at the open window resting his rifle with the barrel on the sill, poking out between the closed shutters. He heard the wagon before he saw it, rolling round the corner from the Rue Rambuteau. He trembled with suspense, for he did not at first recognise the driver as his old friend Antoine. The disguise was good, he thought with a grudging admiration – Antoine's own valet might have taken a pot shot at him for a vagrant. The shabby figure jumped down from the cart and walked along the street with Antoine's unmistakable stride as far as the house opposite. Maurice leaned his shoulder more firmly against the wall and aimed the rifle, nudging it between the shutters and pressing the butt into his shoulder. 'Well, my old friend—'

He relaxed his grip. Not yet, not yet.

He watched the little party come out into the street and cross in front of Antoine, carrying their bundles and boxes like regular peasants, the women dressed in black with kerchiefs over their hair and Bertrand done up like an old gardener in a dirty blue smock coat and yokel's cap. Maurice did not smile at the eccentricity of the outfit. He was the executioner intent on his task. He let Antoine move to the cart and waited until he had climbed on to the long driving seat, watching as he leaned forward and pulled Phoebe up beside him. Maurice took aim, the gun pointed squarely at Antoine's back, and in that moment he remembered their friendship, the long idealistic discussions at café tables and the optimistic revolutionary dreams they had once shared. A strong sadness engulfed him and his eyes misted with a sense of regret. He hardened his heart. Antoine had proved his bourgeois soul by abandoning his revolutionary friends. He saw the deserter lean forward and stoop to assist Tessa. It was now or perhaps not at all – quickly, before his own nerve failed. Maurice's hand trembled as his finger squeezed the trigger. At the same moment, the horse, as if anticipating the retort of the gun before it broke the stillness, shifted uneasily and the cart rolled forward a few inches.

Phoebe clung to Antoine and the seat of the wagon as the rifle fire split the silence of the street. The horse reared and the cart lurched violently. She heard the frantic neighing of the horse and Antoine shouting, and saw Tessa, her arms raised to them, her mouth open in an expression of surprise, the upper half of her face shattered and bloody as she fell backwards to the cobbles.

Antoine leaped down from the cart to hold the horse's head, struggling to soothe the frightened animal and Bertrand, making a move towards Tessa, glanced up swiftly at the buildings, his face agape with a bewildered sort of fury, as he scanned the upper storeys.

Phoebe climbed from the seat as the wagon steadied. She dropped to her knees beside Bertrand who was bending over Tessa, calling her name. Tessa lay with her arms flung out on the cobbles, her hair in a bloodied curtain across her face; Phoebe pulled it aside and saw that the bullet had crushed her fine broad brow.

Antoine shouted to them, 'Take care, it may be an ambush.'

Phoebe stood up. Tessa's blood had smeared her hands and she wiped them against her dress. 'I don't think so. They've stopped shooting.' She took the reins from Antoine and watched him talk to her brother, placing a hand upon his shoulder and then helping him carry Tessa into the house. She hugged her arms about her to stop the tremors which swept through her body. For Bertrand's sake she must not give way to hysteria. A small crowd had gathered at the end of the street, arms folded, murmuring to one another. Someone cried out in terror, 'It's the Versaillais! They're coming!' but was hushed down. Phoebe said, 'There's nothing more to see. You'd better go away,' surprised by her self-control and by the fact that they obeyed her.

After a while Antoine returned. He entered the house from where the shot had come and after a moment appeared at one of the upstairs windows. 'Nothing. Whoever it was is far away by now.' He came back to the street.

'I must go to my brother,' said Phoebe.

Antoine nodded. 'He says you're to leave without him. And I agree.'

Phoebe was dismayed. How could she go now, when Bertrand needed her? She saw at the same time that Antoine could not delay; if he was questioned by the Communard police they might discover that he was deserting from the National Guard. She said quickly, 'You must go without us. We shall leave some other way.'

Antoine hesitated then climbed on to the cart. 'I'll come again at the same time next market. Be ready and waiting near Les Halles.' Before she could protest he flicked the reins and drove away.

Phoebe went into the house. A dark ribbon of blood led from the pavement and up the stairs as far as the apartment where Tessa's body lay on the sofa. Bertrand was trying to wipe away the blood from her eyes with a towel. He looked up and said brokenly, 'Phoebe – who would do that?'

Phoebe stared at the dark stain spreading into the sofa. 'Her golden hair. Tessa was always so proud of her hair.'

She thought of the people in the neighbouring streets. Could someone have taken 'spy mania' further than the rest? A few had become suspicious of their foreignness, one or two had even hinted they thought they were spies, but there had been little of the harassment to which many English residents had been subject. She put her arms round her brother and did not know how to comfort him.

They buried Tessa near Thomas's grave. No inquiries were made, no police came visiting; the authorities were too taken up with the chaos within their own departments to investigate the death of an Englishwoman and Bertrand and Phoebe were too distraught to do more than accept that someone had a grudge against them.

The sun shone gently through the trees in the cemetery and Bertrand said as they walked homeward, 'You should have gone with Antoine.'

It was then Phoebe told him that Antoine had not left Paris but intended coming for them again with the farm wagon. 'We must be ready the day after tomorrow.'

'I'm not leaving.' Bertrand spoke very calmly, as if the decision had been made some time ago and he had already given it some thought. He smiled at Phoebe's look of dismay and her angry, 'But you're not like Maurice. There's nothing for you to stay here for.'

'What is there for me outside Paris? You'll go back to Griseley—' he cut short her protests that she would not leave him. 'You'll go home eventually, but I shall never go back to Yorkshire. I'd made my life here with Tessa. Paris is the only place I've ever been really happy.'

Phoebe saw that he was right: the pulse of Paris which she had found so stirring was everything to Bertrand. But she was not going to leave him without a struggle. 'Come with us,' she begged, and the next day she said again, 'Come with Antoine – at least until the fighting's over.'

It was a Sunday and they walked along the boulevards, light with blossom and filled with people strolling in their best clothes as if it was any Sunday in May. A little crowd of children watched a Punchinello show under the trees at the Place de la Concorde where the fountains sparkled in the sun. Phoebe's hand tightened on Bertrand's arm. It seemed as incongruous that people should be enjoying themselves when Tessa lay cold in the cemetery as that they should do so when the Versailles troops were outside the Paris gates. All was peaceful except for the distant sound of the cannonade and the activity at a vast barricade being built at the end of the Rue de Rivoli. Phoebe recalled a proclamation by the Committee of Public Safety that they would blow up Paris and bury everyone under the ruins rather than surrender and she shivered as she watched the children laugh at the antics of Punch and Judy. People stood around the base of the barricade, watching its construction with interest as more paving blocks and soil were added.

'Perhaps we shall win.' Bertrand was unaware that with that 'we' he had allied himself with the Parisians. But Phoebe could not think of herself as a Parisian: the defiance which was embodied in the barricades and would be crushed at them made her want to weep for the madness which had seized this beautiful city. She saw now that its civilised splendour was only surface deep. She could not endure to stay and see Paris destroy itself. She prayed for Maurice and tried to sustain the thought that perhaps after all the Communards might succeed. Yet behind the brilliance of the May morning, the fountains and the music playing in the Tuileries Gardens, Phoebe sensed a current of fear and a certainty of catastrophe; it was in the shuttered shops, the closed hotels and sad dreary streets which stood deserted on their route home, and in the abandoned attempts to erect barricades made from paving blocks torn from the roads.

Phoebe woke early with a start, remembering that today Antoine was coming and she must dress again in peasant garb. She went to the windows and opened the shutters, wondering as she glanced at the blank houses opposite, who could have borne Tessa such a terrible hatred. Sounds carried on the still air – drums and a confused clamour, as if in the distance people were shouting; then she heard the tocsin pealing in distant churches. She saw a neighbour below and called to her, 'What has happened?'

'The Versailles troops entered Paris last night, mademoiselle,' the woman said.

Phoebe dressed hastily and woke Bertrand. 'We must go to Les Halles at once and wait there for Antoine. *Please*, Bertie. You must come too.'

Bertrand was slow and she was in a torment of impatience with him, but at least he had agreed to come. Phoebe's mind filled with images of hordes of the 'red-trousers', the Versailles soldiers, marching down the Rue Rambuteau. She hurried Bertrand towards the markets, carrying their bundles of food and clothes.

Bertrand halted. 'You go and wait at the meeting place. I've forgotten to pay up the rent.'

Phoebe released a cry of fury. 'The house may not be standing tomorrow!'

'Nevertheless, we can't leave owing money.'

She said savagely, 'Don't be so like Father!'

He smiled. 'Father ought to be proud of you, Phoebe. I hope he is.' He hugged her swiftly and then kissed her, saying tenderly, 'You were always more like a mother to me than a sister.'

He strolled back along the street with his pack over his shoulder and she felt compelled to call after him, 'You will come back?' He did not answer and Phoebe stood for a while watching him before she turned reluctantly towards Les Halles.

Bertrand went to look for the *concierge* and was told that the man had left that morning for his brother's house; he walked from the apartment and did not turn again towards Les Halles, wandering instead towards the Hôtel de Ville where an immense new barricade several yards high had been built across the Rue de Rivoli. Fresh barricades were going up in panic everywhere, but Bertrand felt detached from the fear around him. He had left all he possessed behind him; in the rough peasant smock he was free even of his old identity and for the first time in his life he was unconstrained by thoughts of self-preservation, indeed he had little consciousness of self at all.

He walked westward towards the city, heading against the flow of population which fled from the areas of fighting. National Guards were stopping people, forcing them to help prise up paving blocks from the road, some at bayonet point; those who protested were made to carry extra blocks. Bertrand offered no resistance but contributed paving block after paving block to several barricades as he moved from street to street. Some barriers were made of upturned cabs and omnibuses, the gaps filled with soil and bricks and piled up with the ubiquitous *pavés*; others were little more than piles of sandbags and mattresses. Now and then he asked for news and learned that seventy thousand government troops had poured through the breaches in the defences at the St-Cloud gate the previous night. It was a crime that the wall had not been adequately defended and that fifteen hundred National Guards had surrendered, and shocking that prisoners were being beaten and murdered by the regular soldiers. Rumours spread from one group to another all that morning. Thiers's men had invaded the Left Bank as far as

384

Montparnasse station; another column had already occupied the Étoile and installed cannon in the Champs-Elysées. There was a battle raging at the Place de la Concorde and the Versaillais had been beaten back. Bertrand prayed that Phoebe and Antoine had escaped.

Near the Opéra house a barricade of water-carts had been strung across the boulevard. The Vendôme column no longer dominated the view southwards, for it had been torn down by the Communards in a gesture of destruction just under a week earlier. As Bertrand worked his way towards the fighting he found himself heading towards the Boulevard de Clichy, making for his old haunts in Montmartre. The sound of artillery and cannon was dense, shattering the air between the buildings, for the government troops were only a few streets away.

Now and then he came upon pockets of confusion as citizens and National Guards ran to and fro; some of the soldiers were panicking: he saw a man stripping off his National Guard uniform as he ran and stuffing the jacket and *képi* down a cellar opening. Others sang the 'Marseillaise' boldly as they marched towards a barricade.

The nearer Bertrand came to the fighting the more careless he grew of his own safety. He walked upright, hardly aware of the flying bullets and only pausing when ordered to carry the obligatory paving block and set it in place on a barricade. His progress was slowed by the frequent barricade duty and it was afternoon before he reached the Place Pigalle.

Phoebe did not look back as Antoine drove through the final checkpoint north of Paris. She clutched the small bundle on the seat beside her which consisted of a shawl wrapped round a couple of loaves of bread. The orchards were filled with blossom and workers in the fields were calmly tilling their plots of earth as if they did not know there was a civil war or if they did, it was of no concern to them. It was her first view of the countryside in over a year. They passed a hawthorn tree in full flower and the scent of the white blossom made tears mist her eyes. 'The maythorn is out.'

Antoine touched her arm. 'Don't worry. Bertrand will follow us. He will be with us in a day or two.' But Phoebe sensed as they left the city behind that she would see neither Paris nor her brother again.

By late afternoon the army's attack was less intense, slowing because of the fear of booby traps and mines. The troops were coming to a halt in a line which ran roughly north to south, from the area round Bertrand's old school in the Rue de Rome to the Montparnasse railway station on the Left Bank.

The relative calm which enveloped the streets gave people a new confidence and the business of erecting barricades went on with a firm and more organised purpose. Bertrand's tireless performance in carrying *pavés* had won him friends on the Boulevard de Clichy and he spent the evening on the floor of a café cellar with a group of a dozen or so National Guards. They laughed at his gardener's costume, treating him with a rough affection, suspecting him of being simple-minded. His reputation spread and it seemed that everyone in the area had heard of *'l'Anglais'* who was a bit of a clown, but a good fellow who had allied himself to their cause. The next morning men shook his hand warmly and shared their bread and wine and gossiped over what might be expected that day. The sound of cannon had started up again in the early hours. 'They're moving round to the north,' someone said. Fear made them fall silent as men went to the barricades and one handed Bertrand a rifle with a curt nod.

386

Bertrand carried the gun reluctantly and would have liked to discard it, for he could see again Tessa's body and the gaping hole in her head. The others told him to aim at the snipers which popped out along the street beyond the barricades, that it was no different to shooting rabbits, but he could not bring himself to fire and after a while the men grew tired of his odd behaviour and let him wander away.

The dead were lying in the street and Bertrand wondered idly why he had not also been hit. The main attack drew closer as the morning wore on to midday and, when they heard that Thiers's men had raised the tricolour at the top of Montmartre, the National Guard began to fall back. The Place Pigalle had been taken and the streets as far south as the Opéra; it was only a matter of time before the government troops broke through the great barricade at the Place de la Concorde.

There was nowhere to go except eastward and Bertrand followed the general retreat, alone and separated from his companions of the previous night. It was evening when he came upon the quarter near his old apartment where he had lived as a student sculptor. People were panicking. By now the Versailles troops had captured the Opéra, the Place Vendôme and, at last, the Place de la Concorde. The streets to the south were a mass of retreating National Guards. In the distance a red glow lit the sky: it was said that the Communards had blown up the Tuileries Palace. A woman ran towards him as if to ask for help and her mouth worked with emotion.

'My husband is killed, the National Guards have looted the house. They say the Versaillais are murdering everyone. They've shot forty-nine of the rebel scum in Montmartre – lined them up against a wall.' The woman began to weep. It was clear that she was terrified.

Bertrand felt detached and had curiously little pity for

her. The woman spat on the cobbles, seeing where his allegiance lay.

'Go join your friends.' She dried her face on her skirt and gestured wildly behind her. 'They're all madmen.' She began to weep again.

Bertrand saw the National Guards on a barricade at the end of the street. To the north and west of La Villete and Belleville the streets were still held by the Communards. By the eerie light of the glowing skies he recognised Maurice, leaning against an upturned water-cart buttressed with mattresses. He was laughing over something.

Bertrand felt a sudden lifting of his spirits and a sense of brotherhood with the Frenchman. It was fate that had brought them together again. He would help him fight those murdering Versaillais. He began to run towards him.

Maurice turned at the sound of Bertrand's cry of recognition and his laughter died on his lips. His expression became a look of terror – as if he had seen a demon rather than an old friend.

Eighteen

M stands for money, where's the poor man's share?
With rent and with taxes, his pocket's soon bare.

People's Alphabet c. 1870

'That old devil can hold out as long as we can,' said Matt.

'Longer, now those traitors in the foundry have joined the machine shop knob-sticks.' Walter was hammering a nail into a placard which read in crimson letters: *Unity is Strength*. He gave the placard a further vicious blow.

Jack pulled on his jacket and cast a critical eye over his brother's handiwork. 'He'll not get his lions cast, though. That's what matters to him.'

Some of the paint had run and Walter, seeing Jack looking at it, said, 'Looks like blood, that.'

'So long as it's only fake.'

The strike had been on for three months and though most of the men had stood firm through the worst of the winter, many were now drifting back to work as if it was the mild May weather itself which had mellowed them.

'Jack's right. Clough hasn't the skilled men for the big castings,' said Matt. 'Not while us men on the committee stand fast.'

'And we will stand fast.' Walter glanced at Jack, not quite trusting him.

'Aye, we'll stay fast.' Jack went to the pump and sleeked his hair with water from the bucket, but the truth was he was weary of the strike. The protest had been necessary, and he could not say he had suffered as others had suffered – his own brother for one; he looked at Matt, gaunt and embittered, hardened to the strike like Walter – but as the weeks and months dragged by and they made no progress Jack's heart was going out of the struggle. Their main hope lay in Edwin Clough's obsession with casting his lions, but Jack was uneasy about the intimidation necessary to keep men from giving in and going back to work. Walter was all for 'thumping unity into them'; there had been some bad moments and he was unhappy to see old friends go in dread of his own brother. Neither he nor William Burns would have the power to restrain Walter and the other hotheads if it came to a fight. The only restraint so far had been their fear of what would happen if Clough got an excuse to call in the militia.

Jack straightened his necktie and collar; now that his days were not filled with work in the foundry he spent much of his time at Gerald Clough's house, painting scenery, gossiping or rehearsing for *And All That Makes a Man*. He knew that his allegiances were shifting from his workmates and brothers to the more seductive world of Gerald and Olive's theatre.

'You'll be back for the meeting?' Matt was watching him closely.

'Aye, I'll be back.' He wished their watching him did not make him feel so guilty. 'Christ, I'm only going to a rehearsal.'

'Rehearse one with the lovely Cissy for me,' Walter said, turning his back.

Jack pulled on his cap and left the yard. Of course, Walt would have to think he was playing around with a woman. He felt a certain superiority over him. As he crossed the town from Griseley Bank he reflected how Walter could not be further from the truth. Cissy was a good actress but like many minor players – like Tessa who had run off with Bertrand Clough – she could not escape the fact that she had begun her career as a tart. No, if there was any feminine attraction it lay elsewhere. He thought of the grave-faced, beautiful Olive – remote yet so accessible: *You must treat me as a sister, Jack, I want you to feel that you can always talk to me*. And he *could* talk to her, he marvelled: he felt at ease in her company in a way which he might have resisted had he thought there was the least danger of its being misinterpreted; but Olive's pure and generous spirit included everyone in the company, man or woman. She was like a sister to them all – Lamplugh, Ben Dunn, Lulu, Cissy and Victor. What was more natural than that her affectionate nature should embrace him as well?

The maid admitted him to Gerald and Olive's drawing room. Olive had suggested they run through the scene in which he, as the rebel leader, persuaded the tyrant's wife to support the rebels' cause.

The house was very still and Jack was nervous as the seconds ticked by and no one came. Gerald would be at the foundry this afternoon, but the house was usually filled with laughter and conversation and the sounds of other players practising their lines. The room was on the first floor; he stood by the window where from behind the crisp lace drapes he could see the road. Traffic in this part of town was thin, the road was quiet, the houses well spaced, very tall and in an earlier decade would have been rather grand. He watched the roofs of one or two cabs with their swaying top-hatted cabbies perched aloft and the occasional delivery cart. He could hear his heart beating in his chest and his palms sweated a little in the stuffy warmth of the room.

Jack jumped as the clock on the mantelshelf chimed three o'clock. Almost immediately, though he had heard no sound of her approach, the door swung wide and Olive stood in the opening.

'Dear Jack!' She came forward and took his hands in hers, smiling at him affectionately. She reached up and smoothed back his hair with a little tidying motion. 'How hot you look. Let me order some lemonade.'

Olive rang for the maid and as they waited she smiled at him again with that soothing intimacy. Jack said, clearing his throat a little, 'Aren't the rest of the players about today?'

'Didn't I tell you?'

He racked his brain for the information which he surely could not have forgotten so easily.

'They've all gone off to Leeds for an outing. I *must* have told you.' He shook his head and she looked crestfallen. 'Oh, and you could have gone with them. Would you perhaps rather have gone for an outing too?'

He answered that he would rather rehearse the scene and she smiled again as the maid came in with a jug of lemonade. 'So would I, Jack. Isn't theatre so *satisfying*.' She turned to the maid. 'Thank you, Rachel. We've some lines to go through. We'll not want to be disturbed again.'

Had he imagined the emphasis in her look, the ensuing intimacy in the smile which she gave him? He drank the cooling lemonade which she handed him, wiping his mouth with the back of his hand.

'Should we go through the lines up here?' Olive suggested. 'It's so grim and barnlike down in the theatre.'

They began.

Jack had forgotten the intensity with which the scene

was written – the rebel leader impassioned by a conviction of right and justice, the queen tortured by divided loyalties – but its importance lay in the fact that the hero had fallen hopelessly in love with the queen.

It was all so different here, upstairs in the living room instead of down on the stage with the painted scenery and the safety of an audience of players. Olive stood by the mantelpiece, the back of one hand pressed to her brow to express a listening pose, the other held towards him, as if she was torn between loyalty to her husband and surrendering her beliefs for his own. She wore a long velvet robe, draped in folds across her breasts and stomach; her figure was full and clearly outlined under the fabric as if free of the constraints of corseting.

'My queen – if you could tell the furious passion which beats within this heart—'

She made him halt. 'I think at that point you should take hold of my hand, Jack, and perhaps press it to your breast.'

He knew that he was doing the scene badly and wished he was not so nervous. He caught hold of her hand and repeated the lines with it held firmly against his chest. How small and cool women's hands were when they did not wear them out with labour in a factory. He remembered Phoebe's hands and realised that he had not held a woman since holding Phoebe and that a woman's body could be soft and desirable. He could not remember the next line. He apologised and began the speech again: *'My queen – if you could tell the furious passion—'* The velvet of her gown was green, like soft dark moss where it swelled over her breasts.

'My dear, if you could tell the passion which beats within my own heart.' Olive looked at him with a swooning lustrous gaze and as he saw that her eyes were also green, he realised that her words were not the lines of Gerald's play. Quite suddenly and deliberately she wriggled her hand

393

from his grasp and transferred it to his crotch. She lifted her head and parted her lips to meet his own. Her cool reserve had fallen from her as if discarded like the stuff of her gown which, with her free hand, she parted at the neck.

Jack was drowning in sensations as she slipped several more neck-fastenings from their moorings and spilled white mounds of flesh against him. He kissed her and kissed her again. It was his first sight, his first taste, his first possession of a naked female. Their coupling was fierce on the Indian carpet and when it was over Jack was overwhelmed by guilt. He dressed, and when she kissed him he wanted her again.

'You're worrying about Gerald.' She fastened her frock and went to the mirror over the mantelshelf to rearrange her hair.

He watched her, curious about the contradictions in her. Once again she was the woman of the grave manner and cool restraint. 'I don't reckon he'd be too pleased.'

'You men are all the same. You take your pleasure then feel badly about it afterwards. Victor actually cried. Would you believe it? Cried! *Poor Gerry. After all he's done for me.*'

Jack, taken aback at this evidence that others had trodden the same path before him, thrust a hand through his hair. 'Don't you feel badly?'

'My husband can't satisfy a woman.' She wondered how much to tell him. Poor Gerald, he had wanted Jack so much. 'I know it's not his fault.' It was obvious from his expression that he had no idea what she was talking about and Olive felt a sudden misgiving about his innocence. 'He knows I must have some diversions,' she said briskly. 'We've learned to accept the people we are and to discard all such notions as guilt.'

Jack shook his head. 'I don't think I could do that.'

'You'll be surprised.' She smiled. 'Tomorrow you won't feel nearly so priggish. Have some more lemonade.'

'You'll cop it from our Walter,' Sarah said as Jack burst into the kitchen shouting for his working clothes. The strike meeting was to have been at five and it was already quarter past. 'He was swearing you'd given up on them and were going to join the knob-sticks. He says he'll hang for you if you back out now.'

'I'm not giving up on nobody,' Jack said, except women, he swore to himself. Once and for all. He recalled Olive's voluptuous flesh and knew he was wrong and that he would want her again. He dressed swiftly, flinging his best cap and jacket on to his bed.

The meeting was in the tap room; the committee, consisting in Jack's absence of Walter, Matt and William Burns, sat in a row behind a trestle table placed across the window alcove. The room was thick with the choking smoke of two dozen or more tobacco pipes and a clamour of excited conversation dominated the drinking tables.

The men by the window looked up as Jack entered. His brothers glanced away again, Walter with a flicker of a secret smile, Matt looking shifty. Jack took his seat beside William Burns.

'Why the devil didn't you get here sooner?'

Only then did Jack comprehend the mood of the meeting; something out of the ordinary had happened, though he could not tell what.

Walter banged on the table for silence. 'So we're all agreed?'

There was a loud murmur of assent.

'You should have got here sooner,' Burns said again as the din of comment grew louder. 'You and me between us could have stopped all this daft business.'

Walter was sweating but he looked triumphant and grinned when Jack said, 'Now what are you up to?'

'You keep out of this one, lad. We voted when you weren't here.'

A knot of anxiety gripped Jack's stomach as the men got up from the tables, scraping back their chairs, and pulled on their caps and jackets in preparation for a mass exit.

William Burns drew him aside. 'They're going to confront Clough when he comes out of town hall's committee business this evening, shame him in front of his friends – leastways that's the idea, but you know your Walter once he's roused.'

Jack watched the men leave the Nag's Head, wishing he did not have to make the choice to go with them.

Matt shrugged. 'It could work,' he said without conviction. He looked uncomfortable. 'You know how it is with Walt.'

'You could have voted with William against him,' Jack said bitterly.

Matt looked him in the eye. 'And you could have been here instead of messing about with some woman.'

Jack did not defend himself. He felt a longing to stay behind in the pub and let them get on with it. Then he pulled on his cap and followed: he was one of them however much he tried to pretend different. All his flirting with theatre playing, pretending he could raise himself out of his class, it was nothing but a miserable dream.

Sarah pulled on her shawl and bonnet and hurried first to Charles's, then, finding no one at home, to Gerald's house.

Olive came down into the hall. 'My dear child. Whatever is the matter?'

'I've got to talk to Mister Gerald,' Sarah panted.

'And do you think my husband would agree about it being so urgent?'

Sarah pleaded that it was a life-and-death matter concerning Gerald's father. Olive twisted her mouth disbelievingly, then curiosity got the better of her and she let the girl inside.

Olive laughed when she heard Sarah's story. 'The men are going to attack the town hall during a council meeting? Is your brother Jack in this too?'

'All of them. They're going to mob Mr Clough when the council comes out. Oh, get Mister Gerald to call the constables, ma'am. The men will stop short of bother like they have other times if they see the Constabulary there.'

Olive pictured the workers converging on the town square with Jack, dear glorious Jack at their head, and Gerald's father, ranting and posturing and shouting biblical texts, confronted by an angry mob. It was too good – a revolution right here in Griseley. Edwin Clough was about to meet his Armageddon.

'My husband is not home yet,' Olive said. 'Sit down, my dear, and catch your breath. This I must see. But I don't think we need hurry ourselves. Do you?'

The square was a sea of waving placards. The swelling crowd of foundry workers blocked the central steps of the town hall.

From one of the upper windows Murgatroyd the brush-factory owner was shouting in a high-pitched voice at the men, but the meaning of his oration was drowned out by shouts of 'Down with the masters!' and 'We want Clough! Send us Clough!' which soon became a rhythmic chant.

'We should have fetched the constables,' complained Sarah, puzzled because Olive, apparently insensitive to the urgency of their mission, had taken ten minutes to put on a fox-fur coat and hat and high-buttoned boats and, ignoring the route to the police station, had dragged her straight to the town hall.

The men were organising themselves into groups in front of the building, some splitting off and positioning themselves at the corners and to the rear, effectively sealing off the exits. Sarah could see the main entrance doors now; they were opened a crack and the town clerk was visible, remonstrating with the deputation leaders, among them Walter and Matt.

'Where's Jack?' she said anxiously, forgetting their mission to fetch Griseley's police force.

'Where's Edwin Clough?' said Olive, scanning the crowds as well for Jack, hoping Edwin Clough had not escaped by a back way before the men had surrounded the building. The demonstrators were urging those at the front forward and the town clerk's position as door keeper was swiftly becoming untenable. Someone cried, 'If Clough won't come out and talk to us, we'll go in to him!' followed by a roar of approval. The double entrance doors were forced open and the clerk disappeared among the flood of figures which pressed into the building.

Olive seized Sarah's hand and pulled her forward. 'Come on!'

'But we should do something.'

Jack was thrusting his way towards them. 'Sarah – go back home!' Seeing Olive he halted, startled to see her there. How marvellous she looked, and cool-headed as always, as if she were going on a shopping expedition. 'I think you should get off home too, Mrs Clough. It isn't very safe for you to be here.'

'Oh, don't look so dour, Jack. Where's your sense of fun?'

Jack pulled her to one side and said in an undertone, 'This might look like a bit of theatre to you, but it's real enough for some of the men here and if they get rough, you and my sister had best be out of the way.'

Olive, seeing Sarah's bonnet bobbing away through the crowd, said, 'I think your sister already knows where she's going.' She laughed at him and lowered her voice so that he only just caught the next sentence. 'Lord, Jack. I want you. Let's go back home again. The house is still empty.'

Jack felt his face grow hot. He remembered the whiteness of her skin and the triumph of his possession of her. He wanted to have her again and looked at her helplessly, baffled and exasperated by her.

Olive laughed. 'All right. I'll go away.'

The rest of the crowd was moving forward. Jack saw her walk away to the edge of the square and he turned again to the town hall. He pushed his way up the steps under the pillars and through the doors.

The shouts had died as the demonstrators reached the interior of the building. For many it was the first time they had set foot inside the town hall, whose echoing walls and palatial staircase seemed to demand a lowering of voices; indeed, the splendour of the vestibule had rendered some of the men speechless. They came to a halt before the double sweep of stairs, confused by the choice of routes to the first-floor gallery and uncertain about the location of the council chamber and their quarry. The town clerk sat on a chair which one of the demonstrators had the forethought to fetch for him; he nursed a bruised cheek and kept up a whining complaint about the invasion of his territory.

Murgatroyd came hurrying along the gallery and his feet clattered as he descended to the central landing. He came to an abrupt halt as if suddenly aware of his exposed position. Silence greeted his appearance. Then he called, 'You ruffians! How dare you enter this building!'

Walter pushed his way to the left-hand stair, mounting a

few steps so as to be clearly visible. 'We've come for a word with Mr Clough, isn't that right, lads?' He turned to the men.

A shout echoed from the walls, shocking in its volume but inspiring the demonstrators with fresh courage and dispelling their sense of reverence.

'You insolent scoundrels!' shouted Murgatroyd. 'How dare you disturb a council meeting!'

Other members of the council had begun to filter from the chamber and approach the upstairs gallery. The fact that the councillors had braved a confrontation subdued the demonstrators briefly, but at the appearance of Edwin Clough a roar of triumph swelled to the domed ceiling. The men knew they were in sight of victory. Alfred Underwood could be heard, trying to dissuade Edwin from driving out the rioters single-handed. The cheers died and the men waited as Edwin shook himself free of Underwood's restraining arm and walked, puffing and trembling, to join Murgatroyd on the stair.

He scanned the crowd below him and addressed Walter. 'I understand it's me you've come to see. Bateman, are you spokesman?'

Walter's self-assurance faltered; he turned to the others as if for confirmation. 'I am that,' he said defiantly.

'Well you'd better look sharpish and say what you've come to say. We've a council meeting to finish.'

Walter turned again to his companions; Jack realised that he was looking to Matt or William Burns, or even himself to speak; but Matt was tongue-tied by the situation, William Burns was a reluctant revolutionary and Jack was damned if he was going to lend Walt a hand.

'We want a promise of extra pay for making town-hall lions for you and your friends.' Walter seemed to deflate under Edwin Clough's withering gaze.

'And I've told you you're not getting it.' Edwin jabbed his forefinger, gaining strength as Walter's confidence ebbed. Silence fell in the hall as the men looked to Walter expectantly.

It was in that moment that Murgatroyd lost his head. He turned on Edwin: 'This is all your fault. My wife's expecting me home in half an hour.' A roar of laughter infuriated Murgatroyd further. He clung to the rail of the staircase. 'You men – you ought to be at home with *your* wives!'

Walter, fired again with self-confidence, climbed a few more steps of the staircase and others pushed after him. 'I've no wife, and if I had one, I'll be buggered if she'd tell me what time to come home.'

'You ought to be horsewhipped!' shouted Alfred Underwood from the top of the stairs, provoked at last to contribute a comment.

'We ought to be paid a fair wage!' responded Walter. 'Aye – and your railway men and all. And mill workers. Our turn has come. Down with you masters, I say!'

The men echoed the cry. 'Down with the masters!' They surged up the stairs and the councillors took flight.

Jack turned and had a clear view of the square through the open doors. A large crowd of onlookers had gathered outside. He glimpsed Olive's fox-fur hat and noticed that Gerald and Charles Clough had joined her, but more significantly, he saw that a dozen or more constables and, bobbing behind them, two horse-drawn police wagons, were fast approaching the building. Fear jolted him into action. He pushed his way to the stairs and shouted above the din. 'It's the crushers! Run for it!'

The demonstrators at the top of the stairs wavered with indecision. By now the councillors had barricaded themselves in the council chamber. Some men pushed their way down the stairs, making for the door, then turned as they saw the

401

approaching dark wall of blue-coated police. Men fell in the confusion. Some panicked as the police entered the building. A few of the rebels surrendered quickly; others fought back with fists and boots. Jack was forced by the crowd against the wall and saw Walter, his face bloodied, dragged from the stairs by his hair. Then he too felt hands seize his jacket and he was hauled out to the square where the crowd were yelling their support, some in favour of the strikers, others cheering for law and order.

Jack, dragged down the steps with the others to the waiting wagons, heard Sarah shriek, 'Don't arrest my brother!' and the grip on his collar slackened. He was dropped like a parcel on the cobbles and scrambled to his feet.

All around him men were being dragged across the square while the crowd howled insults at the police, at the strikers and one another. Fights had broken out on the steps and Murgatroyd was trying to bang the head of one of his brush workers up against a pillar. Jack saw Walter, still flailing with fists and feet, as he was thrown into a wagon. He saw Gerald talking to the police, who were preparing to lay hold on him again.

'Let this man go, sergeant,' he said easily. 'My wife is convinced he went into the building to try and stop the riot, while his sister sent for your constables. Jack Bateman is no insurgent.'

Jack glanced at Olive and saw her look of unperturbed amusement. 'I'm much obliged, sir.' Jack straightened his collar as the constables moved away. 'I'm grateful to you both.'

'My queen – if you could tell the furious passion which beats within this heart—' Jack pressed Olive's hand to his chest and felt her squeeze his fingers.

'More passion, Jack,' shouted Gerald from the wings. 'You are in love with this woman, remember. She is about to surrender her loyalty to her husband for you and your cause.'

Was he in love with Olive? Jack only knew that he was bewitched by her, that after the affair in the town-hall square, he would have gone to her without thought of Walter or Matt or William Burns.

'Your mind doesn't seem to be on the play, Jack.' Gerald drew him on one side when the rehearsal was over. Jack watched the rest of the cast move away up the auditorium. 'Will you stay with us for supper tonight?'

Jack imagined Olive's insinuating glances across the table and knew he could not match her composure.

'I think not, Mister Gerald.'

'Are you worrying about your brothers, dear boy? Believe me, they deserve whatever punishment they get.'

'By rights, I should be with them. I'd no more thought of helping your father out of a fix than flying, Mister Gerald.'

He laughed and placed an arm about his shoulders. 'Well, I know that, my hearty.'

'Then why?'

'Because I'm fond of you. Very fond.' He hugged him then let the hand on his shoulder fall loosely to touch Jack's shoulder blade, rest lightly at his waist and stroke his hip. 'And I think you are, aren't you, just a little fond of me?'

Jack felt a shock run through him. He turned and saw the limpid look in Gerald's eyes and flush of excitement on his cheek. He stepped away and Gerald's hand fell to his side.

'You do understand—?'

Jack thought of Victor, who had been Gerald's favourite and had cried over his betrayal. He remembered Olive's, *we've learned to accept the people we are.*

'I got you out of a scrape, Jack. As you said yourself, you

should by rights be with your brothers in gaol.'

Jack was saddened by Gerald's poor attempt at blackmail. He had admired the man. He was attracted to his fleshy flamboyance and flattered by the pains he had taken with his coaching – more than that, he *was* fond of him. 'People go to gaol for what you're talking about an' all.'

'So they do, Jack. It's a sad old world.'

Jack put on his cap. 'I think you've got the wrong bloke, Mister Gerald.'

Gerald sighed deeply. 'Ah – such a pity. No ill feelings?'

Jack remembered his possession of Olive and his spirits lifted, for the evening's incident had seemed in some way to lessen his own culpability. 'None at all.'

'It's a shame, though.' Gerald recovered his former ebullience. 'You and I would have made such wonderful allies.'

Nineteen

How much blood, how many tears, have been shed!
What treasure wasted! What hopes blasted! What
pride humbled!

George Augustus Sala,
Paris Herself Again, 1878

Bertrand felt the bond of companionship with the
revolutionaries more keenly as he moved eastward with
Maurice and his companions. Everyone's nerves were frayed
and tempers were short, for it was becoming clear that the
leadership of the Commune was disintegrating. For the first
time since Phoebe had gone, Bertrand began to contemplate
the outcome of the revolution. The self-destructive frenzy of
violence was increasing from day to day. Three days after
the Versailles troops entered Paris, the Commune evacuated
the Hôtel de Ville and put the building to flame. Now it
seemed as if all of Paris was on fire and that the Commune
planned to destroy the city. Nature itself had joined in the
orgy of destruction, for the summer heat had made buildings
tinder dry: strong winds fanned the flames so that they
leaped from building to building.

Bertrand stayed with Maurice. A peculiar sentimentality
made him cling to the notion that in all this madness there

remained a bond between them – if not exactly of friendship, then one forged by their long acquaintance. Maurice had behaved oddly at first, asking only where Phoebe was and then losing interest when he said that she had left Paris with Antoine. When Bertrand told him about Tessa's murder, he insisted with a peculiar fanaticism that he would shoot a Versailles supporter in vengeance. After he had recovered from the surprise of their meeting he had established himself as a kind of guardian, telling everyone how Bertrand had once rescued him from the imperial police, exaggerating the role he had played.

How long ago his first experience of life in Paris now seemed and how the city had changed, thought Bertrand. Like a mistress who was once captivating and generous, Paris had turned in her bitterness into a vengeful harpy.

Maurice began to hate the Englishman because of the secret which was forever nagging at his conscience. The memory of what he had done made him sweat and tremble at night. How could it have happened? Christ! He was not the world's best shot, but to have killed the woman outright and missed Antoine altogether! At the time he would have given himself up, begged their forgiveness and gone on his knees before Phoebe – until he saw that he must think of his own skin and get as far from the place as he could. He had made for the maze of connecting alleyways near the apartment, back to the fighting, where killing had a reassuring regularity and the gun had stopped shaking in his hands. Reason told him that the killing of Bertrand's woman was an insignificant accident compared with the summary executions and massacres committed by the Versaillais as they took prisoners and moved in closer. And Tessa was no loss; she had been a drag on Bertrand from the start. He had probably done him a service. Yet the fact that Maurice had shot

Bertrand's mistress made him nervous and at times ingratiating in his company. And it seemed increasingly that all that had happened since the accident, even the disaster which had overtaken Paris, was in a perverse way connected with Bertrand.

Maurice was puzzled by the Englishman's apparent indifference to death, for he had always considered him in a disparaging way to be of milk-and-water courage. Yet, when faced with the Versaillais, Bertrand had gained a reputation for bravery superior even to his own. It was unnerving and it was another reason for hating him.

Maurice was glad that Paris was burning. It was right that they should purge the city of the last traces of empire. Fire was clean, it purified. Whole streets blazed, making barriers of flames to halt the enemy. Yet as the fires spread Maurice became increasingly disillusioned with the revolution. He saw that the only outcome now could be a fight to the death. The leaders of the Commune were disappearing – Rigault, the Public Prosecutor, dead in a gutter, shot as he cried at his executioners, *'Vive la Commune!'* Maurice gloried in the picture of such a heroic end, yet to perish in a gutter was not an ambition he cherished for himself. He began to plan his escape: there were still ways out of the city for those who knew them or had the right papers. Increasingly he saw the world beyond Paris as sweet and clean and free from corruption, where the guilt of Tessa's killing would fall from his mind and all the madness would end.

After several days Maurice and Bertrand were still together. They manned a barricade to the east of Les Halles, where pockets of resistance still held out and where behind them lay the strong barricades of the Place de la Bastille and the Place du Château d'Eau. Paris was still on fire. The ministries, the palaces, the Prefecture of Police – all the grand buildings had gone. Black smoke hung in clouds which blotted out the sun, the stench of burning was in their nostrils and the sky rained fragments of charred paper which floated about the streets.

The government troops were gaining ground as the morning wore on. 'The only thing for it is to hold out here until the ammunition runs out and then fall back into Belleville,' said one of the men.

Bertrand did not ask himself, as did Maurice, And what then? Bertrand did not think of death, not his own nor Maurice's nor even Tessa's any more with fear. He had lost his reluctance about using a rifle. He fired and loaded with a calm purpose and in silence, not with the embittered intensity of Maurice, who would aim and grunt, 'Take that, you government arsehole!' and a triumphant 'Fuck you!' when he scored a hit.

Bertrand looked on his former horror of battle curiously and did not know what he had feared. One got used to the noise of guns and the yelling, and if it was death he had dreaded – well, dying no longer seemed so terrible. Sometimes he wondered about Phoebe and Antoine and prayed that they had reached safety: but he did not think about his own future. The men fighting with them talked of his fearlessness as suicidal, for he exposed himself to the fire of the Versaillais quite casually. Bertrand knew however that his indifference to the enemy was not courage. If he did not care whether a bullet hit him or not, how could he be called brave?

As the day progressed the government troops took possession of the buildings at the end of the street. Suddenly they were moving towards them, firing as they came.

Two of the men on the barricade fell and the others took their rifles and ran for cover. 'Come on!' shouted Maurice.

'Come on Bertrand, you bloody fool!'

Bertrand continued firing, saying they still had ammunition.

Maurice hesitated but he did not wait to urge him again. He ran for the nearby building. There would be a way out to the rear in the warren of streets off the Rue Rambuteau. He threw off his gun and ammunition, the decision to abandon the cause made in that instant. 'Fuck the Englishman! Fuck them all!' he intoned with a bitter exultation.

He came to a halt, thankful that troops had not yet reached that stretch of the Rue Rambuteau, and saw that he was close to Bertrand's apartment. The little street was shadowed and silent except for the sound of muffled shots and men shouting in the distance. The buildings had a deserted air. A rat, scuttling from between the double entrance doors as he opened them, made him start. Then he was inside and mounting the stairs to the apartment two at a time, stripping off his National Guard uniform as he went. The rooms were shuttered and he flung one of the windows wide so that he could search cupboards and chests for the clothes he would need. He tore off his belt and his red scarf, the badge of the Reds, and flung his *képi* into the hearth as if it held a nest of ants.

He went through Bertrand's wardrobe systematically, pulling out frock coats, shirts and trousers. In a bundle of old clothes on the sofa he came upon Bertrand's passport. Maurice marvelled at his good fortune as he dressed in grey trousers and a clean shirt, a mulberry frock coat and a pair of grey leather boots.

He left the apartment as swiftly as he had entered and made again for the Rue Rambuteau, but the sound of shouting brought him to a halt. He turned in panic looking for an escape: the nearest hiding place lay in the house from which he had only a week before shot Tessa in mistake for Antoine.

Bertrand continued firing after Maurice had gone, holding the Versaillais from the barricade until he ran out of ammunition. As he released the last shot an instinct for survival drove him to take cover, and throwing down his gun he made for the familiar streets of the area near the Rue Rambuteau. He turned a corner and ran straight into a squad of government soldiers coming from the direction of the Rue de Rivoli. One of the Versaillais raised his rifle to shoulder height and took aim.

'I am English,' Bertrand said loudly.

The man hesitated. One of the soldiers came forward and pulled Bertrand's gardener's hat roughly from his head. 'Do Englishmen dress like this?' He pushed the hat in his face. 'Scum! You're one of the Reds.'

A crowd of onlookers was gathering, people hostile to the Commune and eager to ingratiate themselves with their liberators. Bertrand recognised one of his former neighbours. 'He *is* a Red!' she shouted. 'They used to come and go from his apartment as bold as you please.' The first soldier raised his rifle again.

'I'm a teacher,' Bertrand said. 'I have papers to prove I'm English.'

The leader of the group was troubled by indecision. At last he turned to the woman. 'Show me his apartment.'

The woman led the way, her shawl folded round her body, scurrying along the street with self-importance. The soldiers followed, pushing Bertrand between them. The man who had been ready to shoot him satisfied his passion to use his rifle by swinging the butt down against the back of Bertrand's head, prompting a harsh 'Not yet!' from his commander.

They came to a brief halt at the end of the narrow street and the memory of Tessa's death, her arms spread on the

410

cobbles, flooded Bertrand's mind. One of the soldiers pushed him ahead and they entered the apartment building. Bertrand felt the sharp pain of the wound on his head and a warm trickle of blood on his neck as they climbed the stairs. He could hear the crowd in the street and remembered stories of the atrocities committed by the mob sympathetic to the Versaillais, how suspected Communards had been rounded up, men and women and children with limbs torn and bodies beaten to a pulp. The kind of fear which he had not known since Tessa's death touched him with fingers of ice against his spine.

Bertrand entered the apartment and saw that someone had been there before them. Drawers and cupboards were torn open and their contents spilled on the floor. One of the soldiers turned to him with a leer. 'In a hurry, were we?'

'It's been looted, you fool.' Bertrand looked at the wreck of possessions which seemed paltry in their disarray and to have belonged now to someone else.

The man with the rifle raised it threateningly again, but his companion had moved to the fireplace and was fumbling there with something in the grate; he turned in triumph to the others. 'He's Red scum all right!'

A jeer of anticipation rose from the soldiers and Bertrand recognised a National Guard *képi* and red scarf.

'Liar!' The rifle smashed against his ribs with a blow which made him crash to his knees. The soldier raised his rifle butt again, but the captain pushed the man away and signalled to two others who hauled Bertrand into the corridor and down the stairs to the street.

The crowd let out a howl as the soldiers reappeared with their prisoner, dragging him through a battery of fists and sticks, and a chant filled Bertrand's ears, 'Kill him! Kill!' The crowd fell silent as the men propped him with his face against the wall and tied his hands behind his back.

411

He prayed that his death when it came would be clean. The crowd had set up a chanting again. How could they want him to die? They knew nothing about him. They screamed so readily for death – the death of an empire, the death of their Republic. The death of civilisation, was that what people wanted in their hearts?

His last impressions were not of dying, nor even of Paris as he heard the click and slam of rifles being loaded. The mob fell silent once more and the sounds of the soldiers and the street receded. In the moment before the bullets tore into his body Bertrand's thoughts drifted to Griseley.

Was this death? he wondered. To lose all sense of pain and evil? The scent of may flowers and an image of Phoebe with her arms full of blossom filled his mind.

Maurice watched from behind the shutters as the mob gathered in the street below. He saw the soldiers drag Bertrand out from the building to the opposite side of the street, saw them push him up against the wall and then take aim. A howl of satisfaction rose from the crowd and Maurice turned from the window and fell against the wall. Sweat poured from him and he sank to his haunches, the crash of rifle fire still ringing in his ears. He heard himself praying in terror, his voice gibbering, like old women in church. He had not prayed in years and the realisation made him weep.

After a while he dried his eyes. He felt sick and his body was weak. He calmed himself with thoughts of Phoebe. She had escaped with Antoine to his farm in the country where everything would be clean and good. He would go there too and Phoebe would help him forget.

He could not bring himself to look from the window to see whether they had hauled the body away. He slipped out of the house by the back entrance, running through the streets and alleys. He touched his pocket now and then and felt the crackle of Bertrand's passport.

That night as he looked back on Paris the glare of burning buildings filled the horizon, red as blood, raging like the fires of hell itself. The sky was lit from end to end.

Twenty

O that 'twere possible
After long grief and pain
To find the arms of my true love
Round me once again!

Alfred Lord Tennyson,
from *Maud*

The blossom in the orchards was over. Three weeks had passed since the terrible last days of the Commune. Phoebe tried not to think of Bertrand and held on to a hope still that he had survived. She nursed a dreadful image of Maurice fighting to the end along with the Communards who were driven back into Belleville. The Versaillais had lined more than a hundred against the wall in the Père Lachaise cemetery and shot them, and the killing still went on even now.

Antoine took risks as he came and went and brought news to the farm. He told of the thousands of prisoners marched in long columns to Versailles, the orgies of executions, the suspicions, denunciations and settling of old scores within Paris which was eating up all remnants of decency there. But there was no information about Maurice or her brother. Phoebe could not bear to think that they were among those captured, for there was little hope of reprieve for the Communards or suspected Communards taken prisoner. People were arrested on the slightest pretext, Antoine said – traces of black on hands which could have been involved in incendiary operations during the burning of Paris, a bruised right shoulder from the impression of a rifle butt; a pair of army boots or a red scarf in one's possession. The stories of atrocities against prisoners continued with sickening regularity.

Phoebe walked through the orchards one hot day in June. All the fields for miles around belonged to the farm. Phoebe had imagined by 'farmers' that Antoine's family had been small landholders, but the Latrasse family had owned their estate since the days of the *ancien régime*. Antoine's father had been staunchly monarchist. He would have bitterly regretted his son's involvement with revolutionaries, said Antoine's mother, a wiry would-be dragon but for a streak of sentimentality which she told Phoebe was her undoing. Thank God her husband had not lived to see the fall of Paris. Thank God her son had at last come to his senses. Madame Latrasse thanked God for many things, including Phoebe, whom she assumed to be the cause of Antoine's rebirth as a gentleman. Phoebe understood quickly that Antoine's mother had marked her out as a possible daughter-in-law. She liked the English, Madame Latrasse said. Never mind the past – she had never thought much of the first Napoleon anyway, a nasty little man, and his nephew had not been much better. She had supported the Republican Government during the fight against the Prussians. 'But sadly they were weak. We French do not make great politicians though we are great thinkers and great philosophers.'

'And great talkers,' Antoine had murmured.

'Ah – but look now what has happened to poor France.' Madame Latrasse threw up her hands and looked at Phoebe and her eyes filled with tears. 'Our poor France.' And Phoebe, remembering how beautiful Paris had been, wept with her.

Phoebe reached the broad wooden gates at the edge of the apple orchards. The grass here was long and the trees left unpruned. The land beyond the gates spread in an almost unbroken plain. The already ripening corn shimmered in the heat; in the distance stood a band of yellow-leaved poplars, beyond them a darker line of woodland rising to the horizon – and beyond that, fifty miles to the south, Paris.

Phoebe folded her arms and leaned her back against the sun-warmed gate. She wore a dress borrowed from Antoine's mother; it was quaint and black and primly encrusted at the neck and cuffs with lace, and it hung loosely on her figure. Antoine was away, gone again in search of information about Bertrand and Maurice. He would have to take care, for the local Gendarmerie were vigilant on behalf of Thiers's government; a fat policeman had ridden up to the house asking questions soon after Phoebe's arrival. He had hinted that Antoine was not entirely to be trusted, there were rumours about suspect company in the past, if it was not for the family's good honour – he had shrugged his shoulders to indicate that one could only speculate as to what might have happened. In any case the man had questioned Phoebe thoroughly and had examined her passport and even her hands with fastidious care. Madame Latrasse had lied for her, had said that Phoebe was a dear family friend who had come to them from Paris seeking refuge from the Communards, but the man had looked at her suspiciously, saying that the Reds were everywhere and that the women were the worst.

Phoebe watched the road, a straight, creamy-yellow dirt track which crossed the plain. 'We shall have to call the dressmaker to the house,' Antoine's mother had said that morning, regarding her critically. 'We must equip you properly since all your nice things are left behind in Paris.' When Phoebe had protested that she must return to England just as soon as she received news about her brother, Madame Latrasse had given her a searching look and said, 'I shall have a word with Antoine. Leave it to me. You won't have to go back to England.'

Phoebe smiled as she remembered the conversation. Antoine had been kind, but she could not regard him as a future husband, nor was he in love with her. She considered the notion: he was personable and amusing and she was fond of him; he was also very brave, for he had delayed his escape from Paris to rescue her, all admirable qualities. But Phoebe knew now that she would never marry. She pressed her hands against the black silk skirt: she would continue to wear the costume of a chaste woman into middle age and beyond – sober, self-denying and respectable.

She was on the point of turning back to the house when she saw a stirring of dust where the road met the line of poplars and heard the dull thud of hooves. She shielded her eyes with both hands, trying to see who was approaching. The dust cloud came nearer and she saw that it was raised by a horse bearing two riders. Phoebe's mouth dried, for she recognised Antoine and the other must be – she gave a cry and began to run, joy flooding her whole body. He was safe. She could see his mulberry coat and hat. 'Bertrand! He's safe!'

Phoebe halted as the riders approached and her head swam with confusion, for the man mounted behind Antoine, dressed in Bertrand's clothes, was not her brother. There was a roaring in her ears, as if she was about to faint. She murmured, 'I thought—' Maurice slipped from the horse and held her before she could fall.

Phoebe plucked at the sleeve of his coat. 'I'm sorry – I hoped—' She saw that he understood her mistake. 'Why are you wearing Bertrand's clothes?' Her heart lifted again with optimism. How glad she was to see Maurice and to know that he had not been murdered by the Versaillais, and of course – Bertrand would have lent the clothes to help Maurice escape; he was hiding somewhere and would be following later.

Antoine dismounted. 'Phoebe – I wish I could tell you easily.'

The meaning of his words reached her slowly. Maurice still held her. He said, 'My poor little Phoebe. Your brother is dead.'

No, she would not believe them. She heard Antoine say, 'You must have courage. Bertrand is dead and Maurice has come to us for help but no one must see him, not even my mother, it would be too dangerous for her.' She nodded, though his voice seemed so far away. She heard them talking: 'She has had a shock,' Maurice's voice close to her, and Antoine somewhere distant, 'This is too bad. We should have broken the news more gently. Now what do we do?'

Phoebe forced herself to gather her thoughts: everyone's safety must come first. If the police saw Maurice – they were suspicious of all strangers, and he was a Communard, he was on the run, he would be shot and Madame Latrasse and Antoine too. She said, 'Where can he hide?'

'One of the farm buildings.' Antoine's voice was relieved.

Maurice kissed her hands. 'Phoebe. You are very brave.'

The two men hurried away, leading the horse between them. Phoebe waited for Antoine in the orchard and the words, *Bertrand is dead*, repeated over and over in her head. The apples were beginning to swell behind the brown and crumpled blossom clusters; she touched one and the

419

petals fell like dry paper against her hand. The sky was white and distant and there was a rushing sound in her head like that of turbulent water far away. She watched Antoine come towards her through the trees. His eyes were full of sadness as he put his arm round her and said, as Maurice had said, that she was very brave. But she did not feel brave, only numb as she walked with him slowly to the house.

The brown walls and timbers shimmered in the sun. The lush rose-scented vegetation of the garden was all around them and Antoine held her arm firmly, talking all the time, saying that Maurice had told him how Bertrand had died a hero's death fighting on a barricade. She could not understand what he was saying, for Bertrand would not have fought with the Communards. They met Antoine's mother in the entrance and Phoebe ran to her stiff embrace saying, 'Madame, my brother Bertrand is dead.'

They left her to cry in her room with the curtains drawn to shut out the sun. Madame Latrasse said that grief must be allowed to work itself out, but Phoebe wept all afternoon and all evening and still the pain did not lessen.

The next day she got up late and went in search of Antoine. The well of tears had dried to a hard dry knot in her chest and her mind was calm again. Antoine was in shirt-sleeves, cutting the long grass in the garden. The scent of roses was sickly and Phoebe's head ached from the glare of the sun.

'May I see Maurice?'

Antoine glanced round to make sure they were alone, then continued scything the grass as if he had not heard her. 'It isn't wise,' he said after a while. 'I would not have had him come here—' He frowned, straightening from the work, then began again, swinging the blade with swift strokes. 'Why didn't he make straight for the coast?'

'But we're his friends.'

'You don't understand, Phoebe. I must think of my mother. He's taken all this—' he paused, unwilling to voice his thoughts, '—he's taken everything too much for granted.'

'I have to talk to him about Bertrand. How it happened.'

He halted and looked at her, then put down the scythe. 'Of course. I'm an insensitive pig. It must be terrible not knowing.'

He went with Phoebe to one of the outhouses. The interior was whitewashed and strung with cobwebs; the only light came from the doorway and a small arched window high up near the roof.

As her eyes adjusted to the dim light Phoebe saw that Maurice had made a bed in a corner from a palliasse and guessed that he had been sleeping. He sat up quickly. 'Antoine?' He scrambled to his feet when he saw Phoebe.

Antoine turned to Phoebe awkwardly, sensing that she would prefer to be alone to talk about her brother. 'I shall be in the garden. Take care no one sees you when you leave.'

Maurice spread a blanket over a wine cask and pulled forward a wooden box so that she might step on it to sit on the barrel. 'My dear Phoebe.' He took her hand and kissed it fervently. She felt isolated, like a statue perched on a pedestal. Maurice seemed very agitated and she understood how hard it must be for him to talk to her when he had seen Bertrand die.

'I have to know about Bertie. It's so awful, just imagining.'

'He was very courageous,' Maurice said gravely. He went to the door and stared out at the empty yard with his back to her. He was trembling. 'I'm sorry. I have to find the words.'

'Antoine seemed to say that he was fighting for the Communards.'

He turned suddenly. 'He died in my arms. We were fighting together on a barricade near Les Halles.'

'I'm glad he was close to home.'

'He was defending the Rue Rambuteau. His feelings had changed, Phoebe. He was very strong with us against the Versaillais.'

'Because of Tessa.'

'Perhaps because of Tessa.' He fell silent and looked again out to the yard. 'There's not much more to tell. He was killed almost outright – shot through the chest. There seemed little or no pain.'

'Did he leave a message?' she said pitifully, for a final word, even second-hand, would be a comfort.

Maurice turned and looked at her. He came towards her and stood for a moment and his eyes gleamed with tears in the semi-darkness. 'His dying words were, "Remember me to my dear sister".'

Antoine felt protective towards Phoebe in her grief: he could almost accept his mother's conviction that the English girl should be drawn permanently into the family's care. Was it not his duty as Bertrand's friend to replace him as a brother? And if not a brother to Phoebe, perhaps a husband, for since leaving Paris he knew he had altered, become more sober and aware of his mother's advancing age and frailty. It was time he took over the running of the estate; time he settled down and married.

Antoine was troubled about Maurice. On the one hand there was the danger of sheltering a Communard, on the other he felt uneasy about Maurice himself and his sudden changes of mood and ramblings about his last days in Paris. 'I despised you for abandoning us,' Maurice had said, talking of the insanity which had turned friendship to hatred; he had blinked back tears, confessing, 'Now I see that you were right. The Commune was doomed. It didn't act swiftly enough but wasted its energies in dreams of universal justice.' He had seized his arm. 'They weren't ruthless enough, Antoine. That was the pity of it. They should have marched on Versailles early on and annihilated their enemies.'

But it was Maurice's account of Bertrand's death which troubled Antoine most deeply. Had those really been Bertrand's last words – *Maurice, you must take my passport and get away*? He could not reconcile the feverish and tearful story with the old Maurice of the café tables, nor believe in the relationship with the Englishman whom Maurice had once disparaged, as if at the end they had been blood brothers.

Phoebe found it comforting to talk to Maurice. She went each afternoon to the outhouse and sat in the cool half-light on the upturned barrel with her feet on a box, hugging her knees with her arms. She listened to Maurice's repeated story of how Bertrand had fought like a lion against the Versaillais, not recognising her brother in this valiant hero of the Commune and wondering some days whether to believe him.

Maurice lounged on the mattress with his back against the outhouse wall, repeating his account of how he and Bertrand had fought together with various rebel groups in an area between the Gare du Nord and the Hôtel de Ville, how Bertrand had repeatedly exposed himself to enemy fire as an example of courage to the others, and how he had died with two names on his lips – that of his friend Maurice and his sister Phoebe.

Maurice had been genuinely moved by his story of Bertrand's death. Indeed, he had become convinced that it was the true version, for it was how it should have ended had Bertrand not been stubborn and held on at the barricade until it was too late. Maurice saw that he had been right to seek out Phoebe, she would be his salvation. With Bertrand's passport he might just get out of all this alive; hundreds of others had escaped Versailles justice by fleeing abroad. And he would be a brother to her. It was the least he could do, he told himself. Dear, beautiful Phoebe, even more lovely in her grief. A single shaft of sunlight struck through the window and lit her black-clad figure, motionless on the wine barrel, as if she were in a shrine.

'You should not spend so much time with him,' warned Antoine one afternoon as Phoebe ran in from the garden.

'Hearing about Bertrand helps me. Please, Antoine, try to understand.'

'All the same, my mother was asking for you this afternoon. I had to lie. I don't like lying to my mother.'

The dinner gong sounded. The servants moved discreetly to and fro and a smell of fish drifted down the corridor. Phoebe seized Antoine's hand and kissed it. 'I'm sorry. You and your mother have both been so good to me. It's time I thought about leaving.'

'Maurice hopes to go to England too,' said Antoine.

'Bertie gave Maurice his papers. It's appropriate that he should use his identity. They were very close at the end.'

Antoine looked at her and sighed. 'I wish it could have been different – Bertrand was such a good, decent fellow.'

Maurice had grown bored with telling stories of Bertrand's final days. He talked more frequently of the elation of escape and the freedom of the open countryside after being incarcerated in Paris. He described the exhilaration he had felt as he saw the red skies from the burning buildings grow fainter in the distance. He was bored with his enforced idleness and talked incessantly of going to England. He paced the brick floor of the farm building and cursed the fates which kept him here like an animal in a cage.

'If you are going to England you must improve your English,' Phoebe said one day. 'I shall teach you.'

'Ah – England.' He placed his hands behind his head and leaned back against the wall. 'Do you know I've not seen daylight outside these four walls for two weeks?'

'It's safer to lie low for a while. The local police would soon discover who you really are.'

'Safe!' He pulled a face and his teeth showed between his lips. 'I'm tired with *safe*. My only exercise, to walk up and down, up and down in this miserable hole, only going outside when it's dark. Waiting every day for you to come and talk to me and Antoine to bring my food as if he is my gaoler. Is that the kind of existence for a man like me?'

'No,' she agreed, remembering Maurice when she had first met him, denouncing the Emperor with revolutionary talk. How he had intrigued her with his energy and fervour. She could tell it was bad for him to be confined.

'I have nightmares. Sometimes I dream I'm in prison again.'

'It *is* so like a prison.' She looked at the tiny window, which only needed bars to complete the analogy. She was struck suddenly by a temporary solution to relieve the claustrophobia of his existence. 'No one would see you in the far apple orchard. The only risk would be in reaching it, but Antoine's outdoor servants keep to the stables and garden. Once there, you could walk under the trees unnoticed.'

He kissed her and said that she was amazing.

Phoebe went first, hurrying to the corner of each building to make sure the area beyond was empty, then signalling to Maurice to follow. They continued in this way, keeping to the outer walls of the orchards until they reached the trees furthest from the house. They walked then side by side, emboldened by the stillness of the orchard, the nettles by the wall and tangles of briar choking the tree trunks and the long grass which brushed against their legs.

'Antoine has much to do,' Maurice said piously. 'He has neglected his family's estate.'

Phoebe laughed. Maurice was unshaven and blinked at the brightness of the sunlight, and this slight vulnerability in his appearance contrasted with his oddly sanctimonious turn of mind. She fell silent, realising that she was already freeing herself from the fierce oppression of her grief of the past days and that Bertrand's death was no longer a dark weight on her heart.

'I haven't seen you smile for a long time,' he said, watching her.

'I don't feel so sad any more. Bertrand didn't want to go on living without Tessa. Perhaps they're happy now and in heaven together.'

Men and women were not complete without one another: she regarded Maurice as he walked by her side and her heart quickened a little, for his face had none of that coldness today which had made him such a puzzle in the past.

He turned to her. 'Shall we travel to England together, Phoebe? Will I be your brother?'

'It will be—' she had been going to say 'safer' but changed her mind. 'It would be appropriate.'

They walked to the end of the boundary where the wall formed a corner. Here they were screened by brambles and fruit trees from all aspects of the house and from the main track which led through the orchards to the outside fields. Maurice spread Bertrand's coat on the grass and they sat with their backs to the bricks of the high orchard wall, hot through the black silk of Phoebe's dress.

'How wonderful to feel the sun on one's body again.' Maurice closed his eyes.

She watched him secretly, daring for the first time to examine the scar which stretched from eye to mouth and formed a white line where the stubble of his beard did not grow. Her heart twisted a little with emotions she had thought entirely dead to her.

He opened his eyes. 'Shall we begin with the English lesson?'

His knowledge of English was already good, and he was proud of the fact that he had once been to London. She was surprised at his quickness to learn and saw that it was only through laziness and her own willingness to accommodate herself to the ways of Paris that he had always spoken to her in French. She taught him how to speak with an English accent and they laughed at the contortions of his mouth as he endeavoured to say '*H*alifax, *H*uddersfield and *H*ull'.

They went each afternoon to the orchard and at the end of each lesson they would return the way they had come, Phoebe leading, Maurice strolling behind, whistling a little or stopping to pick her bunches of wild flowers. They never encountered anyone.

One afternoon Maurice fell asleep. The air was drowsy and bumble bees banged against the grasses and Phoebe watched as his head lolled back against the wall. She studied him for several minutes, the dark lashes against his cheeks, his jaw slack and his lips parted a little. She felt her heart beat more quickly. There was something intimate and exciting about regarding him while he slept. The sun was very hot and made her feel light-headed and reckless.

If he were to open his eyes, she decided, he would kiss her and she would kiss him back. And then Maurice made a little sound, half groan, half cry, and opened his eyes wide as if he had been on the point of dreaming and was jerked back to consciousness. His look was startlingly direct and strange, almost as if he were afraid of what he might see.

'I am here,' she said gently. 'I won't leave you.'

He looked at her for several seconds. 'I should like to make love to you, Phoebe.'

She was silent. Her heart pounded and she knew that she wanted the kind of love he was offering and that she desired him in a sinful way. She looked down in distress when he said, 'You do know what I mean?' He laid a hand on her lap, running it firmly along the inner part of her thigh.

Her desire for him had become intense and distinct, centred in that part of her body which was forbidden to the touch. She turned to him when he leaned towards her and as she kissed him her body rose to meet his. He worked swiftly to unfasten the minuscule buttons of her bodice, he pulled back the silk and lace and touched the softness of her breast and she shuddered as his fingers reached the nipple. She thought *this is an abomination in the eyes of the Lord* and a vision rose before her of her father in the pulpit of the Ebenezer chapel, but her legs parted in obedience to Maurice's hand.

Maurice drew back from her and said, 'Take off your clothes.'

She shook her head, full of shame again and he smiled, showing his teeth, knowing that she wanted him. He unfastened his shirt, watching her all the time with a shrewd smile and she trembled to see the whiteness of his skin. A deep bluish purple bruise covered an area the size of her hand on his right shoulder. She reached out to him and caressed the rifle mark and remembered Paris and the barricades and the fact that Bertrand had been shot.

He said again more urgently, 'Take off your clothes for me.'

She bowed her head and undid the fastenings at her

waist. She wriggled out of Madame Latrasse's dress and unfastened her underclothes without looking at him, hearing him move away and take off the rest of his own clothes. Her desire faded with the cumbersome necessity of removing corset and petticoats. She began to imagine that one of the gardeners or Antoine would appear among the trees and saw again her father's admonishing fist calling the wrath of God down from Ebenezer's rafters. She sat on her petticoat, holding her arms across her breasts, her chemise bundled on her lap to cover its nakedness.

'You are very beautiful,' he said, and she was startled and only now did she look at him and saw that a man's body, though exotic and strange, was also beautiful. She gasped as he took her hands away from her breast and desire flooded back as he bent and touched it with his tongue. And then all thought slipped from her as she gave way to the sensations which his mouth and hands awakened.

They lay upon her petticoat. The apple trees made a dark pattern on the blue sky and the leaves danced against the sun and she was astonished by the sensuality of her body.

He paused after the first shock of penetration; he waited, then moved almost imperceptibly within her so that she gasped with excitement instead of fear. He drew pleasure from her slowly, until she was consumed by it and, reaching his own climax, hurting her a little now, he moved with silent, animal intensity.

He rolled from her and she lay with the sun soaking her body, naked to the sky. She lay on her side and stroked his bruised shoulder and ran her hand down the length of his torso to touch the source of pleasure at the base, and still as she explored its fragile contours she felt no shame. She sighed and lay back upon her petticoats and let the sun dazzle her eyes.

* * *

They went every day to the orchard and lay together in the afternoon sun, smelling the scent of the grass and the earth, talking and making love to the sound of bees and the wind blowing in the leaves. One day they must have slept for longer than usual, for when Phoebe lifted her eyelids the sun was low in the sky.

'You will be missed,' Maurice said. 'We should not have stayed so long.'

They dressed quickly and Phoebe was a little disappointed by his coldness. But as they came within sight of the outbuildings he bent and kissed her tenderly and said, 'Make haste and see if the way is clear.'

She kissed him back, desire for him mounting again and catching her by surprise, but he seemed not to notice and gave her a little push towards the yard. She left the orchard and made for the outhouse and as she opened the door to see that it was empty she came face to face with Antoine.

He looked at her, taking account of her untidy hair. 'Phoebe, are you all right? Maurice isn't in the outhouse. Have you seen him?'

'We've been for a walk—' Phoebe flushed a deeper red.

Antoine's expression, bland and puzzled at first, stiffened with anger. Then, as Maurice swung round the corner and Antoine saw them together, he released an involuntary 'Ah—' of understanding. 'I came to tell you that you have a letter from your father, Phoebe.' He handed the letter to her and spoke coldly. 'I would rather you didn't take risks, Maurice.' He looked at Phoebe. 'You could jeopardise everyone's safety.'

Later he said to Phoebe, 'I think, don't you, it's time we made plans for you to go to England?'

Twenty-one

What could have been done more to my
vineyard, that I have not done to it?
wherefore when I looked that it should bring
forth grapes, brought it forth wild grapes?

Isaiah 5:4

Edwin read Phoebe's letter several times. Both dead –
Bertrand and the whore. He had half expected it for so long,
yet he was not prepared. He choked back his grief as
memories of Bertrand's childhood, when the boy had been
innocent and pliable, filled his mind. Why Bertrand? Why
the best of the brood? He pressed a hand to his trembling
mouth and prayed for strength against this latest blow. He
crumpled his napkin and dabbed it against his mouth and
his hand tightened its grip to stop the trembling. His chest
hurt with each breath and he sat with the cloth pressed
against his mouth, then walked slowly to his study where he
collapsed into the chair by his desk. He opened the Bible at
the book of Isaiah, muttering the words before he found
them: '. . . *I will tell you what I will do to my vineyard: I
will take away the hedge thereof, and it shall be eaten up;
and break the wall thereof, and it shall be trodden down;
and I will lay it waste . . .*' He came to the verse and read

431

on, the familiar words steadying the rise and fall of his chest. His lips moved soundlessly with the judgement on all sinners: *Woe unto them that call evil good, and good evil; that put darkness for light, and light for darkness; that put bitter for sweet, and sweet for bitter! Woe unto them that are wise in their own eyes, and prudent in their own sight!* The Lord had punished the men at his foundry who had risen up against law and order, and the magistrate had put them in gaol. In Paris, the Lord of hosts had summoned armies whose *horses' hoofs shall be counted like flint, and their wheels like a whirlwind* to crush the insurrectionists and bring judgement on Bertrand for his wrong-doing. Edwin began to read aloud, the words rolling off his tongue with a rich and satisfying resonance: *'Their roaring shall be like a lion, they shall roar like young lions: yea, they shall roar and lay hold of the prey and carry it away safe and none shall deliver it. And in that day they shall roar against them like the roaring of the sea: and if one look unto the land, behold darkness and sorrow . . .'*

He stopped and the tears rolled down his cheeks as he wept for Bertrand, for his young lion, his son, and for every disappointment which he had suffered; and he was tempted for a moment to rail against that deity in whom he had put all his trust.

'Your brother is killed.'

Gerald and Charles stared, their mouths gaping.

Edwin pulled Phoebe's letter from his pocket with a shaking hand and laid it on his desk in the office. 'He was fighting for those Communists. I always knew he would come to a bad end.' His grief again threatened to overwhelm him. He would feel no pity for the girl, but his son, his favourite son. 'Bertrand has long been dead to us in spirit. We must pray for his soul all the same.'

Charles stared at his father's white head bowed over the desk. Bertrand was dead? His brother had met the sacrificial end of a revolutionary. He felt no pity, nor did he feel any sense of satisfaction, as he had once imagined he might, to learn that the brother who had rivalled him all his life was no more.

Tears rolled down Gerald's cheeks. 'Our poor Bertie. Killed in France. We must pray to the Lord for strength.'

'We shall ask Him to look mercifully on your brother's transgressions,' said Edwin.

Charles prayed with them for Bertrand's transgressions and thought of Christina, who was now a widow.

'A woman may not marry her deceased husband's brother,' said Beatrice. 'You know it. He knows it. So why persist?'

'It's so unfair!' wailed Christina.

'Unfair or not, it's the law.'

Christina dried her eyes. 'At least I may receive him now.' Beatrice hesitated, but could find no objections readily. 'There is no law says a woman may not allow her dead husband's brother to visit?' Christina persisted.

'But the gossip—' began Beatrice.

'Oh hang gossip!' Christina stormed from the room and swung down the staircase to where Charles waited for her in the hall.

'I don't know whether one or other of us should offer condolences,' said Charles as she took his arm. 'I to you in your widowhood. You to me for the loss of a brother.'

'I must admit, I'm hard pressed to feel any sorrow,' said Christina heatedly.

Charles fell silent as they walked across the grounds, for he could no longer sustain his earlier indifference. 'I suppose one feels regret rather than sorrow.' They stopped on the terrace and he took her hands in his. 'Of course, I realise we may never marry.'

'But we shall always be friends,' she said quickly. 'And whatever the law says, our souls will be united in death, for married or not, I shall always be yours in my heart.'

It was a pretty and spirited speech and merited one in return. 'And I yours.' Charles dismissed the ignoble suspicion that a marriage of souls in eternity might prove less than satisfactory in the here and now. 'For me there can never be any other.'

'When are your brothers coming out of prison?' Olive pulled on her stockings as she sat on the edge of the settee.

Jack had finished dressing and went to the window. Rain beat against the glass. 'Beginning of August – two more weeks.' A horse and cart rumbled past, the horse trudging patiently along the wet cobbles and the driver wrapped in oilskins, like a fisherman.

'They're lucky they didn't get worse than a spell in Wakefield. Edwin can be a vindictive old so and so.'

Jack turned from the window and surveyed her critically. She was older than he had once thought, her face harder, her figure sagged a little. She did not attempt to cover her breasts and he was both troubled and excited by her nakedness, for women of his own class were modest about their bodies, and decent women too, or so he had always thought. He remembered Phoebe's anger when he had kissed her among the potted geraniums and their curious reserve with one another after that. Did she ever think of him? he wondered.

He watched Olive, fascinated by the sensuous fluid movements of her body. 'Clough's letting all the men come back to the foundry,' he said. 'They've had to promise not to agitate for more money.'

'He needs them for those silly lions of his, that's all. Edwin Clough hasn't an ounce of compassion in his body.'

'Sometimes I think I understand him.'

'Nobody understands that family.' She gave him a quizzical look and he knew that she too was thinking of the feelings he had once had for Phoebe. 'They're all so rigid. Oh, yes. Even Gerald. All he lives for is his theatre.'

Jack thought of Gerald's other preoccupations. 'And his father's passion is his foundry.'

'More like his reputation as a foundry owner and his position on the town council and among the chapel-going fraternity.'

'That's a failing of his, I'll grant you. But he really *cares* about that works. He's spent a lifetime building it up.'

She fastened her hair with her arms raised above her head and pins between her teeth, smiling at him. She stirred a desire in him even now and he went to her and kissed her neck, running his hands over her breasts to caress her stomach.

'Serve Edwin right if your brothers and the other men tell him what to do with his lions when they come out.' She pushed in a final pin.

He moved away. 'They could get work by going south. Clough knows that. What he doesn't know is that they won't leave Griseley. It's where a man's born that counts.'

She laughed. 'You're all so parochial.' And Jack remembered that Olive was not native-born Yorkshire, but had met Gerald in Nottingham and left home and family for him apparently without a qualm. She dressed and came to stand beside him at the window. She kissed him lightly, clinging to his arm, but he responded only briefly and stared again at the driving rain on the window.

Olive was growing bored with Jack; he was so dour and it was tiresome doing it with anyone so frequently troubled by his conscience. 'What is your passion, Jack?' she said. 'Since it so clearly isn't me. Is it to see justice done?' She quoted from *And All That Makes a Man*, '*My liege, I would that all men live in harmony and be free.*'

He smiled at last. 'Something like that. I just want a bit of peace and to get on with the job at the foundry once Walter and Matt get home.'

'What about your acting?'

He did not answer. The play opened within two weeks but he felt no enthusiasm for it. He felt that Gerald had spoiled his passion for the theatre.

Did Olive know about Gerald's feelings for him? Sometimes he thought she did. Suddenly she seemed more serious. 'You've got talent, Jack. Don't let anything get in the way of it.'

The clock above the empty fire-grate struck four-thirty. He turned and picked up his hat and jacket from the chair by the fireplace. 'It's time I was off.'

Olive sighed and went to unlock the door. 'I'll let you know when it's safe to visit me again.' She touched his shoulder lightly as he passed her, flicking away an imaginary speck of dust.

He hesitated, on the very point of saying he was finished, knowing that if he did she would calmly accept the end of the affair.

He had reached the top of the stairs when she seemed to remember something – or perhaps she had planned it, for there was an exaggerated composure about her as she imparted the news.

'Oh, by the way – Gerald tells me that his father has heard from Phoebe.'

He turned, seeing her framed there in the doorway of her sitting room, her head cocked on one side with a little twisted smile.

'Phoebe is coming home to Griseley next week. It seems she's had enough of the excitement in France.'

Edwin knew there were some on the Griseley council who were saying he was a fool to have taken the half-dozen men on again. Alfred Underwood for a start, and Murgatroyd had called him daft to his face for employing gaolbirds. But Edwin felt pleased with his judgement: the Batemans and the others were among his best-skilled men.

Most of the workers had flocked back after the town-hall fiasco. All had agreed to have nothing more to do with union business and he had been right in his guess that a spell in prison would knock the rebellious spirit out of the rest of them. He had set them to work straight away on preparing the new casting-bed for the lions.

'Only a few more weeks now, lads,' he said to Walter, who touched his cap with a deference which strengthened Edwin's satisfaction. The men had publicly expressed their gratitude for his magnanimity in giving them their old jobs; the status quo was nicely restored.

Jack watched his brother, unsure of him. Walter had altered during the weeks away, had grown more sullen; both Walter and Matt were bitter about Jack's role in the affair and the fact that he had avoided prison. The spell in gaol had left a sour taste, and Walter's apparent surrender made Jack uneasy.

'It's going to be a grand day when we cast yon lions,' said William Burns. He had suffered more than the younger men from the privations of prison life and Jack was saddened to see him so eager to please.

'A bloody grand day,' said Walter when Edwin had passed. 'At least we'll be shot of the buggers and can get back to normal again.'

Edwin went out to the yard. Phoebe was arriving in

Griseley that afternoon and the thought lowered his spirits a little. The truth was he did not know how he felt about his daughter's return. He craved that gladness of heart he had once known, when Phoebe had made a haven of tranquillity in his household. But reason told him that the old Phoebe would be gone, for she had been away more than a year and had witnessed scenes which would have changed her, and which people in Griseley could barely imagine.

Charles was coming down the steps from the office, pulling on his gloves. 'Shall we go now, Father? The train will be here in a quarter hour.'

'Plenty of time.' Edwin climbed the stairs past him.

'You *are* coming?' Charles said tetchily.

He was getting edgy, thought Edwin, but it wasn't because of his sister's home coming, he was worrying already about the casting. He paused on the steps and laid a hand on Charles's shoulder. 'It's a good sculpture. A fine beast. Nothing's going to go wrong this time. The men are with us and you've been over the timings and figures again and again.'

Charles pulled out his watch from his waistcoat pocket. 'Father! Gerald's gone for the carriage. Should we go without you?'

Edwin continued up to the office. 'No, lad. I'll be there.'

The factories and chimneys were as black as ever. The station buildings looked as they had always looked as the train slowed and the platform palings skimmed alongside the carriage.

Phoebe had not supposed that they would all come to meet her. She could see the family carriage in the station yard as the train slowed and a lump came to her throat. She leaned from the railway-carriage window and raised a hand tentatively to the trio which formed a grim reception

438

committee on the platform as the train ground to a halt.

Edwin watched her climb from the carriage and walk towards them. No trace of the child in her remained. She was dressed in mourning, in an outfit made of black silk, very chic, very French – the resemblance to her mother was stronger than it had ever been. She kissed him on both cheeks and he embraced her self-consciously, wanting to hold her close, to unleash his gladness and ease his pain over Bertrand. Pride and anger prevented him, for Bertrand's death had been God's judgement and Phoebe must be shown that her defiance had displeased him.

'You look thin, lass.'

Phoebe smiled, close to tears. How old her father seemed, and how sad. They all looked so old. Charles was quite grey and Gerald was stouter than ever. She had told herself that it would be like this and that coming home would be so much harder than leaving, but a knot of pain hardened in her breast because she had lost the brother she loved best and the rest of her family were like strangers to her.

Phoebe saw their combined gaze drift past her to the railway carriage. She should have warned them, she thought, and turned as Maurice lifted down their baggage.

Charles gave her a questioning glance, Gerald looked at her with an amused lift of the eyebrows, she heard her father's 'Phoebe—?' and said quickly, 'Father, this is Monsieur Chaudet. He and I are engaged to be married.'

Edwin's jaw slackened. He stared at the approaching figure. A Frenchman. Phoebe had dared to turn up with a Frenchman after all this time and call it 'engaged to be married'. He shook Maurice's hand and said with a cold courtesy, 'I won't pretend this doesn't come as a surprise, sir.'

Gerald laughed. He pumped Maurice's hand. 'Well, Phoebe, you might have told us.'

439

'I just did,' said Phoebe and they all, except Edwin, laughed a little.

Maurice smiled, he was in one of his moods to charm. Phoebe watched him converse with Charles as they walked to the waiting carriage. They were all overcome by the uniqueness of the situation and their unfamiliarity with one another. Maurice seemed superior and exotic beside her brothers; he was trying out his grasp of English conversation with great earnestness and in his eradicable French accent and desire for him welled within her.

'Well, Phoebe,' said her father in a low voice. 'You've shocked me this time and no mistake. Though it's no more than I'd expect, not after your brother's behaviour.'

She looked at him earnestly, saddened by the great distance between them. 'Don't be bitter, Father.'

'Not be bitter? When my children have proved so wilful and frivolous!' Edwin's hurt welled up in his chest and the effort of silencing a sob made his breath tight and hard.

'Bertie changed.' Phoebe's eyes filled with tears. 'You misjudge him to say he was frivolous.'

Edwin turned away. 'I don't want to talk about him.' He opened the door of the carriage and hesitated as Maurice tossed the baggage on to the carriage rack, regarding him with suspicion.

Phoebe said quickly, 'I thought Monsieur Chaudet might take a room at the Nag's Head – after he's had a bite to eat with us.'

Edwin nodded, relieved that the matter of propriety had been adequately dealt with. 'Well then. Let's be off.'

Maurice had begun to enjoy the novelty of his situation; he felt himself to be a fair emulation of an English gent. He looked around Edwin Clough's sitting room, approving of the expensive carpet, the good prints and solid furniture. He congratulated himself on the way things were turning out. He had guessed, though Phoebe had not said as much, that her family were worth a few sous. Life could become very comfortable here for a while. He smiled at Phoebe across the room, lovely clever Phoebe, the best prize of all. Sometimes he thought that he would have wanted to marry her even if she had not proved so useful to him, even if fate had not decreed that Bertrand should sacrifice himself so that he might escape. He would never tell her the truth, of course. It would only upset her, and he was not a brute. He did not like upsetting women.

'What trade are you in, Mr Chaudet?' asked Edwin, deciding to make the best of a bad job and give Phoebe's fellow a hearing.

'The war interrupted my work.' Maurice judged it too soon to admit to a background of stoking furnaces. 'Alas, so many people lost everything.'

'It must have been a terrible time.' Gerald spoke with the gravity of one who imagined himself sensitive to others' suffering. 'Poor Bertie.' He remembered the fate of his brother and took out a handkerchief and blew his nose.

'Thank goodness that in France at least the insurrectionary working class has been tamed,' said Edwin.

Phoebe said calmly, 'Sometimes rebellion is justified.' She looked at Maurice, expecting him to be roused to anger, a little fearful even of what he might say, for there was hostility to the Commune even here in England and Griseley would be no exception, but Maurice remained impassive.

Gerald said blandly, his thumbs in his waistcoat pockets, 'The Empire of Napoleon III *was* corrupt, and the Government of National Defence let the French people down.'

'It could never have happened in England,' Edwin said. 'What government could have the interests of its people at heart more than Mr Gladstone and his party? And we have our dear virtuous Queen Victoria at the helm. England has a repugnance for disorder. You only have to look back to our own troubles for proof of it.'

'You won't know about the riot.' Charles looked at Phoebe with a wry smile.

Edwin smiled too, for now that it was over, and the men had learned their lesson from it, one could afford to look back on the episode from a more tolerant perspective.

Phoebe was startled. 'A riot? Here in Griseley?' Her thoughts flew at once to Jack, recalling with a startling clarity their antagonism towards one another because of the foundry and her own pious insistence that there could be no comparison between the repression in France and the foundrymen's bid for a higher wage.

Charles, as if embarking on an entertaining story, told them about the strike and the riot at the town hall. 'Quite a little débâcle. The men knocked the town clerk about a bit and Father read the riot act from the town-hall stairs. The Batemans were at the centre of it all, of course. As you might expect.'

'*Jack* Bateman?' said Phoebe sharply.

Maurice was frowning as he struggled to understand their English.

'Not Jack,' Edwin said amiably. 'It was Jack who got his sister to fetch in the police, according to Gerald.'

Maurice looked from one to the other, feeling a stirring of interest in the men who had been provoked to riot. 'What has happened to the men who were on strike?'

'A spell in gaol cooled the riot leaders off,' Edwin said. 'Now they've learned their manners, I've set the men on again at the works.'

'But you've not listened to their grievance at all?' Phoebe said with a touch of asperity.

'Now that *would* be a sign of weakness, lass.' Edwin shook his head at the lenience of women.

Gerald turned to Maurice with the merest hint of xenophobic complacency in his smile. 'We know how to treat our wrongdoers in England.'

Maurice said politely, 'We who have left France prefer not to recall how she has treated her own insurgents.' He stood up. 'But now I must thank you for your hospitality. I shall seek a room at your inn, the Nag's Head.'

'Charles and I will take you there and see you settled in,' offered Gerald.

Maurice shook everyone by the hand and kissed Phoebe's hand tenderly, arranging to meet her the following afternoon.

Gerald turned to Phoebe and kissed her hand with a flourish. 'We'll look after your Frenchman, have no fear. *Adieu, mes amis!*'

Phoebe returned to the sitting room when they had gone. How strange everything was – the house the same as ever, yet everyone, not least herself, so changed. She looked at the harmonium with its candles on either side and the mirror above it, remembering how they had all learned to bang out chapel hymns, and her mother had played waltzes for her to dance to when she was small. Memories of their childhood made her think of Bertrand. She turned to her father who sat by the fireplace; his massive figure seemed to have shrunk into the chair, his hands rested on the arms. He did not look at her and did not stir except for the fingers of his right hand which drummed lightly on the polished wood. What was he thinking? Did he not care at all about Bertrand?

'I think I'll turn in for the night too. It was a long journey.' Phoebe went to the door.

'Do you know what it was like, not knowing from one week to the next what my daughter was doing?' Edwin said suddenly. His hands gripped the chair. 'Have you any idea?'

'I wrote to tell you—' Phoebe held the door handle to steady her.

'You wrote! What use are letters? Learning from a letter that my son – my son—'

Phoebe ran to him and knelt by his chair, grasping his knees in her arms, shocked by their bony lack of substance. 'Bertie died a hero's death, Father. Ask Maurice.'

Edwin summoned the last of his pride as the tears coursed down his cheeks. 'I certainly will not ask Maurice.'

'Bertie could never have come home to Christina. He really loved Tessa. And he changed, Father – oh, I know he used to be shallow and unthinking, but he grew up in France. You ought to be proud of him.'

'I loved him—'

'I know.' She rested her head on his knees and his hand stroking her hair was comforting. They sat for several minutes until she felt the weight of his hand leave her.

'Your Frenchman—' Edwin said abruptly. Phoebe, raising her head, saw that he had dried his cheeks. His face was blotched with red and his eyes bloodshot. He endeavoured to pretend that nothing had happened. 'What's his line of business? Has he any capital?' Embarrassment at his display of emotion made him aggressive. 'Well, I've a right to know if the man my daughter's marrying is likely to keep her in the style she's been used to.'

'I've been used to a very strange style this past year.' Phoebe stood up, straightening her skirt.

'You chose to stay. You'd have been welcome home any time,' he blustered.

She looked down at him, wondering at his small perception of the tremendous upheavals she had witnessed. 'Paris was besieged, Father! The country was at war – national and civil!'

'You know I'm right. Don't bandy words with me.'

'Oh, I'm going to bed.'

'He's penniless, I dare say.'

'Most refugees are. There are men starving in London who got out of France with nothing but the clothes on their backs.'

'But they are Communists!' Edwin said harshly.

She did not answer, afraid suddenly that even here, among her own kin, Maurice might be in jeopardy if his revolutionary activities were known, for there was talk of the government extraditing Communards to France for trial.

Edwin's tone softened. 'It's come as a shock to find out my daughter's to wed a Frenchman. Seems your letters didn't care to include as much. But I want to see you set up, lass. I might be able to lend your man enough capital to start up again here. Now tell me, what was his business?'

'Maurice was hoping to find work here. I wondered if perhaps you might take him on. He's been employed at a foundry works.' Edwin stared at her. 'He was a foundryman.'

Edwin could no longer suppress the feelings which had been gathering inside him all evening. Deeper than his grief over Bertrand, deeper than the long-standing hurt over his children's behaviour and of Phoebe's long absence was a fury against her for her rejection of home and family. It had been aggravated by his instant dislike of the Frenchman; and now there was the fact that Phoebe had kept this last thing a secret from him. At last all his disappointments burst out. 'You're going to marry a foundryman!'

'It's not a crime.'

'It's a folly. And it *is* a crime against your class.'

'Father, you were once an engineer—'

He interrupted her. 'Aye, and I'm not ashamed of it. But I raised myself in the world and I vowed to raise my family too. Are you determined to drag yourself down to the bottom of the pile again?'

She turned. 'I'm going to bed.'

Edwin said steadily, 'There's a place for you in this house as long as you want it, Phoebe. But don't think there will be a welcome for your Frenchman after today, because there will not.'

A summons from Chillingdale, an invitation to Sunday lunch, arrived the next morning.

'You go with Charles. But I hope you'll attend chapel first,' Edwin said and Phoebe nodded, not wanting to provoke further discord between them.

How oddly nostalgic it was to sit in the family pew and to sing the familiar English hymns. A stranger sat in her old place at the chapel harmonium. Phoebe glanced involuntarily to the gallery and saw Sarah Bateman, who sat with a pink-faced young man and offered her an excited smile. There was no sign of Jack. Phoebe thought of the quarrel with her father, and knew that it had been inevitable. She dreaded renewing old acquaintanceships in Griseley and the embarrassment of meeting Philip and of encountering Jack. How easy these obstacles had seemed from afar, yet how confusing it all was close at hand.

Later, seated in the Underwoods' conservatory after lunch, Phoebe felt herself to be a stranger among old friends. Her brother and Christina seemed already to be middle aged: Charles's greying hair and Christina's arid appearance seemed outwardly to endorse the narrowing of their lives. She became conscious of the subtle understanding which existed between them. At the same time, and with a growing heaviness of heart, she saw that no spark of vitality enlivened their communication with one another; it was as if the adventure of life was all behind them. Whereas mine is only just beginning, Phoebe reminded herself with a sudden hunger for Maurice's company.

She felt that she had long ago outgrown her family and the Underwoods and could not restrain a growing sense of moral superiority. She was embarrassed for Philip and his weak attempts to make polite conversation.

'You must bring your fiancé to meet us,' Alfred said. Clearly, thought Phoebe, he had not yet heard that Maurice was not a gentleman.

Charles stood in the doorway, as if he would rather have escaped across the lawn than remain in the suffocating conservatory with its hothouse smell of gardenias.

'Now you must tell us all about your adventures, Phoebe.' Beatrice sat beside her on the wicker sofa. 'We were in such agonies of consternation every day for your safety.'

'I was really quite safe for most of the time,' Phoebe said. 'The Prussian shells didn't reach our part of Paris and though we went hungry we were not really starving during the siege.' She fell silent. A nostalgia for the Rue Rambuteau swept over her unexpectedly and she pictured the destruction which must have taken place there. The deadening effect of the weeks at Antoine's were slipping away from her. Here in Griseley thoughts were clear: recollections of childhood and older memories of Bertrand than those in Paris sharpened her mind to a level of pain. For the first time since leaving France she understood fully that she would never see her brother again.

The others waited for more revelations about the siege and when Phoebe added nothing they looked disappointed.

'I saw an advertisement in the newspaper yesterday for travel tours to Paris,' said Philip. 'One can go by special excursion to view the ruins.'

'The very idea!' murmured Beatrice with an air of being intrigued with the prospect.

'Did the Communists really set all of Paris on fire?' pressed Christina with a shudder. 'They say the women were the most ferocious among the Communists, that they threw petroleum fire-balls and attacked men with their bare hands.'

'I escaped before the worst.' Phoebe remembered Bertrand and saw again the blood and the hole in Tessa's head. She thought of the thousands who had died in the streets or on their way to trial at Versailles and the stories of atrocities committed by the Versaillais. How easy it would be to shock them and give them more than they wanted to hear.

'Foreigners,' said Alfred. 'You can't begin to understand them.'

Beatrice threw him a glance to remind him of Phoebe's attachment to one such outlander. 'I'm sure Phoebe's fiancé is very English in his ways.'

Phoebe decided to provoke consternation among them after all. 'It's strange that I should meet a man whose occupation is so close to home.'

'Close?' enquired Beatrice.

'A foundry, no less.'

Alfred said with interest, 'Mr Chaudet's family have a foundry?'

'His *employer* had a foundry before the war. Monsieur Chaudet is a plain foundryman.'

There was silence, then shockingly, Charles laughed. Christina looked at him and frowned and bit her lip.

'You Cloughs are all tarred with the same brush!' said Beatrice indignantly.

'I'm sure Phoebe wouldn't consider marrying anyone who wasn't nice,' protested Christina. 'And Frenchmen are very well mannered.'

'Oh, his manners might be handsome and French enough, I don't doubt that. But I refuse to believe any person from the working classes is a fit husband for a girl of your upbringing, Phoebe Clough. You could have had our Philip if you'd stuck at home.'

'I went to France at your request,' Phoebe reminded her.

Philip glanced away uneasily, cured of his former aspirations towards Phoebe – if not by her long absence, then certainly by the change in her, for the stay abroad had made her brazen and unfeminine.

'You've no self-discipline. Not one of you!' declared Beatrice. 'No girl of refinement and genteel feeling could degrade herself by such an association.'

'You really were very wicked to upset them like that.' Charles turned to look at her as they drove out past the gatehouse. The wheels clattered on the road and he flicked the whip to speed up the horses. 'You don't know how refreshing it is to have you back.'

'No one mentioned Bertrand,' Phoebe said sadly. She saw Charles's jaw tighten and the laughter fade from his mouth. She wondered how deeply Charles had suffered during the past two years. He had not asked a single question about Tessa.

'So, is your Monsieur Chaudet really a foundryman?' Charles said after a while. 'Have you told Father yet?'

'I told him last night. I hoped he might find Maurice employment at the works.'

'That was very optimistic of you. And does he welcome him with due Christian charity?'

'He refuses to have Maurice in the house again.'

'You can meet at my house,' Charles offered. He shrugged at her look of surprise. 'I don't see why you shouldn't marry who you want. Father's getting more cantankerous and rigid in his ideas.'

'Poor Father.' Phoebe was depressed by the bleak image of her father alone at Belle Vue. She turned to study her brother. She wondered if she had been wrong about him and Christina for he seemed now to have been invigorated by their afternoon at Chillingdale.

'Are you happy, Charlie?'

'As much as I'll ever be.' He glanced at her sideways. 'Christina is a splendid girl. She's very fond of William and I'm fond of young Christopher.' His eyes clouded for a second before he added brightly, 'The situation works very well.'

They passed through the town and the carriage slowed on the cobbles. Phoebe stared at the town hall, trying to picture it under siege. People walked under the trees in the park; the sound of traffic and trains on the railway line formed a disciplined clatter of sound.

'Tell me about the strike,' Phoebe said.

'Jack Bateman got the men organised into a sort of union over the lions. They did well, persuaded Father to reinstate their old wage, but then they wanted extra for the big casting. The foundry's had a few difficulties – the first lion went wrong and the strike didn't help of course and the business of the riot turned everyone even more sour.'

'Will four lions *ever* sit there outside the town hall, do you think?'

'To tell you the truth, I'm tired of the whole business. If the casting goes wrong this time I shan't work on it any more.' Charles urged the horse towards the steep slope of Griseley Bank.

'Has Jack given up his acting?' They reached the Nag's Head and halted.

'Far from it. You must go and see the first night of Gerald's new play. Take Maurice. It's a drama – all about revolution!'

Phoebe climbed from the carriage. She glanced up at the public-house windows. She had expected Maurice to come

450

out and meet her but after a few minutes the street remained empty. She turned to Charles. 'You go on.'

'Don't forget what I said. Come to the house later if you like.'

She nodded and watched him drive away before she entered the pub yard.

Maurice's arrival at the Nag's Head had caused much curiosity. It was customary on Sundays for lodgers to eat with the rest of the family. Kitty fretted about Sunday lunch and the arrangement of her dining room: Maurice was their only guest that weekend and she had heard ominous rumours about French cuisine and Parisian taste and style. Jack, Walter and Matt, used to the comings and goings of commercial travellers, remained indifferent to the stranger, until Walter learned that he had arrived with Phoebe.

'He's Phoebe Clough's intended. You ask Sarah.'

Jack stared at Sarah as she came into the dining room. 'He's making it up.'

'He's not. Phoebe's brought home a Frenchy.'

Walter nudged Matt. 'You know what they say about the Continentals.'

'Don't be coarse, Walt, in front of Rebecca!' Sarah banged a dish of Yorkshire pudding down in the middle of the dining-room table. Since taking up with her clerk in the railway office, Sarah thought herself a cut above the rest, reflected Jack. And didn't he do the same, making love with Gerald Clough's missus? he told himself with a touch of self mockery. Hadn't he given himself a few airs too when he had fancied Phoebe Clough in love with him? And yet it could never have been, for a girl of his class could raise herself by walking out with a railway clerk, or even, if she was lucky, one of the quality, but a genteel girl like Phoebe could only have lowered herself by marrying the likes of a Bateman.

'One of you'd best call our guest.' Kitty smoothed out a crease in the starched white tablecloth. 'We don't want the meat to get cold.'

Sarah went out obediently. They stood behind their chairs and waited. Jack told himself it was of no concern to him who Phoebe was marrying, he felt no curiosity about the stranger, it was all the same if she had returned to Griseley with a Chinaman. He was not prepared for the rush of raw jealousy which filled his throat with bile as Maurice walked into the room. He looked down at his hands, white-knuckled as they gripped the back of the chair.

Sarah ushered Maurice to a place beside their father. Kitty, pink and shining from the heat of the kitchen, introduced everyone self-consciously. She said, 'Sit yourself down, Mister Chaudet and make yourself at home.'

Jack had imagined all Frenchmen to be thin and effeminate, with graceful hands and small feet and a fondness for bowing and kissing. The stranger spread his napkin with square-fingered, blackened and calloused hands, not drawing-room hands Jack noted, and his attention was drawn to the scar which pulled the man's clean-shaven face into a hint of a sneer. How could Phoebe consider marrying the man? It was like Olive had said – no one should try understanding any of the Cloughs: the whole family was tainted with something peculiar.

They ate Kitty's batter and gravy and Maurice declared that 'Yorkshire pudding' was 'the food of the gods'. Kitty glowed with pleasure and said that she supposed people did not eat Yorkshire pudding in France.

'More accustomed lately to rat pie, I shouldn't wonder,' Walter said.

Kitty frowned. 'Manners, Walter. Father, will you carve?'

452

and Joseph stood to confront the side of beef.

'But one ate rats, yes,' Maurice said easily. 'Cats and dogs too.'

Sarah gasped with horror and Walter laughed at her. 'They eat snails and frogs' legs in France an' all.'

'Well, really!' Kitty fanned herself with her serviette, sure that the conversation was not at all proper – neither for the sabbath, nor in the company of her side of best beef.

'Did Miss Clough eat rats in the war?' Sarah's curiosity overcame her squeamishness.

'Miss Clough was very brave. She helped to make balloons you know, and the balloon factory was shelled by the Prussians.'

Jack watched each slice of meat as his father carved. He spoke for the first time, compelled by a desperation to know what had attracted Phoebe to the man.

'Did you work at the factory as well?'

'No. I served in the National Guard – before the uprising.'

'And before that?'

The Frenchman's expression was wary; he regarded him for a moment, as if weighing his answer before he spoke. 'I worked in a foundry. Like you.' If he had said, 'But I am the foundryman who got her,' he could not have struck Jack more cruelly.

Joseph paused in his carving. 'Well, I never did. Fancy you, a Frenchman, having something in common with our three lads. And fancy Miss Phoebe working in a factory! I always knew she was a game lass.'

'Our Jack used to think she was a game lass an' all,' Walter said in a low voice.

'Now then,' murmured Matt. 'That's all water under the bridge these days.'

'Game lass? Water under the bridge?' Maurice shook

453

his head as if the conversation had become too much for him.

'They're just sayings.' Jack glowered at Walter. 'Ways of talking. It's of no consequence.' He looked at the man and saw a sharpness in his gaze which contradicted his supposed lack of understanding.

'Will you be going back to France when you and Miss Clough are married, Mister Chaudet?' asked Kitty.

There was a slight hesitation before Maurice replied. 'We may stay in England for a while.'

The word 'married' hummed in Jack's ears. The realisation that this smirking stranger was to have Phoebe, would call her his *wife* and one day spirit her away again to France filled his mind.

Matt was asking about the Communards and the Frenchman seemed evasive. It was in that moment that Jack understood – the man was himself a Communard. He had not fled the disorder of civil war but was on the run and had come to England to escape government retribution. Jack remembered the newspaper stories of how the National Guards had gone in for an orgy of looting and burning. Phoebe was to marry a revolutionary, a man with calloused hands – just as if no difficulties of class or the foundry or ideologies had ever dogged their own friendship. He said, 'Does Miss Clough intend to keep you, or will you scrounge a job at her father's foundry?'

His mother gasped.

Walter said in a low breath, 'You daft bugger!'

Joseph laid down his knife and fork, his face red with embarrassed fury. 'Mr Chaudet is a guest in our inn, Jack. You'll apologise to him for your discourtesy.'

'I'll not take it back. I don't trust him.'

'Then leave the table!' His mother's voice was cold, like the times when he was small and had offended them, and he

454

felt like a lad again as he scraped back his chair.

'Don't worry. I'm going.'

Jack reached the door and knew that he should apologise. The remark had been unforgivable. He had succumbed to jealousy and that suspicion of foreigners which marked him as an ignorant buffoon.

What was worse, he thought as he reached the street, he had forsaken a good Sunday dinner for nothing. Phoebe Clough was nothing to him. He kicked a stone in the road viciously and it skittered off and hit the wall with a rattle. He walked on up Griseley Bank, past Clough's house without looking at it, as far as the moor and the track to the knoll where he and Phoebe used to meet.

He sat on the springy grass among the bracken and heather with the turf warm to his backside through his Sunday trousers. The sun was high, its rays hot on his bare head and face, and his heart ached for what he had once almost held and then lost.

Maurice brushed aside their apologies. 'The young man was upset about something.' A former love affair? he wondered. He had not asked Phoebe about former lovers, supposing her to have been a virgin.

The incident was immaterial, he decided, and any speculation about it was bourgeois and petty. Yet he was irritated by Jack's behaviour. He had not foreseen complications over Phoebe and did not particularly want to make enemies in Griseley.

Maurice had been alert to the discord between the brothers and it occurred to him that Walter might make a useful ally. After lunch he engaged Walter and Matt in conversation, asking them about the rebellion at the town hall. He felt the old flame of anger against social injustice ignite in his breast as he learned of their grievance and Edwin Clough's intransigence. It was the same everywhere, he said, the capitalists always exploited the workers for their own gain. 'But a successful revolution can only be won by a dedicated band of men.'

'Dedicated to what?' said Walter sceptically.

'To winning. Dedicated to violence if necessary.'

Matt shook his head. 'We tried forcing it and look where it led.'

'So now what do you do?'

'We do nothing. Clough has won,' Walter said bitterly.

'Jack is all for talking Clough round through the union,' added Matt.

'You must *do* something, not talk!'

Walter, his interest roused, said, 'What do you know about it?'

Maurice told them about the strikes in Paris and was tempted to tell them more – how he too had been gaoled. Oh, he would make their eyes goggle if he told them as well about the moments of glory there had been, the thrill of marching shoulder to shoulder with comrades and fighting for a cause, the splendid hours when the National Guards seized the Hôtel de Ville and held the government captive – and would have won then, if it had not been for the men who put their faith in negotiations and talking.

He studied them. Perhaps he *would* tell them, for they were men after his own heart – men of action, not words.

Phoebe found them in the Nag's Head that afternoon, seated round a bar table with their heads together like conspirators. Kitty had greeted her like a long-lost daughter. Sarah had wept a little. Phoebe had been thankful to see that Jack was not there.

Sarah pushed open the door of the bar for her. 'Walter!

You're keeping Mister Chaudet. Miss Clough's called to see him.'

The atmosphere in the bar was one of male exclusivity with its smell of stale tobacco and beer. Phoebe saw in the light in Maurice's eyes and the heated expressions of Jack's brothers a shadow of those evenings in the apartment near the Rue Rambuteau and the ghosts of Georges Marin and Henri.

'We were to walk out together this afternoon, Maurice.' The reproach in her voice was discernible and Phoebe knew she sounded like a shrew.

Clearly Maurice had forgotten that he had arranged to meet her. An expression of annoyance crossed his face. 'We will talk again,' he said before addressing himself to her. '*Ma petite*, don't agitate yourself.'

Outside he was attentive again. 'How could I have forgotten!'

'I believe men find it very easy to rate women of secondary importance when they're in male company.'

'Never again.' He kissed her hand.

'What were you discussing?' She remembered their conspiratorial manner.

'I was becoming acquainted. They are lion-hearted men.' He added in French as people passed them in the road, 'By the way, their brother accused me of being a ponce – intending to sponge off you.'

She was startled and felt an immediate anger against Jack. So he had not changed, he still had a chip on his shoulder.

'I'm sorry,' she said stiffly. 'Jack once fancied himself in love with me. I hope he didn't upset you.'

'No more than a gadfly upsets a stallion.'

Phoebe was a little saddened to hear Jack diminished in that way, and ashamed for betraying him with that 'fancied

457

himself in love with me', for had she not also been in love with him?

They were approaching Charles's house as they climbed Griseley Bank. She explained quickly, 'My brother has suggested we avail ourselves of his hospitality today,' not wanting to tell Maurice yet about her father's hostility.

Maurice followed her through the gate to the painted front door. She rang the bell and they smiled at one another as they waited. '*Je t'aime*, Phoebe.'

'And I love you,' she echoed, desire for him making her reach up on tiptoe and kiss him swiftly.

The housemaid showed them into the front parlour. Phoebe had not been there since Tessa had lived with Charles. The room had an air of the neglect which permeated bachelor residences, no matter how well managed by the servants.

As soon as the girl had left the room Maurice pulled Phoebe into his arms. 'I have not had you for two whole days.' They kissed hungrily and Phoebe thought, when we are married I shall know this feeling for ever and ever. Yet there was a melancholy in the chilly cramped parlour which was invasive and spoiled her mood of joy. They heard Charles in the corridor and they parted.

He hailed them with an uncharacteristic cheeriness. 'Well, so you found him.'

'Maurice was gossiping in the pub. Soon he will be more English than the English.' Phoebe looked at Maurice fondly.

Charles motioned them to the chintz sofa. 'The point is, what are we going to do about Father?'

'About your father?' queried Maurice. 'There is a difficulty?'

Phoebe flushed. 'I told him you were a foundryman and he didn't take too kindly.'

'But you said you would win him round, that he would soon give me work in his foundry.'

'As for that, I don't think there's much hope of it.'

Charles said that he would talk to Edwin and try to persuade him. But Maurice was sullen and said he had been counting on Phoebe's influence with her father.

'It doesn't matter,' she protested. 'I've an allowance. We can live on that for a while, until you find work – perhaps in Manchester or Leeds.'

'Love will find a way,' said Charles with false joviality.

Maurice looked at him mockingly and Phoebe remembered the old Maurice, the one she had first known who would have said then as he said now, 'Love, my friend, does not pay the bills.'

The moment passed, and they talked of other things. Charles mentioned the casting of the lions.

'I have heard about these lions. The men feel strongly against them.'

'You've been listening to the Bateman brothers,' said Charles. 'Perhaps Father should listen harder.'

Maurice said coldly, 'It's a rare master who listens to the voice of his workers.'

Phoebe had expected that Maurice would walk up to the house with her, but he had a distant air when they left Charles, saying outside on the pavement, 'I suppose it is finished – this job for me at the foundry.'

'I think so. Once Father makes up his mind—'

He nodded, but he did not seem angry now and had a preoccupation about him as they parted. 'I shall talk to the foundrymen at the Nag's Head tonight. I will tell them they should not give up hope.'

Jack saw a figure walking towards him as he came down Griseley Bank in the early evening. He continued towards

Phoebe, aware that they would have to acknowledge one another. He told himself it was best that way, without others there to gawp and speculate, without the Frenchman watching him, best now to get it over with. He would look her in the eyes and show her that she meant nothing to him.

He gave a curt nod, 'Miss Phoebe,' and his voice sounded unnatural, his head filling with the word 'Phoebe' as he added, 'It's good to know you came out safe from all the French troubles.'

'Hello, Jack.' Her voice was soft and musical as in the old days. She had not altered much, a little thinner perhaps and her face harder, with a more resolute look to it. 'How are you keeping? I heard about your brothers and the strike at the works and everything.' She pressed her gloved hands against her skirts.

'Aye, well, that's all done with now.' He hesitated. 'I was right sorry about Mister Bertrand—'

A look of distress crossed her face and his heart went out to her as she nodded and said, 'Time heals.'

He prepared to move on but knew something else must be said so that the next time they met it would be easier. He braced himself. 'I wish you well in your future marriage.' There, it was done. She would see that it did not affect him, this engagement of hers to the sneering Frenchman.

An expression – not quite pity, but a strange surprised anguish flew across Phoebe's face as she stumbled out a rigid kind of thanks.

As they parted and went their separate ways Jack dwelled on the way she had looked – the flush on her cheek, her old habit of pressing her hands flat to her skirts. Two things occurred to him; one was that he had not fooled her, and the other that she had found the meeting just as difficult as he had.

Twenty-two

Then comrades, come rally,
And the last fight let us face . . .

Eugene Pottier, Communard,
'International Anthem of
Socialist Workers', 1871

Phoebe had believed that her engagement to Maurice would
be a defence against Griseley. Her love was a protective
shell from which the future glowed brightly and the past
was excluded for ever. She knew now that it was impossible
to stay here, and yet Maurice seemed disinclined to move
on.

Seated in the darkness of Gerald's theatre she felt the
warmth of Maurice's arm close against hers and his knee
pressed to her skirts. He was impatient to make love to her
again: they had done it once, hurriedly in the front parlour
one day when Charles went out to buy cigarettes and she
had been tormented by desire and guilt. Griseley
righteousness had pervaded every second of those hasty
minutes, memories of chapel and her father's
pronouncements on the sins of the flesh, even Beatrice
Underwood with lips pursed in disapproval, and Christina's
face, white and tear-stained on her wedding day – all these

and other images had mounted upon one another from behind the lace curtains of Griseley Bank as Maurice pumped out his passion and she lay on the hearthrug with her head against the fender.

She could not dismiss her encounter with Jack from her mind. It had been inevitable that they would meet and she had known that such a meeting would stir up old memories, but she had not anticipated the nervous restlessness it would arouse in her. She could not settle to anything, could not even make plans for leaving Griseley and she lost patience with Maurice's growing interest in the foundrymen's grievances. Could he not see how trivial Griseley business was after the way people had suffered in France?

The stage curtains rose to reveal a rectangle of brilliant light backed by a colourful scene of castle and mountains. A smell of dust and gas, scenery paint and stage costumes drifted towards them. The warm excitement of a brilliant and artificially created world thrust itself upon Phoebe and she quickened with excitement as Victor, dressed in a Garibaldi shirt and pantaloons, leaped on to the stage.

She squeezed Maurice's hand, sensing his concentration as the plot unfolded. Gerald strode about in a purple velvet robe, shouting despotically and ordering executions left, right and centre. Olive, regal and noble, watched as a captured rebel soldier, Victor, was put to death off-stage with convincing gunshots. The explosion of sound filled the theatre and the audience shrieked with appreciative horror.

Maurice drew in his breath sharply. He half rose as if he would leave the auditorium, for the drama had impinged too closely on reality. People in the row behind began to grumble that they could not see and Maurice sat down with a bump. He was appalled by the intensity of the picture which had thrust itself into his memory. For several seconds he felt his heart pound, until the image of Bertrand's body against the

462

wall faded; he turned to Phoebe with a rueful smile, as if to say, how foolish, when we know it's only make believe.

Phoebe's heart too had surged with fear, her mind filled with the memory of Tessa's death, with images of war and of Bertrand dying on a barricade. She touched Maurice's arm in sympathy. How much more frightful it must be for him, having been there at the end.

The leader of the rebels did not appear until the second scene. Phoebe recognised Jack, costumed in a white shirt and blue pantaloons, a set of pistols in his belt. She heard Maurice murmur, as if mesmerised, 'Flourens!' and then Phoebe was locked in a separate spell as Jack began to speak. A chill of suspense gripped her and her hands tightened in her lap. She was back in the darkness of a theatre rehearsal, the broadness of his speech and strength of his diction intoxicating her, thrilling her with its power.

The play continued and the first shock of recognition lessened, but Phoebe remained spellbound by Jack. She followed his every move, flooded by memories which she could not hold back: the frightened innocence of that first kiss, his *woman, if you're too stupid to see*, and the confusion of first love. Unconsciously, silently she wept, until, feeling the tears reach her chin and neck, she came to her senses. She felt dazed and her head ached when the play was over.

Maurice touched her cheek as the lights brightened and people began to clamour, 'Author!'

'You have been crying. You were moved by the hero's death?'

She nodded. 'I think it must be Gerald's best play ever.'

'It was very exciting,' he agreed, 'but I shall challenge your brother about the ending.'

* * *

463

They went backstage and Maurice at once accosted Gerald. 'My friend, I question the morality of your play. Why must the hero die and the despot live?'

Gerald, receiving the praise and congratulations of everyone around him, looked alarmed at this note of dissension.

'It's the sort of ending which occurs in real life,' Phoebe reminded Maurice gravely.

Gerald, reassured of the validity of his creation, smiled. 'One's aim *is* to mirror real life.'

'I disagree. The theatre must mirror the ideals of man. The King must be assassinated in your play so that Right can triumph.'

'But it *does* triumph,' protested Olive. 'The King is convinced in the end of the justice of the men's cause.'

'Ha! Then you do not mirror real life, for in real life a despot is not convinced by reason. Justice occurs only when the oppressed rise and crush their rulers.'

'*Let the people take their destiny into their own hands,*' said Jack, who had appeared unnoticed in his stage costume beside them.

Maurice stared at him, the hostility of their previous encounters forgotten, the name Flourens again at the forefront of his mind. 'It is a line from the play?'

Jack nodded.

'Then I agree. It is only the ending which I dislike.'

Maurice's antipathy to the conclusion of Gerald's play was not shared by the critics. Word went round the players that men from Manchester and Leeds had been in the audience, men who were 'big in the theatre'. *And All That Makes a Man* had, it seemed, caught their fancy. Gerald was drawn deep into conversation with a stranger dressed in a checked coat and top hat.

Olive murmured, 'I wonder if our fortunes are about to

be made, Jack?' and Phoebe looked at them swiftly, for Olive's hand on Jack's arm seemed possessive and Jack's manner with her sister-in-law was strange, intimate and at the same time faintly hostile.

Phoebe's headache was fierce and the claustrophobic smell of the theatre made her feel ill. Maurice spoke to her but she hardly heard him, for she was confused still by Jack's effect on her and she sensed that he was watching her as she moved among the players with Maurice. Gerald was shaking hands with the man in the checked coat and the stranger raised his hat and left the theatre. Gerald's voice came through a buzz of other sounds, Olive's laughter, people congratulating one another, Jack talking to Victor. Gerald was smiling. He said he had been offered a run in Leeds, the whole cast was to be uprooted. He turned to Jack. 'Well, my hearty. The moment of truth at last. What's it to be for us? Leeds or the foundry?'

And then Olive was hugging Gerald and the cast were cheering and kissing one another. Phoebe saw the look which passed between Olive and Jack and she turned away, shocked beyond anything she had experienced, no doubt in her mind as to the significance of that shared glance.

'Phoebe?' Maurice took her arm. 'Shall we leave?'

She nodded, wanting to be far away.

Outside, the theatre-goers had dispersed and the street was empty of people and carriages. The gas lamps were lit, a fine rain cooled Phoebe's hot forehead and she took off her hat, for the pins hurt where they pulled her hair tight. Maurice drew her out of the sphere of light from the streetlamp and attempted to kiss her, and irritated she said, 'I think I should like to go straight home.'

He sulked a little and there was a constraint between them as they walked through the town towards Griseley Bank. She said, 'We must talk about going away. I can't stay in Griseley. It suffocates me and I don't think we could be happy here.'

Maurice was angry. He felt that things were going wrong and it was all Phoebe's fault. If she had treated her father more carefully he would still be in the old man's good books. He felt a deeper anger against Edwin, an employer, a despot whose tyranny went unchecked.

He waited outside the Nag's Head the evening after the theatre performance and leaned against the wall of the pub smoking a cigar as he watched Jack come up the hill from his work. Maurice recalled the splendour of the play, Jack's uncanny resemblance to the magnificent Flourens still faintly suggested in the swing of his stride though he was dressed in a working jacket and fustian trousers and covered in the dirt of the foundry.

Jack nodded a grudging acknowledgement as Maurice stepped away from the wall and was immediately wary. 'Are you looking for me?'

'I think we can talk.'

'I don't know that we've owt to say to one another.'

'You don't trust me. But you must, my friend. I'm interested in your struggle at the foundry.'

Jack laughed. 'What do you know about us? You're a Frenchman, and you're going to marry Edwin Clough's daughter.'

Maurice shrugged. 'Edwin Clough is my enemy too.'

Jack found Maurice tiresome, stirring up trouble with Walter and Matt, but he felt cheered by the revelation that the Frenchman was not on the best of terms with Clough.

'You cast the first of the lions tomorrow,' Maurice said.

'You seem to know plenty about the foundry. You'd best carry on talking to Walter and Matt for your information.'

'Perhaps, but I know that you have led them. You could do it again.'

'Why should I keep flogging myself for them?'

'I have seen you in the play.'

Jack shook his head. 'You want to talk to my brothers, not me.'

'Your brothers are good fellows, perhaps they have the fighting spirit and you are only a play-actor. You will not win your struggle unless someone leads the revolution.'

Jack took a step towards Maurice angrily and pushed him against the wall. 'Look, Mister Chaudet – this isn't Paris.'

Maurice regarded him with an amused expression, then raising his elbow he eased the weight of Jack's arm from his chest and drew on his cigar.

Jack hesitated. Walter and Matt were coming up the hill. He watched them, then turned from Maurice. 'You talk to them, lad.' He brushed past him into the yard. 'They're your revolutionaries.'

There was the usual apprehension in the foundry which affected the men before a big or important casting. They were tensed up about the new lion now it was all under way. The metal was glowing in all the furnaces, the casting-bed was ready, but everyone was conscious of how it had gone wrong before.

Edwin paced the foundry in a tail coat, shaking his head if his sons talked to him, sweeping aside remarks, restless with unleashed energy until the pouring began. He stood by the casting-bed then, his hands gripping one another behind his back as each team came forward in turn.

Jack tightened his hold on the crucible tongs and thought, 'If it had been different, if Phoebe had not been Clough's daughter, if I was not the clod I am, it would be me she's marrying and not Chaudet.' The molten bronze bobbed with the crust of dross as he stepped forward with Matt. He glanced at Walter and William Burns on the opposite side of the casting-bed: their expressions were tense with concentration. 'If I had been a Frenchman,' he thought, 'if I had fought against the Prussians, if I had been in a real revolution instead of Gerald's play, I might have stood a chance.'

The last teams of men had begun to pour. Jack marvelled at their combined determination to make it a perfect cast, for what did any of them care if Clough got his lions or not? The men hated the master's guts, Walter and Matt were likely hatching up more trouble and he was off to Leeds – not because of Gerald's, 'You must, my hearty. We can't take the play anywhere without you,' nor because of Olive's persuasion – but because when he had watched Phoebe walk out of the theatre with Maurice his decision had been made. But there would be no more messing with Olive. 'If I come with you, it's because of the acting,' he had said. 'You and me are finished.' And she had smiled coolly and told him, 'You're showing your class. You know, you really are a prig.'

Jack concentrated on steadying the crucible. There was a pride in getting it right. If anybody was going to bugger up the casting this time, it wouldn't be him, nor Walt, nor any of the rest of the men.

They stepped back as the metal reached the top of the risers, and still some left in the crucible. Jack turned to Matt and grinned for it was about as accurate as it could have been. Walter gave a shout to signal the finish and an involuntary cheer came from the men.

Edwin Clough raised a hand for attention. A silence, growing with resentment, followed his, 'Well done lads, I'm right proud of you. Let's hope it's as good as it looks.'

'Pity him being proud of us don't run to more money,' muttered one of the men.

It was not the only murmur of dissent as Edwin moved away.

The plan was that the remaining three lions should be cast, one each fortnight, over the following six weeks. Edwin had not dared to give way to an early mood of euphoria, for the statue's success could not be properly judged until the metal had cooled.

Now that Charles was supervising the fettling and polishing, Edwin felt a surge of acute joy, for the bronze had emerged from the mould without a flaw. He touched the cold metal lovingly, each ripple of muscle clearly defined, the tresses of the mane heavy and solid, yet alive. He knew that he had never known such gratification nor would again in the same way. If only Annette could have seen it. If only his sons understood how much this moment meant to him. Emotion threatened to overwhelm him, for he wished with all his heart that Bertrand could have known this triumph.

Edwin spent every spare minute in the workshop, watching the men buff up the bronze to bring out its sheen. He imagined the lion with its comrades, guarding the municipal hall. All who passed by would look on it and tell themselves that Edwin Clough had created a wonderful asset to Griseley. The long wait with all its frustrations – the strike, the disaster of the first casting – had almost been worth it. The Lord had tested him and here was his reward. Edwin raised his eyes to the roof of the workshop and offered a prayer of thanks to his own Maker.

One thing alone troubled him, for he had not during the past twelve months found the opportunity to tell the council about the reduced dimensions of the lions.

* * *

469

It was already late July and the councillors, frustrated by delays, had thrown caution to the winds and fixed the inauguration ceremony for September; but they were growing anxious as the list of dignitaries to be invited to the ceremony from the outlying manufacturing towns grew longer and more impressive. It was decided that Murgatroyd and Wormauld should 'inspect' the first finished lion before invitations went out, on the pretext of congratulating Edwin. Gerald opened the workshop door one afternoon and announced, 'Father, there's a deputation from the town hall to see you.'

Edwin turned with a start to confront his fellow councillors.

'This is a grand day, Edwin.' Wormauld shook first Edwin then Charles warmly by the hand.

Murgatroyd nodded a brief greeting and made straight for the lion which stood on a brick platform at the centre of the room. The competence of the sculpture clearly startled him for, after walking all round it, he could at first think of nothing to say.

Wormauld turned to Charles and clapped him on the shoulder. 'Well, I'll be damned. It's a splendid beast. Eh, lad you've done your father proud.'

Murgatroyd halted beside the lion's flank, his eyes narrowed. 'Wait on – I thought the statue was going to be bigger than this.'

Edwin prepared to brazen out the situation. 'I don't think you'll be disappointed, gentlemen—'

'"Ten foot nose to tail," you said. It was agreed.'

'This is as big as you'll get, my hearty,' Gerald laughed. 'And worth a corner of the town hall at half the size.'

'It *is* half the size!' exploded Murgatroyd.

Wormauld was pacing out the length of the sculpture.

'Now, now. Not half,' protested Edwin, hoping that by

insisting on accuracy he could escape his predicament.

'Bloody near enough though.' Wormauld had finished his pacing.

'The mighty King of the Beasts, reduced to looking like a pet poodle alongside our town hall building!' wailed Murgatroyd.

'Don't talk rot,' said Charles, finding the whole business of size immaterial. 'What do you know about sculpture?'

They stared at him. Murgatroyd said, 'Now then. Show a bit of respect for a town councillor and a member of the Arts Council.'

'You know no more about art than you do about brushes,' muttered Charles.

Wormauld put on his hat. 'I think the council should have been informed about this, Edwin. This could spoil the whole balance of the project.'

Murgatroyd followed Wormauld to the door. Edwin shouted after them that the council did not know when it was well off. Charles and Edwin watched them go; for once father and son were united, and Edwin was comforted by Charles's spirited defence of the lion, but his own bravado had concealed a deepening fear. Would the council's disappointment over size be enough to imperil the whole project? He touched the cold metal for reassurance. No, he told himself fervently. Nothing must go wrong now.

News of the dispute over the lion soon reached the rest of the town. It came to Maurice's attention and he puzzled how the incident might be turned to the men's advantage, for no ill luck for an employer was too insignificant to go unexploited.

'Is it possible the councillors may refuse the lions?' he asked Walter when they met one evening in the rhubarb field where they were hidden from the road and the eyes and ears of the inmates of the public bars.

'I don't know about refusing them, but there's a devil of a hullabaloo.' Walter sniggered. 'Serve Clough right if they turn it down.'

Maurice walked away from Walter and Matt and leaned against the wall. He was impatient with their enjoyment of Clough's squabble with the town councillors. Fate did not bring misfortune on an enemy for man's entertainment but for acting upon: the moment must be seized and the upper hand gained. That was where the Commune had gone wrong. It was where everyone went wrong, they did not grasp the advantage. He swung round to face them. 'If the next lion can be delayed, will that not embarrass Clough more?'

'We've no way of doing that now,' said Matt. 'Not without another strike – or if something went wrong with the next casting.'

'It would be a good time for a strike.' Walter watched Maurice closely: he was clever, there was no two ways about it. 'Clough would be afraid of losing face and we'd have him.'

'I'll not strike again.' Matt kicked his heel against the wall, remembering Rebecca's suffering that winter and his own weeks in prison.

'But it would work this time,' said Walter.

Matt, however, was obstinate. And so were the rest of the foundrymen when Walter called a meeting after work; the men gathered reluctantly on a patch of waste ground near the railway line, nervous of provoking another confrontation with the police. Walter explained to them how the council were unhappy about the way the statues were turning out, how the lion had been a disappointment because of its size, how it only needed the men to arrange another setback and Clough would be so frightened of the council turning round and saying 'you can keep your lions' that he would agree to their higher wage.

The men were sullen. Someone shouted, 'That lion was a grand bit of casting. The council need their brains testing if they can find owt wrong wi' it.'

'That's as maybe. I'm not disputing it's a good lion, now it's done, but do you want extra money for making it or not?' said Walter, exasperated.

'We weren't all involved in the making of it,' someone grumbled. 'Why should we fight your battles? We've got wives and children. We're not fancy-free like you.'

Maurice had agreed to speak at the meeting and to put the idea of striking to the men. He stood in the shelter of the railway arch near the back of the crowd, listening to Walter talk. He saw that the fellow was not going to win them over. How milk-and-water these people were! He remembered Flourens, who had marched up and down on the table when they had captured the Hôtel de Ville. These workers had no fire in their bellies. He pushed his way forward to stand beside Walter and the men fell silent. A murmur of misgiving ran through them, for few knew who he was and as he began to confer in a low voice with Walter, his foreign accent made those near the front shift their boots and look at one another in an attitude of deeper mistrust.

'Mister Chaudet has come to us from France,' said Walter.

'Aye, and he can go back home again,' someone cried at once.

'My friends – I understand your grievances.' Maurice spread his hands in a gesture of apology. 'I am here to help you.'

'What does he know about it?' murmured Jack to William Burns.

'A lot, according to Walter,' said William. 'He's organised strikes afore. And he's a fighter.'

Yes, he was that, thought Jack, listening to the man speak, seeing again the scar on the left side of his face which was thrown into relief by the low rays of the evening sun. And the Frenchman knew how to make a crowd listen, for the others had stopped murmuring among themselves and seemed suddenly mesmerised by his voice.

'. . . I am a worker just like you. In France we workers rose up to avenge ourselves on our rulers. I have fought on the barricades, my friends. I have seen blood flow. I have stood shoulder to shoulder with brave men glad to die in a glorious cause.'

'Wait on—' shouted one of the foundrymen. 'There's no glorification about wanting a shilling or two more in our wages.'

'You are wrong. The workers' fight *is* a glorious one. Have you not seen the greed of your employer? Have you not seen his splendid house above the town, with its fine carpets and furniture? Rise from your festering slums! Avenge yourselves against him! Strike for your rights and join with me in the cry, *Down with Clough!*'

There were a few obedient cries of 'Down with Clough!' urged on by Walter, which were swallowed by the roar of a passing train. Jack stepped forward to speak and Walter groaned, 'You can go back home out of it for a start.'

'Let Jack have his say,' said William Burns, and others echoed him as the rattle of the train died. 'Let the lad speak. At least he never landed anybody in quod.'

Jack climbed on to the pile of bricks and rubble which formed a natural platform. He had not intended to speak nor even to attend the meeting; he had come out of curiosity, to discover what ideas the Frenchman had been putting into his brothers' heads. He was surprised to find himself in agreement with him and Walter, for there had never been a better time to threaten a strike than now, with Clough getting edgy about completing his project. A respectful silence fell. Jack looked round at the meeting and saw men he had known since his apprenticeship, men he had grown fond of over the years, on whose faces years of worry and heavy labour were etched.

'I agree that it's a good plan to get at Clough while he's down, but if we confront him, it should not be in the heat of the moment.' He looked at Maurice. 'And there'll be no blood spilled. We should ask for the same terms as before – an improvement in hours, an annual review of wages and recognition of our society.'

'We'll not go to gaol again for your brother!' shouted one of the men and the others took up the cry.

'I have been in gaol too!' shouted Maurice. 'It is not so terrible. What are you – cowards? Do you not know that I would have died for the Commune!'

'There'll be no need for dying – nor even gaol,' said Jack. 'Not if you do it legal this time. No breaking heads nor town halls. And we'll win.'

'You daft bugger!' said Walter. 'Do it like that, and by the time everyone's finished argy-bargying about it and union's brought in as well, the lions will be finished and it will all be too late. We should strike now!'

Walter was a man after his own heart, thought Maurice, remembering all the cowards in the National Guard who had run away when it came to a fight. There were so few real soldiers. He thought again of Flourens and his uncanny likeness to Jack Bateman, who might have been a good man to have on one's side if he wasn't so cautious. 'You must fight!' he shouted. 'And if blood is spilled, then blood is necessary!'

'We'll abide by Jack,' said William Burns.

'Aye. We'll not go to gaol.'

'Bloody cowards!' Walter shouted.

His old followers shuffled their feet but they were obstinate.

'It's like water wearing on a stone,' Jack told them. 'We keep at Clough for long enough, show him we mean what we say and we'll get there.'

'We!' snorted Walter as the men dispersed. 'What do you care? You're off out of it come September.'

Maurice met Walter alone the next Sunday evening, the night before the casting of the second lion. He thought of Phoebe and was surprised how little he needed a woman when he was intent on some intrigue. He recalled that he had arranged to meet her this evening: they might 'walk out together' she had said, as if they were some bourgeois genteel couple, but she would have to wait. Phoebe would have to learn that she must take second place.

'The lads might strike yet,' said Walter. 'Some of them feel right badly about the past year. We just need a bit of time.'

'We don't have time. We must act before tomorrow, when they cast the second lion.' Maurice told himself he must carry on the fight for justice. He would raise the glorious flag of revolution here in Griseley. In his heart, he thought of the years ahead, when he might have enjoyed a leisured lifestyle if Edwin Clough had not turned against him. Now he would have the hard toil of supplementing Phoebe's modest income, of supporting a nagging wife and, before too long, children. He knew that, revolutions aside, revenge against Edwin Clough would be sweet.

'Do you want an adventure, Walter?'

Walter grinned, 'Do I heck!' He would have followed the Frenchman in anything, would have fought on the barricades like those Communists with someone like Maurice to urge him on.

Twenty-three

Lions are Kings of Beasts, and yet their pow'r
Is not to rule and govern, but devour.

Samuel Butler

Phoebe's relationship with her father was strained. He could not prevent her from marrying Maurice and so he did his best to ignore him, talking as if Phoebe was again part of his household and, when she went to see Maurice, pretending that he did not know where she had been. She supposed that if he did not see him or hear her talk of her fiancé he could pretend that Maurice was not there.

To prevent a feud, Phoebe went along with the pretence, avoiding talking of plans for her marriage, keeping her thoughts to herself. The trouble was, Maurice showed a reluctance to discuss their marriage almost equal to her father's. He spent too much time talking with Walter Bateman. The sooner she persuaded him to leave Griseley the better.

He had promised to walk with her by the river. 'Will you come with me to chapel?' she had said. 'It would please Father no end and might win him round a little.'

'It is a little late to win him round, *ma petite*,' he had laughed.

She had lost her temper. 'If you won't even try!' Then she had softened, 'Well then, come for a walk this evening with me, instead of wasting your time smoking and drinking with Walter and telling your tall stories in the pub.'

She had offended him. He said that men like Walter would have made good allies in their fight against the Versaillais.

Phoebe sighed as she walked down Griseley Bank and wished that Maurice could forget a little. His head was stuffed full of the glamour of revolution, as if he had already forgotten the sordid end to it all. He had kissed her, quick to forgive her bad humour. 'You are becoming a scold, *ma petite*.' And it was true.

She neared the Nag's Head where Maurice had promised to meet her. A figure was leaning against the wall overlooking the rhubarb field. As she drew closer she saw that it was Jack, dressed in his Sunday clothes in a black braided jacket and good bowler. She would ignore him, she decided. If he was having an *affaire* with Olive – and she was sure that he was – she wanted nothing at all to do with him.

'Now what do you think those two are up to?' Jack said without looking up, as if he had known she was approaching long before she reached him.

Phoebe shielded her eyes against the evening sun and looked for the object of his interest, forgetting her resolve as she saw Maurice and Walter skirting the far side of the field, making their way down towards the town. She released a cry of exasperation. 'He said he would meet me this evening!'

Jack swung round and leaned with his back against the wall, surveying her critically. 'He neglects you a bit for a fiancé.'

His look, his implication that she was a fool stung her, but she directed her anger against Maurice. 'I shall go and

478

talk to him.' She made for the path between the houses.

Jack called after her, 'I've got the pony-trap harnessed to take my mam to my aunty's. You'll give him a piece of your mind quicker if I drive you down the Bank.'

Phoebe hesitated, looking along the narrow path to the rhubarb field, and saw that he was right: if she went by the road she would intercept Maurice at the bottom of the hill. She returned to the pavement and saw that Jack was already on his way to fetch the cart.

They drove in silence. Phoebe was hot with embarrassment; she told herself there was something very peculiar in her former lover driving her to pick a quarrel with her fiancé. She was aware that people would watch them pass and comment on the two of them together. The cart jostled and jerked down the cobbles and near the bottom of the hill, as Phoebe had feared, the crowd around the Ebenezer chapel turned to stare. Phoebe prayed that her father had already gone inside off the street and would not see her. She flushed as she saw Murgatroyd with his wife and wondered what Jack was thinking and whether he was enjoying her dilemma. If he did he gave no sign of it, for he drove in stolid silence looking neither to left nor right.

Jack reined in the horse at the bottom of the Bank, where the road curved towards the town hall, giving a clear view of the square. 'They can't have gone that way, else we should see them,' he murmured. 'They've not had time to get right out of sight.'

He turned the pony to the left and they trundled in the direction of the foundry. Phoebe, glancing down the road, was the first to spot their quarry and in her surprise she seized Jack's arm.

Jack sucked in the air between his teeth as he followed the direction of her gaze, for Maurice and Walter were clearly silhouetted against the foundry roofs as they sat astride the wall before they dropped to the yard on the other side.

'What do we do?' Phoebe still held Jack's arm and she clung to his sleeve, her teeth chattering with fear, for she guessed that Maurice's entry into her father's foundry was no innocent Sunday-evening outing. She recalled his constant talk about the revolution, his frustration with peaceable living and his insistence that Walter would have made a superb confederate.

Jack handed her the reins of the pony-cart and jumped down from the driving seat into the road. 'Wait here. I'll talk to Walt and find out what they're up to.' He set off towards the foundry and turned suddenly. 'Wait on, mind. Don't go fetching the constables nor anything daft like that.'

Phoebe watched him go, saw him take a run at the wall and scramble over the top. The road was quiet and up in the town the church bells were ringing. The horse whinnied and she willed it to be silent, fearful suddenly – not for Maurice but for Jack.

Jack hauled himself over the wall, conscious of Phoebe watching him and remembering too late that he was wearing his good clothes. He asked himself what he was doing, walking into trouble like he was witless, but the feel of Phoebe's hand on his arm was still strong, as if she were there beside him, the two of them against the Frenchman and Walter. The notion made him burn with courage and he felt twice the man his brother was – and three times the Frenchman.

The yard was empty but the foundry doors stood open. Jack dropped lightly to the ground and made towards them.

Once inside, the contrast of the evening light in the yard with the darkness of the foundry rendered him sightless for several seconds. He could hear the two men talking at the far end of the building as he slipped round the door to the protection of the wall by the furnaces.

He waited, his heart thumping in his chest until his eyes got used to the gloom. The dusty smell of coke and metal was familiar; the foundry was cool like in the early morning before the furnaces were lit and the quietness calmed him a little as he watched Walter and Maurice. They stood close together by the casting-bed, which contained the mould ready for the second lion. They were bending over the feeders, funnelling something down into the mould.

He understood instantly what they were doing – a bit of loose sand, just enough to mix with the molten metal and ruin it, and no suspicions raised, for inclusions were a natural enough cause of defective castings.

Jack stepped out from the shelter of the wall and walked down the centre of the building. Walter stopped what he was doing and he and Maurice stared, paralysed in mid-action. Jack wanted to laugh. It was like a drawing in an adventure story – two robbers caught red-handed by the law, except that he was not the law only Walter's kid brother, he reminded himself, and a confrontation with Walter, especially if Walter was up to something, would most likely end in a punch-up. He saw his brother's look of alarm change slowly to a comfortable grin.

'Take no notice. It's only our Jack.' Walter continued scooping sand from the floor into the mould.

Jack watched him. 'Why bugger up the casting?' he said after a while.

'Revenge, lad. We're going to show the old devil we're not beaten.'

Maurice had watched in silence all the while, letting Walter do most of the work. He began cleaning off the edges of the feeders when Walter had finished. Only then did he speak. 'It will put back the casting for a few weeks and give you time to organise a strike.'

Walter dusted off his hands. He grinned again. 'Well, are you with us?'

Jack shook his head in disbelief rather than denial.

'We need you to be with us, Jack,' said Maurice. 'It will be for you to organise the strike.'

'After this? Knowing there's dirty tricks been played?'

Maurice looked at him scornfully. 'You think the masters don't ever play dirty tricks?'

'It's the only way to win,' said Walter. 'Come on, Jack. What do you say?'

Jack looked at Maurice. 'What's all this to you? Your fight was in France and it's over. You *lost*,' he reminded him.

'My fight is wherever there's injustice.'

For a moment it seemed to Jack that the man was perhaps a little mad.

'If you're not with us, you're against us.' Walter was learning quickly the jargon of the revolutionary.

Jack laughed and turned away. 'Bugger off, will you!'

He did not see the glance which passed between Maurice and Walter, a look which said that one did not allow a spy to go free. Jack sensed rather than saw Maurice come after him. He started to run but moved too late as the Frenchman's arm hooked round his neck.

'We cannot let you go, I fear. Not without a promise.' Maurice tightened his arm against his throat.

Walter moved in closer and Jack thought of the beatings he had taken from him. 'Used to this, aren't we, Walt?' he grunted and, struggling to escape Maurice's grip, he kicked out, making contact with his brother's groin.

'You bugger!' Walter doubled in pain.

Maurice still had his arm against Jack's throat; Jack

smelled his breath and thought of the Frenchman with Phoebe, touching her, having her. He summoned up a roar of fury, twisting and fighting to be free; but Maurice held him fast until Walter had time to come at him again and this time Walter's blood was up. Maurice said in a quiet voice, 'You know we may have to kill him,' and Jack saw that Walter, swinging his arms like steam hammers, was furious enough to take the Frenchman literally.

Phoebe waited in the street. No one came to that part of the town except on working days. The silence unnerved her and she tried to imagine what was happening in the foundry. She tried to understand her feelings about Jack, for the feel of his arm had been familiar and reassuring and her heart had quickened with pleasure at being close to him. After a while she clicked quietly to the horse and flicked the reins and the cart rumbled towards the foundry wall. She tied the reins firmly to a lamppost. After which it was an easy enough matter to stand on the driving seat and pull herself on to the wall. Swinging her legs over and tucking up her skirts she dropped down to the soft sand in the yard.

She could hear a noise from the foundry, a repetitive uneven thud. Then from the door she saw them – Maurice holding Jack in his arms and Walter hitting Jack's body with a mechanical and silent intensity.

They did not notice her, so engrossed were they in their business. Phoebe felt a rage mount inside her with each thump of Walter's fist into Jack's slumped body. Was Maurice inhuman, and Walter crazy that he could so abuse his own brother? She had not seen men behave like that. It was barbaric. Someone must stop them. She picked up a shovel from the wall in both hands and ran at them with a cry of fury, bringing the flat of the blade down with a crack on the back of Walter's head. He fell quite slowly, buckling

483

at the knees, then rolling sideways to the foundry floor.

'Have I killed him?' She looked up and met Maurice's eyes. Then she saw Jack, his face bloody like meat, his body sagging in Maurice's arms and strangely inert. She forgot Walter. 'What have you done! He's killed Jack!'

Maurice felt the weight of the man in his arms and let him fall to the foundry floor.

'What have you done!' Phoebe raised the shovel again, feeling a murderous rage against him, for behaving like a madman and for the way he had beguiled her all this time into thinking she was in love with him.

Jack drew a slow choking breath and coughed.

'I could kill him just like that,' Maurice said with a sneer and snapped his fingers. 'Cowards deserve to die.'

Phoebe dropped the shovel and fell on her knees beside Jack, and Maurice watched her cradle his head in her arms. 'He will mend,' he said dismissively. 'And his brother is alive. His skull is extremely solid.' As if to confirm it Walter began to stir. Maurice looked at Phoebe and felt a fleeting tenderness towards her. 'Nobody knows we are here, Phoebe. You don't have to tell anyone what has happened. Perhaps *you* can persuade Jack to join us—'

'Be quiet.' Phoebe felt an overwhelming nausea and threw him a look of disgust. She spoke to Jack. 'Why did they do it? What was it about?'

'We can continue the revolution, Phoebe!' Maurice dropped to his knees beside her and seized her arm. 'You remember how it was in France.'

Phoebe turned to him swiftly and scornfully. 'But this isn't France. People here don't want your kind of revolution.'

'It's necessary.'

'Perhaps—' For a moment she remembered how she had once admired him. 'Perhaps it *was* necessary. But it failed.

It was a horrible mess. Nothing could have justified all that killing.'

'Ah – you are a woman,' he said impatiently. 'Women are too soft and stupid for revolution.'

Phoebe caught his arm and gripped it, digging her fingers into his wrist. 'The only stupid thing I've done was to ever want to marry you. I don't know what you were doing in my father's foundry, and I don't really care very much, but I'll see that you rot in gaol for what you've done to Jack.'

'No – let him go,' Jack mumbled, struggling to sit up.

'You won't harm me. You love me.' Maurice smiled and his eyes were dark and unfathomable, as she remembered them in the old days. 'You have seen the injustice here. The working man must rise up. Force must be met with force.'

Phoebe hesitated, for it was true that she had loved Maurice as intensely as she now loathed him.

'Let him go,' Jack repeated more insistently.

She was still gripping Maurice's arm. She saw the white scar on the inside of his wrist and thought of Bertrand. If they had not all fallen under Maurice's spell, would Bertie and Tessa still be alive? 'I don't love you,' she said coldly. 'I snap my fingers at you.' She flicked her fingers in his face in an imitation of his own dismissive gesture and was gratified by his swift look of hurt. She released his arm. 'You're a fraud, Maurice! Worse – you're a self-deluding one.'

He stood up and said with a sneer, 'I always knew you would end up on the side of the bourgeoisie.'

'And you will most likely finish on the gallows.'

'Phoebe—' he spread his hands, his mood changing quickly. 'After all we have been through together? Come, it's not too late.'

'Go away,' she said harshly. 'Before I forget I'm a *bourgeoise* and hit you.'

Maurice's expression darkened again and he spat on the foundry floor. 'Very well. Stay as you are, you cowards!' He went swiftly, without looking back. People always disappointed in the end, he told himself as he scaled the foundry wall – Georges and Henri and Jean Tissier fallen to the Prussians, Antoine had turned against the Commune, Jack could have become another Flourens if he had not lacked the nerve. Even Walter, who was stout-hearted enough, was sadly deficient in brains. He should have known that these people were not strong enough for him. He despised them for their weak-headed conformity, for their lassitude, and most of all he despised Phoebe, whining at him over the moaning Englishman. He wondered how he could ever have believed that she was a daughter of the revolution.

Jack groaned and struggled to his knees with his arms folded across his ribs. Phoebe helped him to his feet, wrapping both arms round his waist so that he might lean on her as they moved slowly to the foundry entrance.

'What were they doing?'

'It doesn't matter. It's not important now.' Jack leaned against the door then went to the tap in the yard and splashed water on to his face which made him cry out.

After a while Walter came out from the foundry blinking at the light and staggering a little.

'You'd better get off home,' Phoebe shouted. 'Your captain's left you to it.'

Walter looked at Jack for confirmation and he nodded. 'Chaudet has gone – I should think for good.'

'I'll not say anything to my father,' said Phoebe, 'since it looks like Jack put a stop to whatever you were doing.'

Walter looked again to his brother with an expression of stupefaction, and Jack murmured, 'Least said the better.'

Walter did not wait but climbed on to a stack of foundry bricks and scaled the wall.

Phoebe dried Jack's face with her shawl and spoke carefully. 'The gate is locked. Do you think you can get over into the road?' There were purpling bruises around his eyes, and his nose and lips were swollen and still bleeding. She dabbed the improvised towel more tenderly as he winced at her touch.

'Mind your clothes,' he mouthed, seeing the blood on her shawl.

She repeated the question. 'Can you climb over the wall?'

'If you can in a frock, I can with these ribs.'

They clambered as if they were drunk on to the pile of bricks and to the top of the wall, with Phoebe pushing from behind and Jack pulling her after him. Walter was already a small figure in the distance as he hurried towards Griseley Bank.

Phoebe felt curiously jubilant. There was a freedom in sitting with Jack beside her and the foundry behind and looking over Griseley, as if Maurice and all that had happened no longer had any significance. She had ceased to be an engaged woman and should have been heart-broken, instead she wanted to shout to the world that she was free and sitting on top of the wall. They clung together, panting for breath, and she felt hysteria bubble up inside her.

'You were grand, hitting our Walt like that.' Jack began to laugh, groaning with pain at the same time, so that she was afraid he would fall from the wall.

Phoebe grew sober. 'If it hadn't been for me bringing Maurice here—' She looked at his poor, battered face, wanting to hold him close and thinking, 'I have loved you all this time, Jack, and I did not know it.'

Jack interrupted her. 'Where's the horse?'

'I tied it up—' Phoebe's voice died as she saw the empty lamppost.

Jack stared at the empty street. 'The bugger! The thieving Frenchy bugger!'

Two days later Edwin stood with Charles in the foundry as the men hoisted up the cooled lion from the casting-bed. A twitch of a nerve in his cheek betrayed his anxiety; it was a tense moment, breaking the sand away from the casting.

Charles said, 'It's a pity Gerald's not here to see it.'

Edwin frowned. 'Gerald's a damned fool. I'm not a young man, Charles. He would have come into all this if he'd bided his time.'

And now I shall, thought Charles, aware of the added responsibility which would fall on his shoulders and saddened by his brother's sudden abdication in favour of the precarious business of theatricals. He summoned up an enthusiasm for breaking off the mould, though he felt infinitely weary of the foundry, of his father and in particular of the lion project.

'Well, lad. The business will be yours one day.' Edwin tried to muster a pride in the one son who had stuck to him, yet he was aware of a disappointment, for it should have been Bertrand standing there, and even Gerald might have made a successor preferable to the lacklustre Charles.

The men had begun banging off the sand to reveal the metal underneath. Charles stepped forward and touched the surface. He turned to his father. 'The core must have broken up.'

'The core?' Edwin pronounced the word as if it was foreign to him.

'There's inclusions in the metal. Look—'

The men broke off more of the mould and the top surfaces of the lion were seen to be pitted and marred with sand.

Edwin's heart pounded in his chest and the blood hammered in his brain. Ruined. The second lion ruined. And the council expecting them all finished in a matter of weeks. An icy fog enveloped him, in which the sounds of the foundry came faintly, echoing in his head from a distance. Men mouthed senselessly at one another. Only one lion. Only one lion to show still after all his hopes and dreams. He let out a roar of anguish and turned in his wrath on Charles.

Jack, watching the mould break from the casting, saw the look on Clough's face as it dawned on him that his lion was ruined. He felt only a fleeting pity for the master as he began to rant and roar and blame his sons and everyone else within range. He might, he supposed, out of a sort of loyalty, have told Gerald what Maurice and Walter had done; he should perhaps have told Phoebe, instead of letting her think nothing but a punch-up had gone on in the foundry. But Gerald had gone to Leeds, and when he considered all that had happened he owed Phoebe no sort of loyalty.

He stared at the extent of the damage to the casting without emotion. At the end of the week he would give his notice too and follow the players to Leeds, for he owed even less loyalty to Edwin Clough.

His mother had supposed he was leaving Griseley because he could not stand living with Walter any longer. 'It's Walt should move out,' she had said. 'Whatever were you fighting about for him to go for you like that?'

Jack felt the pull on his bruised body as he shifted his position. A memory of Phoebe's spirited and tender ministrations was sweet but transitory. No use thinking like that, he told himself, and wondered if she was regretting sending off Maurice.

The theft of the pony and cart had been another matter. The Frenchman's departure with the family's transport had caused a storm of indignation at the Nag's Head. His father

489

threatened to scour the country for the culprit. His peaceable mother promised to flay Maurice alive. Jack did not suppose they would find him, for the Frenchman would be miles away by now.

Jack listened to the consternation over the spoiled casting, the shouting and bawling which raged in the foundry: Charles Clough swearing it was the last straw, he wouldn't touch another blasted lion, and Clough himself going on about the town council, family honour and not losing face. As he stepped back from the lion Jack was aware of a sense of pure satisfaction. He shared a glance with Walter; it was a strange look, almost one of truce.

Phoebe sat at the table in the dining room waiting for Edwin to come home. She had not told him yet of her broken engagement and she prepared herself for the smug judgement, his 'I told you how it would be'.

She had discovered her camera that afternoon and had polished the brass where it was tarnished with neglect, recalling her excitement when she had first unpacked it all that time ago and her first attempts at taking pictures. It stood now on the table, the brass and rosewood gleaming. She had sought out her photographs and found Tessa, lovely in her transparent costume, vibrant, alive. Among the pictures were those of the foundrymen. She looked long at Jack, hard-necked in his working clothes beside his brothers, a labouring man among other coarse and surly labouring men, and yet she knew now that the camera lied.

She looked up, hearing the front door open, and heard the slow footsteps, more suggestive of fatigue than usual, as her father crossed the hall. He paused by the dining-room door and laid a hand on the frame to support himself.

'The second lion is scrap. The core or else the feeders

broke up. There's a fortnight's work to do all over again.'

'I'm sorry.' Phoebe was unable to stir an interest, but she saw that he had perhaps come to the end of his tether.

He moved away from the door.

'Father—' She drew in her breath, she could delay it no longer. 'Maurice has left Griseley.' She stiffened her shoulders defiantly; she would not give him the satisfaction of seeing her disillusionment. 'He'll not be coming back and I'm no longer engaged to be married.'

He stood for a moment, then said, 'I'm right glad to hear it,' before moving off into the hall.

Phoebe, surprised, even a little disappointed by his subdued reaction, turned back to the table and the photographs spread on its surface. She would take it up again, she decided. She would set up another studio and take *real* pictures of real people, like those of Tessa. She picked up the photograph of the foundrymen and gently touched the awkwardly posed figure of Jack, regretting that it was all she had.

Edwin learned the full circumstances of Maurice's disappearance during chapel gossip that weekend. He was the last to know, it seemed, that Maurice Chaudet had been a criminal, a man whose criminality was now common knowledge in the town, since it was the landlord of the Nag's Head who had been chosen as his victim.

Edwin, detecting the satisfaction on the faces of his willing informants, burned with silent humiliation. His lion project was in jeopardy – the men, led by Walter Bateman, were already muttering about strikes again – Gerald had deserted him and one of his best workers, Jack Bateman, had given notice to follow, and there was only one decent lion ready for September. And now to be told that his daughter had contemplated marriage to a 'horse-thief' –

Murgatroyd had used those very words. Edwin was mortified and drove home in high dudgeon.

He slammed the door to signal his mood on reaching Belle Vue. He could ignore the facts no longer. A foundryman he could have tolerated; a common horse-thief was the last straw. His daughter was no longer his daughter; she was not pleasing in his house.

Phoebe was sitting at the harmonium, playing a mournful little tune of her own making. Edwin, noting only fleetingly that she seemed to do little else these days, refused to be moved by the charm of the scene, nor deflected from his purpose by considerations of a future in which Phoebe would no longer gladden his house with her playing. She had blackened it with her corrupt ways. His lamb had turned out to be as wicked as her brothers. *O generation of vipers*. He flung down his hat and cane.

'You would have done better going to chapel and praying to the Lord for your sins!'

Phoebe stared. 'Whatever is the matter?' She was quite calm. It was almost as if it were he who were at fault for interrupting the peace of the sitting room.

The realisation that his anger did not touch her with dread fuelled Edwin's wrath further. 'You will vacate this dwelling within the week for you've brought shame on the family!'

She frowned tolerantly. 'I really don't—'

'You brought a thief into this dwelling. He sat on that very couch!' Edwin pointed a shaking finger at the corrupted sofa. 'You would have married the blackguard! Get out of my house!'

He had expected her to plead for forgiveness. At the back of Edwin's mind there had been lurking a tender scene in which, after a day or two of suitable remorse and having made it known in chapel that he was praying for her, having asked all the congregation to pray likewise, he might have forgiven Phoebe and allowed her to stay. But Phoebe made no protest. She packed her bags and went to live with Charles.

Murgatroyd and Wormauld had called an extraordinary meeting of the town council. It was extraordinary in more than name, for it took place furtively in Murgatroyd's house after chapel one evening and it excluded Edwin from its proceedings and also its chairman Alfred Underwood and the few councillors suspected of loyalty to Edwin.

'I was against the damned lions from the start,' declared Larkin. 'He's delayed for years over these beasts, then tells us they're going to be half the size, and now he says he can't finish them for September, just as we're about to send invitations all round.'

'Clough's going to make us look damned silly one way or another,' muttered Murgatroyd. 'And this latest is a tasty business, eh? His daughter's foreign fancy-man running off with the publican's horse and trap? Just wait till that gets round!'

'Who's to say what the next thing might be?' wondered Wormauld.

Murgatroyd was prepared to speculate. 'It only needs Leeds and Bradford councillors expecting champagne and biscuits and Clough to tell us he's got another strike on and everyone in Yorkshire will be having a damn good snigger at our expense.'

'The point is, do we do something before it's too late?'

They looked at one another. They knew why they had gathered. The motion was as good as carried already, for the men present formed the majority of the council. The only thing left was to choose who would put it to the next council meeting that the town-hall project was off – the lions were no longer required. They waited expectantly for Murgatroyd, knowing they would not be short of a volunteer.

Phoebe told herself that to devote her life from now on to her brother and young nephew was a fitting destiny for her: William was growing fast and needed a mother figure. Never mind that Christina had ten times more patience with children, and that William's infant games and snivelling irritated her. She would do her duty and fill her days playing mother to her brother's child.

Gerald, having heard what had happened, wrote from Leeds after a day or two and said that Phoebe might go and live with them. She was briefly tempted, for Leeds was far from Griseley and there was a ring of adventure in starting anew. But she refused, telling herself that she would not fit in with Gerald's eccentric household; besides which it was impossible, for Jack would soon be living there.

She had been with Charles for a week and already she was bored. She sat in the parlour in the evening sunlight, mending a pair of William's drawers. Charles was visiting the Underwoods and, sensing that she would be playing gooseberry, she had elected to stay at home.

Every so often she sighed and stared out of the window. Traffic moved up and down Griseley Bank with a slow rumble, the clock ticked in the hallway, the rattle of crockery from the maid in the scullery was the only indication that she was not entirely alone.

The sound of the doorbell made her jump, for she had been dozing and had not seen anyone come up the path. She heard Charles's housemaid scurry along the passage, the click of the latch and the sound of voices, a man's and the servant's, and then the maid tapped on the parlour door, 'Please, mam. It's Mr Bateman wants to know are you at home?'

She nodded, rising to her feet and letting the sewing slip from her knee.

Jack's presence seemed to fill the small front room. 'I hope you don't mind. I'm off to Leeds tonight. I thought I'd come and say goodbye.'

She cleared her throat. 'It was good of you to bother.' She offered him a chair.

'Well. You know,' he said awkwardly. 'For old times' sake.'

Jack sat on the chair by the empty fire-grate and Phoebe turned on the sofa to face him. She bent to pick up a bundle of sewing from the hearthrug and he leaped to pick it up for her. She smiled, blushing a little as she accepted it from his hands.

Her stateliness contrasted strongly with Jack's last memory of her as he thought of her sitting on the wall of the foundry beside him. He thought of the night she had hidden in the beer-wagon at her brother's wedding and wondered at how much, and how little, she had changed.

'I'm sorry your father turned you out.'

She stiffened. 'I've a home here as long as I want, and Gerald—' she paused '—Gerald has offered as well.'

He nodded, but the quiet of the cramped house on Griseley Bank did not seem to suit her and he felt saddened by the thought of the life ahead of her, living in Griseley above the mills and the foundry as a spinster aunt.

'So,' she said, 'you're going to exchange the smoke of Griseley for the greater grime of Leeds.'

He laughed. 'No moors to escape to there.'

'None of your mother's home cooking.'

'No getting up at five in the morning for the foundry. No more Walter to plague me.'

'No *obligations*,' she said with a touch of envy.

No more memories, he thought. No Phoebe.

495

'I hope you'll have great success, Jack,' she said. 'And I hope you'll be happy living with Gerald and Olive.' She pronounced the last name rather coldly and he blushed, wondering how much she had guessed about Olive.

'I shan't be living with them. I've got myself lodgings. I shall play the lead in *And All That Makes a Man* with them and then perhaps try my luck in Manchester. Who knows?'

'Who knows?' she echoed. 'So, I might have gone to Gerald's after all,' she thought.

'Your father said I could have been running the foundry shop in another ten year. He called me a buffoon.' Jack laughed. 'Ten year! I should be getting on for an old man.'

'We shall both be quite, quite old,' she reflected, imagining ten years in Charles's house, watching life pass by through lace curtains.

They sat, looking at one another, and their silence was full of strange possibilities which grew stronger as the stillness lengthened.

Jack stood. 'Well, I'd best be getting on.'

They shook hands very formally. She saw that the cuts on his face were healing into a scar below one eye. She released his hand slowly and the firmness of his grip made her feel faint with memories.

'I suppose—' he hesitated '—Leeds isn't a million miles away. Will you come and see Gerald's play?'

'Perhaps I shall. It will be a much grander production than it was here.'

'I remember the first play I did with them. I was that scared at the first rehearsal my knees were knocking together.'

'I remember it too. I thought you were so fine as Lysander.' They looked at one another and Phoebe saw that she must not let him go. She said, holding his gaze, 'I think I fell in love with you that night.'

'I fell in love with you years before that, when you were a kid with ringlets.'

She laughed a little breathlessly for she was afraid that he was teasing her. 'I don't believe you. You pulled my hair. You Batemans were atrocious.'

His eyes were dark and serious. 'Phoebe, I wish—'

She stepped towards him and raising her hands drew his face tenderly down to her own. 'Tell me, Jack. Tell me what you wish,' she whispered and the years rolled away and the years in the future spread out before her. How stupid she had been. Life was not over until one drew one's last breath.

He pulled her into his arms, kissing her eyes, her cheeks, her lips. 'Woman, if you're too stupid to see.'

Twenty-four

Never before has the king of beasts been so nobly and so truthfully treated in sculpture, and it is difficult to know which to admire most, the vitality of this creation or its majesty.

The Trafalgar Square lions,
The Times, 1 February 1867

A clatter of pigeons distracted Alfred Underwood from his speech. '. . . and so,' he concluded, 'Griseley is proud to have this magnificent work of art to grace its municipal park, a statue not inferior to those stately lions in Leeds and Sir Edwin Landseer's masterpieces in London's Trafalgar Square.'

'Hear! Hear!' Philip Underwood stirred Murgatroyd and Wormauld and the other councillors to applause and a muted cheer rose from the crowd of onlookers under the trees.

A platform had been erected in the park. In the distance stood the square building of the town hall. The children from the various Griseley Sunday schools, assembled near the platform, burst enthusiastically into their prepared anthem in response to the placarded signal that they should begin to sing, and the band of the local Rifle Volunteers stood by in readiness for their finale piece. The local Oddfellows and Foresters, representatives of the Working Men's Institute, and the Griseley Arts Council, the Chief Constable with a battalion of police 'just in case', and workers from the mills, the factories and workshops and Clough's own foundry had turned out to witness the unveiling.

Coloured bunting was strung among the few yellowing leaves on the sycamores. The draped statue, placed between the memorial fountain and the bandstand, looked like a white shroud under the skeletal trees. The councillors, having formally rejected the town hall project in favour of a single modest statue in the park, had elected to wear black coats and top hats instead of their official costume, which might have intimated a somewhat grander do, and resembled mourners at a funeral rather than celebrants at a festival.

Edwin gave a little sigh as the mayor pulled the cord which lifted the sheet by means of discreet pulleys arranged in the branches of a large chestnut and whisked it away from the statue. A cheer rose from the onlookers and grew in strength as the full beauty of the bronze lion became evident. Edwin saw his family gathered alongside the platform: Gerald, come over from Leeds, who was thought of well in the theatrical circles of that big city; Charles, who had settled down in the past months to the responsibilities of the foundry, standing with Christina Underwood, and Phoebe, his beloved Phoebe, talking with Jack Bateman, who had come with Gerald and Olive especially to see the ceremony.

He thought of Bertrand these days with fonder memories, his boy, who could have done so many things if he had not been led astray by a woman.

The Rifle Volunteers began to play a march and gradually the crowd edged away.

Beatrice Underwood, arm in arm with Alfred, said, 'It's

perfectly exquisite, Edwin – a right credit to the town.'

Edwin nodded. 'You'll be along presently with the others for a bite I hope, Alfred?' He watched them walk away across the park to the carriages waiting in the square.

Phoebe came towards him. 'I'll go up to the house, Father, shall I, and make sure the tea's got ready?'

He squeezed her waist affectionately, 'You do that, lass,' turning again to view the lion, so that he did not see her walk back to Jack Bateman and link her arm in his.

Jack walked with Phoebe across the grass. Drifts of leaves swished gently under their feet. Phoebe felt his strength against her side and saw the curious glances of people as they passed. Jack walked with his head high and a swing to his step for he had learned only that day that he had got the part in a new comedy in Manchester. She had said she would go with him, they would throw caution to the winds. 'There won't be much money, Phoebe,' he had told her seriously and she had laughed, saying she did not care, she was going to open a studio. 'I shall sell photographs, art pictures as well as bread-and-butter cartes de visite.' Jack was proud of her, for he knew that she would do whatever she wanted.

'You're beautiful,' he said against her ear, feeling the brush of her silk skirts against his leg. 'I want them all to know you're mine.'

'You'll come back to the house with me, won't you?' She tucked her arm more firmly in his. 'I want to show you off to the Underwoods.' They reached the park gates and the row of carriages and a crowd of people milling in the road near the town hall.

'Your father's going to raise every objection he can think of to us marrying.'

'Let him.' Phoebe looked at him, smiling into his eyes.

He swung her round on the pavement in front of the

startled gaze of Murgatroyd and Beatrice Underwood, lifting her on to the steps of her carriage. He held her hands, her pale hands, soon to be stained black again with her photography, but beautiful, always beautiful. 'Phoebe Clough, I love you.'

Edwin stayed in the park until the town-hall workers began to clear away the chairs and trappings on the platform. Not one from Murgatroyd's faction had congratulated him. Still, the statue was there, and with 'Clough's Foundry' stamped neatly along its tail. There was no shifting it now.

It *was* a magnificent beast. The sun gleamed on the bronze, softening its features, but also confirming its strength, the rippling muscles, the proud head, lifted in recognition of what it represented. Britain's pride, thought Edwin, the pride of an industrial nation, a nation which would not be beaten, nor cowed by rebellious elements.

One of the town-hall servers came to stand beside him. 'It's a grand lion, Mr Clough.'

'Aye,' said Edwin gently. 'It is that.'